Without

Air

To Shari —
just
breathe!

Mary
Perrine

Mary Perrine

2022 White Bird Publications, LLC

Copyright © 2022 by Mary Perrine
Cover design by BZHercules.com

Published in the United States
by White Bird Publications, LLC, Austin, Texas
www.whitebirdpublications.com

ISBN 978-1-63363-574-6
eBook ISBN 978-1-63363-575-3
Library of Congress Control Number: 2022931236

PRINTED IN THE UNITED STATES OF AMERICA

ACKNOWLEDGMENT

A huge thank you to Evelyn and crew at White Bird Publications for helping me bring this story to life. Their support has been endless.

Thank you to my Beta-Readers: Bridget Christianson, DeeAnn Eickhoff, Barb McMahon, Ruth Novack, and Linda O'Neil. Their masterful critique of my rough draft helped enhance the story, making it so much better. Also, enormous gratitude goes to Beth Lynne at BZ Hercules. There is no one I would rather have in my corner when it comes to the *next round* of editing and revising.

I also want to thank my readers. You lift me up with your words, messages, and stories. Thank you for continuing to believe in me.

And, as always, a special thank you to my husband, Mitch. He is my first reader, top critic, and best friend. Without his support, I would have thrown in the towel long ago. Mitch comes with an unending supply of chocolate, water, and support. And somehow, he has the innate ability to know when I am running low on all of them. Without his love and encouragement, I wouldn't be following my dream.

Taking a story from the first keystroke to a published novel takes a team. These people are all part of my team. I am forever grateful for every one of them and of you! Thank you!

Life
Without
Air

**White Bird
Publications**

PROLOGUE

LIFE WITH NORAH—Norah Van Pelt

Life Without Air
A three-part series on the loss of a child

It has long been believed that having a child fills an emptiness in the heart, which people do not even know exists until the dream begins. Just the mere anticipation of this stranger's arrival changes them so profoundly and makes them love so fiercely that they would sacrifice their own soul for this cherub. The two become one—bonded for life, not easily separated—even during the abhorrent adolescence years.

But what if that bond is broken? What are the repercussions? What happens if the child, or even the dream of a child, ceases to exist? What if the child is lost to infertility, miscarriage, a stillbirth, an ugly custody battle, an adoption that does not materialize, or, God forbid, a death after the child has settled into the family? How does one navigate the agonizing pain of whitewater that pulls them under, submerging them in a grief so deep, they cannot see the future?

How do parents maneuver the suffering when it becomes so tenacious, it feels as if an appendage has been ripped from their body? How do they navigate the rage coursing through them, spilling over at the most inopportune times and in the most inappropriate ways? How does one survive the gaping, Grand Canyon-sized hole left in the middle of their heart when their child is torn from them? How do they stop the bleeding, the gushing of hope? How does a parent ever become whole again? Trust again? Love again?

The truth is—it is nearly impossible. The heart will never completely heal. It will scar over, leaving a jagged, ropey cicatrix, a torturous reminder that never ceases to exist. The best one can hope for is to become a pathetic shadow of oneself, rife with holes and shattered bits. Parents strive to make it through each day without drowning in a sea of despair, constantly mired in what they have lost. They will forevermore guard their heart, always knowing that at any moment it could crumble into a million little pieces, nothing larger than a speck of dust—not breathing—just living a *life without air*.

How do I know? Because *my* pain is still fresh; my heart is still bleeding, and the hole is still tearing. I have a dozen bad days for every good one. On my good days, I push my shoulders back, plaster a phony smile across my face, and pray to make it through without falling headlong into a tailspin.

On my bad days, I pray my next breath will be my last.

Norah Van Pelt is a syndicated columnist

PART ONE

LOSING

To hold a child
in your heart
or in your arms,
only to lose them,
is to miss out on
every dream,
every possibility,
every tomorrow.

NORAH VAN PELT

Daughter
Wife
Mother
Journalist

CHAPTER ONE

Norah shivered violently as she flipped up her hood and tightened the laces at the neck of her sweatshirt. She locked her fingers together inside the open front pocket of the worn gray top. The words *Yale University* had faded over time and from multiple washings. The blue printing had cracked, and the once-thick material was threadbare. Yale had been her dream school, a far cry from Parker College in the small town of Parkerville, Iowa where she had earned her English degree.

Back in high school, Norah had done everything right to secure admission to Yale, so, when the rejection arrived, she was positive there had been a mistake. She laughed as she called the Dean of Admissions. He had assured her she was an excellent candidate, *but* no mistake had been made. He wished her well and landed, what amounted to, a humiliating verbal pat on the back before he hung up on her dream.

A fallback school had never been in her plan. Norah had no Plan B. She did not do Plan B's. But, after a year of wallowing, serving meals at the local Denny's, hoarding every penny she made, all the while smiling through her heartbreak, she picked herself up and drove her 1983 yellow Volkswagen Bug the two miles to Parker and begged to be accepted for late admission. After four years of committing her entire life to her studies, work, and helping her mother die with dignity, she and her dad brushed the Iowa limestone dust from their lives and moved to northern California for a fresh start. Why there? Simple. It was somewhere they had never been, a place with no memories, yet was filled with possibilities.

The cool breeze cut through the two-decade-old sweatshirt. Goosebumps rose on her bare legs as she walked toward the water on the nearly empty beach. She was focused on only one thing, so much so, that she barely noticed when she stepped into the rogue ankle-deep waves that splashed nearly to her thigh. The angry gray morning clouds rolled swiftly across the sky, muddying the color of the water even more than the waves. It was fitting she had chosen this day to die.

Waves lapped at her waist as she trudged deeper into the salty water. The sand swirled around her legs, poking at her with what should have felt like thousands of pins, but she didn't notice. Even by San Diego standards, the water was cold, yet she didn't feel it. She heard the wind call to her, screaming for her to stop, to keep fighting, but instead, she continued to wrestle her way deeper into the ocean. A massive wave broke over the top of her, and she let go, diving head-first into it. Norah was afraid of the water; she had never learned to swim. She couldn't save herself if she wanted to. It was the reason she had chosen to drown; there could be no turning back.

As the waves tossed her about, instinct kicked in and she fought back. She held her breath as a swirl of water sucked her down, slamming her against the ocean floor. She opened her eyes, but the greenish water she had expected to see below the surface had begun to turn black; she wasn't sure if it was the grayness of the day or if she was losing consciousness. Finally, her lips parted, and she drew in a mouthful of the briny water. The pressure squeezed her chest from the outside as the liquid rushed into her lungs. For one brief second, she fought to save herself, but the moment passed as quickly as it appeared. She closed her eyes and remembered what had driven her to take her own life, and she let go.

FIVE YEARS BEFORE

San Diego was always sunny. The temperatures were almost always in the sixties and seventies, picture-perfect. And even on the rare days when it wasn't, it still felt that way. A week before, Seth had surprised her with two tickets for a flight to the vibrant coastal town. He had arranged a stay at a five-star resort, Sunset Shores.

As a couple, they had visited San Diego many times, but always for business, with friends, or with co-workers; they had never gone alone. This trip was different; it was a celebration. Seth had been promoted to detective, and Norah had finally been gifted with her own column at the *Clearwater Chronicle* in Mason Hills. The column, *Life with Norah*, had always been her dream. After ten years of marriage, things finally felt like they were falling into place.

From candlelit dinners, bouquets of flowers, expensive champagne, dancing until dawn, and moonlight strolls on the beach, the long weekend was perfect. Seth had pulled out all the stops. It was the beginning, the launch of something new. They were ready to start a family, add a little one to their home.

Late one evening, when the beach was empty and a full moon glistened overhead, they built a small fire on the beach and burned Norah's diaphragm. They could barely contain their laughter as the rubber melted into a bubbling puddle amidst the burning driftwood. There was nothing keeping them from their dream.

Liliana had been a glint of hope in the sparks of that fire; she sprang to life in the warm flames as they made love on the beach. Exactly nine months later—almost to the minute, Norah gave birth to the most perfect part of her life—her daughter—the light they had agreed to call Liliana before they ever said *I do*.

FIVE WEEKS, THREE DAYS, AND FIVE HOURS BEFORE NORAH WALKED INTO THE WATER

For years, they had put off having a family, just waiting for the perfect moment, for the moon and the stars and the earth to align. But after everything fell apart, Norah wondered what they had waited for. She was a thirty-eight-year-old divorcee with no one in her life except her father, a sixty-four-year-old widower who had found a new love of his own.

Five weeks, three days, and five hours before, give or take a few gut-wrenching minutes, they had buried their dream. On the day Liliana's casket was lowered into the ground, she was eight days shy of her fourth birthday. The pastor repeatedly explained to Norah that the lowering of the casket would not take place until after everyone had gone, but Norah insisted it was done in front of her. She had been with her daughter from the very start, and she would be there until the bitter end.

Throughout the service, Norah held an armful of gerbera daisies in pinks and yellows and white. Once the tiny white casket reached the bottom of the hole, she plucked one at a time from the bouquet and dropped it into the open grave, watching each one tremble in the light breeze before landing on the shiny, white surface. When her arms were emptied, Norah never felt more alone. She fought everything inside her not to jump into the hole with her baby girl. Sliding her foot forward, she watched the soil trickle into the open grave. Seth had grabbed on to her elbow as she teetered on the edge; she knew he was keenly aware of what she was thinking. But as soon as he touched her, she jerked her arm from his grip and stepped backward.

After the final prayer, when the pastor closed her Bible, Seth turned and walked away. She had seen his tears, but she had nothing left for him. He was just another painful reminder of their dead daughter. His eyes were her eyes; his thin lips were also Lili's. The two were a matched set. She could not even look at him without bristling.

There was not a word powerful enough for what she felt for Seth. She hated him, despised everything about him, from his voice to his touch. This man she had once loved, she now loathed. Cancer does that. It takes your love and turns it inside out, stomps on your heart until you can no longer love. It drives you to detest both people and God.

Lili had been her life, her joy, the best part of Norah. God had given her exactly what she had prayed for, a beautiful, blond-haired angel with blue-green eyes the color of the ocean. He had offered her a baby to love, a toddler to hold. He had given her the joy of Lili's chubby hands against her cheeks. God had blessed her with sloppy kisses, giggles, the amazing baby smell, and spit-up on every outfit she owned. Oh, God had kept His promise; it was Norah who had screwed up. She had forgotten to pray for the long term—for Lili as a child, a teenager, an adult with children of her own. But even though it was her fault, Norah was still angry with God. He knew exactly what she had wanted. He had just refused her dream, and for that, she would never forgive Him.

INTROSPECT

Katelyn Li: "I was wrapped in a blanket, watching my son and husband build sandcastles, when I saw that woman walk into the water. I couldn't believe she was going swimming—fully dressed, no less. No one was in the water that day. The lifeguards weren't even on duty because of the wind."

Conn Vernon: "That woman ran into me, literally plowed into my shoulder. It was like she didn't even know I was there. I dropped one of the coffees I was carrying, but she said nothing. I honestly don't think she even noticed. I'll tell you this. I've never seen such empty eyes in my entire life."

Pat Ammala: "We were having breakfast on the hotel deck when my husband, Darwin, saw her walk into the water. He raced toward the shore and called to her. Instead of looking back, she looked up into the sky as if God had called her name. By then, two other men had run into the water and started searching for her."

Ruth Novack: "My husband and another man pulled her out. Her body had already turned a bluish shade and the corners of her mouth were covered in foam. Her hair and clothes were caked in sand. They gave her CPR until the ambulance arrived, but it was too late; she couldn't have survived. I'm sure she was on drugs. I don't know what she was thinking. She put more than her life at risk that day."

CHAPTER TWO

FOUR DAYS BEFORE LILI'S FUNERAL

Norah hated that the hospital had become Lili's second home. It infuriated her that her daughter had grown comfortable with the bright lights and the sounds of the machines pulsing day and night. She despised that her baby girl no longer cried at the sight of a needle but instead, just turned away. The remnants of Lili's short childhood had been torn to bits and pieces, leaving Norah nothing to hold on to. And instead of playing with her friends, she was confined to a bed with railings, attached to machines whose sounds marked the little time she had left. Her only friends were the doctors and nurses who checked in, smiling when they talked to her but frowning when they turned away. Lili no longer cried when it was time for more tests, but Norah cried for her.

Near the hush of dawn, on the day Lili drew her last breath, a grandmotherly nurse wandered into the room. Norah watched as she methodically disconnected the machines that kept her daughter alive. The details had exhaustively been discussed until Norah wanted to scream. *The Plan*, as the oncologist had referred to it, had more pieces than she could absorb, beginning with when it would be put in place—when nothing more could be done to save Lili. That moment was upon her, and her chest felt like it was caving in. A lump the size of a golf ball grew in her throat, and she could barely breathe.

Strictly by chance, Shanice was the nurse assigned to Lili that day. Her voice was soft and as gentle as her own mother's had been. She spoke slowly and matter-of-factly. Norah wanted her to leave, but even more, she *needed* her to stay. When the moment came, she didn't want to be alone.

"How long will it be?" she whispered over the top of Lili's head.

Shanice rubbed Norah's arm before giving it a gentle squeeze. "I don't think it'll be long, hon; a few hours at most."

Norah pressed her forehead against her daughter's, willing life into her, begging the universe for another day, another week, another year. "I, I'm not ready," she whispered. "Can we wait just a little longer? What if…" But she stopped. Lili was ready to go, even if she was not. Her heart jackhammered in her throat and her ears.

"Honey, none of us are ever ready for death. It's all in God's hands now." Shanice held her hands out to her sides, palms facing upward as she spoke. "You've got nothing to be worried about. He'll take good care of your little girl 'til you get there."

Rage engulfed Norah. She angrily cleared her throat before speaking. "You'll have to forgive me, but I'm pretty damn mad at God at the moment."

Shanice patted Norah's shoulder. "It's okay, hon. God can take it. He's a big boy. Give Him all you've got." Nurse Shanice walked over to the window, opened the blinds, and stared at the deep purple of the morning sky. She folded her arms across her chest. The stitches on the sleeves of her maroon scrubs stretched at the shoulders and looked like they would burst. "Nobody can understand God's ways. That's called faith." Shanice turned around. "You okay, hon?"

Norah just nodded.

Shanice silently pulled the door open and held it with her foot. She watched Norah for a few seconds. "I'm here for you—both now and after. I'll be back in a little while." Then she was gone.

Norah squeezed out a "thank you," but it was muffled by the cacophony of hopelessness swimming in her head. She wasn't even sure Shanice heard it.

Less than an hour later, Liliana opened her eyes and looked at Norah. "Momma," she whispered so quietly, Norah almost missed it.

"I'm here, baby girl," Norah cooed as she kissed the peach fuzz that had emerged on the top of her head since ending her chemo treatments. "I love you, sweet pea."

The corners of Liliana's lips turned up in a weak smile before she closed her eyes again. She drew a breath and moaned softly as she released it in a long, gurgly exhale. Norah knew it was her last. Yet she held her breath, listening for her daughter to inhale. Seconds turned into minutes. Norah clung to Lili's lifeless body. "Don't leave me. Please don't take her, God. Please!" She sobbed. But, from past experiences, she knew her pleas were falling on deaf ears. God wasn't listening. He hadn't been for years. At 6:02 a.m., on April 29th, Lili stopped existing. At that moment, Norah was keenly aware that for the first time in over ten years, she was all alone.

Still sobbing, Norah crawled out of bed, picked up her daughter, and carried her to the rocker Dr. Weston had sent in. She covered them both with the baby quilt her mother had made years before, for the granddaughter she would never meet until now—if heaven were real. She wrapped her arms around Lili's tiny body and softly hummed "Edelweiss." It had always been Lili's song.

Just days later, Liliana would have celebrated her fourth birthday. Three gifts she would never play with were wrapped and tucked under Norah's bed. She didn't know why she bought them—wishful thinking, confident of a miracle, or because that was what a mother did. No matter which it was, she knew they would remain wrapped forever.

The stillness of death was thunderous. Lili's chest no longer rose or fell; her heart no longer pulsed against Norah's arm, but Lili no longer struggled for each breath either. Sitting in a wooden rocker, unable to draw a full breath, Norah felt as if her heart would implode, cave in from the sheer lack of oxygen. She had prayed that if God were real, He would take her too. "Please don't let this be the end. Please!" Norah had wailed. She choked on a sob that banged against her words and caught in her throat. "If you can't give me more time with Lili, take me too. I don't want to be here without her," she cried.

The door creaked, and Seth stepped into the bright room. "Is she…?" His eyes were wide, and he held his breath as he waited for her answer.

Norah laid her cheek against her daughter's. "She's gone," she whispered. Seth moved toward them. "Don't!" she growled. "Not one more step."

Seth dropped to his knees onto the tile floor; she heard the thud as he made contact. "Come on, Norah. She was my daughter, too."

A laugh escaped, a hard, ruthless mockery meant to hurt. "I guess you should have remembered that before you walked away," she huffed. "*I* faced this, Seth. I did this, all by myself. I was here every day for her." Her glare was sharp; she knew the truth cut him. "I will never forget your words. Do *you* remember them?" she asked sarcastically. His dark eyes told her he remembered, but she needed to turn the knife. She had lowered her voice to mimic his, repeating the words he spewed. *"I didn't sign up for this, Norah. Cancer wasn't part of the plan."* Norah kissed Lili's forehead. "You were a coward. You didn't just leave me; I could have lived with that. You left your daughter, your flesh and blood. You abandoned her when she needed you." Her voice was brittle. "Lili needed you, Seth. *I* needed you."

"Norah, please…"

"You know what, Seth? None of this was part of *my* plan either. I didn't plan on our daughter getting cancer. I didn't plan on her dying. And I sure as hell didn't plan on you walking away and leaving me to deal with all of it by myself." Her words floated through the silence, poked at him enough to elicit physical pain. His mouth twisted as he drew a sharp breath. "I didn't plan on any of it. We *needed* you. But you weren't there. You went on with your life as if everything was just peachy. You went to work and out to *happy hour* with the boys." Her face filled with disgust as she spat that phrase at him. "Happy hour, Seth. Where was my happy hour? Why did *you* deserve to be happy?"

Seth gulped several mouthfuls of air; his chest heaved as he tried to speak. "I don't know what to say. I can't even find the words to tell you how sor…"

"Stop it, Seth. Just stop! I was the one who watched our daughter die, the one who saw her take her last breath. It was me. Me, Seth." She poked a finger into her chest. "I was the one who cared for her, took her to appointments, watched them pump chemicals into her tiny body, trying to kill the poison growing inside Lili." Norah choked on a sob. "And I held her while she died." She glared at him until he looked away. "You have no right to claim her as your daughter. None!"

Norah continued to gently rock Liliana's body as she watched the tears roll down Seth's cheeks. For a moment, her heart softened. She shuddered as she stared at Lili's ashen face. "Look at her, Seth. We made this beautiful little girl. You and I, we did this."

"I know." His voice cracked as he spoke. "She was so perfect."

Instantly, her emotions spun to fury. "No, she wasn't, Seth. She was sick." Norah rubbed her thumb along Lili's chin. "She was so sick, and I couldn't help her. I couldn't save her." She leaned over and kissed her daughter's cheek. "Sweet Lili, I tried. I tried so hard to save you, sweetheart, but I failed. I'm so sorry." She wept.

Seth scooted toward her, stood up, and pulled her and Lili from the chair—cradling them in a tight embrace. "Nor, there was nothing you could have done. Lili couldn't have had a better mother." His arms tightened around her as she sobbed against his shoulder, Lili's limp body resting between them. "You did everything you could."

Norah sucked in a deep *How dare you?* breath and stepped backward. She looked into his watery blue eyes. "Well, maybe *you* could have done something, then." Her words stung; she could see it. "Oh, wait. You did, Seth. You left. Lili sure as hell deserved a better father than the one she got."

Norah moved to the bed and sat down, still holding Lili in her arms. She faced away from him and hummed "Edelweiss" again as her tears dripped onto her daughter's face. The two-minute song lasted nearly five minutes before Norah pressed the red button on the side of the hospital bed. She laid her daughter on the bed, softly planted a kiss on her cheek, and returned to the chair.

"Say your goodbye, Seth. You have until the nurse gets here, so you'd better make it quick."

INTROSPECT

Leslie Frink: "I've been an oncology nurse for a very long time. I've seen a lot of things in my career: miracles and devastation. But the death of a child? It's heartbreaking."

Sara Johannsen: "I remember when Norah told me Lili was sick. I didn't even know what to say. I just held her and let her cry. That night, I showed up at her house with dinner and a big bottle of wine. I let her talk well into the night. I slept on her couch, and I went with her to see the specialist the next day. I don't recall why her husband didn't go or where he even was. Norah held my hand the entire time we were with the oncologist."

Lori Vang: "I worked with Seth at the station. He wasn't as personable as the other detectives. He had a hard exterior that few people could penetrate. I remember the night he learned his daughter had cancer; he went out for drinks with his old partner. I thought it was odd he didn't go home to his wife."

Bridget Christianson: "Lili attended the preschool where I served as principal. I loved that family. I didn't often see her husband, but Norah volunteered for everything. If anyone needed her, she was there. We will miss all of them, especially sweet little Liliana."

CHAPTER THREE

There was an unsettling sound in the distance, a buzzing with a pitch like fingernails on a chalkboard. Norah grimaced as it grew louder, pulsing. Slowly, she felt herself begin to rise, floating, weightless. A sense of warmth washed over her. The white light summoned her; even with her eyes squeezed shut, she could feel it. "Lili," she called in a sing-song voice. Her words sounded hollow; they had a low, echoey timbre as they bounced off the walls of a long, hazy hallway. "Lili, it's Mommy." She laughed as she clapped her hands together, locking them in front of her chest. "Come out, honey. You win." An eerie stillness fell. Norah's panic swelled. "Lili?" she called again, more frantic this time. "Lili?"

Wildly, she jerked her head from side to side, as she ran down the long hallway. Her arms cut through the white foggy mist as she searched for her daughter. At the end of the long hallway, she turned around and screamed, "Lili! Where are you?"

Someone touched her arm, pulled her from what must

have been a bad dream. "Honey, wake up." She felt the hand shake her arm again, rougher this time. "Norah, honey, wake up."

Norah's eyes slowly opened but immediately snapped shut. The light was too bright. It was not how she imagined heaven to be. It did not feel welcoming; instead, it felt cold and frightening.

"Come on, sweetheart. We've been waiting for you." The voice was soft and warm; it had a familiar cadence and tone.

Norah opened her eyes again, blinking multiple times to clear her vision. "Dad?" Her voice didn't sound right. It sounded hoarse, like she had been screaming. Every breath she took burned as oxygen filled her lungs.

"I'm here, honey." Her dad smiled. "You're okay, Norah. Everything's going to be okay. It's *all* going to be fine." He tenderly laid a hand against her cheek.

"I'm here too, Norah." She felt someone lift her other hand. Seth awkwardly smiled when she made eye contact. She tried to return the compassion, but the rawness of her throat forced the corners of her lips down and she closed her eyes to swallow.

"Seth," she whispered, "where's Lili?"

The two men exchanged a knowing look. "What?" she questioned through clenched teeth. "What's going on?"

The door opened and a nurse breezed into the room. He grinned when he saw her. "Well, well, well. Looks like Sleeping Beauty is finally awake." He moved to the side of her bed, squeezing past Seth. "I just need to check your vitals," he said as he lifted her hand out of her husband's.

Norah watched all three men. Each had something they were hiding; stories left untold. She felt it. She had been a reporter long enough to read people.

Finally, the nurse stopped moving. "How's your throat?"

Instinctively, her hand touched her neck. "It hurts. Bad," she added.

"I'm sure it does," the man said. He pointedly looked at her father. "Hang in there, Miss Norah. It'll get better." He turned toward the bedside table and lifted a small thermos and a spoon. "Do you want some ice chips?" Norah opened her mouth in answer and let the cold chips he spooned in melt in the back of her raw throat.

"More," she whispered. He spooned a few more chips into her mouth before returning both to the bedside table. "Slow and easy," he warned. "We have to make sure you can swallow okay before we give you too much." He wrote something on a clipboard and hung it back at the bottom of the bed. He squeezed her toes and winked at her. Then he nodded to the men and disappeared again.

Seth moved back to her side. "Why am I here?" she asked him. His eyes shifted to the floor and he said nothing. "Dad?" she eked out as she turned her attention to him. "Why?" That same look she saw before passed between the men.

"Sweetheart, we can talk about all of that later." He pulled up her covers and tucked them under her arms. "It can wait. For now, you just need to rest."

"Where's Lili? Who's watching her?" Norah asked with a hard swallow. "I want to see her. Seth, can you bring her to me?" She tried to tuck her hand behind her head, but the movement pulled the cannula from her nose and tugged on her IV. She cried out in frustration. "I just want to see my little girl."

Her dad unfolded a metal chair and pulled it next to the bed. He lowered himself onto the front edge and leaned forward. He took her small hand in his soft, blue-lined big one. Just as when she was small, Norah felt warm and safe with her hand in his. He pressed her hand against his rough, unshaven face before drawing in a breath and releasing it. "Norah, do you know where you are?"

Her face tightened as she tried to swallow. Clenching her teeth tightly together, she answered slowly, "In the hospital. But why?"

She touched Seth's hand. "Why am I here?"

"Do you know *where* you are, Norah? What city you're in?" Seth asked.

Norah melted into the bed as the memories flooded back. Her daughter was gone and she was not. She had failed as a mother, and obviously, because she was here, she had failed at joining her daughter.

She wanted to scream, wanted to cry, but she could not. Every inch of her body throbbed in pain—no longer just physical.

"Get out, Seth! Get the hell out of here," she whispered.

INTROSPECT

Brad Van Pelt: "Norah has been through so much in her lifetime. Seeing her eyes when she realized why she was in the hospital was gut-wrenching. She may be a grown woman, but she is still my baby girl."

Rafe Garcia: "I lost my only son in a boating accident. For a year, I wanted to crawl into a hole and never come out. Therapy and support groups were the only things that helped. Norah needs help. I hope she gets it."

GRACE WILSON

Daughter
Stepdaughter
Stepsibling
Mother
Teacher
Mistress

CHAPTER FOUR

Grace could hear the clock ticking behind her; she cringed. It was the sound of her childhood, waiting for her father and his belt, her stepsiblings taunting her from the other side of the bedroom door.

As far back as she could recall, this was the first time she had ever been called to the principal's office, even as a child. She had never had so much as a late assignment out of fear of her stepmother. Her heart raced as she gripped the arms of the uncomfortable chair. Principal Holbrook was not a man of formality. Usually, her conversations with him were casual, conducted in a non-threatening environment such as her classroom or teachers' lounge—so when the Dean walked in and whispered that Bart wanted to see her— Grace immediately panicked. She quickly asked the students to explain to Mr. Groves what they were working on.

Mick nudged her toward the door. "I've got this, Grace. I can read a lesson plan. Bart's waiting for you." His arched brows and wide eyes told her it was serious.

In just under two minutes, she slipped through the front

door of the office. Noelle nodded to the chairs against the window. "He told me to have you wait here." Grace tried to read the secretary's face, but she gave nothing away. If her job was to terrify people into never being summoned again, she deserved a raise. Clearly, she had been the best candidate for the job.

Grace crossed her legs and uncrossed them multiple times before picking up the local newspaper. She opened it wide and lifted it in front of her face. Words and headlines passed in front of her eyes, but not a single story drew her attention away from her impending meeting. The letters on the pages blurred together, and suddenly, she wanted to cry. She had spent the last twenty-five years doubting herself— the same way others had always doubted her. Instead of trying to stand out, she hid. She kept her head low as she focused on making it through each day.

Her father had remarried when Grace was eight. Before that, she had been an only child. Until the moment the minister pronounced her father and Cynthia husband and wife, she and her father had been a team. That phrase—*I now pronounce you husband and wife*—changed everything. Before then, her stepmother-to-be had played nice, but after the vows, it became clear the new woman in her dad's life didn't care for Grace any more than her own mother had. Neither of them had wanted her.

Grace was positive *she* had been the reason her mother had deserted the family when she was just two years old. She had no memories of the woman, but, if she were to believe what her new stepfamily told her, *she* drove people away. There were no pictures of her mother, none of the two of them together. Her new mother had destroyed them all. If she met her on the street, she wouldn't even recognize her. What color was her hair? Was it curly or straight? Did they share the same eye color or any of the same features? Grace had so many questions her father chose not to answer and her stepmother refused to acknowledge.

When her dad married Cynthia Powers, a woman as

pretentious and strong as her name, she and her three horrid children, who made a game out of tormenting Grace, stole her father's love and attention. While her step-siblings called her father *Dad*, she had been given strict instructions to refer to her stepmother only as *Miss Cynthia*. If there was a disagreement in the house, Grace had always been at fault. If something went wrong, she took the hit—literally. In the early years, she missed more meals than she ate, and, because of her raw backside, she stood more than sat.

Every night before going to sleep, Grace had crossed off the date on her calendar, moving her closer to the day she could leave the hellhole her stepfamily had created. The day she left had been the happiest day of her life—until her daughter was born.

Bart cleared his throat. "Grace?" It came out as a question. She wondered how many times he had called her before she noticed his arrival.

She quickly stood up, catching the toe of her pointed flats on the carpet, stumbling into Bart. Awkwardly, she folded the paper, leaving it more bunched than creased and flattened; she knew Noelle would refold it before fanning it out with the magazines.

"Are you okay?" the principal asked as he waited for her.

"Yes," she answered sheepishly. Grace followed him through his door and settled on the edge of a chair matching those in the main office. Bart closed the door and walked to the other side of his desk. He was a big man, both tall and broad. His chair groaned under his weight.

"If this is about…" Grace said at the same time Bart asked, "Do you know why…"

Bart stopped talking and Grace let out a nervous titter. "You go first." She nodded toward him.

"Okay," Bart said. "Do you know why I wanted to talk to you?"

"Not really." Grace shyly shrugged. "Is it about the yearbook?"

"No." Bart laid a heavy hand on his desk. "But now you have me wondering. Is there a problem with the yearbook?"

She wrung her hands nervously in her lap, chiding herself for saying anything. "Clarice and I have been having a bit of a creative disagreement lately. We just see things differently. But we'll, ah, work it out. It'll be fine."

Bart nodded slowly. "Okay, then." He leaned back in his chair, crossed his legs, and tented his fingers in front of him. "The reason I wanted to see you is because I got a call from the father of one of your students. His son seems to think you don't like him and therefore are choosing to ignore him—even when he asks you for help." Bart sighed. "He also claims you embarrassed him in front of the class."

Grace's shoulders tilted back, and her chin came up. "I would never! I love *all* of my students." She absently ran her hands down the front of her slacks. "Who's the child?"

"Henry Franzen."

Her mouth flew open, prepared to defend herself, but she shut it just as quickly. For the second time in ten minutes, she heard the clock's driving tick. Again, she opened her mouth, and again, she closed it.

Bart nodded knowingly. "That's what I thought."

"He's not an easy child, Bart. You know that," Grace said. "I'm sure you've seen him multiple times just this week."

"I know that, but those are the kids who need us the most and, if Henry even remotely appears to be interested in help, he should be the first person you go to." Bart uncrossed his legs and folded his arms before leaning forward and laying them along the edge of his desk. "Do you understand?"

Grace nodded. "But…"

"There are no *buts*, Grace. This isn't the first time you and I have had conversations about students. Remember Beau Marvin? Neil Lyons? Jillian Blakeley? All this year. This just happens to be the first time I've called you in to have a formal discussion." Bart pulled a file from his drawer and dropped it on top of his desk. "You know, Grace, you're up for tenure after next year. If you asked me right now if I planned to keep you, my answer would most likely be no." Grace averted his stare; she tipped her head down and focused on the yellow memo on Bart's desk, obviously the call from Henry's dad. "Do you even want to be a teacher? Are you willing to put in the effort it's going to take to improve?"

Grace's mouth suddenly felt as if it was stuffed with cotton. Her words just barely eased past the massive lump growing in her throat. "I-I am," she whispered. She had always been a crier. Her eyes stung as they filled with tears; she glanced at the ceiling to keep them from falling, a trick she learned when dealing with her stepmom.

"Okay then," Bart said softly. "I'm willing to keep you around for one more year because I think you *could* be an excellent teacher. Honestly, you're good with most of your students, but you seem to have a blind spot to the Henrys of the world. I'll work with you, but if things don't change..." He stood. His height alone was enough to make her heart race. "Well, you know where I'm going."

Grace nodded as she rose. She stared down at her pointed shoes, a garage sale purchase she'd made back in college. The toe had separated from the sole when she had tripped moments earlier. The tears she had been trying to keep at bay finally made their descent, dotting her navy blouse. Bart pushed a box of tissues across his desk. She took one and wiped her face, dabbing at the mascara she was certain had left black smudges below her eyes.

Bart sighed when the bell rang. "Listen, Grace. There's only one class left for today. I'll cover for you. Go home and pull yourself together. Tomorrow's a new day."

She sniffed loudly and wiped her face again. He didn't have to tell her twice. She hated this place lately, but she needed the job so she could take care of her daughter. The thousand dollars a month she received from Finley's father was barely enough to keep them afloat.

"Thank you," she said as she jerked the door open and hastily vacated his office.

INTROSPECT

Eric Larson: "I was coming into the team room as Grace was leaving. She had her purse and jacket and seemed to be in a hurry. She looked like she'd been crying, but she didn't say a word. She didn't even respond when I asked if she was okay."

Nancy Allen: "I've worked with Grace for two years. She's an incredibly nice person, but nice doesn't make you a good teacher. She's definitely creative, but her classroom management could use some serious help."

Terri Shuck: "I honestly feel bad for Grace. She's trying to do her best. But teaching and being a single parent isn't easy. Between home and school, she's with kids 24/7. She has no downtime."

CHAPTER FIVE

Grace aimed her car toward the town's park. The raging river and the dangerous waterfall kept Halston Park from becoming a popular place for families with young children. The uneven terrain made it nearly impossible for the elderly to navigate. Even the high school students, who once viewed the park as *party central* after football games and on weekends, had moved to a more secluded location, one the cops had yet to locate.

A barely legible sign on Highway 78 was the only indicator the park even existed. It was nestled in the middle of a grove of towering trees along a section of the Rock River. From the highlands, the water roared downstream, wildly breaking against enormous boulders, sending a spindrift of water skyward before tumbling toward a waterfall about a hundred yards east of the park. The townies chose safer places to picnic and play, while the day-trippers and vacationers passed the sign without so much as a second glance.

The older blue Escape bounced through the potholes of

the deteriorating road. Grace guided the car through the entrance and into the neglected lot. Weeds sprouted from the deep ruts of the once gravel space. She glanced at the clock on her dashboard as she turned off her car. *2:20 p.m.* It surprised her to see another vehicle. An elderly couple ate a late lunch at a rickety old picnic table that looked ready to collapse. Because of the walker next to the woman, she was confident they would not venture beyond the table. As Grace passed them, she smiled and nodded before turning her attention to the uneven ground. Cautiously, she made her way down the incline to the river's edge.

⊱⋅ ⋅⊰

Not long after moving to Ponderosa Falls, Grace accidentally stumbled on the park. Finley had never been a good sleeper. In the spring, summer, and early fall, when daylight refused to relent before bedtime, her daughter could not fall asleep. Finley hadn't learned how to let sleep wash over her. Riding in the car over bumpy gravel roads seemed to be the only thing that would lull her to sleep. So, each night, Grace put Finley in a sleeper, covered her with a quilt, and strapped her into her car seat. After an hour or so on the road, her daughter was nearly comatose.

Once she had discovered Halston Park, Grace's nightly course was set. The road was rough enough to jostle Finley to sleep. Halfway down the narrow drive, her daughter's crescendoing screams always began to soften and, by the time she reached the parking lot, silence almost always ensued. Some nights, Grace would roll down the windows and listen to the crickets and frogs as the breeze lightly touched her face. Other nights, she would lock her door, leaving Finley's window open just enough to listen for her while she sat on the riverbank, daydreaming about her best life.

Because of the park's seclusion, Daniel, Finley's father, often met them there. There were no prying eyes, no one to judge their age difference. Grace was twenty-five; Daniel was over twice her age. Crow's feet had grown near his eyes and deep lines ran from his nose to the corners of his mouth. The hair of his youth was now a hybrid of soft brown and unruly gray, revealing his evolution to middle age. His belt no longer fit over his stomach; instead, it rested just below his slightly rounded paunch.

In Grace's eyes, the most wonderful thing about Daniel, other than the fact that he had given her Finley, was that he was a highly respected psychiatrist—Dr. Daniel Fischer MD—a medical doctor with a specialization in mental health. He lived in Hollister, Colorado, a ninety-minute drive from Ponderosa Falls. However, Daniel wasn't just any psychiatrist. Dr. Daniel Fischer had been *her* therapist— the person who convinced her she was not crazy.

When Grace was in high school, Cynthia had worked every angle, concocting elaborate stories to convince Grace's father she was certifiable. Unable to say no to his wife, her father agreed to ship her off to the Big Woods Ranch for girls deep in the southern Rockies. Behavior was their focus. The headmaster guaranteed that by the time Grace returned home, she would be a changed girl, a teenager without the attitude. He promised they would see a woman of morals and etiquette. But Grace had no personal *glitches,* as Cynthia called them. Still, she spent the better part of a year locked up in the woods with a dozen other girls and a group of counselors who saw punishing the girls as their entertainment.

The camp director had been right about one thing; it had changed her. The time away had broken her. When she returned home, she was silent and withdrawn. She spoke only when spoken to and never asked for anything. If she wasn't in school, she was locked in her bedroom, avoiding the rest of her so-called *family*. It took several weeks before her dad noticed the changes. The daughter he once knew had grown apathetic and indifferent. As far as Grace was concerned, his worry was too little too late. He should have noticed the change when Cynthia and her brood moved in, not after she had been exiled to the far corner of Colorado.

Several months before she turned seventeen, her father agreed to pay for weekly therapy sessions with a well-known local psychiatrist, Dr. Daniel Fischer. He not only was highly recommended by the school district, but his walls were lined with awards and honors. Dr. Fischer appeared to be the perfect person to bring Grace out of her funk.

Grace was not sure which of them fell in love first, she or Daniel, but the love they shared made her happier than she had been in an exceptionally long time. For four of the five years her father footed the bill for her sessions, the two of them had a clandestine affair. He had sworn her to secrecy because he was married, had been married for more than twenty years, most of Grace's life.

Daniel and his wife were childless by choice and loveless by circumstance. Simply put, they were two people living in one house sharing separate bedrooms and interests; they were housemates at best. At least that was *his* story. Grace had no reason to doubt it. For one hour each week, she was genuinely happy, and that happiness spilled over into the rest of the week. Those sixty minutes were not enough, but they had to be for the time being. Instead of moping around, she smiled. Instead of crying, she laughed. Instead of hiding, she joined the family. This, of course, irritated her stepmother and Cynthia had insisted her father stop paying for the meetings, but he was so remorseful over destroying his daughter, he not only continued to pay for her therapy sessions but college as well.

When she moved out from under Cynthia's thumb, she continued her weekly sessions. Four days after Grace graduated from college, she discovered she was expecting. Nothing made her happier than to feel Daniel's love growing inside of her. She could not wait to share the news with him. Knowing he wanted a life without children, she knew he wouldn't be as excited as she was. Still, she figured he would come around to the idea of their little family. It wasn't until Grace was five months pregnant, and their ultrasound revealed they were expecting a girl, he finally confessed their affair to his wife, a woman who was more than happy to quietly leave him without reporting his transgression to the medical board, as long as it involved a healthy payout. His wife had signed a prenup agreement, leaving her without a penny of Daniel's money in the event they split, the sole reason she stayed. Their break-up had brought tears to her eyes—tears of joy.

When the first Mrs. Fischer exited *stage left*, Grace wrongly assumed she was the understudy who would step into the role as the new Mrs. Daniel Fischer. But instead of flaunting his young girlfriend, Daniel hid her away in a city nearly two hours from his office, in a place where no one would connect the dots of an illicit affair that had started when Grace was a minor. Word of an affair with *any* patient, much less a minor, would destroy his career. So once again, Grace waited in the wings for her scene to begin.

The stretches between Daniel's visits widened, especially after Finley was born. His excuses became flippant and illogical. But Grace had learned early in life what making waves got her, so she remained silent. She knew the end was near when, during one visit, they met a neighbor in the hallway of her apartment, the one, which Daniel paid for while she was in hiding. Not able to avoid a greeting, Daniel introduced himself as *Grace's* father, not Finley's. For the rest of the weekend, Grace walked on eggshells, waiting for the curtain to fall.

On Sunday night, standing at the apartment door with his duffle bag at his feet, Daniel handed Grace a checkbook and a debit card for an account he had set up months earlier. He promised he would take care of her until she landed a teaching job, and then he would put money into the account each month for his daughter's care. But as far as a relationship between them—it was over, *finito*. He was moving on and he expected her to do the same. She begged him to reconsider, promised him the moon, but, in the end, he walked away.

Watching from her living room window, with her

daughter balanced on one hip and the envelope with the bank book and card in the other, Grace felt her heart break. For years, she had believed Daniel loved her as much as she loved him, but, obviously, she had been wrong. Finley was all Grace had left. Once she found out she was pregnant, Daniel had forced her to abandon her father to keep him from learning of their affair. With Daniel by her side, she called him and told him goodbye, claiming he had chosen Cynthia's family over her. When she hung up, she felt nothing but relief. Daniel was her family, he and the new baby they would meet in seven-and-a-half months.

After Daniel departed, Grace fell into a deep depression. She spent weeks crying, stress eating, and throwing up. Finley's diapers rarely got changed and neither of them bathed. They both cried themselves to sleep. Then one morning, after her daughter nearly choked on food that had been abandoned on the floor days before, something inside of Grace snapped. She became human again. She pulled her life together and began applying for jobs. Within weeks, she landed a position teaching English at the high school in Ponderosa Falls, a town of nearly eight thousand residents, not more than twenty minutes from Boulder.

The account Daniel had left her had become her lifeline. To fund the beginning of her new life, she dipped into it again and again. She never wrote a check; instead, Grace used the debit card to withdraw money. She paid cash for everything to keep Daniel from knowing she was moving. She hired a moving company, settled into a small two-bedroom rental, and purchased furniture for the rundown cottage she would share with her daughter.

It wasn't until Daniel got the bank statement that he tried to call her, but, by then, she had dropped his phone plan and blocked his number. If he could abandon them, they could just as easily leave him.

After spending the better part of a month searching for Grace, Daniel finally tracked her down. In the living room of her house, the two had a knock-down, drag-out fight. At the end, they came to an agreement about visitation and money. Grace and Finley settled into their new life, one in which Daniel only made an appearance on the third Saturday of each month.

～～～～～

From the bank of the river, Grace dialed Daniel's number. As angry as she was with him, somewhere deep inside, she still fantasized about reconnecting, becoming family, not like they were before, but a *real* family. However, that was not what she wanted from him at the moment. She needed his therapy services, someone to listen, to help her get past her angst over the possibility of losing her job. After deserting their family, he owed her that much.

The phone rang six times before going to voicemail. Grace did not leave a message. She knew he wouldn't listen to it until late into the evening, and the likelihood of him returning her call based on her voicemail was almost nil. Instead, she pressed the *end* button and texted three numbers to him—*911*. It was less than a minute before her phone rang.

"What is it?" he angrily whispered. "I'm with a patient."

"I need to talk to you," she whined in the child-like voice she knew Daniel couldn't resist. He had always loved playing the role of *father figure* with her—even in the bedroom. Grace, with a daughter of her own, now saw this as disturbing.

"Not now!" he hissed. "I'll call you after this appointment." Then he was gone.

Grace set her phone on the ground and stared into the rapids. The air held a fine mist, but she didn't notice until she ran her hand through her hair, flattening it as the drops melded together. With the heel of her shoe, she pulled a small branch toward her. She snapped off a piece about a foot long and side-armed it into the wild swirl of leaves and mud. Immediately, it was swallowed up by the raging waters. She flung a second and then a third stick into the water while she waited for Daniel's call.

After several minutes, she stood up and walked along the river's edge, stepping over rocks and avoiding the small craters left by water that had overflowed its banks. Her phone finally rang as she neared the waterfall. She hastily made her way up the uneven slope, over some boulders, and away from the thundering noise of the plunging water.

"Daniel?" she said in the form of a question.

"What do you want?" His voice was sharp. Grace flinched.

"I just need to talk. I have a problem. Can you make time for me?" Silence fell on the other side of the call. "Daniel?" she questioned. "Are you still there?"

"I'm here," he said in a softer voice. "I was going to call you this evening anyway." Grace felt her heart flutter. "I was supposed to see Finley next weekend, but how about if I come Friday afternoon instead? I know it's still four days away. Can you wait until then? Will you be able to take the afternoon off and meet me at Halston?"

Grace laughed. "That's where I am right now. Yes, I can take time off. What time do you want to meet?"

"Just a minute," he said. Grace could hear him shuffling papers. "One thirty. I'll let you know if I need to change the time, but, ah, I should be able to make that work."

"Okay. I'll see you then." Grace sighed loudly.

"So, why aren't you in school right now?"

"That's what I need to talk about."

His voice deepened. "Did you..." he began, but she answered before he finished.

"No, I didn't get fired." She rolled her eyes at his pompous tone.

"Okay. I have to go. I have a patient right now. See you Friday. And, Grace, please make sure Finley's dressed for the weather. You don't always dress her warmly enough. Put her in that sweater I bought her for Christmas."

Grace cringed. "Wow!" was all she said before she hung up. Her heart had gone from happy to doleful in less than twenty seconds.

INTROSPECT

Dr. Daniel Fischer: "Grace has always been rather…off. She lives in this fantasy world that separates her from—what a psychiatrist isn't supposed to say—but *normal people.* I first saw her as a patient when she was seventeen. From the moment she walked into my office, her infatuation with me was undeniable. I made the mistake of being sucked into her fantasy. That one misstep led to a baby. It wasn't something I had planned."

Charmin Erickson: "I often see Grace Wilson in the grocery store. She lives in a rental on the other side of my landlord. When I suggested a playdate for our daughters, she stiff-armed me, telling me it wasn't a *good idea.* She even used air quotes. When I asked for an explanation, she rushed into the next aisle. It made no sense to me."

Sara Obermeyer: "I met Grace her first day in town. She seemed a bit scattered, but I chalked it up to being stressed out over the move. There was one thing that really bothered me. She kept leaving her daughter in her stroller on the sidewalk while she went inside to talk to the movers. Who does that? That kid could have disappeared in a heartbeat."

The Ex-Mrs. Denise Fischer: "I met Daniel after his residency. He was a few years older than me. We were drawn together by our mutual decision *not* to have children. He was from a large dysfunctional family, as was I. Looking back, I don't believe we were ever truly in love. I think we stayed together more out of convenience than anything. I wasn't shocked when he told me he'd had an affair. I was surprised it was with a patient, though. It was completely unethical. But I used that knowledge against him to garner myself a little nest egg. I didn't know his mistress was pregnant. Had I known, I could have held out for more. I guess Daniel got what he deserved."

CHAPTER SIX

Under the guise of an unavoidable, last minute doctor appointment for Finley, Grace raced out of school at noon on Friday. She hastily ran through the shower, her second of the day, and slipped into a red sundress and a white sweater before meticulously redoing her hair and make-up. With seconds to spare before she had to leave, she pulled a matching red sundress over Finley's head. On her way out the door, she grabbed the worn pink bag that had once housed diapers but now held snacks and toys. She settled the little girl into her car seat and ran her fingers through Finley's hair in a feeble attempt to tame her daughter's wild brown curls. Conceding defeat, she slammed the car door and hastily backed down the driveway.

"Crap!" she complained loudly.

"No!" Finley yelled from the backseat. "Bad word, Mommy! Bad girl!"

If she hadn't been so frazzled, Grace would have laughed. "I know, honey, but I forgot your dad wanted you to wear that sweater he bought you."

Back at the top of the driveway, she left the car running and the driver's door open. She raced into the house to retrieve the hideous sweater, tossing the torn-off tags onto the entry floor as she hurried out the door. She gritted her teeth, angry with Daniel's request. For all she knew, the sweater didn't even fit Finley.

In the still of the night, when sleep evaded her, she had imagined her time with Daniel. She had planned to arrive before him, to be provocatively sitting at the top of the bank when he drove into the parking lot. *His* girls, heads pressed together, would be playing on the soft white blanket, laughing. Daniel needed to see what he was missing, catch a glimpse of what he could have had. She had watched the video play out in her mind until it was no longer a plan but her reality. It was nearly 2:00 a.m. when her eyes closed for the remainder of the night.

But, like always, Grace was late; Daniel was already at the park when she arrived.

Before the car even came to a complete stop, he jerked the back door open. He unbuckled his daughter, picked her up, and lifted her above his head.

"Daddy!" Finley squealed as she threw her arms around his neck. "Daddy! Daddy! Daddy!"

Daniel grinned. "Finley! Finley! Finley!" Then he put her down and took her hand. "Does she have a sweater?" he asked Grace in his usual condescending way.

She bit her tongue and counted to five before she answered. It was a strategy he had taught her to use with others, but it was one she often used with him. "Of course, she does. It's in the backseat next to her. It was too warm in the car."

Daniel leaned in, grabbed the multicolored sweater, and slipped his daughter's arms into the sleeves. "Stay away from the water. Understand?" he warned her. But Finley just giggled and ran toward the bank, tumbling down the hillside toward the river. Surefooted, Daniel followed, making every effort to catch her before she hit the water. He grabbed one arm just before she rolled into the beastly river that had yet to give back any of its victims.

Grace clumsily followed Daniel down the hillside, arriving a full ten seconds behind him. She grabbed Finley's arm and fell to her knees. "No!" she yelled in the little girl's face. She pulled her hand back and swatted her daughter's backside. "Bad! Bad! Bad! You never go near the water. Look at you. Your feet are soaked, and your dress is filthy."

Finley's chin lifted upward as her lips curled down; she let out a howl that sounded almost animalistic. Her shoulders arched forward, bouncing as she wailed. She rubbed her eyes with her round fists and turned toward her father. Daniel picked her up and held her close. "M-mommy hit me," she sobbed.

"Mommy was scared, honey," Daniel told her softly. He rocked her back and forth, as he glared over her shoulder toward her mother.

"We talked about this, Grace," he hissed.

Grace's face clouded with anger. Her brows pulled tightly together, and her eyes narrowed as she scowled at him. "Screw you, Daniel," she seethed. "You think it's easy being a single parent? You see her one day a month. I'm with her every single day. *You* try taking care of a three-year-old. She's quite delightful!" Sarcasm dripped from every word.

"Mommy's mad!" Finley whimpered as she covered her ears. "Mommy's yelling." She looked at her mom. "Stop yelling! Bad Mommy! We don't yell."

Daniel took a deep breath. "No, we don't yell." He set his daughter on the ground as Grace spun around and stormed off toward the falls on the path that ran along the river. Finley was five steps behind her.

~~~~~

Grace needed time to cool off; it was just how she was. At best, they had tenuous relationship—at least when it came to Grace and her ups and downs. When they fought, Daniel always gave her time to pull herself together, to put into practice the techniques he had taught her. She had been gone for nearly ninety minutes when she heard him walking up the path behind her.

"You okay?" he asked softly.

She sat on a large boulder on the edge of the river. "I'm fine," she nodded, her back still toward him. "I just needed some time to cool off."

Daniel looked around. "Where's Finley?"

Grace turned toward him. "Don't!" she threatened. "I don't want to play your stupid games."

Daniel stepped forward, climbing over the smaller rocks that ran along the edge of the falls. Frantically searching the riverbank, he yelled, "Where is she, Grace?"

Grace felt her panic rise. "I left her with you."

"No, she followed you here. I watched her go. I thought you knew she was behind you."

"Finley!" Grace bellowed. "Finley! Finley!"

The two of them raced along the path at the edge of the falls and back toward the park. They screamed Finley's name repeatedly. One called and then the other, sounding like an eerie echo. They stopped yelling only long enough to listen for a response. But there was none.

As they neared the park, Daniel froze; Grace ran into him from behind. "What is it?" she asked.

But Daniel only pointed. Her heart sank, heavy with grief and dread. Finley's multicolored sweater tossed about in the rough waters, holding tightly to a low willow branch. But there was no sign of their daughter.

Grace dropped to the ground and sobbed hysterically as Daniel raced back along the river toward the falls, searching for his daughter in the rapids that slammed against the rocks. She pounded the ground until her hands bled. When she finally dialed 911, she could barely get the words out through her struggle to breathe.

INTROSPECT

Butch and Dixie Granger: "We saw that woman at the park on Monday afternoon. She was sitting alone near the river, throwing sticks into the water. She seemed quite interested in seeing how far they would go before they disappeared."

Principal Bart Holbrook: "Grace has some issues. Sometimes she has it together. Other times she will crumble with just a look. She wasn't the best teacher, but she wasn't the worst either. I didn't know her as a mother. She kept her home and school life separate."

School secretary, Noelle Strum: "I have never liked that woman. She didn't really fit in with our staff. But then again, it's not like she tried to either. From the day she walked through that door, she had a chip on her shoulder. I hate to say it, but I wouldn't be a bit surprised if she had something to do with her daughter's disappearance."

High School Dean, Mick Groves: "My son is a freshman this year. I worked his schedule so he wouldn't have to have Grace for English. He's not much into the whole school scene, so I handpicked teachers who are good with kids like him. For obvious reasons, I didn't choose her."

Kristen Lea: "I know Grace tried, but sometimes I think she didn't try hard enough. Don't get me wrong, I'm sure she's a wonderful person, but I saw her with her daughter on several occasions. There was something that never seemed quite right."

COLTON STONE

**Resident in Seventeen Foster Homes
Husband
Father
Carpenter**

CHAPTER SEVEN

Colton tugged the leash out of his front pocket and pulled the back door of his truck open. "Humphrey!" he called. "Humphrey!" he yelled again. A giggle drifted from the back of his silver F150 pick-up. His heart skipped a beat as he came around the corner and saw his daughter with her arms wrapped around the massive sheepdog. The two were never far apart.

The side of Addison's face was pressed against the dog's thick neck as she sang his name. "Hum-fee! Hum-fee! I love you, Hum-fee!" The two of them filled him with an incredible sense of joy. Since she was two, his daughter had been speaking in full sentences, but she still could not say the dog's name. With all the love Addy lavished on him, the big dog did not seem to care if she mangled his name.

"Hey, pumpkin," he said as he peeled her loose from the dog. He tried to kiss her, but Addy threw herself sideways, whining and reaching for the dog. He finally gave in and set her down. Addy pressed her forehead against Humphrey's side and rotated in a circle until her back was to him and her arms were spread outward along his back. Humphrey waited patiently as she wound his long, silky hair around her index fingers.

Colt laughed and his daughter mimicked it. "Are you two finally ready to go?" he asked. "Humphrey, in," he commanded. The year-old dog instantly obeyed, and the little girl followed him toward the truck. Colton lifted her into the backseat and strapped her into the car seat on the passenger's side. Once she was settled, he tickled her and listened to her hysterical giggles. Something inside him went soft. It had been a long time since he had heard his daughter laugh.

Humphrey clumsily turned in a circle before plopping onto the seat; he rested his massive chin on the little girl's lap. Colton watched her gently take the dog's hair in her chubby hands, running her fingers through it. She leaned forward and planted a kiss and a pat on the top of Humphrey's head. "That was so sweet, Addy. Humphrey loves you too."

"I love you, Hum-fee!" she laughed. "Love, love, love!"

Colton closed the door and walked to the other side of the truck. He drew in a deep breath before opening his door. Today was their new beginning, a fresh start. Life was finally going to begin again after a year of misery. He could feel it. But yet… Something didn't feel quite right. Before climbing into his truck, he searched the horizon but saw no one. Someone was watching him; he could feel their prying eyes. It was a feeling he had experienced often in the last year. Who it was, he couldn't imagine, but it frightened him. A shiver ran down his spine and he shuddered as he climbed into the truck and raced from the lot.

Addy laid her head on top of the dog's and hummed softly. She planted hordes of kisses on him. From time to time, she would wrinkle her nose and loudly complain *Yucky!* or *Icky!* before spitting the dog's fine hairs from her mouth. But within seconds, the cycle would begin again.

Periodically, he would recognize the tune she hummed, but often, it was just random notes strung together.

They hadn't been on the road for more than thirty minutes before Addy's humming slowed and her eyelids began to flutter. Colton tipped his mirror and looked at his daughter. A wide smile crossed his face and his heart felt full. There was no one he loved more, but, even as much as he loved her, he was grateful she was asleep. The hum of the tires against the pavement was comforting—mindless stretches of time to do nothing but remember. Driving was when he could breathe; it was when the memories of his past returned—the ones he needed to relive so he wouldn't forget.

The foster care system had not provided him with a forever family. Every night, he knelt on the floor of wherever he laid his head and prayed for someone to love him enough to make him part of their family. He'd had some wonderful foster families, but none of them had wanted him as much as he wanted them. Twice he came close, but something always happened, and he was inevitably returned to the system. By the time he turned thirteen, he knew he was too old to be adopted. From experience, most families wanted babies, toddlers, or at the very least, young children they could still influence and mold. They weren't interested in adopting a child who had moved headlong into the tumultuous adolescent years.

Colton had never been a bad kid—in fact, quite the opposite. He had always been a rule follower and a pleaser. So, it made no sense that his mother had abandoned him at an amusement park when he was five years old. The deep emotional scars of that day stayed with him. And, like sticking your tongue into a cavity, even though it causes pain, Colt continued to poke at his past, never letting it heal. The emotional festering nearly drove him insane, but, from time to time, the pain was drowned out by the good—his mom.

❦

The sun woke him the morning everything changed. He felt the warmth as it streamed through the open window and spread like a ribbon across his face. His mother was already up by the time he opened his eyes. The tiny apartment looked emptier than it had the night before when he had fallen asleep to one of his mother's unusual records and the smell of her funny cigarettes.

Colt sat up and called for his mom, but she didn't answer. He called again, his voice echoing in the two-room apartment. He threw back the covers to the strong smell of urine; he had wet the bed again. A flood of color raced up his neck and onto his cheeks; they burned with embarrassment as he climbed off the old mattress that lay on the floor in the middle of the empty room.

In the bathroom, he found clean clothes hanging over the side of the tub. Stripping down, he filled the sink with water and dunked his pajamas in and out the way his mother had taught him. He squeezed his pj's with his tiny hands, trying to remove as much water as he could before climbing onto the edge of the tub and tossing them over the top of the shower rod. Then he turned on the shower, grabbed the hand-held sprayer, and washed off in the tub. He had just finished drying off when the front door opened.

"Mom!" he called as he slipped on his clean underwear.

She stuck her head through the doorway. "I'm right here, buddy."

"Where's all of our stuff?" he asked, hopping on one foot as he poked a his other through the leg of his pants.

His mom walked into the tiny bathroom and sat on the toilet; she pulled him onto her lap and ran a warm hand against his naked back. "I think it's time for an adventure. What do you think, Colty?"

He wrapped his arms around her neck and whispered, "What kind of an adventure?" He had heard that line enough times to be wary. From past experiences, it could mean stealing things without getting caught or hanging out with a group of people he didn't know, or sleeping in their car for days on end, eating food they found in dumpsters behind restaurants.

"Well, I was thinking maybe we'd go for a little ride and spend the afternoon at an amusement park."

Colton's eyes narrowed as he leaned backward and studied her face.

"You heard me," his mom said. "An amusement park!"

Enthusiastically, he jumped off her lap and danced around the black and white checkered floor. "An amusement park?" he yelled in question, not sure he believed it. "An amusement park?" he hollered louder. "Woo-hoo! An amusement park!"

Something slammed against the ceiling in the apartment below. He felt the vibration against the bottom of his feet. His eyes grew wide, and he slapped a hand across his mouth. "I'm sorry, Momma," he whispered. But instead of getting angry, his mother just laughed.

"Hell, yes, an amusement park!" she screamed. "Screw you, old woman," she shouted as she repeatedly stamped her foot against the bathroom floor, laughing. "Colt baby, you keep celebrating. Dance like there's no tomorrow."

Colt stared at her for a moment, but her smile told him it was okay to continue his celebration. He loved his mom more than he ever had. Even when it wasn't, their life together was perfect.

"Now get your shoes on, and let's go have us an adventure."

The car was filled with boxes and bags when he crawled into the front seat of the rusted car his mother referred to as her *tin can*. "How long will it take to get there?" he asked his mom, but she never responded. Colton knew enough not to ask twice; he did not want her to change her mind.

The long car ride and the haunting music coming from

the cassette tape lulled him to sleep. He wasn't sure how long he had been out when his mother shut off the noisy car. Colton's eyes grew wide. Huge signs surrounded by moving lights announced their arrival. Rides sprouted into the sky off in the distance; smiling families raced toward the gate. "Where are we?" he asked, surprised she had kept her promise.

His mother smashed her weird smelling cigarette in the cupholder between the seats and put what was left in a little pouch. "At the amusement park, silly." She tickled him before she opened her door. "Come on. Let's go."

His door no longer opened, so Colton climbed into her seat and out the driver's side door. He tightly grabbed her hand. They laughed as they ran toward the park entrance. His mom opened her wallet and paid the woman with two twenty-dollar bills. He had never seen that much money in his entire life.

The woman at the counter wrapped a bright green bracelet around his wrist. Colt felt his shoulders arch backward; he had never felt so proud of anything. He touched the band, promising himself he would never take it off. His mom took his hand and started to run again. Her eyes were wild; he had seen that look many times before, but he had always been in a place where he could stay out of her line of sight when she got like that. His short legs moved as fast as they could to keep up. Colt's feet slapped the pavement as he ran. The oversized garage sale tennis shoe slid up and down on his heel. He curled his toes to keep them from falling off. His right shoulder ached as she pulled him through the crowd. Because of his height, his face often brushed against the stomachs or butts of strangers. He begged her to slow down. "Momma!" he called. "Momma, I'm tired."

She dropped his hand, threw her arms out to her sides, and spun in a circle with her chin aimed toward the sky. "Colt, baby, you can't be tired. We have so much to see and do." She bent down and pressed her forehead against his. He couldn't tell if she was looking at him, because her eyes darted all over his face. They had that glassy look like she wasn't really inside. When they looked like that, he always remained silent.

"Now quit being such a damn baby and keep up." She grabbed his hand and squeezed.

He wanted to cry out in pain, but he was afraid. His mother pushed her way through the crowd, running into people as she stumbled time and again. Colton wanted to make his mother happy, so, like usual, he kept his pain locked inside.

When they reached the merry-go-round, she finally let go. The line was short, too short for Colton. His stomach flip-flopped and he prayed the ride would break down before they reached the gate. The man pulled the chain back to let riders in. His mom ran ahead of him and jumped on a white horse with a blue saddle, but he froze at the gate.

"Come on, kid," the man yelled. "Are you riding or ain't cha?"

Colton was pushed forward by the momentum of the crowd behind him.

"Come on, baby. Get on," his mom said, patting the plastic horse next to her. Still, he didn't move. A woman finally took pity on him and lifted him onto the pink horse. His heart raced; he could feel it hammering in his chest. When the ride started to move, he wrapped both arms around the horse's neck, pressed his face into the hard plastic, and wept.

"Don't be such a chicken-shit, Colt." His mother poked him in the side. "If you can't enjoy life, you might as well be dead." She threw her arms into the air and let out a whoop. After a few minutes, the ride began to slow, and he realized he had done it—he had faced his fear.

As the sun slid across the sky, Colton grew braver. He rode the small boats and the airplanes while his mom watched him from behind the chain barrier. Before they left, he begged to ride the merry-go-round one more time; he had to prove to her he wasn't a baby.

"Momma, please?" he pleaded. "I want to show you how brave I am."

His mom looked toward the gigantic clock at the top of a tall tower. She stared at him, but he knew she wasn't looking at him. She had that same empty, faraway look she got on nights when she dropped onto the mattress with her clothes still on, instantly falling asleep. "Whatever." She dropped the wand with the long, brightly colored ribbons that she had been twisting in the air for the past few hours and started toward the merry-go-round.

"Momma." He pointed to the wand she had stolen from a booth when the man was helping someone else. "Your ribbon," he yelled. But she ignored him. He left it lying on the ground and ran after her, afraid of getting lost.

His mother didn't join him on the ride. Proudly, he went through the gate alone, prepared to show her how brave he was. Her eyes had softened, and she looked tired or sad or both. Like always, Colton took it upon himself to make her laugh. He blew her a kiss, but she didn't notice. He called her name, but she didn't respond.

When the ride started, he sat upright, holding the reins of the brown horse with the diamond on its forehead. He had chosen it because it was the biggest horse, not like the little pink one he had been afraid to ride before. He let go with one hand and waved to his mother as the carousel turned and his horse moved up and down. The second time around, he smiled when she called to him. "I love you, Colty. Be brave, my big boy." By the third time around, she was gone. Colton searched for her, snapping his head from side to side as the carousel circled, but the movement of the people passing by made him nauseous, so he stopped looking. Surely, she would be waiting for him at the gate when he walked out.

All the other children jumped off the horses and raced to the gate, but Colt hung back. Something didn't feel right. His stomach flopped again.

"Hurry up, kid," a different worker yelled at him. "You

gotta get off before I can let anybody else on."

Colt was embarrassed. He jumped off the side and shuffled through the gate. "Momma?" he called softly. "Momma!" he said louder, but she didn't answer. Then, with his best big-boy voice, he yelled again. "Momma?" But she never came. The crowd continued to pass by him like he didn't exist. Families laughed, children skipped, and parents held their young children's hands. But none of the people were *his* mother—his family.

Too afraid to leave the merry-go-round, he stood near the gate. If she came back for him, he didn't want to miss her. He didn't know how long he stood there, but he knew it was a long time. He was tired and his legs hurt. His stomach loudly complained. Tears slowly rolled down his face, but, before long, he was sobbing so hard, he could barely see.

A group of older boys gathered around him. They were laughing at him, passing him around the circle they had created. "Look at the widdle baby!" a kid with red pockmarks on his face said in a childish voice. "He pissed hisself."

INTROSPECT

Cheryl Gould: "I was a friend of that little boy's mother back when she disappeared. I'm not proud of those days. The drugs were flowing, and you did whatever you had to for your next fix. I know Sunny loved Colton; that's why I was surprised when Hector told us she was gone, that she'd ditched the kid a couple hours away at some amusement park. Sunny didn't just leave her son, she completely disappeared. We never saw her again. And you *know* Hector looked for her. She was his top girl; she made him more money than the rest of us combined."

Gavin Torrey: "I was running the merry-go-round on the day the kid got left. He stood there for a long time before I finally asked him where his old lady went. He couldn't stop blubbering long enough to tell me nothin'. It ain't my job to keep track of these kids and their folks. Some lady finally took pity on him and hauled him to the front gate. I have no idea whatever happened to him. I'm sure he's a grown-ass man with kids of his own by now."

Julie Vangsness: "I worked for social services back then. The police called me when they left the park with Colton. I met them at the station. He knew his name, but he didn't know anything about his mom except that she had *yellow* hair and everyone else called her Sunny. I figured someone would want to adopt him, but he ran up against a patch of bad luck. I had a special place in my heart for the little boy."

CHAPTER EIGHT

Addy yawned noisily, drawing Colton from his string of memories. He drew a deep breath before turning to check on his daughter.

"Hey, honey. Did you have a good nap?" He smiled at her before turning his attention back to the road. Addy closed her eyes again, but he knew it would not be for long. She was a talker.

They had a good ten hours, without stops, before they reached their new home. He had purchased the house after seeing only online photos and a few other snapshots a local realtor, Helena Nikolaou, had taken and emailed to him. The realtor had the inspection done for him. The house was fine except for a few minor issues he could fix himself. Helena had promised to be at the house when the moving company arrived that day. He was counting on her to tell them where things should go. It likely would not look the same as if he had been there himself, but it didn't matter. Just having it partially set up would make it so much easier, especially with Addy underfoot.

"Mommy?" Addy said as she looked across the backseat.

The hair on Colton's neck stood on end. He thought they were past this question.

Addy squirmed in her car seat, trying to see into the front passenger's seat. "Mommy?" she called louder.

Colton sucked in a deep breath and blew it out through tight lips. "Honey, remember, Mommy lives in *heaven* now." Those words cut. He had quit believing in God long ago. If Brit was in the place he once called heaven, he would never see her because he and God were at a permanent impasse, which meant Colt wouldn't be heading there after he died.

"Mommy!" Addy screamed. "I want Mommy!" The passenger's seat bounced as she pressed her feet against it, stiffening and bending her knees repeatedly. "Mommy!" A raspy sound gurgled in her throat as she screamed. Sweat and tears streamed down her reddening face. Snot ran from her nose as she screamed for her mother again and again.

Humphrey stood on the seat and tried to lick Addy's face, attempting to calm her outburst, but she pushed him away, kicking at him from the side. "No! No doggy! No Hum-fee!" After a few minutes, he moved to the far end of the seat and laid his head on Colton's shoulder near the driver's window.

"I know, boy. I don't know what to do either," Colt said as he reached over his shoulder and scratched the dog's muzzle.

A blue *rest stop* sign came into view as he rounded the next corner. Addy's shrieks made him cringe. He guided the truck off the road and into the lot. "Should we get out and play with Humphrey for a little while? Would that make you happy?"

The screaming slowly quieted while Colt waited for her to calm down. Addy looked at the dog, who stood on the opposite side of the bench seat. "Hum," she sniffed, "fee?" She wiped her eyes with her fists before beckoning the dog with her plump hands.

Colton felt his shoulders relax. Distraction was the key; it had been since the night Brit died. "And maybe, *maybe* if you're really good, we can get a treat before we get back into the truck." Addy's face lit up. "I thought you might like that." He grinned.

Addy nodded her head, still sniffing.

"Do you want some water, sweetie?" He opened his bottle and handed it to her. She took a long drink. When she was done, she wiped her mouth on her arm before handing it back to her dad.

"Hum-fee!" She giggled. "Hum-feeeeee!"

Colton smiled. They had made it through their worst Mommy crisis yet.

～～～～～

Sitting on a picnic bench watching his daughter run with Humphrey made Colton's day. These were the two people... He laughed out loud when he realized he thought of Humphrey as a person. But it was true; the dog belonged to the family every bit as much as he and Addy did. Yes, these were the two *people* he loved more than anyone else in the world. Actually, they were the only people he loved—since he lost his wife.

If you had asked Colt if he believed in love at first sight before he met Brittany, he would have emphatically said *no*. But then that moment played out, like in every cheesy movie ever made. He saw her across the crowded room and his heart felt like it would explode. It was so painful, for a moment, he thought he was having a heart attack. She was the most beautiful woman he had ever seen. The way her long wavy brown hair swung when she walked made him weak in the knees. Her vivid blue eyes were intoxicating. He felt like he had too much to drink. If he spoke, he knew his words would have been garbled and he would have stumbled over them. So instead, he spent the entire night watching her from a distance, stalking her every move, avoiding every other woman who tried to corner him.

Finally, when it looked like she was getting ready to leave, he followed her outside. Next to her car, Colton struck up a conversation, making her laugh with the light and easy comedic humor he was known for. He invited her for dessert at an all-night café, where the two drank coffee, sampled every flavor of pie, and laughed until the sun broke over the horizon.

They dated for nearly nine months before he worked up the courage to pop the question. Brit enthusiastically accepted, and they were married in her parents' backyard, in an elaborate fall wedding, less than two months later.

Short on dough, but long on ability as a carpenter, Colton bought a fixer-upper and turned it into her dream home. All day long, he worked a job that earned him money to survive, but the exhaustion of the day melted away each night when he began working on their future. Nothing was too big or too elaborate. If Brit could dream it, he could build it.

In the evenings, while he tore out and replaced walls, flooring, and cabinetry, Brit attended book clubs, hung out with her friends, or visited her parents. Colt was an introvert. He did not need people; he never had. Since his mother had abandoned him, he spent his entire adult life avoiding close relationships; he had learned people did not hang around. Because of that fear, his relationship with Brit surprised him.

His wife was his opposite. She craved a good conversation or a night out. It was what made her shine. At night, when Brit fell asleep, Colt would lie awake in their cramped apartment, exhausted, yet too wired to sleep, and watch his wife softly snore. What he felt for her was beyond love; it was something he could not put into words, something that filled his heart, voiding out all the bad things that had ever happened to him.

On the day the house was completed, as they raced around getting ready for work, Brit had asked him how things were coming along. Standing in only a towel around his waist, hair wet, dripping down his chest, he took her hand and lied. He convinced her it would be at least a month before he finished. The soaker tub was on backorder and the blinds were the wrong size; the backsplash in the kitchen had come from two different dye lots and the appliances had not been delivered. A smile never passed his lips, but his nerves almost gave him away. It was her birthday and, with the promise of all the beer they could drink, several of the guys he worked with helped him finish the house ahead of schedule—as the perfect gift.

Before he left for work, he told her he was taking her somewhere special to celebrate another trip around the sun. At exactly 6:30 p.m., he blindfolded her and helped her into the passenger's seat of her new Toyota Corolla.

"Where are we going?" She reached over and laid her hand on his arm.

"You just have to wait." He laughed. "Besides, you know you love surprises."

"You're not even going to give me a hint?" she whined.

Colt chuckled. "Nope. My lips are sealed."

Brit playfully slapped his arm. "Fine," she said as she settled in for the ride. To distract her, Colt talked about everything but the house, vacations, her family, and their future children. After the house was completed, that was their next goal.

When he stopped the car, he instructed her to wait for him to open her door. "Okay, be careful getting out," he said when he reached her side. She held his hand as he helped her out of the car. He wrapped an arm across her lower back and guided her along the walkway.

"Do I look ridiculous?" she asked. "I bet I do. I bet people are staring at me, aren't they? Can I take this off?" She reached up to remove the blindfold, but Colton caught her hand.

"Not yet," he told her. "You always try to cheat." He laughed. "You're just a cheater."

"I am not," she said quietly. "It's so peaceful here.

Listen, I can hear the birds singing."

Colt could not contain his excitement. "Yes, it's beautiful. You'll love it. It's a little out-of-the-way place I found on the way to one of my construction jobs."

He steered her along a paved surface he knew to be their driveway, but she believed was a sidewalk leading to a restaurant. Finally, he stopped and turned her to the right. "Okay, go ahead and take it off."

Brit lifted the blindfold from her face; the static had turned her hair into a wild mess of tiny dancing threads floating in the breeze.

"What?" She jumped up and down in her high heels. "What?" she cried again. She threw her arms around Colt's neck and planted a handful of kisses on his face. "It's beautiful! It's exactly as I pictured it. I'm so glad you made me stay away until you were done." Suddenly, she turned toward her husband. "Wait! You are done, right? Because this morning…"

"I lied." He laughed. "Happy birthday, hon. We can move in tomorrow…or tonight if you want."

She dropped her head against his shoulder. "Oh my God! This is so perfect!"

"I am so glad I made you wait to see it. Seeing your excitement was worth the wait." He tried to kiss her, but she kept turning her head toward the house. "Okay, you win. Let's go see the rest."

Brittany wandered from room to room and back again, excitedly wearing a path through their newly remodeled home. When she returned to the living room with the vaulted ceiling and dark wood beams, Colt had already laid out a blanket and a charcuterie board he had purchased earlier in the day. He had poured two glasses of wine and handed her one.

"To our future." He tapped his glass against hers.

"May it be as perfect as you are." She smiled.

They spent the evening talking, eating, and making love in different rooms of their new home.

A month later, Addy was the size of a grain of rice, but she was growing every day—the same as Colton's love for the two of them. Brit happily suffered through the morning sickness because she knew the end result.

While she was expecting, Brit still spent many of her evenings with friends and family; Colton continued to work late at one job site or another, stashing away money for their future, for their baby. But even though they were busy, they always found time to spend together, both before and after Addy was born.

Life was good, more than good. It was perfect—until it wasn't.

Shortly after his daughter turned two, Colt walked into the dark house after working later than normal. There wasn't a light on anywhere in the house. Something was off. He knew it before he opened the door; he could feel it.

"Brit?" he called from the entryway. "Brittany?" he yelled again. She had purchased a new Enclave just a few days before, and it was parked in the garage. He turned on a lamp in the living room but noticed nothing amiss. It wasn't until he flipped on the kitchen light that his world came crashing down. Brit was lying on the floor. A glass of water was tipped over and the liquid had puddled on the wood floor, an empty pill bottle next to her limp body.

His heart slammed in his chest. Panic raced through him as he dropped onto the floor and rolled her over. He felt for a heartbeat but found none. Sobbing, he called her name over and over, begging her to respond. Her body had already grown cold, and he knew it was too late; he just didn't want to believe it. Colt picked her up and cradled her in his arms as he begged God for mercy. It was during a slight pause in his sobbing that he saw the small piece of paper lying under the edge of the cabinet. Two words had been written in a fat black marker: *I can't*.

Colton didn't know how long he sat there, hysterically crying. But it was nearly morning by the time he had pulled himself together enough to call Brit's parents. He didn't call the police; he left that to Mark and Nichole. They arrived in less than fifteen minutes, holding him as the siren sang in the distance.

⚜

A year had passed since that horrific night. It had taken him that long to give up on the dream of his wife coming back. He had always been on shaky terms with God, but when he drove out of the driveway on the day she died, leaving the dream house he had built for his wife, he vowed never again to trust God—if God even existed.

INTROSPECT

Nichole Brooks: "I loved my daughter so much. When she and Colt married, my husband and I were thrilled. He was a wonderful son-in-law; at least until... It isn't fair. Nothing is fair. I lost my only daughter that day. How did Colton not see it coming? How did he not know she was suicidal?"

Mark Brooks: "Colton was the perfect husband and father. At least, that's the way I used to see him. I thought of him as my own son. But afterward, it was like he became someone we didn't even know. Do I blame him for my daughter's death? Yeah, I think I do. He was her husband for God's sake. He should have known. He should have told us she was struggling. Why didn't he tell us? Why?"

Carter Brooks: "I wish to God my sister had never met Colton Stone. That meeting led to the chain of events that sent her down this path of self-destruction. I miss her so much."

Kevin Patrick: "I worked on that house almost every night helping Colt finish it for his wife's birthday. It was an amazing place. I thought Brit would be so happy there, but... Well, things happen, things that are out of our control. Everyone else is blaming Colt. I think that's completely unfair. All I can say is that I'm glad he left Hollister. I think it'll be better for everyone now that he's gone."

CHAPTER NINE

It was nearly 2:00 a.m. when Colt drove into his driveway in Podany, Arizona. The silvery crescent moon disappeared and reappeared as the clouds floated across the dark sky. The stars followed suit, fighting the clouds to be seen.

The outside lights illuminated the long front porch. A small ray of light reached up from the deck, casting a yellow glow on the house number. The house looked better than the photos had indicated. He had chosen it for its location more than for its looks. Cosmetic work was something he could do when he had time.

Their new house was situated close to the Colorado River. It was an exaggerated stone's throw to California in the west and to Mexico in the south. He had chosen Podany because of its location. It was far enough from where he had lost his wife and where his mother had destroyed his childhood by discarding him on a whim. He was grateful to leave Colorado in his rearview mirror. It would take a lot for him to ever return to the place laced with so much loss.

His other reason for choosing to call Podany *home* was

because he had lined up a job with a company whose sole purpose was building houses for the homeless. It was not his usual commercial construction work. No, this job gave him a sense purpose. Colton needed that.

He switched off the ignition and stared at the house. A burst of air passed through his nostrils and his shoulders fell. He was past exhaustion; it was a fatigue that ran deep into his soul. He rested his head against the steering wheel and sighed. *Finally*, he thought. *Finally, a new beginning.*

Addy was asleep in her car seat, but Humphrey was anxious to get out of the truck. He licked Colt's neck until he finally conceded. Colton climbed out and opened the backseat door. The dog jumped from the seat and raced around the yard, searching for the perfect place to attend to his business. Colton stretched as he watched Humphrey sniff the trees and grass along the edge of the road, clearly checking for *social media posts* from the local four-legged residents. Immediately, he noticed the lack of humidity, something common to Colorado afternoons and evenings. It felt amazing.

Keeping a watchful eye on the dog, Colton crossed to the passenger's side and opened the back door. His daughter still did not move. He unbuckled her and thought about moving her into the house but changed his mind; he wanted to make sure her bed was ready first. Colt gently pushed the door closed, leaving it slightly ajar so as not to wake her. Then he opened the front door of his truck and grabbed a few bags and a large cardboard box marked *Important Files*. With his arms full, he used his foot to gently close the door before climbing the stairs to the house.

Helena had left the keys inside the planter. Colt set the box down, fished them out, unlocked the door, and shoved it open with his hip. Humphrey nearly knocked him over as he ran through the doorway. "Whoa, boy," he told him as he rubbed the dog's head. "Slow down. The house isn't going anywhere."

Colton glanced toward the truck. The ceiling light was

on, and Addy was motionless, so he closed the front door and made a once-through of the house. "Wow," he muttered. Helena had done an excellent job of supervising the moving process. Except for a stack of boxes in each room, the house was move-in ready—that was until he opened the door to the third bedroom. Except for a couple of boxes marked *Addy*, the room was bare. It was supposed to have been her room.

"What in the hell?" he said aloud. He rechecked the second bedroom. His desk and two large bookshelves had been placed there, just as he had instructed Helena. So, where was Addy's furniture?

He pulled his phone from his back pocket. There was a message from his realtor. Somewhere along the route, he'd had no service. The call had gone directly to voicemail. Helena told him precisely what he already knew. Addy's stuff hadn't made it to their new house. He was positive it was still all sitting behind the secret moving bookcase entrance into his daughter's room back in Hollister. The movers had missed her bedroom entirely.

Again, he sighed. Frustration was nothing new lately. For Colt, this was yet another blip in what amounted to a lifetime of unfortunate events. That was what his mother used to tell him. "It's just another *unfortunate event*, Colt, baby. Eventually, the universe will straighten itself out and good things will begin to happen." *When will that be?*

For tonight, he would put Addy in with him.

Humphrey whined as Colt shifted the boxes around in his bedroom, searching for the one with sheets. He pulled a pocketknife from his jeans and carefully cut open the top of the one labeled *blankets*. "What's the matter, boy?" he asked as the dog's complaints grew louder. "Didn't finish your business? You're going to have to wait a minute."

Colt hastily made the bed, throwing only a blanket over the fitted sheet. "Let's go get your sister," he said as he headed toward the door.

By the time Colton reached the entry, Humphrey was standing on his hind legs, scratching on the metal door. His nose was pressed against the wooden frame near the opening as he whined loudly. "That bad, is it?" Colton laughed as he pushed him down and pulled the door open. The dog took off like a shot and let out a deep bark, unlike any Colt had heard before.

Suddenly, he understood why. The moment felt surreal as the events moved in slow motion. The car's headlights bounced up and down as Addy stepped into its path. He heard the sickening thud and the squealing of the brakes. Colt knew he was running, but it felt exaggerated and slow. No matter how hard he tried, he could not get to his daughter fast enough.

The lights on the porches around him flashed on after he yelled. Colt wasn't sure if he was dreaming or if it was real. But when he dropped to his knees, when he saw the blood—so much blood—he knew. He was numb. The man in the car was already talking to 911, but Colt couldn't hear anything.

INTROSPECT

Davis Hall: "I didn't see her. Honestly, I didn't. Now I don't know if I will ever *not* see her. When I close my eyes, when I look in the mirror, when I drive at night—I see her. That little, round face, those chubby hands, that curly hair—all coated in blood."

Barb McMahon: "*Welcome to the neighborhood.* That runs through my mind constantly. *Welcome.* It's a downright shame this had to happen on the night they moved in, or at all. How do you get over something so horrific?"

Ellie Woller: "You can hate me if you want to, but I have no sympathy for that man. Who in the hell leaves a child alone in a vehicle in the middle of the night? I don't care what he was doing. That poor little girl deserves a much better father. Her blood is on his hands."

CHAPTER TEN

Only two other people were in the hospital waiting room as the dark sky slowly began its shift toward morning. The woman slept restlessly with her head pressed against the wall. The teenage girl's head lay in the woman's lap; her long legs were pulled into her stomach and her feet poked through the space under the arm of the short couch. A rolled-up jacket served as her pillow. Her arms were tucked inside her t-shirt and folded across her chest. She shivered several times.

Colton left the room, returned with a worn white blanket, and laid it over the girl. One of her eyes slowly opened. "Thank you," she mouthed. He smiled and nodded. Colton wished he would get the opportunity to see Addy at that age, but, until someone walked through that door with good news, he only saw the worst. A breath caught in his throat; a sob and a sigh wove together as a sound of pure distress escaped from him. He turned away, hoping neither of the others had noticed.

Colton pretended to read. Every few minutes, he

dropped the magazine on the table, got up, and paced the room. On each trek, he counted the twenty-two steps to the door and back again. Always on his third trip, he would leave the room and walk toward the door marked *Surgery*.

By some miracle, the paramedics had been able to keep his daughter alive. There had been no heartbeat, but they got it going. When they were pressing so hard on her chest, Colton was afraid they would break her. But she was already broken. He had shoved Humphrey through the front door of the house and jumped into his truck. He almost beat the ambulance to the hospital. Colton was grateful it wasn't more than a few blocks away.

Before the paramedics pulled the gurney from the ambulance, he was standing at the entrance of the Emergency Room. He never left Addy's side until they pushed her through the set of doors where he stood—the ones marked with the words he did not want to obey: *Do Not Enter*. It was where he last saw his baby girl alive; the last place he saw her take a breath. Colton pressed his forehead against the narrow glass panel and watched people scurry in and out of rooms. He needed to believe she was still breathing. If she died, he would have lost his last reason for living.

A man in scrubs on the other side of the door signaled for him to back away from the doors. He stepped to the side as they swung open, and the man walked through. The deep lines in his face told Colton he was not new to medicine.

"Mr. Stone?" the man asked.

"Yes?" he answered with a question of his own. His eyes narrowed and his back stiffened as he braced himself for bad news.

The man held out his hand. "I'm Doctor Theelin." He shook Colton's hand. "Your daughter is being prepped for surgery right now." He met Colt's eyes with a moment of silence. "I'm not going to make you any promises. Your daughter's lost a lot of blood. She has internal bleeding and a lot of broken bones. I don't even think we know all of her injuries yet."

Colton's eyes stung. The doctor laid a hand on his shoulder. "I can promise you this, though; I will do everything in my power to save your little girl."

A lump formed in Colt's throat; he tried to clear it, but it was no use. "How long?" he whispered.

The doctor shrugged. "I can't say, but I'll have someone let you know how things are going from time to time." Colt nodded. "In the meantime, your daughter's going to need blood."

Something inside Colton stirred. "I can do that." It was the first glimmer of hope he felt. It was the one thing he could do to help save Addy.

"We won't be able to use your blood for this first surgery, but I can assure you there are going to be many more in the next few days. It's a good idea to donate as soon as possible."

The doors swung open again. An older nurse walked through; her head was tilted down as she focused on the paper she clutched in both hands. Doctor Theelin stepped backward, blocking her path. He put his hand out to stop her from colliding with him. "June, can you set Mr. Stone up to donate blood as soon as possible?"

"Yes, doctor." She turned to Colt. "I'll contact the lab and have someone come get you."

"Thanks," he said. "Is there anything else I can do?"

The doctor gave him a weak smile as the nurse hurried down the hall. "Just say some prayers, son." He pressed a code into the keypad and reentered the restricted area.

Colt's legs ached with weakness. He watched the doctor rush down the hallway on the other side of the door. He was still standing in the exact same spot when the lab tech called his name fifteen minutes later.

His adrenaline was waning by the time he returned to the waiting room. If he thought he was tired before, he had been wrong. He was numb with exhaustion, but he would not let himself give in. Through his sleeve, he absently touched the cotton ball bandage on his arm as he dropped into one of the uncomfortable tan chairs.

Again, he picked up a magazine and flipped through the pages; he saw nothing. He rolled it up and squeezed it in his fist. If he did not set it down, he knew it would hit the window on the far side of the room. Angrily dropping it on the table, he stormed out of the room to the vending machine on the far end of the hallway. He pulled two one-dollar bills from his wallet and aimed them at the slot. One after the other, the machine pulled them inside and waited for him to make his selection. Shifting from one foot to the other, he scanned the snack selection. Who was he kidding? Even if he was hungry, he couldn't eat. With a sigh, he turned and walked away, leaving the money for the next person who needed to pass the time while they waited for a crumb of good news.

For what felt like hours, he walked the hallway, taking great care to step only inside the carpet squares, not on the seams. The rhyme he learned in one of his foster homes played in his head. *Step on a crack, break your mother's back. Step on a line; break your father's spine.* In the beginning, it had been only a game, something that made him feel like every other child, but then the teasing started, and it was not fun anymore. "Ah, don't chase *him*. Don't matter if he steps on nothin'. He ain't got no mom or dad anyhow. Pick somebody who's gonna care." And just like that, the game was a miserable reminder of being abandoned. For years, he went out of his way to step on every crack he could find. Rage flowed through him as his desire to punish his mother grew. In his mind, he saw her, back broken, lying on the floor writhing in pain. It brought a moment of peace, but the moment was always followed by a deep bout of sorrow.

Colt never thought of his dad. He didn't know why. When he was young, it had always been just the two of them. It was like his father never existed.

Colton was aware he was missing the lines and the

cracks as he walked through the hospital corridor. Maybe it was true for children too. From what the doctor told him, Addy didn't need any more cracks in her tiny body.

The hours passed and the waiting room began to fill with people arriving for early morning surgeries. True to his word, the doctor sent someone to speak with Colton every hour or so. With each report, he was grateful to know his baby was still living on this side of death.

Around noon, Dr. Theelin appeared in the doorway of the waiting room. He looked as drained as Colt felt. Colton jumped up as soon as he saw him. The doctor pointed a thumb over his shoulder, toward the doorway. Colt grabbed his jacket and followed.

"How'd things go?" he asked anxiously. "Is Addy okay?"

The surgeon continued to walk. "Let's talk where we have some privacy."

Halfway down the hall, he pushed a door open to a small conference room. He held it and signaled for Colt to enter. Dr. Theelin shut the door and seated himself in a chair on the opposite side of the table.

Colton's eyes grew wide, his stomach churned, and it became difficult to breathe. "Please, just tell me," he begged.

The doctor nodded. "Addison's…"

"It's Addy. That's what I call her. Addy," Colt said.

Dr. Theelin gave him a thin-lipped smile. "Okay. *Addy.*" He leaned back in his chair and crossed his legs before folding his hands in his lap. "Addy's surgery went as well as can be expected. She is in critical condition, however."

"What does that mean?"

The doctor looked at the wall above Colt's head. "Well, it means she could go either way. There are too many unknowns right now."

"So, she could still die?"

Dr. Theelin sighed. "Yes, but, Mr. Stone…"

"My name's Colt," he said. "Addy and I are a team. It's

just the two of us."

The doctor's mouth dropped open slightly. "Just you two?" he asked slowly. "May I ask about the girl's…Addy's mother?" He corrected himself midstream.

Colton looked up at the ceiling before returning his gaze to the doctor. "She committed suicide a year ago."

Dr. Theelin's eyes never left Colt. "I'm sorry. What about your daughter's grandparents?"

"Brit…" It pained him to even say her name. "That was my wife." The doctor nodded. "Well, once she died, they wanted nothing to do with Addy or me. They blame me for her death."

"Colt, I'm so sorry. I can't imagine anyone turning their back on a child."

Colt's breath hitched in his throat. If only the doctor knew his whole story. "So, can you imagine…well, if Addy dies…"

"It sounds like you've had a pretty rough year."

He shrugged, and then dropped his shoulders with the release of a long breath. "Addy and I just got here. It was supposed to be a fresh start. The beginning of something…better."

"Son," the doctor said, "sometimes things happen in life that we just don't understand."

Colt snorted. "There's been a lot of those things. I haven't understood any part of my life since I was five. Until that point, most things made sense."

Dr. Theelin stood up and moved to the chair next to Colt. He laid one hand on his shoulder and leaned his other elbow on the tabletop. "I'll do my best to explain everything." Colton could do nothing but nod. The kindness of the doctor made it impossible to speak.

"Addy's surgery went well, but we just don't know what the next twenty-four hours will bring. Anything could happen. She's being monitored constantly. There could still be internal bleeding we missed, or an infection could settle in. It's up to Addy now. If she's a fighter, she'll likely make it. If not…" The doctor squeezed Colt's shoulder. "Well, let's not go there. Do you understand? Do you have any questions?"

Colt drew a jagged breath. "Yeah," he whispered. "Why? Why did this happen?"

The doctor grimaced. "That's something I can't answer, son." He bit his lip and squeezed Colt's shoulder. "There is something else you need to know."

"What?" Colton shifted in his seat. He swiveled his chair to the right. "What is it?"

"I got your blood work report back from the lab just before I came to find you." Doctor Theelin paused.

Colt's shoulders rose with uncertainty. "And?"

"Son, do you know your blood type?"

His shoulders dropped and he drew a small breath. "I do. It's AB negative. I was *blessed* with the rarest blood type. Why are you asking?"

The doctor opened the folder he had set on the table. "Colt, Addy's blood type is O positive. Do you know what that means?"

Colt shrugged. "Isn't O the most common blood type? That's what her mother's blood type was."

"Okay, but, Colt, with both of them having O blood, you can't be Addy's biological father."

Colt laughed. "There must be a mistake. Brit and I *planned* to have Addy. She wasn't an accident." His eyes narrowed as he stared at the doctor. "You need to check again."

The doctor shook his head. "There was no mistake, son. They typed your blood twice. Each time, you came out as AB negative. And since we gave Addy a transfusion, we know she's O positive."

Colton's mind raced as the two men silently struggled with the truth. He tried to make sense of the news the doctor laid before him. "So, what you're saying is that my wife cheated on me? Is that right? Is that what you're telling me?"

The doctor leaned back. "Colt, why did your wife

commit suicide?"

Tears began to stream down Colton's face as the realization began to take hold. "I don't know. I honestly don't know."

Dr. Theelin leaned closer to him. "Was there a note? Did she say anything at all to you beforehand that might have made you suspect an affair?"

Colt thought back to the night he found his wife lying on the kitchen floor. Her cold body, the pill bottle, and the paper with two words—*I can't*. His shoulders sagged. "She cheated and I had no idea." Colt crossed his arms, laid his forehead on the table, and sobbed. His back rose and fell in rapid succession. "I was such a fool."

The doctor laid his hand on Colt's back. "No, son, you were a man in love."

Suddenly, Colt stood upright; his chair slammed against the wall of the small room. "No. You don't get it?" he yelled. "A year ago, I lost my wife, and today, I lost my daughter."

"Colt, for now, your daughter's still very much alive."

Colton kicked a chair as he walked past. "No, she's not! That girl in there is not *my* daughter." The door handle fought back as he attempted to jerk it open. He clenched his jaw and glared at the doctor. "I know you don't know me from any other person who's sat in a waiting room waiting for news." He repeatedly pulled the door open, banging it against the inside of his boot each time. "But here's something you might get. I've lost every female I've ever loved."

He slammed the door and he walked out of the room and down the corridor toward the front of the hospital. The doors slid open but not fast enough. "Sonofabitch!" he muttered as he slammed his shoulder into the metal frame on his way through. "Sonofabitch!" he whispered into the sky.

INTROSPECT

Dr. Theelin: "I've delivered a lot of bad news in my day, but this is one time I'm not likely to forget. Colton Stone is a broken man if I ever saw one."

DeeAnn Eickhoff: "I saw him when he first walked into the waiting room. He was clearly distraught, and yet, I knew he had a kind heart. He went out of his way to get a blanket to cover my daughter while we waited for my mother to get out of surgery. Not just anyone would do that."

Life without Air

THE VOICES WITHIN
(a choral poem)

NORAH	GRACE	COLTON
I lost my daughter to a disease I can't understand. Why, God?	I lost my daughter.	I lost my daughter.
	I can't understand why God would take away my child.	I can't understand.
		Take away my child, and I am nothing. My child is gone; the one I believed was mine.
I've lost all sense of hope.	I've lost all sense of hope for the future	I've lost all sense of hope.
She was my everything.		Everything I did, I did for her.
My precious baby girl. Why have you destroyed me, God?	My precious baby girl.	
		God doesn't exist. If so, why has he has destroyed everything I love?
	Everything I love was lost that day. How do I go on?	
How do I go on? How do I stop the hurt? The pain?		How do I go on?
	The pain!	The pain is more than I can bare.
	I can bare none of this. I want to die.	
I want to die. I don't want to go on. Where are you, God?	I want to die.	I want to die.
	God!	God doesn't exist. I said it before.
	I said it before; I will never give up hope for, my daughter.	
My daughter!		My daughter, never existed.
Lili	Finley	Addy

Mary Perrine

PART TWO

ONE YEAR HAS PASSED

LONGING

Empty arms. Aching heart.
Scars with jagged edges.
Longing to love and receive love.
Wishing to hold the child who is no more.
Yearning for what will never be.
Lost.
Drifting in a sea
of memories.

LIFE WITH NORAH—*Norah Van Pelt*

Life Without Air
Part two of a three-part series on the loss of a child

A year—one year since the dream of parenthood has sifted like white ocean sand through the fingers of the once happy parents. Well-meaning friends and family say it's time to move on; let go of the past and focus on the good things in their life. But they have never lost a child, or the hope of a future with one. Because it did not happen to them, they cannot feel the jagged edges of a broken heart; they have no idea how shattered it is. They do not understand the anxiety over never feeling whole again.

Grief is stubborn; it is sneaky. No matter how often it is pushed away, it lurks in the shadows, plotting its return. It appears like a burglar in the night, attacking at the most inconvenient times: at the grocery store, out for dinner with friends, in a meeting, or driving down the interstate. Even the slightest memory can unlock the door of this anguish, making it nearly impossible to close it again. When it happens in public, people stare. Their eyes dart away when they are caught watching the meltdown. For a few brief moments, they are satisfied with the life they constantly complain about, the workaholic spouse who rarely helps around the house, and the kids who drive them crazy. They will choose all of it over the grief-stricken life of a parent who has lost their tomorrow.

These distraught parents are no longer seen as individuals who *recently* lost a child. Compassion is waning. Suddenly, outsiders expect these one-time parents or parents-to-be to snap out of it, to host parties or celebrate occasions they do not have the energy for. There is an expectation to get excited over brightly colored wrapping paper with insignificant baubles inside, seasonal songs, colorful candles on top of cakes dripping in sugar, holiday lights that illuminate an entire city, and the 4th of July fireworks. They don't understand why smiling is hard and laughing is nearly impossible.

These heartbroken people want their well-meaning friends and relatives to talk, but they don't want them to say anything of significance. They want to forget, but they are more afraid they *will*. They want to remember everything, but it's too painful. What was once right-side up feels upside down. Their lungs are perfectly fine, and yet they struggle to breathe. One friend stops calling. Then two. Then three and four—until suddenly, the parents are left with silence, a phone that no longer buzzes with a call or text, and a birthday that passes without notice.

So what? they tell themselves. *I'll make new friends.* And they do, ones who do not know the baggage they carry, ones who are not bogged down in finding the right words. But those friends become close, and eventually the story pours out because, *surely, they'll understand.* The loss slowly begins to control the friendship, and once again, silence grows as the fissures grow deeper and longer.

The heartbroken parents want to talk, they need to talk, but they are afraid. So they bottle everything up inside until it feels like they're going to explode. They cry themselves to sleep, wake with puffy eyes and a throbbing headache, always making excuses of allergies or a little too much celebrating. Because after all, they have learned silence is right for everyone else—but it does nothing to heal their own heart.

It has been one year.

Norah Van Pelt is a syndicated columnist

NORAH VAN PELT

**Mother of an angel
Divorcee
Orphan
Columnist**

CHAPTER ELEVEN

The walls of Norah's office had been painted *anger brown*. Not long before Lili died, Mateo chose to update the building. An interior designer should have been consulted, but, based on the fact that the place looked like the Benjamin Moore paint factory had exploded, it was clear that hadn't happened. Her boss, a researcher at heart, discovered production increased when people worked in a space they loved. His goal: to make it homey, warm, and personal.

Two weeks before Lili died, Mateo showed up at the hospital with flowers and magazines. He also had a booklet of paint samples in his satchel and asked her to select a color when she had time. He did not notice *she* had all the time in the world; her daughter did not. Anger seethed through her as she grabbed the paint samples and twisted them open to the darkest colors. Once there, it took her twenty-three seconds to pick one. The color wasn't important, the name was.

"Are you sure?" he asked. "Anger brown?"

In a series of expletives she reserved for horrific

situations and dreadful people—both qualified that day—
she told him in no uncertain terms to paint her office that
color and to get out of Lili's room.

It had been a year since Lili died. One year of no hugs
and no one calling her *Mom*. Attending therapy and grief
meetings had helped her glimpse the future. Breathing did
not hurt like it had three hundred sixty-five days before or
even fifty days. She was finally able to move on.

A cardboard box of personal items sat in the center of
her empty desk. The only thing that had not been packed was
a photo of Lili. Norah lifted the 11 x 14-inch frame from the
wall. She turned her back toward the window and let the
sunlight wash over the non-glare glass. Her daughter's smile
was warm, but her eyes did not have the spark Norah
remembered. Now, it was evident she had already been sick.
Seth had taken the picture just days before Lili's first
symptoms appeared. For weeks, her daughter had lodged a
variety of complaints. Sometimes her stomach hurt, other
times her head. At night, she cried because her elbows and
knees ached. She wanted to eat, but when Norah brought her
food, she refused it. The mother in her chalked it up to the
stomach bug that had been passed around her daycare.

For two days, they cuddled together on the couch,
wrapped in blankets, watching movies on Netflix or half-
hour programs on public television. Lili slept much of each
day while Norah just held her, grateful for the time together.
But that blessed feeling turned to panic when on the second
night, while Norah was changing Lili's pajamas, she noticed
large bruises on her back and legs. After tugging on a clean
nightgown, she carried her lethargic daughter to the car and
raced to the ER. There had been no diagnosis that night, but
the doctor scheduled her to meet with an oncologist the
following morning. Norah felt the rug being yanked from
under her. Lili couldn't have cancer. It was a disease
reserved for older people—like her mother—not her sweet
baby girl.

The next couple of weeks moved at a snail's pace.

Norah spent too much time in her head. She wanted answers, but they were not quick in coming. The oncologist had told her what she did not want to hear, but a definitive answer would not arrive for weeks. Norah waited. By the time the doctor called with the results, Norah had already resigned herself to the diagnosis. She had researched childhood cancer. Once they knew they were fighting leukemia, Norah dove headfirst into a rabbit hole, investigating day and night while her daughter slept. She knew, according to the American Cancer Organization for Childhood Leukemia, thirty-five hundred children in the United States were diagnosed with it every year. The five-year survival rate was ninety percent. But the survival rate for acute myelogenous leukemia, the kind Lili had, was less: sixty to seventy percent. The stats went on and on, and within days, Norah could recite them in her sleep.

Fight, Lili! Fight! became her mantra. She prayed, she cried, and she cussed out the universe. The one thing she did not do—was get support from Seth. The minute she mentioned *cancer*, his flame went out—for Norah, for Lili, for their wedding vows. The *in sickness and in health* apparently did not apply to his daughter. He made excuses for not coming home and for not calling. When he was home, he never touched his daughter. He acted like cancer was contagious and just being around Lili might give him the big C also. After a while, Lili stopped asking for him. Norah was glad. She did not have the energy to care what Seth did. The only thing she had the strength to focus on was her daughter.

That had been over a year ago. She could finally look at photos of Lili without falling apart. Remembering the good times brought happy tears, just as remembering her illness brought tears of heartbreak. Life was not perfect; it never would be, but it was slowly getting better.

A double knock on the door frame stole her attention from the photo. She smiled as she laid the picture on her desk. "Mateo, I was sort of expecting you."

He scowled as he looked around the nearly empty office. "You don't have to leave, you know."

"I know," Norah said, "but actually, I do. I need a fresh start."

Her boss leaned his head against the wide door frame and sighed. "Norah, I fought to get your column into syndication. That's huge!" Then, like a child, he stuck his lower lip out and pouted. "Are you still going to leave me?"

Norah laughed. "I'm not leaving the column, just the *Chronicle*." She shifted the items in the box to make room for Lili's photo. "I'll still be writing *Life with Norah* and it will still appear in *your* paper."

"Nonetheless, you're leaving us. And not just us, but all of California."

Norah moved toward her boss and rested her forehead against his chest. She wrapped her arms around him and patted his back. "I doubt very much that California will miss me," she said with a smirk.

"Oh, you don't know that." He sighed. "I sure as hell hope Podunk, Arizona knows what a treasure they are getting."

She frowned. "It's Podany."

"Same thing," he teased.

"Not even close." Norah walked to the window and looked out at the city. "I will miss this place." She crossed her feet and leaned against her desk. "The people, the town, the good memories." She turned toward Mateo. Her voice grew soft. "What I won't miss are the bad memories. The ones *after* Lili."

Mateo sat on the desk next to her and draped an arm over her shoulder. "You've had more than your share of heartbreak. Your mom, Seth, Lili, and…"

"And now my dad," Norah nodded once. She released the breath she hadn't realized she had been holding. "Just when I thought I was finally getting my act together…" She stepped sideways, out from under Mateo's arm. "Okay." She pointed toward the door. "Enough. I've got to go say my goodbyes and you've got to find someone else to fill this office—another stupid person who'll put up with your mind-numbing crap." She chuckled.

Her boss walked toward the door. "This will always be *your* office, Norah." He tapped the door frame as he walked through it. He spun around and pointed at her empty desk. "Even with someone else sitting in that chair."

Norah grinned. "Then can I take the desk with me?" she teased.

"Hell no," Mateo frowned. "You own your own paper now. Let the *Podunk Press* buy you a desk."

She sighed. "Again, it's Podany."

"Whatever," he said with an exaggerated eye roll and a smirk as he walked away.

Norah plopped into her chair and ran her hands along the front edge of the mahogany desk. She would miss the *Chronicle* and her colleagues, but it was time to move on. The next chapter of her life would be so much different. Being a mom was no longer one of her dreams. No child could replace Lili; she did not want them to. Instead, the paper she bought with a small portion of the money her dad left her would be her baby. It was the start of something new, something she could watch grow. Taking chances had never been her thing, but as scared as she had been when she signed the papers to purchase it, she knew it was the right move.

INTROSPECT

Brent Staller: "I heard Norah bought a small newspaper in Arizona. Seems like a big jump to go from writing a column to owning a paper. I give her a year, year-and-a-half tops, and she'll be back here begging Mateo for her job back."

Justin Castillo: "I didn't even know Norah was leaving until last week. Here's to hoping this fast-tracks my movement toward the top. I'm sick of writing obituaries."

CHAPTER TWELVE

Norah poured herself a glass of chianti; she took a long sip before returning it to the wooden tray on one end of the massive coffee table. The sleek leather sofa randomly dotted with throw pillows in shades of red, yellow, and cream faced the wall of windows. Other than frames, the French doors were the only break in the floor-to-ceiling glass. Two days had passed since she moved out of the home she and Seth had shared for nearly fifteen years. A handful of boxes was all that made the cut when she left. Most of those contained photos and important papers. The furniture, knickknacks, and decorations of her past were just things, reminders of what once was. It was all baggage she did not want in her new life. Those barriers included her wedding photos, which she ceremoniously burned in her backyard firepit—on an evening that may or may not have included a full bottle of wine and an entire box of chocolates. She could not quite remember, but, based on her deep fog and debilitating headache the following morning, she wouldn't have bet against it.

Two weeks after signing the paperwork to take ownership of the *Podany Press*, she returned to Arizona to find a house. Somehow, she had always imagined it to be similar to their house in Mason Hills: a single-family home situated in the middle of a close-knit neighborhood. But the realtor had changed her vision of *home* when she showed her a listing for a condo that had just come on the market. It was love at first sight. The marble countertops and cathedral ceiling with the dark beams and open trusses, the long glass fireplace that ran the length of one wall, sharing the warmth and light with her home office on the other side—was not who she was; it was not anything she could have even imagined. She had been born and raised on Iowa soil; that alone kept her feet on the ground and her head out of the clouds. No, the condo was not her. But since Lili's death, *she* was not herself anymore either. During the past year, she had become someone entirely different than the woman who laid her daughter to rest and gave her husband the boot. The condo fit her *new* persona—Norah, a wealthy, single businesswoman who was driven.

The building had been built with four condos on the fifth floor, the top of the building. Each level below housed nearly two dozen apartments. The residences were each unique, exquisite, and tasteful. The architect had designed all four condos with a grand view of the Colorado River. A gathering room, complete with a professional kitchen, restaurant-style dining room, bathrooms, game room, and elevator took up the space on the backside of the condos. Each condo opened into the shared space used by only those on the fifth floor. Stairs led to a rooftop terrace built to resemble a restaurant patio, complete with tables and chairs covered by an oversize pergola.

Norah came from old money. At one time, her grandparents had owned thousands of acres of land in Iowa. It was a goldmine for those who wanted to farm it. By the time her grandfather was in his seventies, he had begun to sell off the land little by little, tucking away money for a rainy day. After her grandparents passed, her father held the reins to the land, still thousands of acres. Like his father, he began to sell it off, investing the money in high yield stocks. When he died, he left Norah more money than she could spend in a lifetime—more money than a hundred people could spend in a lifetime. She sold off the rest of the land and left her only connection to the state.

After purchasing the condo, Norah was at a loss. With the staging furniture gone, all she saw was a dauntingly enormous, empty space. She needed someone else's input. No, what she needed was someone to turn it into a magnificently cozy abode. *Words* she could weave together into something sterling, not a house. The saltbox she and Seth had owned had been eclectic and functional at best. Nothing matched. Clearly, it would never have been featured in *Good Housekeeping* magazine. More likely, it would have shown up in a *how not to decorate* segment on HGTV. The house had not been their focus. It had been a place to lay their heads while they built their careers, a nest egg for the future, nothing more. It was their first step toward starting a family.

Every wall was as white as the day they moved in. Neither the walls nor the woodwork had ever received another coat of paint. The hue of their furniture could be found in every section of the color wheel. There had been no complementary or adjacent colors. It lacked a color scheme completely. There was no rhyme or reason to any of it: location, design, or color. If a piece of furniture served a purpose, they bought it. Norah's father had once described their house as looking like the Lucky Charms rainbow threw up. And once Lili was born, there had been no time to worry about the place they lived.

What had, before their daughter was born, at least been clean, was covered in baby puke and crayon scribblings. Looking back, Norah realized how messed up they really were, not just her and Seth as a couple, but their entire life. She could point her finger solely at Seth, but she had plainly been part of the problem. Norah had allowed Seth to control everything. In her new life, she wanted better.

For an entire day, she pored over ads for interior designers in the area, reading reviews and looking at photo galleries before settling on one just down the street from the newspaper, in the old part of town filled with small shops and crumbling storefronts yet to be restored. The owner, Tracy Hentges, met her at the door late one evening after work. After a long conversation, Tracy gladly accepted the challenge. It was not often she had a client give her free rein to design a space befitting a magazine cover, all with an *unlimited* budget.

As the evening wore on, the two women moved from owner-client relationship toward friendship. Norah needed friends in Podany. In the few hours they spent together, she knew Tracy would design the perfect space; she could trust her. And when it came time to see her condo, it was wildly beyond her expectations.

Norah stared out at the Colorado River. Her hatred for water had only been exacerbated by her attempt to drown herself the year before. But her condo sat high above the water, a safe distance from death—purposeful or accidental. From her window, the boats that cruised the river looked like toys in a turquoise-blue stream. The mountains and the magnificent, gnarled trees in the distance completed the perfect picture.

One by one, she hauled her boxes from her SUV, up the elevator, and to the top floor. Each one was emptied as it arrived in the condo. A handful of rare books and some of her mother's most treasured decorations she could not part with found a home on one of the many tables or shelves. Norah laughed once she hung the dozen or so pieces of clothing she had packed in her bedroom-size walk-in closet with the long center island; the room resembled a business going under and was hosting a fire sale. Clothes shopping was first on her to-do list.

Before leaving Mason Hills, Norah had Marie Kondo-ed everything in her house. If it did not *spark joy*, it went. There was not much from her previous life that gave her pleasure at all. She joked she had even Marie Kondo-ed Seth, but that happened long before she ever started packing.

⁓⁓

A few days before she was set to leave Mason Hills, she hired a couple of neighbor kids to help her haul everything to her front lawn. With a thick black marker, she made a huge sign out of a chunk of an old appliance box. *Free! If you need it, take it. If you know someone who needs it, give it to them. Don't be greedy. Be kind!* By noon, the lawn that, at 7:00 a.m. had been heavily strewn with furniture, clothing, and household goods, was nearly empty. Her sign had worked. As far as she could tell, people took only what they could use: a can opener, a set of sheets, a pair of curtains, a frying pan, or a setting of dishes. Seth's belongings, the ones he had not collected when she kicked him out, walked away with new owners as well: golf clubs, tools, and exercise equipment.

At 3:00 p.m., a man, who had helped himself to only a pair of muffin tins earlier in the day, arrived with his teenage son and a U-Haul truck. He offered to haul the remaining items to the Salvation Army where he volunteered one weekend a month. Norah was incredibly grateful. For reasons unknown, she had not thought through the ending of her free sale. In her mind, it had all vanished, found a happy home with someone who needed and wanted it. What was left was loaded into the truck in less than ten minutes.

The brakes on the rental truck squealed as the man stopped to check for traffic at the end of Norah's driveway. Her stomach lurched. "Wait!" she yelled as she raced toward the driver's door. "Please stop!" she called, pounding on the white door with the abstract splash of orange. "I have a few more boxes."

"Okay." The man shrugged before backing up the short driveway. His son jumped out, lifted the latch, and shoved the door upward on its rollers. The creaking resounded in Norah's brain as she struggled with her last-minute decision. Finally, she led the strangers inside the nearly empty house and pointed toward a stack of boxes, each labeled with a large cursive L.

"Were these boxes you forgot to put out today?" the man asked, nodding toward the stack.

Norah's eyes brimmed with tears as she shook her head. She swiped her hands across her face and pressed her tongue to the roof of her mouth to stop the flow.

The boy's eyes grew wide. His shoulders raised as he tucked his hands into his front pockets. He shifted his glance from Norah to his dad. She knew he was waiting for his father to say something to rectify the situation.

"Ma'am, I'm sorry. I didn't mean to upset..." The man stepped toward her.

She held her palms toward him as she took a deep breath and released it through her pursed lips. "No, I'm okay. It's fine. Sometimes..." She looked at the boxes. "Sometimes it just hits me." She turned back toward the man and his son. The boy was nearly as tall as his father. She and Lili would never grow into what the man and the boy had. "Grief," she said.

The man's nod was slow and methodical. "Lost my wife a few months back. I completely understand. Grief's a sneaky bastard."

Norah threw her arms around the man's neck. "Thank you," she whispered. "Thank you for understanding." When she let go, she smiled at the boy. "I'm so sorry about your mom." She gently touched his cheek. "Life's not fair, is it?"

The boy shook his head. "No," he whispered. He cast his eyes toward the floor and clenched his jaw.

"It gets better," Norah told him as she wrapped her arms around him. "I promise you."

At first, his body was rigid, but suddenly, he lifted his hands and hugged her. "Thank you." The words were broken as he tried to squeeze them out.

"Okay. Let's get these boxes into the truck," the man said.

Norah let go of the boy and touched his shoulder. "What's your name?"

"Josh," he whispered. He pressed his finger and thumb against his eyes.

"You've got this, Josh," she said quietly.

After several moments of silence, the three of them moved from a shared heartache to loading the remnants of Lili's life. Ten boxes of varying sizes and three brightly wrapped birthday gifts marked *Lili* went into the back of the truck.

Before the man and his son departed, she handed the boy two $100 bills and told them she wanted to pay for the truck rental and dinner. "Thank you," the man said. "It's nice to meet someone who has walked the same path as Josh and me."

Norah stood in the driveway and watched the truck drive away with the last of Lili's belongings. For a brief second, she wanted to chase after it, but she fought the urge. The truck bounced as it traveled along the uneven pavement on the road. Even after it turned north, and she could no longer see it, she did not move. She needed to hold on to the moment a few seconds longer. Once she moved away, Lili would be left behind.

She wiped her hands on the front of her capris and headed toward the front of her yard. Norah tried to remove the sale post, but she had pounded the stake in farther than she thought. With her teeth gritted, she wiggled it back and forth until the ground let loose and returned it to her. She folded the cardboard around the square stick and shoved it into the trash can, pushing it down along the inside edge of the overflowing container.

Memories of Lili and Seth haunted her as she wandered the yard one last time. At the front door, she saw them as a family of three, first-time parents, nervously laughing and whispering as their daughter slept soundly in Norah's arms.

Lili's chalk drawings popped onto the driveway as Norah walked across it: rainbows, misshapen hearts, smiling faces, and Lili's name spelled with four straight lines and two big circles dotting the I's. The apple trees Seth had planted their first summer in the house were already snowing white blossoms. The lilac bush was in full bloom, a reminder of the row of lilacs her mom planted along their fence line back in Iowa.

As she stepped around the corner of the house, Norah dropped to her knees; the ghost of Lili playing was so clear, for a moment, she thought it was real. She was afraid to move, frightened that even a solitary blink would destroy the vision she had been gifted. The image slowly faded. "Don't go, Lili," she whispered. "Please, don't leave me again." But in a heartbeat, the vision was gone. Slowly, she stood and walked across the patio where she had spent hours watching Lili and her future children play.

But all those memories were part of her old life, the one she was determined to bury. She could not look back; it was the future that needed her.

A short stack of boxes remained in the corner of the living room. Norah opened the door between the house and the garage and loaded them into her Land Rover. Those boxes contained everything she owned. Little had made the cut from her old life to her new one.

The house was heavy with silence. Norah's eyes burned as the hush of nothingness pressed down on her until she thought she would go crazy. She plucked her phone from her back pocket. "Hey, Siri, play nineties pop hits." Music filled the kitchen as she turned on the tap and tilted her face under the stream of water, catching the ice-cold liquid in her mouth. She had not thought to keep a plate, cup, or anything else. It had all gone in the free sale.

Her stomach grumbled, complaining loudly about its lack of attention. She had not eaten since the night before, and the cheese and stale crackers had done little to curb her hunger. For much of the day, she dreamt about the turkey, swiss, and cranberry sandwich on wild rice bread and the Diet Coke she had picked up late the night before at Delia's Deli. She typically avoided gluten, but today was a day worth celebrating—the beginning of everything new and good.

Norah had just unwrapped the sandwich when the doorbell rang. "Come in!" she yelled before taking a big bite. Her neighbors had been stopping by all week, bidding her farewell. But it wasn't a neighbor who rounded the corner into the kitchen. It was Seth. Her throat constricted. It tightened around the crusty edge of the bread. The bite felt too big; it would not slide down and she couldn't cough it up. She popped the top of the soda can, opened her mouth wide, and poured it down her throat, softening the bread as they melted together. Slowly, the bite slid down.

"You okay?" her ex asked.

Norah touched her throat as she continued to battle for a full breath. "Why-why are you here?" she asked. Then she took another draw from the can.

Without a word, Seth left the kitchen and wandered through the house. Norah let him go. She had no interest in small talk with anyone, but especially not her ex-husband. She took another, smaller bite of her sandwich, then wrapped it up in the white paper and returned it to the empty fridge. Seth had ruined her celebration.

When he returned, his face was white; his mouth twisted as if he were trying to say something but couldn't form the words. He leaned against the wall and watched her as she brushed invisible crumbs from the countertop where she had been eating.

"Why are you here?" Norah asked him again.

Seth walked toward her, stopping close enough for her to feel his breath on her face, close enough to smell the thick, sweet smell of whiskey. "We had it all, once." His eyes bored into her, and her cheeks began to burn. She stepped back with one foot, creating distance between them. "We could have it all again, Nor. We could try again. Marriage, another baby. It couldn't happen twice. It would work this time. I know it would."

With the tiniest of movements, Norah shook her head. "No. It wouldn't. And I don't want it to." She watched his face. "There'd be too many reminders of what we lost, Seth. Can't you see that?"

He tried to grab her hand, but she pulled her arms back and side-stepped out of his reach. "I still love you, Norah."

Norah laughed out loud. It was pointed and cruel. "You love the idea of who we *were,* the us *before* Lili got sick. That's what you're in love with, Seth."

He shook his head. "No, Nor. I love *you.*"

She tightly clenched her jaw and leaned toward him. "Well, I don't love you." She glowered. "Honestly, I'm not sure I ever did." Seth jerked back as if she had slapped him.

Norah locked her hands together behind her back and circled around him. He turned with her, always facing her. "Seth, *you* left," Norah hissed. "You were here when things were good, but you ran when things got bad." She clicked her tongue. "How do you ever expect me to forgive you?" His face fell. Norah was not even close to being done with her tirade. "Do you know how many times Lili asked for you when she first got sick? Do you have any idea how many times I lied for you? Or how many times I told her about your *important* job helping people? She needed you, Seth. More than that, she *wanted* you." Norah leaned closer to him. "Lili wanted a dad. There were nights she woke up begging for you." Norah glared at him. "But she got me instead. You know why, Seth?" Three times, she poked a finger against her chest. "Because I stayed. *I* was here for her."

Seth's eyes grew glossy. A lone tear rolled down his cheek. Everything in Norah hardened. He could go to hell as far as she was concerned. She had nothing left for him: no empathy, no love, nothing. They were done.

Seth grabbed her hand and held it tightly, refusing to let it go no matter how hard she fought. "Please, Nor. Can we try? I'll go to counseling. I'll do whatever you want. Just, please, don't let this be the end," he begged. "Don't shut me out."

Norah stopped battling. He loosened his grip as she lifted their hands and laid them against her chest. Tenderly, she said, "I'm broken, Seth. *You* broke me. *You* did this." Angrily, she thrust his hands back at him. "You could have supported me; you *should* have supported me." Norah wrapped her hands behind her head and moved toward the breakfast nook. "I'm not saying it wouldn't have been hard, but if we'd been there for one another, if we'd gone through it *together*, there might have been a chance for us. But you didn't want that. You couldn't do it. You thought only about yourself—not me, not Lili—just you." The low afternoon sun bled through the vertical blinds scattering light the color of saffron across the room. "I loved you, Seth. *Past tense—* loved. I loved you because you gave me Lili. But you and your selfishness destroyed that love. And now you want it back. But you just want the good times, the happy times. You want *good old Seth and his perfect life, perfect wife.*" Norah turned toward the island. "How do I know you would stay the next time we hit a wall? Or the next? How could I ever trust you with my heart again?"

Seth looked sadder than Norah had ever seen him.

"You don't. You can't," he said softly. "I screwed up. I know that. All we can do is try. Aren't we worth that much? Isn't that what Lili would have wanted for us?"

Norah's anger flared. "How dare you ask me what Lili would have wanted!" She moved toward him. "Back then, she wanted *you*. But in the end, she barely remembered you were her father." Norah pulled her hand back and slapped Seth across the face; the sound reverberated across the empty kitchen. Guilt instantly washed over her. She had never hit anyone; it was not who she was.

An angry red handprint grew on Seth's cheek as he turned away from her and moved toward the window. He stood there for a long time before speaking. "I suppose I deserved that," he said, still staring into the backyard.

From the empty window seat in the breakfast nook, Norah studied the backyard also. She was confident her ex was focused on something other than the ghosts of their past. Lili's tire swing swayed ever so slightly in the light breeze. Seth pointed toward it through the grimy glass Norah never got around to washing.

"Do you remember the day we put up that tire swing?" He nodded toward it.

"Why?" she asked, coldly.

"You made a promise to me that day. Do you remember?"

Norah remembered, but she was not about to confess. Instead, she tipped her eyes downward and sighed.

"You told me that swing was like a pendulum. No matter how far it went in the wrong direction, it would always return—just like our love. Remember?"

Suddenly, he was standing in front of her. He grabbed her slender arms; his fingertips nearly touched. Norah could feel his grip tighten, digging into the flesh as her hands stiffened and edged toward numbness.

"Yes," she finally whispered. "But that was before." Twisting sideways, she jerked her arms free and stepped away from Seth. "*Before* you showed me what kind of a man you really are." Her eyes narrowed as she held his in a callous stare. She pointed toward the door. "Get out, Seth. Now!"

Neither of them moved. Norah's arm began to ache as she continued to point, but she wasn't about to give in. Seth would never again control her; he would never win.

Finally, Seth took a step toward the door. "We're not done, Norah. We're not done by a long shot. I'll be back, again and again, and I *will* wear you down."

Norah's loud guffaw surprised even her. "Like hell you will. Now get out!"

Seth stepped toward her again. "You better watch yourself, Norah. Because this isn't over." Then, he spit in her face and let himself out. Norah wiped her cheek with the bottom of her t-shirt and followed him outside, watching until he drove away. When his car disappeared, she raced down the stairs, heading next door to borrow a saw. It took her the better part of half an hour, but she cut the tire swing out of the tree and threw it on top of the trash can near the street.

If Seth remembered that swing as a metaphor for their life, she wanted to make sure it ended the same way their marriage had—in a pile of garbage.

Norah had yet to meet her three fifth-floor neighbors; she would when she was ready. While arranging to leave her old life, she thought a lot about how to know who to let into her past and who to keep at arm's length. After a lot of soul searching, she realized the answer was easy; no one could ever know about Lili—or Seth. As far as anyone else was concerned, neither of them ever existed.

There was only one problem with her plan—her syndicated column. She was under contract to write one more column on the death of a child. She would write it, but then she would let the column go. With any luck at all, people would never connect her with the syndicated columnist Norah Van Pelt. To make certain they didn't, she went back to using her married name: Norah Burke. That way, no one would ever know they were one and the same. If they asked, she would simply deny it.

INTROSPECT

Seth Burke: "I met Norah at Parker College back in Iowa. We became close, but we were never an item. We never dated. I was in love with her from the moment I first saw her, but I knew she didn't feel the same. I frequented the Denny's where she worked, sometimes with my buddies, but often with a girl I lavished with a lot of attention. I hoped to make her jealous, but she was so focused on school that she barely noticed me. When she moved to California with her dad, I stayed behind and finished my last semester of school. Then, I moved west.

I wouldn't say I stalked her, but I orchestrated a chance meeting at the newspaper where she worked. One thing led to another, and before she knew it, I had convinced her to marry me. Norah only thinks we're done. It's amazing the information you have access to when you're a cop. It gives you a lot of power."

Walt Canter: "I loaned Norah the saw. My wife and I watched her from our back porch. I offered to help her cut the swing down, but she refused. She said she had to do it herself. We saw Seth leave earlier. Watching how angrily she wielded that saw, I am sure she was destroying more than that swing."

CHAPTER THIRTEEN

Just as the golden rays of the sun flooded the sky in a glorious burst of color, Norah opened her eyes. Lately, her daydreams and the vivid and often chaotic ones playing out in her sleep were almost always about the newspaper. Her new adventure was never far from her mind, especially on this day, her first one at the helm. But then again, as hard as she tried, her daughter's memory was never more than a blink away either.

Norah rolled over and stretched; her hand bumped the framed photo of Lili. Her daughter filled the pillow space where the ghost of her ex used to lie. Not in this bed, but in a different one, as Lili would have said, *many sleeps ago.* "Good morning, sweetheart." She leaned sideways and kissed the glass. Carefully, she opened her nightstand and wrapped the wooden frame inside several sheets of pink tissue paper before closing the drawer. She did not dare leave the photo out since her fictitious biography claimed neither wife nor mother. No one had yet to visit, but there was always a first time.

She was showered, dressed, and out the door in under forty-five minutes. Butterflies fluttered in her stomach, giving way to the anxiety she felt since waiting at the first stoplight near her condo. Her timing was impeccably off. Every stoplight turned red just before her arrival. Each stop added to her nervous stomach. She wasn't sure if she was relieved or terrified when she pulled into the parking ramp across the street from the *Press*.

According to her online search the night before, the bakery, just down from the parking ramp, had a five-star rating. Less than ten minutes after it opened, Norah walked out the red and white checked door with a large pink box filled with a variety of treats for her first staff meeting. Traffic raced up and down the street as she attempted to jaywalk her way to the paper.

"It's a lot safer to cross at the light," a man called from down the street.

Norah laughed. "I see that now," she said as she turned in his direction and walked toward the corner.

"Luke Simon," he said.

"Norah Va..." She cringed. "Burke," she corrected. "Norah Burke."

Luke squinted and tipped his head. "Really?" he teased. 'Cuz, it sounded a little like you weren't quite sure?"

The blood instantly rushed up Norah's neck and onto her cheeks; a mirror would have reflected the brilliant color. "Positive." She laughed softly. With her arms full, she wagged her head toward the newspaper building across the street. "New owner of the *Podany Press*. Today's my first day. I have to confess, I'm a little nervous."

"Really? I would never have known, what with those fluorescent cheeks and forgetting your name like that." Luke winked at her. "You had me completely fooled." His laugh was warm. It reminded her of her dad's. "How about you give me the box of...whatever this is you're bribing your staff with, and I'll carry it over there for you?"

Afraid he would change his mind, Norah handed him

the box, as it had grown heavy during their conversation. She shifted the straps of her tote and purse higher up on her shoulder. They chatted as they waited for the light to change before crossing.

"Well, this is me," she said, balancing her tote on a lifted knee as she dug for her keys.

Luke chuckled. "That sounded like the way you'd end a date. I guess if this were a date, it was the shortest date in the history of dates. And I should know," he said. "I've been on some really short ones. One time I got ditched by a girl with no front teeth. And another time, the girl didn't even show up, but her *mother* did. I kid you not! I am the king of bad dates. I could tell you so many stories."

"Ooo-kay." Norah cut him off. "Nice to meet you, Luke, but I need to set up for my meeting." She pushed the door open and held it with a hip. Instead of handing the box to Norah, Luke walked through the door and toward the conference room. She followed him across the main part of the office. "What are you doing?"

He set the box on the table and grinned as he walked past her and into the office next door.

"What's, ah, going on here?" she asked from the doorway.

Luke stepped out of the office and pulled the door closed. "Luke Simon." He pointed a finger toward the placard on the door. "Norah Va-Burke's right-hand man." He offered her his hand as he laughed out loud.

Norah slowly nodded; a sideways smile gradually grew. "You are a character, aren't you?" She chuckled. "I think I like you, Luke Simon."

"Everybody does," he said. "Everybody except the women I try to date."

＊＊＊

Fourteen people shuffled out of the conference room and past Norah after their first staff meeting. Each one stopped to greet her, taking a few moments to share their name and role again. Luke stayed behind, watching. He knew more than she wanted him to.

"Got those names now?" he asked.

"For your information, I'm actually quite good with names...Larry." She walked away with a grin.

"Luke!" he yelled. "It's Luke."

"Whatever you say, Lenny."

Norah smiled as she sat down for the first time since crawling out of bed. The new shoes she bought had been a bad idea; they were killing her feet already and the clock had not even tolled 10:30. She kicked herself for her choice of clothing. Most of her staff wore jeans and tennis shoes. And why wouldn't they? Reporters were always on the go, literally running after stories. She had been in their shoes before. This wasn't the *Chronicle*—the elite newspaper of northern California; it was small-town Podany, Arizona. Mateo may have been right. At the moment, it felt a little Podunk-ish, not her condo, but the downtown area, and certainly, the people who worked for her.

She slipped her shoes back on as someone knocked on her door. "Hey, Boss. You got a minute?"

"Open door policy," Norah told her. "I'm always available. And, please, call me Norah."

"Okay." The woman shrugged. "Elizabeth Ramos," she reminded Norah. "But everyone calls me Beth."

"Good to know." Norah smiled. "What can I do for you, Beth?"

"Well..." She stepped inside the office but kept her hand on the doorknob. "Do you, ah, mind if I shut this?"

"By all means." Norah's brows furrowed. Was this going to be one of those tattletale exchanges, the ones Mateo had warned her about? *George isn't doing his job. Bailey has some issues. Susan leaves early every day.* If so, she would stop it before Beth blurted out even one newspaper secret.

Beth slid into a chair opposite Norah. "So, here's the thing..." *Yes, this was it,* Norah thought. She could feel it.

"I do research for the paper. If reporters need to know something, they send their requests my way. Well, Boss, I mean, Norah..." Beth shook her head. "Honestly, Norah doesn't work for me. I'm just going to refer to you as Boss. If that's okay?"

Norah laughed. "Go for it."

"Okay, Boss. So, here's the thing. As a researcher, I know you write a syndicated column under the name of Norah Van Pelt."

Norah's face turned white; her stomach flipped. The jig was up. They had already figured out who she was. "Who else knows?" she asked dryly.

"Are you kidding?" Beth laughed. "No one. The rest of these clowns are too focused on trying to write their next big story and kissing your ass in hopes of earning a big raise."

Norah chuckled; her shoulders dropped as she relaxed. In a different situation, Beth would have been hilarious, but this was her situation—the one she was trying to hide. "So, no one here knows?"

"Well, I didn't say *no* one." She pointed to the wall that separated Norah's office from her right-hand man. "Luke knows. He's a nosey-ass assistant." Beth's grin was short-lived. "But you aren't going to find anyone more trustworthy or loyal than him."

Norah stood up and limped to the wall she shared with Luke.

"Ah, new shoes. You might want to put your money into some flats," Beth said.

Norah pounded on the wall. "I'll be shopping tonight, if I can still walk by then." She frowned.

The door burst open. Luke skidded through the doorway on his slippery loafers, almost falling onto Norah's desk. The old *Laverne and Shirley* show she and her mother used to watch popped into her head when he hit her desk. He could have been Lenny or Squiggy. "You rang?" he said, righting himself.

Norah raised her hands out to her sides. "Are you

always like this?"

Beth nodded. "Always." She punched him in the shoulder as he flopped into the chair next to her. "Shut the door, dumbass," Beth told him.

"Wow!" Norah chuckled. "It's like *Animal House* around here."

"Mmm...more or less," Luke agreed as he reached back and shoved the door closed.

Norah's face grew grim. "So, Beth tells me the two of you know who I am."

"Ah, yeah." Luke arched an eyebrow. "You're the infamous Norah Va Burke. Right?" He giggled as he elbowed Beth. Evidently, Beth had already heard the story of their meeting.

She rolled her eyes. "Very funny. But since you know, I feel like I need to explain."

"Hey, Boss. You don't owe us any explanations," Beth told her.

"I think I do. You see, I've always written under the name Norah Van Pelt. As you know, I write a syndicated column under that name—*Life with Norah*. Some of the things I write about can get...well, rather personal, so I've never revealed my photo to the public. I'm shown only as a generic female. I guess I'm sort of the Betty Crocker of columns." She chuckled. Neither of them laughed. *Betty Crocker clearly was a Midwest character*. Her eyes flitted between Beth and Luke. "Do you understand?"

The two nodded like a couple of bobblehead dolls. "I don't get the Betty Crocker reference, but..." Luke smiled.

Norah waved a palm toward him. "Never mind. Bad joke." She looked directly at Beth. "Are you okay with keeping my secret?"

Beth leaned forward, "Did you really lose a child?"

The question threw Norah; she felt like she'd had the wind knocked out of her. Her face grew pale, and her answer released in a rush of air. "Yes."

Beth rounded the corner of her desk and warmly

wrapped her arms around Norah's neck. "Thank you for writing those columns. You put words to what I have felt for so long but could never express." She stood up and pointed to her chest. "Researcher here, not writer."

"You lost a child?" Norah asked empathetically.

Beth returned to her chair and reached for Luke's hand. "Luke and I both. I had several miscarriages." She folded and unfolded her hands. I know that's not like losing a real baby. I never got to see or hold the ones I carried, but…"

"Don't ever marginalize your loss, Beth. Your hope for a baby and a future with one was every bit as real as mine. A loss is a loss whether you held the child or not." Norah's heart broke for her.

"Thanks," Beth said as she looked at Luke. "And Luke, well."

She looked at him with a softness that surprised Norah. Norah saw him squeeze Beth's hand.

"Well, Luke and I were married during that time. The loss tore us apart as a couple, but over the years, it strengthened our friendship." Beth made a funny face at him. "So, anyway, if you want to date him or anything, have at it."

Norah laughed.

"Well, on that note, I'm going back to work." Luke popped up, pulled the door open, and disappeared around the corner.

"I'm sorry," Norah whispered to Beth as her researcher leaned against the door frame of her open office door.

"Your columns have helped a lot. I'm looking forward to your next one."

INTROSPECT

Beth Ramos: "Norah is going to be all right. I've known her for like five minutes and I already like her."

Luke Simon: "It still hurts to talk about the children we could have had. Everyone thinks about the mom and what

108

losing a baby does to her. No one ever really considers how the dad-to-be feels. Listening to Norah and Beth talk, I sort of felt invisible. I know they didn't mean to leave me out, but... Anyway, I'm a man, right? I'm supposed to be tough and macho and all that other crap they teach you from the time you pop out of the womb. Only, I don't really ever feel that way."

CHAPTER FOURTEEN

A massive bouquet of flowers walked into Norah's office on a pair of short legs. "Where would you like me to put these?" the pinched voice asked.

"Oh my gosh!" Norah jumped up and took the enormous arrangement. She misjudged the size and the weight as she wrapped her arms around it; her hands barely connected on the other side of the large metal can. Norah stumbled toward the table, nearly dropping it before she set it down. She wondered how the woman she now knew as Maxine had carried it all the way from the front office. "That's quite the bouquet! Where did it come from?"

The woman tried to shake out the cramp that had started in one forearm. "Tiffany, from the flower shop, just delivered it. Her words, 'The sender asked to be kept anonymous, so tell Norah if she even thinks about trying to find out who sent it, my lips are sealed.'" Maxine rubbed her thumb on the inside of her arm. "I didn't think I was going to make it back here."

"I can't believe you did. It's huge." Norah pulled a

yellow rose from the vase and handed it to her administrative assistant. "Thank you."

Maxine smelled the rose and winked at her. "Someone has quite the secret admirer."

"Not so much a secret admirer. I'm pretty sure this came from my old boss."

Maxine walked out of Norah's office. Her words faded as she moved farther away. "He must really, *really* miss you."

Norah pushed her door shut and hit Mateo's number on her cell phone. "Well, well, well. If it isn't the owner of the *Podunk Press* in Podunk, Arizona," he teased. "Shouldn't you be bossing people around by now? I mean, it is your first day, right?"

"Well, obviously, you know it is." She smiled as she looked at the bouquet. "Thank you for the flowers. They are gorgeous. I've never seen a bouquet that big."

A few seconds of silence fell across the line. "What flowers?" Mateo finally asked.

"What flowers?" she repeated, laughing. "You're such a joker."

Mateo cleared his throat. "Ah, now I feel kind of bad, Norah. I never sent you flowers. I probably should have."

Norah seemed genuinely confused. "Seriously? These aren't from you?"

"Wasn't there a card?"

"The florist told my secretary they were from an anonymous sender, and she wasn't allowed to tell me who sent them. I seriously thought they were from you."

"Sorry, Norah. It wasn't me." She could tell Mateo was walking as they spoke. "I hate to do this to you on your first day, but I'm already late for a meeting. Can I call you tonight? I want to hear all about your first day, but duty calls."

"Sure," Norah said. "Later." She pressed the end call button and studied the flowers. The only other person who could have made this grand gesture was Seth. She didn't want them to be from him, but she knew better.

A massive blister had grown on the side of her little toe and it rubbed as she walked to the center of the main office. "Can I have everyone's attention?" The office slowly quieted. Norah turned around in a circle to make sure everyone was listening. "It turns out, the flowers that were delivered are for all of us." She turned toward Maxine. "Are there vases around here?"

"There are. If not, I'll improvise."

"Perfect!" Norah folded her hands together in front of her waist. "Maxine's going to make everyone a bouquet and bring it to your desk. Is everyone okay with that?" Heads bounced up and down as her staff returned to work.

Maxine amassed fifteen vases and set to work dividing up the flowers. "You only need fourteen," Norah told her.

"Oh, I'm sorry. I thought the big vase would be too large for a smaller bouquet. Do you want me to keep a bigger one for you?"

Norah shook her head. "No. No. Don't leave me any." Maxine looked confused. "Those flowers come with a price," Norah told her.

⚬⚬⚬⚬⚬

Around noon, Norah limped out of the office in her pumps and returned fifteen minutes later in a pair of Coach tennis shoes. They looked ridiculous with her $400, black designer dress and jacket, but, with a large bandage over the top of the blister, she never felt better.

Norah, Beth, and Luke spent the remainder of the afternoon meeting with reporters about the stories they were working on, what needs they had, and ideas they wanted to pitch for future articles. When she finished with the reporters, she visited the printers in the back warehouse. By 5:00 p.m., the office began to quiet and by 6:00, nearly everyone had gone home.

Luke stuck his head into her office. "Hey, want to go grab a drink somewhere?"

"Wow! Are you taking what Beth said seriously?" She grinned.

Luke tilted his head slightly. "About what?"

"Dating me." She laughed.

His face grew red. "This isn't a date. It's just…" Norah could tell he was flustered. "Never mind. You probably want to get home anyway."

Norah stood up. "Luke, I was just kidding. Yes, I'd love a glass of wine."

Beth came around the corner. "Me too. It's been one of those days."

"Great!" Norah was all about making friends. "The more the merrier."

Luke leaned against the wall but turned when he saw movement in the outer office. "Ah, Norah," Luke said. "There's some guy standing at the front counter."

Norah nearly spit out a mouthful of cold coffee when she saw who it was. "Seth," she whispered. "What the hell?"

INTROSPECT

Luke Simon: "I have no idea how that guy even got into the office. Maxine always locks the door when she leaves at 5:00. I'm not even sure who this Seth character is. But Norah sure did. And she didn't seem very happy to see him."

Beth Ramos: "Something wasn't right. I could tell from Norah's face and the way she said the guy's name. She kind of spit it out of her mouth—along with the coffee—which was kind of funny. But she said his name more like a hiss. We offered to stay, but Norah insisted we go. I told Luke we should stay anyway, but he's a guy and… Well, he's a guy."

Maxine Miller: "Of course I locked the door. I remember because I dropped the keys when I pulled them out of the lock. We had that lock replaced not that long ago. We might have to have it changed again."

Seth Burke: "Norah is mine. She's been since the minute I decided she was. A guy's gotta do what a guy's gotta do. I told her it wasn't over. I'll never let her go."

GRACE WILSON

Mother of an angel
Former Mistress
Estranged Daughter
Questionable Teacher
Lost

CHAPTER FIFTEEN

The bathroom mirror reflected who Grace had become in the twelve months since her daughter's drowning: a rawboned, lonely, and lost soul with not a single reason to move forward. Not a day passed without the same recurring thought—*no one needed her, no one wanted her, and no one loved her*. Her outside world had gone silent; the noises she heard came from within. Every inch of her screamed for help, begged for mercy, yet no one was listening. She chastised herself for who she was and who she no longer was. She wasn't a mother, but she wasn't *not* a mother either. Grace had brought a child into the world, but because of her irresponsible, self-obsessed need to be loved, her daughter was gone. Did she even have the right to still call Finley her *daughter*? Or had that been taken away too?

On the day Finley disappeared, the only other thing besides the sweater that was found was a lone white sock with lace around the top, but because of the surge of water that churned over the boulders, her daughter's body was still missing. *Too dangerous to go in. Moving too fast. It's a river. She could be miles away. The likelihood of finding her is almost nil.* They repeated those phrases, but she could not hear them. When she attempted to take her own life, wishing to be slammed into the rocks and held down by the angry force of nature, they restrained her. She fought, but they were stronger. She begged, but they stopped listening. She cried, but they ignored her.

Nearly every day, Grace walked the path along the Rock River. Searching. Even in the dead of winter, when the river slowed to nothing more than a sluggish trickle, she braved the elements and continued to search. She wanted to know where her daughter was; she needed to know. Closure was what she longed for, but she wasn't sure she wanted it. If there was no body, there was still hope. But Grace knew better.

Then, one day, just before the witching hour when the sun settled below the horizon for the night, Grace uncovered something: a small leather shoe. Her heart raced as she jerked off her glove and scraped at the ice with her fingernails, digging to unearth it. She prayed there was more: a foot, a body, but it was just the shoe. She pressed the ice-cold leather against her cheek. This gave her hope—hope she could give her daughter a final resting place.

Grace returned to the river every day after that, eager for additional finds, but the river surrendered nothing else.

Grace splashed water on her face as a gentle knock called to her. It was the third in five minutes. "Grace, are you okay?" It was Clarice—once again checking on her after her frenzied escape from their meeting with the student yearbook editors.

Most of the time, Grace *was* fine; other times, out of the blue, the crushing heartbreak would hit her so intensely, she could not see straight. *Grief.* Her line of vision would narrow, a rush of black clouding her peripheral view, creating a tunnel of light, a narrow spotlight. At the end of the passageway, Finley always waited, picking wildflowers along the river's edge and waving to someone beyond the picture. Grace would always try to reach her, arms stretched forward, gauchely running toward what seemed so real but was nothing more than an apparition. Slowly, the vision would disappear, fade to black, and she would plunge to the floor. It had happened in front of her students, on the street, and at home more times than she cared to admit.

The first few times it occurred, Grace thought she had been stricken with epilepsy or a brain tumor. *Punishment.* She believed it was her penance for being a terrible mother. But the doctor had assured her it was nothing more than her brain playing tricks on her, a sort of hallucination caused by the loss of control she desperately wanted. Before she left, he handed her a quarter sheet of paper with the name and phone number of a therapist. Grace had smiled, but when she walked out of the building, she ripped it into tiny pieces, letting them drift from her hand as she stomped toward her car. She swallowed down a fresh swell of rage to keep from making a scene. Daniel had made her distrust therapists.

She saw the handle of the bathroom door wiggle. Ben, one of the night custodians, spoke to her from the other side as he searched for the key to unlock the door. "I'm coming in to check on you, Grace," he said.

"I'm okay," Grace called weakly. "Don't come in. I'm on the toilet." Suddenly, the handle stopped moving. "I'm going to go home, though. I think I may have food poisoning."

Lying came easy to Grace. Since the day her stepmother, Cynthia, sent her away to the camp for girls with unwanted behaviors, Grace had perfected lying. *I'm fine. Never better. Don't worry about me.* She had lied about her affair with Daniel, she had lied to her father about why she was breaking ties, and she had just lied to Clarice and Ben. It was how she coped with life. *I've got it. It's all under control.* But the worst part was that she lied to herself.

"Grace, are you really okay?" Clarice asked from the

other side of the still-locked door.

"Yes. I'm fine. It's just a stomachache. Nothing a little more time in this bathroom won't fix."

Silence met her false admission. "Alright, if you're sure. Call me, though…if you need anything. Do you have your phone with you?"

"I do. I'll call. I promise," she said.

Grace tiptoed to the door and listened to Clarice run down the hallway, her flip-flops slapping against the floor. She leaned her head against the heavy door and wept.

Again, she returned to the mirror. Dark bags had grown under her eyes, much too dark for someone in their twenties. Make-up would not even conceal them. No, that wasn't correct; make-up was an option. She just didn't have the energy or the desire to apply it. Her sloppy ponytail with escaping clumps of hair looked unprofessional, as did her oversized sweatshirt with the torn neckline. Truthfully, *all* her clothes were baggy these days. Her dress clothes had been shoved to one side of her closet, making way for the sweatshirts, leggings, and jeans she opted for daily.

Bart, who threatened not to offer her a continuing contract just a year earlier, had signed the papers granting her tenure. He sent them to the district office and placed a copy in her mailbox in the workroom without any discussion. Even he did not have the heart to take away the one thing she had left.

She was a terrible teacher, and she knew it. Everyone else did too. Less and less time was spent in front of her kids and more of it was spent on the sidelines: watching but not seeing, listening but not hearing, breathing, but not existing. Every Friday, Jen emailed lesson plans for the following week to Grace and dropped off materials for those lessons— always when Grace wasn't in the room. When Finley died, Grace had pushed away even Jen, her only true friend. On good days, Grace could follow through with some fidelity, but on bad days, she left her students to fend for themselves, to glean pieces of knowledge from their textbooks or from one another. It wasn't fair, and it wasn't right.

Each night, just before she collapsed into another night of restless slumber, she promised herself *tomorrow* would be different. *Tomorrow* would be the day she would put her life back together and join the real world. But tomorrow never came. The sun would rise, and the nicer clothes Grace had laid out the night before would get tossed to the floor in favor of something that looked like she had slept in it. Truthfully, many nights, she had.

Still hiding in the bathroom, Grace pressed her ear to the door. Silence echoed loudly. Slowly, she twisted the lock and pulled the door open.

"Well, there she is," Ben called from down the hall. "You okay, Grace? You had Clarice pretty worried."

"I am." Grace hurried toward the team room. "I'll feel better as soon as I get home, though."

Ben shook the dust from his wide dust mop. "Do you want me to take you home?"

"No, I'm okay." Grace gave him a frail smile before slipping into the team room to grab her purse. "No, I'm not," she said out loud to the empty room. "I'll never be okay again."

The river roared as the highland water raced over the rocks and headed toward the falls. A year ago, Grace and Finley met Daniel in this very spot. Her biggest problem at the time had been the possibility of not earning tenure. In the grand scheme of life, losing her job seemed minor. Losing Finley was all that mattered.

On that Friday afternoon, she had let Daniel provoke her yet again. He was good at it. When they were together, she let it slide, too afraid to question him. Since they split, she was a little freer with her words. So, instead of focusing on Finley, she had dropped the ball. No, that wasn't true. The drowning of their daughter rested solely on Daniel. It was entirely his fault. He had thrown digs at her until she couldn't take anymore. She would never forgive him—not today, not ever. The calls he bombarded her with, went unanswered. Honestly, his voicemail messages went into her trash as soon as they popped up on her phone.

Grace stopped walking. A noise floated through the air. The sound was muffled, tossed about by the fierce wind and the roaring water. Again, she heard it. She couldn't tell where it was coming from. Slowly, she turned in a circle, rested a hand above her eyes, and searched into the woods and down the trail. A tiny movement far away drew her attention. Fear clawed at her stomach as she considered her options. It was rare for anyone to visit the park. She could count on one hand the number of times she had not been alone. Was it human or animal? Could it be a bear or a wolf stalking her? After all, she was the one traipsing through their territory.

She stepped behind the trunk of a massive tree and watched as whatever it was closed in. It was walking on its hind legs, which meant only a bear or a human. When she could make out colors, Grace could tell which it was.

"Grace? Grace? Where are you?" the man called.

His familiar voice brought tears to Grace's eyes. She had not seen him in so long, and even though she thought she would never forgive him, she knew she already had.

"Daddy?" she whispered. She stepped from behind the tree, and a sob caught in her throat.

He stopped and held his arms wide for her to fall into. "Ah, honey," he said. He wrapped his arms around her. "Ah, my sweet, sweet girl."

Grace pressed her face against his broad chest and sobbed. "W-why are you h-here?" she whimpered.

"It's a long story." Her father continued to hold her. "Cynthia and her brood are gone."

"Gone?" Grace stepped backward.

"Yes, as in *found* a bachelor with more money and no kids of his own." He looked down at his daughter. "Poor slob." He cackled. His stomach had grown larger and softer since she had last seen him. His fine hazelnut hair had given up and coarse gray hairs had won the battle. But he was still her dad in every sense of the word.

He tightened his arms around Grace and tenderly planted a kiss on the top of her head. "I've been out here all day. I figured you wouldn't stay away today of all days."

Grace's lined forehead and narrowed eyes stored several questions. Finally, they spilled out in one long string. "I didn't see your car. How did you know I'd be here? Why today? How did you find out?"

"Ah, baby girl. I'm your dad. It's my job to know things." He turned her sideways and tucked his arms around her waist as they walked toward the waterfall. "I parked on the other end of the park, down past the waterfall." He sucked in a deep breath and returned it as a sigh. "How did I know about *today*? Well, when Cynthia left, I was devastated; I could barely function. Although, I don't know why." He smiled. "I needed someone to talk to. The only person I knew was that doctor we sent you to, Dr. Fischer. We talked about a lot of things during my sessions, including my relationship with you."

Grace's stomach lurched and surged with adrenaline. *How much had Daniel told him? Had he come clean?*

"Dr. Fischer could get into a lot of trouble for breaking patient-doctor confidentiality, but I am so glad he did, Gracie. I didn't even know I had a granddaughter or that she...passed. Had I known, I would have been here sooner."

Hurt shot through Grace. "Really? After everything that happened, how can you even say that? You would have come just because I needed you?" She jerked herself away from him. "Where were you when Cynthia treated me like an untouchable in my own home? Where were you when she lied to you—told you I was stealing and picking on *her poor babies*?" she asked. "Where, Dad? Where? Because all I saw was you siding with her and never with me. You never asked me a thing. You just took her word."

She folded her arms across her chest and glared at her father. Maybe she had not forgiven him after all.

Her dad looked confused. His head tilted to the side and his eyes clouded. "You're telling me everything she told me about you was all a lie? None of it was true?"

Tears dripped onto Grace's shirt, leaving dark spots on the light gray sweatshirt. She softened her stare. She was still his little girl. "Honestly? You didn't know that every time her kids did something wrong, she blamed me? And you didn't know it was Jimmy who stole money from her purse, repeatedly? And the pot, well, that was Cynthia's. I saw her smoking it. Did you know that?" She watched his face as it twisted with this new knowledge. "You knew none of this?"

Her father shook his head. "I'm so sorry, Grace. I was so busy working, trying to keep up with the life Cynthia wanted that I didn't even realize what was happening under my own roof—to my own daughter." His eyes grew glossy; a single drop rolled down his fleshy cheek.

Grace's shoulders sagged. The father-daughter pair turned and walked toward the waterfall along the narrow path. When they reached it, Grace climbed onto a large boulder and stared at the water hurtling off the high ledge of rocks.

"What else did Da-Doctor Fischer tell you?"

Her father sat beside her. "About your daughter, you mean?"

Grace nodded. "Yes, Finley."

"He told me she drowned here a year ago today." He lifted her tiny hand. "Grace, I am so sorry. I can't believe you suffered through this alone."

Grace crossed her arms and faced him. "What else did Doctor Fischer tell you?"

"He just said he had been helping you through the loss."

"He told you nothing else?"

Her father's eyes narrowed in question. "Should he have? Was there more to tell?"

She shook her head. "No, I lost *my* baby girl, Finley." Daniel had lost her daughter. *Her daughter,* not his.

INTROSPECT

Clarice Gennard: "I don't know what to think about Grace. She has always been a little off. Maybe more than a little, but I have never seen her like she has been lately. Every little thing sets her off. Of course, I shouldn't judge. I've never lost a child. I can't even imagine."

Principal Bart Holbrook: "Grace isn't in a good place. She hasn't been since her daughter drowned. Even before that, she wasn't a great teacher. But I couldn't throw one more rock at her. Yes, I tenured her. I just couldn't fire her. Not now."

Marty Wilson: "I didn't know Grace even had a daughter, let alone lost one. How was I supposed to know? I want to be close to my baby girl, but she's two hours away and I work six days a week."

Cynthia Powers Wilson Brooks: "That girl has been crazy since the first day I met her. I tried to tell her father that, but he didn't listen. It wasn't until we found the marijuana in her room that he admitted there was a problem. Maybe I planted it; maybe I didn't. Either way, it was the push he needed to send her away. While she was gone, our life was heavenly."

CHAPTER SIXTEEN

Two weeks later, Grace was alone again. Her father had returned to Hollister. He had gone back to work and to a new woman he had not confessed to until the day he drove away. Promises made—promises broken. He had assured her he would not lose contact this time, but a week had passed, and she had yet to hear from him. Honestly, she was not shocked. She would have been more surprised had he kept his word.

Summer vacation tormented her with its long, lackluster days. Her twisted and wearisome thoughts battered her through every waking hour. She tried to quash them, but they would not relent. The internet searches stirred new morbid thoughts. *Time it takes for a three-old to drown. Chances of surviving falling into a raging river. How far a river can carry a body. How to survive losing a child. Mental health crisis. Nervous breakdowns.* If she was not at the park searching for clues or punishing herself for being so foolish, she was googling every thought that popped into her head. Several nights each week, often well into the early morning hours, her den was lit only by the glow of her computer screen.

Late one Thursday night when she arrived home from the park, something felt off. Her porch lights shimmered downward; a short, the landlord had yet to repair, caused it to flicker slightly in the stiff breeze. For a year, Grace had left the lights on. At first, she believed it was to welcome her daughter home, but after months of a barren porch and empty arms, it became her way to memorialize Finley. The soft yellow glow attracted flies and other small insects. Cobwebs stretched along the sides of the doorway and hung from the fascia on the ceiling of the porch. Grace slapped a mosquito that violated her arm. She froze in the middle of a second slap when she heard someone clear their throat. She assumed it was the man next door who spent almost as much time awake as she did.

"Grace," the voice called to her as she fished her key from her pocket. The hairs on the back of her neck stood at attention and a shiver raced down her spine. Her heart thudded in her chest. He was too close.

"Get away from me," she hissed in the general direction of the voice.

"Come on, Grace. You won't answer my calls. All I want to do is talk. I just want to make sure you're okay."

She turned toward the dark yard. "Show your face, you coward."

A figure stepped from the shadows of the massive spruce that grew to one side of her front yard. "Please talk to me," he begged.

"Why should I?" She walked to the edge of the rotting wooden porch, teetering on the top step.

"I just want to know you're okay."

"I'm just freakin' dandy, Daniel. Why wouldn't I be?" Her voice flooded the neighborhood, almost echoing. "But I'd be a whole hell of a lot better if you'd get out of my yard and go back to your perfect life where you don't have to remember what you did."

Grace dismissed him. She spun around and returned to the door. Suddenly, Daniel was next to her. His fingernails dug into her wrist as he squeezed.

"Listen, we need to talk. I just want fifteen minutes. Please?"

"No!" she yelled. "Let go! Get the hell away from me!"

The porchlight next door flashed on. The door opened and a burly man stepped onto his porch. "Ma'am," he said. "Do you need help?" He did not wait for her answer. In what seemed like no more than four steps, he was across her yard, climbing the stairs. The steps creaked under his massive size. The curves of his muscular chest tested the seams of his t-shirt. He towered over Daniel, and Grace could see her ex was clearly shaken. Cowering, Daniel dropped her arm and stepped between Grace and the door, shielding himself behind her.

Since Cynthia's appearance in her life, Grace had become a loner; people scared her. Not because of what they wanted, but because of what they took from her: her self-esteem, confidence, and self-appreciation. Because of her poor self-concept, she had not met many of her neighbors, including this man.

"Sam," he said, nodding in her direction. "Former Marine," he said to Daniel.

"Grace."

"Yes, ma'am. I know who you are. If you don't mind me saying, everyone knows who you are."

"Oh," she said softly. She knew she was not seen around Ponderosa Falls in a positive light. "I suppose that's true."

He turned toward Daniel and held out his hand. "And who are you?"

"Dan—Doctor Daniel Fischer." He lifted his hand to meet the man's.

Daniel's face contorted, and he bit his lip as the man squeezed his hand, pumping it up and down. Grace delighted in the interaction.

When Sam let go, Daniel eased his hand behind his back. Grace watched him stretch and twist it, covertly attempting to ease the pain. She smirked at the grimace that marked his face.

"Is this guy bothering you, Grace?" Sam asked.

She looked toward Daniel. "I guess that depends on what he has to say."

"Do you want me to escort him out of your yard?" Sam asked.

Grace shook her head. "No. He has fifteen minutes to say his piece and then he'll be gone."

Her neighbor held out his hand, palm up. "Give me your phone. I'll give you my number." He fixed an angry stare on Daniel. "All you have to do is call, Grace. I can be here in less time than you can say…" He glanced toward the door. "Daniel."

Grace grinned at him. It was so heartening have someone see her. She dropped her phone in his hand and looked over her shoulder at Daniel. Sam entered his number with an agility that surprised her. "It's under S for Sam," he said. He backed toward the stairs, facing the porch as he slowly descended them. "Grace." He tipped his head toward her. "Nice to meet you." Then he glared at Daniel. Sam pointed his index and middle finger toward his eyes and back at Daniel. "Doctor Fischer, I'll be watching you—even when you think I'm not." Then he returned across the lawn toward his house. He stopped as he grabbed the handle. "Fifteen minutes, Danny," he said. Then he disappeared through the door.

"Nice, Daniel." Grace snorted and shot daggers at him. "You were so scared that you used me as your human shield. No wonder you couldn't protect Finley."

"Shut up, Grace," he whispered through gritted teeth. He glanced toward the house next door. "Unlock the damn door."

Grace stepped into the kitchen and flipped on the light switch. Daniel followed her into the disheveled room, silently judging her—as usual. He took three steps across the tiny room and yanked open the birch door of an upper cabinet near the stove.

"Where's the scotch?"

"I don't drink scotch," Grace said. She tucked loose strands of hair behind her ear.

He searched the cupboard again, angrily shoving bottles to the side. "Wine? That's it? Nothing stronger? You know what I like to drink."

Her eyebrows rose and her teeth squeaked when they ground together. "Well, *Danny*," she said, repeating Sam's dig, "*you* don't live here. Next time, bring your own damn scotch. Better yet, don't come back."

Daniel slammed the cupboard door. "You've changed, Grace. And not for the better."

She ignored his brazen comment and walked into the living room. She flipped on a lamp and quickly settled into Daniel's favorite chair. Her ex was headed toward it, but, at the last second, veered right, and dropped onto the couch. Grace smirked. Nothing delighted her more than to take things from him, no matter how small.

"You look like hell."

"Nice! Is that what you tell all your clients? I'm sure that's helpful."

"I'm telling you, Grace, you don't look healthy. Are you eating? Sleeping?" He looked around the room. "Just look at this dump. It looks like you haven't picked up a damn thing since Finley died." He launched a stack of trash off the coffee table and onto the floor.

"Screw you, Daniel. It's my life."

"Wouldn't be the way I'd choose to live."

Grace clenched her jaw. She was done sinking to his level. "I hear you've been talking to my dad. Check off another ethics violation, Daniel." She drew a checkmark in the air with one finger. "You could lose your license if I went to the medical board. I could ruin you." Even in the dim light, Grace could see Daniel's face grow red. Something she had not felt in an exceptionally long time washed over her: confidence. It felt amazing.

"You needed someone, Grace. When your father came to me, I thought he should know." He reached into his jacket pocket, removed a bottle of pills, and set them on the coffee table. "I wrote you a prescription for Prozac. You've taken it before, so…" Daniel shrugged.

She glanced at the clock on the wall. "I suggest you tell me what you came here to say because you asked for fifteen minutes, and you have seven left." Her scowl turned to a sneer. "And don't think for one second Sam isn't watching the clock too."

Daniel's eyes widened and his lips drew into a tight line. "I have something for you," he finally said. He pulled a gold, rolled-up envelope from the sleeve of his jacket. "I thought this might help." Daniel tried to flatten the envelope before he handed it to Grace.

"What is it?"

"Open it. I think you'll like it."

Grace straightened the clasp and lifted the flap. By feel, she could tell it was a photograph. But her eyes were locked on Daniel, not the picture.

"Look at it, Grace."

She removed the picture and gasped in horror. It was Finley—just not as Grace remembered. This photo was an older version of her daughter. "How? How can this be?" Grace's voice was thick. Daniel moved across the room and sat on the arm of her chair; he draped his arm over her shoulder. "Wh-where'd you get this?" She felt almost intoxicated.

Daniel huffed. "It's not real, Grace." His condescension scraped like a knife across a plate. The hair on her arms rose when Daniel clicked his tongue and rolled his eyes. "It's an age-progression photo. I found a guy on Facebook who does them. I thought you'd like to see what Finley might look like now."

Grace didn't want to look at it, but she could not pull her eyes from the photo. She was sucked into the gawker slowdown syndrome. You wanted to know what happened, but you didn't really want to see the aftermath of the accident. You just couldn't stop yourself.

She gently touched her daughter's face. An electric current buzzed through her. *Why would Daniel do this? Why would he remind me of what I lost?* Then suddenly, her rage fell away and joy moved in. *This is how my sweet little girl would look now.* Her emotions cycled for several minutes as she stared at the picture. She had no idea if she was angry or happy with Daniel's gift. Her stomach started to spin, and she thought she was going to be sick right there in her living room.

"You need to leave now, Daniel," she told him softly, pressing an arm into her stomach.

"Grace, there's still something I need to tell you." Her face was grim, and her eyes were cold. She held her jaw in place, waiting for something as equally appalling as the reminder of her dead daughter, but nothing he could say or do could hurt her more than losing her only child. "I'm seeing someone else. We've recently gotten engaged. I'm moving on, Grace. As your therapist, I think it's time you do the same."

The contents of dinner lurched into her throat, and she gagged before swallowing hard. Did she love Daniel? Did she hate him? Did she hope they would reconcile on the other side of their loss—once their grief settled?

Grace jumped up. The chair tipped to the side under Daniel's weight. He stumbled sideways, catching himself with one hand against the door frame. "You need to go, Daniel. Now." She looked at her phone and slid through a series of screens. "I just need to press this one button, and Sam will be here to make sure."

Daniel scowled at her before hurrying across the kitchen and into the entry. When he reached the door, he turned toward her. "She was my daughter too, Grace. I thought you would enjoy reminiscing."

"Get out!" Grace screamed. "Just get out," she whispered.

And then he was gone.

INTROSPECT

Sam Jacobs: "I knew *of* Grace but had not met her before that night. I bought my place not long before her daughter died. I used to see them together in their backyard. It was all so sad."

Dr. Daniel Fischer: "Grace is such a mess. It's been a year since we lost Finley. Come on, a year? At some point, she has to move on. I just don't see it happening. I brought the picture because I thought she might enjoy seeing how Finley would look today. I mean, the girl's gone."

CHAPTER SEVENTEEN

Finley laughed as she ran out of the river and up the uneven bank, kicking her feet wildly out to the sides with each step. At the top of the hill, she stopped and looked around; her smile faded. "Mommy?" she questioned as she rubbed one eye with her fist. Her round cheeks fell as her mouth turned down at the corners. "Mommy!" she screamed. "Mommy!"

"I'm here, baby!" Grace called as she tried to get to her daughter through the white fog that swelled between them. Grace panicked; she could no longer see her little girl. "Finley? Where are you?" In front of her, she heard giggles again, but they were interspersed with her daughter's sobs somewhere on the other side of the thick curtain of mist. "Finley!"

Grace's eyes flew open. She sat up and threw her legs off the side of the bed. That buzzing feeling had returned, making her feel sick to her stomach. Still not fully awake, she stumbled to Finley's bedroom. The early morning light streamed through the small stained-glass unicorn hanging in her daughter's window, painting a rainbow of colors across the neatly made bed. Grace peered around the room, half expecting to find Finley hiding somewhere, but she was wrong. A raspy sigh escaped. Her daughter was not alive; it had been just another illusion in a long line of nightmares that plagued her once peaceful sleep. Grace toppled on top of the bed, bunching the yellow, blue, and white comforter in her arms, burying her face in the thickness. Uncontrollably, she sobbed. *When would it end?*

The photo Daniel had given to her, the one that was supposed to bring her comfort, had made everything worse. Memories of the past and impossible dreams for the future rained down on her, soaking her in a torrent of sorrow. He wanted her to move on, yet his desire to help had sent her reeling backward, to the day Finley drowned. It was cruel. For a moment, she wondered if he had done it on purpose, used the photo to remind her how miserable her life was—especially when compared to his. No. Daniel had a mean streak, but even he would not be that vicious. Maybe he really was trying to help her. Wasn't it Hamlet who said, "I must be cruel only to be kind; thus, bad begins and worse remains behind." What could be worse than losing your only child? Did he think seeing the photo would bring her out of her darkness? Well, he was wrong.

Already late for a summer workshop training at school, Grace pulled her hair into a scruffy ponytail. She snatched a pair of jeans from the bedroom floor and held them to her face; instantly, she rejected them, discarding them in the corner next to her dresser. A second and a third pair also hit the pile. The fourth, a pair of black capris with rips across the thighs and knees were the least offensive; she tugged them on and tightened the belt, poking the end through the loops nearly a quarter way around her. Knowing the air conditioning at school would be set too cold, she pulled a bluish-green sweatshirt over the gray t-shirt she had worn to bed and raced toward the kitchen.

She had been instructed to bring a lunch. Her fridge held nothing but condiments, a case of Coke, and a block of cheese that garnered a layer of tiny white crystals and a small patch of green mold. She threw three cans of soda into her bag along with the block of cheese she would have previously referred to as a disgusting science fair project.

Backing down the driveway, she narrowly missed a woman pushing a stroller. The woman banged on the back of her car and screamed an obscenity Grace chose to ignore. The meeting had already started by the time Grace jerked the front door open. Noelle made eye contact with her as she raced past the office toward the Media Center. She tiptoed through the open door and snuck into a chair in the back of the room. For Grace, she was actually early. But it didn't matter. No one even noticed her erratic arrivals and departures anymore.

By 3:00 p.m., the sugar and caffeine buzz she had from sipping her three cans of soda, half of the day disguised as coffee, had turned into a major crash that left her shaky and more out of sorts than usual. Before the meeting even ended, she was out the door, running across the parking lot to her car.

Anxiety gnawed at her as she pulled onto the highway in front of the school. A horn blew, cutting into the conversation that played out in her head. She narrowly missed a white van that seemingly appeared out of nowhere when she pulled onto the road. The man swerved onto the shoulder to avoid her, but instead of feeling guilty, she flipped him off and returned to her internal banter.

Once she reached the main drag that led to the park, Grace dug into her bag and retrieved the hunk of cheese she had thrown in it that morning. The slide zipper on the plastic bag was broken and the block tumbled onto the console between the seats, where it picked up sand, gray flecks of dust, and tiny particles of food that had settled there in the past year. Steering with her forearms, she snapped the block in half, dropped one piece onto the passenger's seat, and carefully bit small unblemished pieces, avoiding the mold and newly acquired grit. The cheese was warm and soft, but for the time being, it would calm her disgruntled stomach. When nothing edible on the chunk remained, she rolled down her window and sent the piece flying.

A few hundred feet before her turn onto the gravel road that led to Halston Park, brake lights began to pop on. Grace, lost in thought, did not notice. At the last minute, she swerved to the right, barely missing the compact blue crossover just ahead of her that carried a couple of her students. As *she* had done earlier, one of the students flipped her off as she sailed past on the narrow shoulder.

Lights flashed about ten cars ahead of her. She drew deep breaths to slow her racing pulse, but the red and blue shards that splashed across the vehicles as the brilliance of the earlier day shifted to a gray rumbling sky, worried her. Traffic slowly began to move, and Grace edged her way back into the line. Frustration set in; she was positive she could crawl faster than traffic was moving. By the time she reached the officer directing traffic, she was seething.

An ambulance raced toward her, cutting the corner down to the park faster than it should have, two wheels nearly lifting off the ground as it leaned to the right. She flipped her blinker on, indicating a turn into the park. "What's going on?" she hissed at the cop as he put his hand up for her to stop. He had a baby face and looked younger than most of her high schoolers. For all she knew, it was his first day on the job.

"Sorry, ma'am," he said. "The park's closed until further notice."

"Why?" Grace was irate. "You can't just close the park for no reason."

He scowled at her. "Please keep moving forward." He waved his orange safety flashlight back and forth along the highway, indicating an end to their conversation.

Grace inched forward; she stared down the sideroad as she passed. About a quarter of a mile down the dirt road, more lights flashed against the darkening sky. Rain started to fall, first as a mist, then in droplets so big, she thought the windshield might break. But the downpour was short-lived, turning to pea-size hail as Grace made a U-turn farther down the highway.

As she again approached the road to the park, the officer flashed his wand along the road again. Once more, she slowed, trying to see what was happening near the park.

"Keep going, lady," the young officer said. The siren of a rescue truck sounded behind her, and she hit the gas to avoid being rear-ended. Instead of attempting another pass by the park, dealing with the petulant cop, she opted to head home.

Grace turned on the television. The local news would not run for another couple of hours, but she left it on, watching some horrendously terrible talk show with a couple more screwed up than her and Daniel. She hoped for breaking news. Facebook and Twitter offered nothing. News apps were void of information also. At 5:00 p.m., wrapped in a thick red throw, she watched the news for the first time in nearly a year. Disappointment set in as the weatherman immediately broke into the newscast to share about torrential storms and flooding to hit the area. *Take me out,* she thought. *Come and get me. Drown me with my daughter.*

She dug through the cupboards and found an open box of crackers with an expiration date almost a year before. She stuck the box and a nearly empty jar of peanut butter under one arm, then she grabbed a bottle of wine from the line-up on the counter and returned to the living room. There was no need for a glass; it would only slow her down.

Sitting in front of the television, Grace felt a loneliness settle in unlike any she had ever felt. After Finley drowned, there had been people in and out of her house and her life. Someone stopped in daily, brought her food, prayed with her or for her. But eventually, the visits began to fade. By the time they ended, she was so set in a routine between going to school and visiting the park, she did not realize she was alone. Tonight was different. In the dark house, lit only by the flickering light of the television and the brutal lightning storm that had begun to batter Ponderosa Falls, she realized just how alone she truly was.

⤙⤚⤙⤚⤙⤚

When the sun rose the following morning, Grace did not. It was nearly noon before she peeled herself off the leather couch; the television still played in the background. A cracker smothered in peanut butter was stuck to the front of her shirt and the bottle she had in her hand when she passed out lay sideways on the floor, not a drop remaining.

Grace stumbled to the kitchen. Four Advil and a gallon of water were the only things on her mind. Her head throbbed and she pressed the heels of her hands against her temples to relieve the rhythmic pressure. With eyes at half-mast, she searched the cupboard for a bottle of pain-reliever but only found empty ones. Frustrated, she tossed them across the room, sending a blue streak of cuss words behind them. She wanted to cry, but she could not. Her head hurt too much.

Mail dropped to the floor as the carrier slipped it through the slot in the door. Once again, she squeezed her head with her palms. She closed one eye and looked toward the haphazard stack that joined the mail from the past week. A pink envelope stood out among the non-descript pouches and coupons she would never use. It coaxed her toward it, called to her from the heap of junk mail and bills. Except for a couple of weeks after Finley died, the mail offered nothing more intriguing than car warranty extensions and deceptive offers of home equity loans. Grace rented.

With her toes, she scattered the mail and slid the envelope toward her. Afraid bending over would make last night's *dinner*, if she could even call it that, reappear, she stationed the envelope directly next to her chair. She bent slightly to the right and snatched it off the floor on her first attempt. But even so, her stomach gurgled and threatened to rise. Grace froze while she waited for it to settle again.

There was no return address on the envelope, nothing

138

to indicate the sender. Her name and address were written in large, curvy letters, handwriting she did not recognize. Her curiosity piqued and she slid her finger beneath the edge of the flap and tore it open. It was a generic birthday card with balloons and a cake on the front. The words *Happy Birthday* marked the sentiment. The paper was flimsy, one of those you would buy at a dollar store in a pack of ten. Who would have sent her a card? Almost no one knew it was her birthday, and those who did didn't care enough to send a card.

Grace opened the card and gasped before letting out a blood-curdling scream. She closed the paperboard card and reopened it again and again, each time staring at the faint blue scribbles that marked the inside. Below the squiggly lines were the words: *Happy Birthday, Mommy! When are you coming to get me? Love, Finley.*

Everything went black as Grace fell from the chair and onto the floor.

INTROSPECT

Sergeant Pollack: "I was the first one at the river the day Finley Wilson drowned. I've seen hysterical people in the past, but Grace was inconsolable. There was an older man there, a Dr. Fischer, but I still don't think I have the whole story. Dr. Fischer identified himself as a friend of Grace's. Since that day, I've dealt with Grace multiple times. I'm afraid she's headed down a dark, slippery slope."

Anonymous: "Yes. I sent the birthday card. So what? Who did it hurt?"

CHAPTER EIGHTEEN

The bottle of Prozac Daniel had left was nearly empty. Grace had not even opened the bottle until the birthday card arrived. Then she ate them like candy. By the end of the first week, she was numb. There was an emptiness inside her that neither made her laugh nor cry. She literally felt nothing; she no longer cared about anyone or anything. Finley didn't make appearances in thoughts or her dreams anymore.

On the morning she took the last two pills, before the sun painted the sky with the morning spectrum of colors, she called Daniel, begging him for another prescription.

He refused. "Grace, they were just to take the edge off until you could get yourself back to ground zero and start building from there."

"I've been at ground zero for over a year, asshole. I haven't gone anywhere. You did this to me, Daniel. You made me this way!" she screamed at him. "You need to fix this."

"Grace, listen to me. You've got to get help. I can make some calls…"

The birthday card lay on the kitchen table. Grace picked it up and read the inside. "Daniel, did you send me a birthday card signed with Finley's name?"

"What? What are you talking about, Grace? Of course, I didn't. Why would I do that?"

"Well, someone did." She pressed the end button. If Daniel was not going to help her, she would have to weather the storm alone. If she couldn't kill her pain with Prozac, she would subdue it with whatever she could find.

⚭⚭⚭⚭

With the Prozac gone, Grace began to feel again. Suicidal thoughts drifted through her mind several times a day, begging her to take action. It was not often she left home, but when she did, she drove erratically, taking corners too fast, running red lights, and driving on the wrong side of the road. She had a death wish, but nothing she did got her what she wanted. From the three pharmacies in town, Grace purchased several bottles of over-the-counter sleeping pills, stashing them in her medicine cabinet. They were ready when she was. Her nightmares returned and she found herself sleeping on the couch more often than in her bed. *Sleeping, was it? Or passed out?* she wondered. Either way, those nights always started with a full bottle of wine and ended with an empty one. The only two places she frequented were the drug store and the liquor store. Grace no longer went to the park, no longer searched the river.

Then it happened. One morning in July, Grace hit rock bottom—somewhere far lower than the ground zero Daniel talked about. That day, after waking up in a pool of puke, most of which had dried on her face, she knew she had arrived. Determined to change her life, she cleaned herself up and carefully drove to the grocery store. Changing her life began with what went into her body.

Grace had just loaded four overflowing brown paper bags of fresh fruit into her car when a woman walked by with a child in a stroller. Her heart banged inside her chest and the buzzing returned. Grace saw the curls waving in the breeze over the top of the small stroller and snapped. Reality fell away.

"Finley!" she yelled. "Finley!" Grace grabbed the woman by the shoulder and swung her around. "Where do you think you are taking my daughter?" she screamed.

The woman's face flamed red and sweat instantly began to bead on her forehead. "I don't know who you think you are, but this is *my* daughter. Her name is Aubrey." The woman wedged herself between Grace and the stroller.

Grace grabbed the handle and jerked it sideways. The child screamed as the stroller almost tipped onto its side. "Don't cry, Finley. Mommy's here."

The woman stood her ground. She turned and held a death grip on each handle, trying to steer the stroller away from Grace, but Grace was not letting go of the side of the stroller. The woman screamed for help, but Grace did not budge. The strolled jerked back and forth as the women fought for the child. A crowd gathered around them, watching the skirmish, trying to figure out what was going on—who the real mother was.

With her free hand, Grace dug her long fingernails into the back of the woman's hand as the child sobbed. "Stop it! You're scaring my daughter."

"She's not your daughter!" Grace screamed. "She's *my* daughter." She glanced into the crowd of people. "Please, someone help!"

Suddenly, a woman from the crowd pointed at Grace, "Hey! That's the woman whose kid drowned at Halston Park last year," she shouted. "That little girl's not her daughter."

A tall man stepped forward and wrapped his arms around Grace from behind and pulled her backward, away from the stroller. The air was filled with the sharp, terrifying blare of a siren as it moved closer to the store. Grace kicked at the man with the heel of the boots she had slipped on before leaving home, but he was too strong for her and separated his legs so she could not reach him.

With Grace subdued, the other woman quickly buckled her daughter into her car seat, started the engine, and turned on the air conditioner. She locked the doors and stepped into the crowd as the police cruiser pulled up.

"That's my daughter! That's Finley!" Grace screamed, still struggling to free herself from the man.

The first officer handcuffed Grace's hands behind her back.

"I want my daughter!" Grace sobbed as she physically battled with the two officers. The officer, much smaller than the man who had intervened initially, grabbed her elbow and pushed her toward the squad car. She continued to fight, so he stepped back, distancing himself from her. "Finley!" Grace screamed as she slammed her heel into the top of the cop's foot. He yelled and let go. Still struggling to get to the little girl, Grace toppled backward onto the ground. Her head bounced when it hit the asphalt. She felt the sticky, warm blood pool around her head. The crowd went silent as the two officers tried to save her.

"Let me die!" Grace screamed. "Please, just let me die," she whispered.

INTROSPECT

Lynne Porter: "Today was the worst day of my life. That woman accused me of kidnapping *her* daughter. Little Aubrey was so frightened. I don't know if she'll ever get over this nightmare. What in the hell is wrong with that woman?"

Clara Baxley: "I recognized Grace Wilson immediately. I couldn't remember her name, but I never forget a face. The poor mom of the other little girl was beside herself. I can't even imagine."

Officer Collins: "Grace Wilson is not new to any of us at the station. You have to feel for her, but she needs serious help. I'm just afraid it's too late."

COLTON STONE

Widower
Father to a Child that is Not His
Carpenter

CHAPTER NINETEEN

Addy galloped across the living room floor and dropped on top of Humphrey. The sheepdog did not move, except to lick her face. "Hum-fee kissed me." She laughed. "I love you, Hum-fee." She wrapped her arms around his thick neck, lifted his ear, and sang, "I love you!" She giggled when the dog washed her face with a second long swipe.

Most people would not have noticed Addy's slight limp from the night of the accident, but Colt did. She had been perfect when her mother died; he had her for only one year and she was already broken. His wife would never have left their daughter in the truck in the middle of the night; she would have insisted it was an accident waiting to happen. But then again, Brit was not here. She had taken the coward's way out. It was not until the night of Addy's accident he had learned why she had ended the story of her life. Her decision still haunted him.

In the beginning, he had blamed himself, but, after weeks of sleepless nights, the blame turned to hurt. By the time he sought help, it was fury that ran through his veins.

Now, he was simply filled with regret and *what-ifs. What if he had been a better husband? A better father? What if he had made Brit happier? What if the house had been bigger or nicer?* There were a million questions that raced through his mind when he watched his daughter play. The biggest: *What if he had been enough—enough that Brit wouldn't have searched for something he had not been able to give her, in the arms of someone else?*

Suddenly, his emotions flipped, and anger smoldered inside of him, igniting a bonfire of rage. *She* was the one who had cheated. *Brit* was the one who had broken their vows. Brit knew Addy was not his daughter; she just couldn't live with her dirty secret any longer. Even though the facts were clearly pointed out on the day of Addy's accident, he still could not believe she had betrayed him. There had never been two people more in love, but the more he thought about it, the more he realized that was as bogus as Addy being his daughter. Brit had taken Addy's paternity secret to her grave. Maybe she never loved him; maybe that was another falsehood he had wanted to believe. But with Brit gone, he would never know.

Clearly, the weight of her secret had been too much for his wife to carry. For a few hours, it had been too much for Colton also. On the night of Addy's surgery, he had walked away when he discovered he was not her biological father. He was nothing more to her other than a glorified babysitter who had been paid in lies and deception.

On the morning after Addy's surgery, as the dark sky faded to a deep purple and a sliver of orange grew along the horizon, something inside Colt shifted. In the park not far from his new house, he had sat on the edge of the small merry-go-round, pushing himself in a slow circle as Humphrey sat in the grass, watching him, judging his decision to abandon his daughter. That word—*abandon*—was like a punch in the gut. It was exactly what his mother had done to him. She had discarded him like the ribbon wand she dropped at the amusement park when he was not much older than Addy.

Her actions owned him; he could never let go of how that decision still made him feel. He could not let Addy spend her entire life thinking she was not good enough to be loved. She already had one parent choose to leave her; she did not need another.

By the time the morning sky had morphed into a brilliant blue day, Colt had already returned to the hospital, to his daughter's side. He waited for her to wake, waited to fulfill his promise to be the best dad a girl could ever ask for. All he wanted was to hear her call him *Daddy*, but it did not happen that day, or the next, or for nearly a month. But eventually, after reading her books, playing music, and telling her stories about Humphrey, it happened. Once again, the world was right. He was *Daddy*.

Colt watched his daughter *drive* a Barbie doll up and down Humphrey's back, sputtering sounds bouncing her lips. The long thin arms and legs of the doll tangled in the dog's fur, pulling as it bounced along in Addy's hand, but Humphrey never moved or whimpered. If dogs could talk, Colton was sure he would tell him he would do anything for their girl. He was fiercely protective; he rarely let Addy out of his sight. At night, he planted himself next to her bed and would not leave until the morning light. Humphrey picked up where Colt fell short.

Addy's hair had grown back enough to hide the scars from that terrifying night, a night he could not unsee or forgive himself for. A fine white line cut across her right eyebrow, separating the brow into two sections. Another marked her cheek. Both were thread-thin, unnoticeable to almost anyone else, but Colt saw them, just as he knew the exact location of each ropey scar under her hair and arm and the pink puckered line that ran across her stomach. Sometimes, when she fell asleep in his arms, he would trace the scars with his thumb. He was afraid he would forget. He could never let anything like this ever happen again.

On a parenting scale of one to ten, Colton ranked

himself somewhere in the negative. He had failed that night and so many others. What kind of a parent let their guard down with a three-year-old? But maybe somewhere deep inside, he always knew he was not her father—or a father at all. And not being a father, it stood to reason he had no parental instincts and that was why he had left Addy alone in the truck on the night of the accident. *Maybe.* What he did know was someone out there had a daughter they had no clue about. Or perhaps he did. Was it possible this person knew everything Colt had struggled through and didn't care?

Colt glanced out the patio door into the backyard. Something felt amiss. For the first time since bringing Addy home from the hospital, trepidation coursed through him. He rose from the couch and moved to the glass door. Staring off into the distance, beyond the wire-fenced yard, he searched for an invisible danger, something that would drag him down when he least expected it. A shudder passed through him, and his blood ran cold. What was out there? Or who? It was Addy's playful screech that drew him back to reality— disregarding his concern.

Following the accident, the surgeon put Addy into a medically induced coma. For nearly ten days, while her brain healed, Colt wrestled with his worst-case scenario thoughts. Around 7:00 each morning, he drove to the hospital to sit by her side and hold her hand. For nearly five hours, he sat vigil, talking to anyone in his head who was *not* God. He had given up on God and religion when Brit committed suicide. When he was silent, words filled his head. Someone was silently talking to him, but he did not want to listen. So, to keep the voices silent, Colt did the talking. Shortly before noon each day, he kissed his daughter goodbye and returned home to work on Addy's room—a room he wasn't even sure would ever be hers.

Days after Addy's accident, Colton finally called his realtor in Hollister. She told him everything left behind had been donated to the Salvation Army, as he had requested. Apologies were made if she had misunderstood his directions, but she had not. He just had not planned on the movers missing an entire room.

Once they brought Addy out of the coma, Colt lived at the hospital. Sometimes he fell asleep in the aqua vinyl recliner in her room, often waking to a tray of institutional food being pushed in his direction. It usually tasted like thick paste, but he had been grateful for every kindness he and his daughter received. One of his new neighbors had taken it upon herself to feed, water, and walk Humphrey, who spent his days in the fenced backyard or lying on the couch waiting for their girl to return. Colt had increased the size of the doggy door so Humphrey could come in from the heat or go outside to relieve himself.

For nearly two months, Addy lived in the hospital or the rehab center learning to walk and talk again. When she was finally released into his care, her days were spent attending physical, occupational, and speech therapy. Between nursemaid and father, Colt played chauffeur, driving his daughter from one appointment to another.

In the first few days after Addy had woken, she was quiet, too quiet. It worried Colt. Would she return to him? Would she ever be the giggly little bit of a thing he fell in love with? Or had she lost her incredibly joyful spirit? When she was tired or lonely, instead of reaching for him, she often turned away, mumbling a word he believed to be *Mommy*. It was late in her recovery that she finally grew comfortable around him. The rejection had hurt him, but it had not been a surprise. Addy had spent nearly every waking minute with Brit. He had been the absent parent, the one who came home for dinner and watched TV in the evenings with her curled up in his lap. He had never been the one she turned to when she was hurt or sick. That gift had been reserved for her mother.

Addy grew stronger every day. Colt began seeing glimpses of the girl she once was—her loving nature and silly personality; nothing made him happier. But while he had reason to breathe easier, there was something else that clawed at him—*guilt*. He often wondered if he owed it to his daughter's *biological* father to find him. But who was he? Colton considered purchasing a DNA kit for Addy. A database might show a match: a father, a grandparent, or an aunt or uncle.

Colt had gone so far as to put the kit in his Amazon cart, but he could never make the purchase; it lived on the *save for later* page of the website. Clicking *purchase* meant something he wasn't sure he was prepared for—to relinquish his rights to the little girl he had raised since birth. Colt was not; he would never be. Physically, there was no part of him in Addy, but he was her *daddy*; he had earned that title. He would always be there for her: to kiss her scraped knee, beat off the boys who would want his daughter, and walk her down the aisle. He wanted it all—from Daddy to Dad to Grandpa. His entire life had been about rejection and loss; there was no way he would allow anyone else to be taken from him.

His daughter lay on her stomach and lifted the ridge of Humphrey's brow. His eyes grew wide, but he never moved; Addy giggled. "Daddy, look!" she called loudly. "Hum-fee has eyeballs just like mine. They're brown!" She let go of the dog's fur and clapped her hands and sang, "Brown! Brown! Brown! Just like mine, mine, mine!"

Colt sighed. "He does," he agreed. His eyes were blue; Brit's had also been. Addy's brown eyes had not come from either of them. It was just another dagger that stabbed at him, a reminder he was not her biological father. Her eye color was something she shared with someone outside of their circle.

"Dad—dy." Addy rotated herself to see Colt. Her elbows rested on the floor as she laid a cheek on the back of her hands. She kicked the floor with the toes of her tennis shoes in a staccato rhythm that matched her question. "Can. We. Go. Outside. To. Play?"

Colton laughed as he scooped her into his arms. He matched his tempo to hers. "Yes. We. Can. Goo-fy. Girl."

There was no more extraordinary sound than his daughter's laughter.

"Come on, Hum-fee," she called to the dog as Colt carried her over his shoulder. "Let's go play." The dog jumped to his feet and followed.

INTROSPECT

Addy Stone: "Daddy plays with me and Hum-fee a lot, and he cooks me maca-woni and cheese. He's the best daddy."

Anonymous: "Sometimes we are fooled by what we see and hear. People aren't always who we think they are."

CHAPTER TWENTY

The Kids' Cave Daycare Center was a mile from Colton's house. When he received the all-clear for Addy to safely return to normal activities, Colt signed her up for two weeks of partial days before enrolling her full time. Addy never fought drop-off; she never cried when Colt walked away. Instead, she would throw her arms around his neck, plant a big kiss on his cheek, and whisper, "See you later, alligator." To which, his response was the inevitable, "After a while, crocodile." Then Addy would giggle and run off to make new friends. No, *she* never cried, but Colt came close a few times.

Because of the accident, he had lost the job that had brought him to Podany. By the time he was able to call the foreman to explain his situation, the job was gone. He pled his case, but the foreman's response was as firm as the rebar reinforcing the cement flooring in the homes they were building. Volunteer? Sure. But he had no money to take him on as an employee. The money from the sale of Brit's dream house, along with the life insurance settlement, and the savings Colt had stashed away, had kept them afloat while Addy recuperated.

For six months, he cared for the sweet little girl with whom he did not share DNA. During that time, he met with an attorney who assured him that, as with property, possession was nine-tenths of the law. And according to Colorado law, when Brit gave birth, and listed Colt on the birth certificate, he was legally Addy's father. That was all he needed to hear. He was her father in every sense of the word.

After making sure Addy could handle full-day daycare, Colton began digging through online leads and pounding the pavement in search of a job. After a couple *underqualified* and an equal number of *overqualified* rejections, he landed one, doing custom work at Ned's Custom Cabinetry. It was an independently owned small business that employed a dozen people. Impressed with Colt's know-how and understanding of the building process, Ned hired him as foreman of the small crew, his right-hand man. The job, along with a few side gigs, provided a decent income. He was able quickly pay off Addy's hospital bill and pad his savings.

It was not all smooth sailing though. Colt and Ned often butted heads over jobs that walked through the door. His boss believed in two things: speed and making as much money as possible. Colton believed in quality. They often argued over projects, but in the end, Ned almost always bowed to Colt's decision.

Cabinetry was not all they built. They tailored anything customers could envision. Colt had been handed sketches on napkins and old receipts. He had even built a nightstand from a picture of a drawing on a man's hand. Nothing surprised him anymore. Bookshelves, benches, and boxes of assorted shapes and sizes were their biggest demand. But they also constructed window seats, desks, tables, dressers, and ornate, one-of-a-kind, pieces of furniture.

Before Colton had been hired, the crew had built an

elaborate casket for Harvey Salazar, the wealthiest man in Podany. Ned showed him the photos: maple with marble inlays. Silver-plated handles and a secret compartment for the jewelry and money he planned to take with him—all to keep his ex-wives and ungrateful children from staking claim to it. No one knew for sure if anything of value made it into the casket, but regardless, the compartments were there. During the coffin building, production of everything else came to a screeching halt while every employee worked on a specific part of the casket to ensure it would be completed in time for the burial.

Colt was always the first to arrive and the last to leave. Before beginning work on his own projects, he would check in with each person, discussing their plan, quality of their work, timeline. When he was sure his crew was set, Colton would pull on a pair of oversized headphones to drown out the noises of the machines. Once in place, he rarely spoke. He got lost, deep inside himself. Thoughts and memories piled on top of one another, and he silently argued with them, resurrecting a slew of *whys* that had returned since before Addy's accident. He knew he spent too much time in his head and not enough time with people who did not want to play Barbie or Hide-n-Seek, but, for now, stepping into a world beyond his daughter, was not an option.

A red light in the corner of the workshop began to pulse, signaling someone had entered the showroom. Sonja could handle it, but there was always the chance he would be called in for a consult. He continued to work but kept a vigilant eye on the door. When twenty minutes had passed without a sign of her, he returned his full attention to the dresser he was building, a project that did not need to be completed until late fall when the snowbirds returned south.

Suddenly, the light flashed green, and movement burst from the shop. Team members removed their headphones and started toward the restrooms and breakroom. Colt straddled his headphones over a sawhorse before checking in with them.

"Everybody good?" he asked. The nine men and three females all nodded before returning to their conversations. "Okay, then. See everybody at lunch." Then he headed through the fireproof door and into the showroom.

Ned was once again gone. Lately, he and his recently retired wife spent more time traveling than in the shop. Since Ned's last departure, Colt often spent his evenings working on a proposal to buy the business. He knew Ned was zeroing in on the freedom of a life without work; Colt just had to convince him it was time. After reviewing his finances and polishing his speech, often falling asleep with his computer in his lap in the early morning hours, when Ned returned from Hawaii, Colt would be ready.

Colton walked around the back of the counter and stuck his hand in the empty order basket. "I saw the light flash. Orders or window shopping?" he asked Sonja.

"Just finishing up an order." Her fingers raced across the calculator as she worked on material costs.

"Big or small?" Colt asked.

"Small," she said. She gave him *the* look. "Just let me finish, would you?"

He grabbed a soda from the small office fridge and drank nearly half the can while he waited.

"Okay, here's the order." She handed it to him over her shoulder as she reached for the ringing phone. "Hello, Ned's Custom Cabinetry," she sang into the phone.

Her familiar deep voice was nearly an octave higher than normal. Colt laughed at the sweetness she projected; he knew better. Sonja could hold her own.

He perused the order. Small, but unusual. The man had precisely drawn out the project on graph paper. Notes were written in small boxes he had sketched on the side. Arrows pointed to specific directions.

The box had a thick hollow lid, which housed a hidden compartment that could only be accessed through a pair of screws hidden below a pair of wooden plugs. There was a tiny hole in the front of the box, disguised as the top part of the latch.

"What the hell is this?" he asked Sonja when she finished the call.

The lines near her eyes grew deeper as her cheeks pressed upward. "I don't know," she admitted. "It was just all a little creepy. The guy, the box, everything."

Colt picked up the paper and read the name. "Who is this guy?"

She tapped her fingers on her desk. "Well, he was dressed in a police uniform, but he wasn't a local cop. He just said he was passing through, saw the shop, and decided to order a gift for his wife."

"What's with the hole and the hidden space?"

"I asked."

"I knew you would." Colt laughed.

"He claims they have a nanny who they want to keep an eye on. His wife has wanted this for a long time. I'm guessing he finally gave in."

"He's a cop? Why does he need to hide a camera in a box? You'd think he could plant small cameras anywhere."

Sonja shrugged. "I just took the order. He put money down and said he'd be back through the end of the week. I figured you could have it done by then, right?"

Colt nodded as he stared at the order; pages of detailed drawings and directions were stapled behind the printed order form. "I'll take care of it myself. It's still pretty bizarre."

"I agree," Sonja said. "Hey, you want to know something else?"

Colt looked up at her.

"He would only give me his first name. *Seth*."

"Wasn't his last name on his uniform?"

"No. And I looked. He was wearing a wedding ring, though. So, I suppose he could be telling the truth."

"Maybe." Colt took the order with him into the shop. People ordered all kinds of weird things. How was this any different?

INTROSPECT

Sonja Waller: "I am never surprised by what people order, but this Seth guy gave me the creeps. It wasn't because of what he ordered; it was more this sinister vibe he gave off."

Ned Newton: "Colt's a top-notch employee. I trust him, but I often wonder what he's hiding. There's more to his story than he's letting on."

Seth: "Respect the uniform. Respect the man. Respect the power. I earned this uniform."

CHAPTER TWENTY-ONE

Cutting and sanding the pieces to construct the unusual box the mystery man ordered whittled away at Colton's afternoon. With his headphones in place, thoughts of the officer, Addy, and Brit wove through him as he worked.

Before his daughter was born, he had built a wooden keepsake box to house all of Addy's important information. It was the one thing he had carried with him when he left Hollister. Trusting it to the movers was not something he was willing to do. The box was filled with memories. He had not looked through it since his wife's death. It was something the two of them had done together, sharing the memories over a glass of wine late in the evening whenever Brit was feeling nostalgic. Addy's birth certificate, memorable photos, cards, her baptismal certificate, and newspaper clippings had all been organized by date, carefully lined up front to back.

Colton had spent days building the birch box. On the top, he had inlaid slices of amethyst stalactite. Amethyst had always been Brit's favorite stone—purple her favorite color.

When Colt decorated Addy's room, he matched the paint of her walls to the pale purple of the stones. The final decoration was the box. He centered the box on the top of Addy's dresser. One day, he would share it with her but, for now, he kept it locked. The key was taped to the back of Addy's dresser.

Too tired to cook, Colt settled on McDonald's for dinner. He picked Addy up from daycare and headed to the PlayPlace a few blocks west of the daycare. He could have devoured two Big Macs in the time it took his daughter to nibble through a quarter of her hamburger and six French fries. Addy looked at the pictures and then *read* the book that came in her Happy Meal.

"Daddy, I want to go play." She leaned her chin on the back of one hand and poked at a sticky spot on the table with one finger.

"Are you done eating?" he asked.

Eyes wide, she nodded.

"You're sure?"

Addy swiped her finger across her chest in a big X. "Cross my heart and hope to die." She giggled.

Colt cringed. Daycare had taught Addy all kinds of thing he didn't not want her to know. That phrase was the one he hated the most. "Just say yes or no, sweetie," he told her as he grabbed the remains of her burger and devoured it in a couple of bites.

Addy put her hands on her hips. "No, no, Daddy. That's not how we eat," she chastised him as she wagged a finger in his direction.

"Sorry, baby girl," he said. "You're right. He took a swig of his soda and set it back on the table. "So, who wants to go play?"

Addy raised her hand. "I do. I do, Daddy. Pick me!"

Colt smiled as he grabbed her from her side of the bench and planted a kiss on her cheek. "Really?" he asked as he wiggled a finger into her side.

"R-ee-ally!" She screeched as she tried to escape.

Colt finally set her down and watched her disappear into the tunnel that headed to the top of the structure.

Addy high-fived him each time she raced past before heading back into the pint-sized tubes.

More than two dozen times, he heard her yell, "Daddy, look at me!"

How could he not? He never took his eyes off her.

"You ready to go, kiddo?" he asked when she came down the slide and did not move. She yawned and stretched as she nodded. "Bath time and then bed, okay?" Again, his daughter silently agreed. He set her on a bench, slipped on her shoes, and tied them tightly. He took her hand, but she did not budge.

"Can you carry me, Daddy? I'm too tired." Dramatically, she crumbled onto the rubber mat. "See," she said quietly. "I can't even walk."

Colton laughed. She had always been a drama queen. He picked her up and tossed her over his shoulder and spun in a tight circle. She closed her eyes. Sleep settled in before they even left the parking lot. He could hear her shallow breathing as he pulled onto the main drag.

A quick bath followed by a short story was all it took before Addy was out for the night. It was earlier than usual, but she had worn herself out. Colt's proposal for Ned was not quite ready; the early bedtime gifted him an extra hour to fine-tune it. Ned planned to be back at work the following day. Unless the perfect opportunity presented itself, Colton would give him the weekend before making the offer to buy the business.

Just after midnight, Colt snapped off the lamp on his nightstand. He raised the window just enough to let a breeze drift over his bed. With only the moonlight as his guide, he walked down the hall to check on Addy. She had not moved since Colton had tucked her in.

"Come on, boy," he told Humphrey as he poked him with his toe. "Let's go outside so you can do your business. Then we won't have to get up at the crack of dawn."

Humphrey followed him out of the room. Colton pulled Addy's door closed. Humphrey was not out longer than a minute before he barreled into the house. "Good boy." Colt rubbed the top of the dog's head.

By the time Colt reached the hallway, Humphrey had his head pressed against Addy's door, whining. "Come on, Hum. How about you sleep with me tonight? You can even sleep *on* the bed." He laughed. "Because that's where you'll be by morning anyway."

Always the one to take advantage, Humphrey raced to Colt's bed and jumped under the covers on Colton's side. "Oh, no, you don't. Move over, you big oaf," Colt said as he pushed the big dog toward the far side of the bed.

It was only minutes before they were both asleep.

Around 4:30 a.m., Humphrey grew restless. He gave a low growl, so soft Colt mistook it for snoring. He shoved the dog. "Stop snoring," he told him. "Otherwise, go sleep somewhere else."

When the dog quieted, it was Colt's turn to feel restless. The dog had woken him, and he could not get back to sleep. After deciding a pitstop might alleviate his discomfort, he threw back the covers. It was freezing in the house, freezing by Arizona standards. A stiff breeze, which had not been there the night before, blew through the window. The curtains danced inward as he shoved his window closed.

Colt pulled on the jeans and sweatshirt he had thrown in the chair the night before. With Humphrey at his side, he opened his bedroom door and padded down the dim hallway, lit only by the early dawn. He was not surprised to see Addy's door ajar. She often used the bathroom during the night.

Colt shoved the door open and froze. Humphrey raced across the room and stood on his hind legs at the window. He barked twice before Colt called him down. The window was wide open, and the screen was missing. A lump lay in the middle of Addy's bed. He lifted the covers to find his daughter curled into a ball.

"Hi, Daddy," she whispered.

"Why'd you open your window, pumpkin?" He started toward the open window.

"I didn't," his daughter told him. "That man did."

Colt froze. His heart thudded in his ears as his stomach twisted in an explosion of heat. "What man, honey?"

"The man who was at McDonald's last night," she explained. "Daddy, I'm so cold. Shut the window."

Colt was sure his heart was going to explode. What man was she talking about? Had someone been watching them? He did not want to touch the window; it might contain fingerprints or DNA.

He sat next to his daughter, who was still nothing more than a bulge under her comforter. "Honey, this is important. When was the man here?"

A mumble came from beneath the blanket. Colt lifted it and asked his daughter again. "He left when he heard you. Close the window, Daddy, please," she begged. "I'm so cold."

"Go crawl in my bed, sweetie. I'll be there in a minute."

Addy rolled off the side of her bed, pulling most of the covers with her, and ran to her dad's bed. Humphrey followed. Colt touched nothing in his daughter's room.

He tiptoed past his bed and checked the lock on the window before unplugging his cell phone, shutting the door, and going into the living room.

"Nine-one-one, what's your emergency?" a woman on the other end of the line asked.

"Someone broke into my house. Into my daughter's room," he said.

"Sir, is the person still in your house?"

"I-I don't think so," Colt told her. "My daughter said he went out her window."

"How old is your daughter?" the 911 operator asked.

"Four."

"What's your name, sir?"

"Colton Stone."

"And the address, Mr. Stone?"

Colton verified his address as she dispatched a squad. Almost instantly, he could hear the sirens in the distance. He stayed on the line until he heard a noise at his door.

INTROSPECT

Addy Stone: "That man was nice. He told me to be really quiet because we were playing a game. I'm good at games, especially quiet games."

9-1-1 Operator: "We don't get many intruder calls from that area. Usually, it's things like barking dogs or noise complaints in that neighborhood."

Anonymous: "I only needed five more minutes."

CHAPTER TWENTY-TWO

For the second time in a year, sirens wailed, and red and blue flashing lights battered Colton's neighborhood. People stood on their lawns, gawking toward the Stone home. Unsure if they were dealing with a madman with a gun or a random cat burglar, an officer got on his speaker and announced for everyone to return to their homes. "Lock your doors and windows. Stay out of sight. Close your blinds and curtains and remain vigilant. If you see or hear anything that makes you suspicious, call 911 immediately." People scrambled in all directions. If you listened hard enough, you could hear the collective click of doors locking.

Colt sat in his living room with two officers while several others processed evidence in Addy's room, outside, or in other parts of the house. Poised with a pen, a small pad of paper, and his phone, one officer recorded the conversation and jotted down notes. The more senior of the two asked the questions. "Mr. Stone, what exactly did your daughter tell you?"

"Call me Colt," he said. He looked up as he recalled the

short conversation he had had with his daughter. "All she said was that there was a man in her room, and he went out the window when he heard me."

"Anything else?"

"No. After that, I sent her to my bed, and by the time I checked on her, she was asleep. I didn't wake her. I assumed you'd want to talk to her."

The officer nodded. "So, nothing then?"

Colt's eyes flashed. "Wait. There was one thing. She told me the man was at McDonald's last night when we were at the PlayPlace."

"Which McDonald's?"

"The one on Main," Colt said.

"What time were you there?" The officer looked at his partner instead of at Colt.

"Mmm. I'd say we got there around 6:00, maybe a little later. We probably left sometime around 7:10 or 7:15."

"Hill," the officer called to a cop walking through the living room. "Call the McDonald's on Main and see if they have security cameras inside. If so, get any footage from between five and eight last night. I also want video from any surrounding cameras that aimed anywhere within a thousand feet around the McDonald's for that same timeframe."

Officer Hill nodded. "On it, Chief."

"We'd like to talk to your daughter, Mr. Stone. You can sit with her, but please don't lead her or encourage her to speak. Let us do the questioning. Understand?" the officer asked.

"Yes." Colt stood. "I'll go get her."

"Wait. We'll let you know when we're ready for her. When you go in there, don't talk about what happened. We'll come and get you in a few minutes. Carter," the chief called, "go with him and stand outside the door where the girl can't see you." He turned back to Colt. "Officer Carter will let you know when we're ready."

"What if she says something about it?" Colt asked. "How do you want me to handle that?"

"Change the subject." He looked back at his notes.

Colt sat on the edge of the bed and watched his daughter sleep for over seven minutes before Officer Carter instructed him to wake her. He was keenly aware that if Humphrey had not woken him up, he could have been staring at an empty bed. His shoulders fell and a contemplative sigh rushed out. He picked up Addy and held her tightly as he rocked back and forth. Minutes later, with his daughter wrapped in the comforter from his bed, he carried her to the living room.

A woman in jeans and a t-shirt had joined the two men. She pointed toward the chair where he sat before. She took the chair adjacent to the father and daughter.

"Hi, Addy." A warm smile crossed the woman's face as Addy turned away from her and buried her face beneath the quilt. "My name's Tammy Clarkson. I'm a police officer."

Addy's eyes slowly appeared above the edge of the bulky fabric. She scanned the room. "Nuh-uh," she corrected the woman. "Where's your costume?"

All three officers laughed. "Not all police officers wear *costumes*," she said. "That's how we trick the bad guys."

Colt could tell Addy was processing what she had just heard.

"Ohhhhh." She laughed as she dug her way out of the comforter. "That's tricky."

"It is," the officer agreed. Officer Clarkson pressed her finger to her lips. "But that's our secret, okay?"

"Okay," Addy agreed happily. Then she tried to wink at the woman, but instead of closing one eye, both closed tightly before reopening.

"Good." The officer winked back. "Addy, can I ask you some questions? I'd like you to help me catch a bad guy. Do you want to do that?"

The little girl sat up straight. "Can I be a police girl then too?"

The woman nodded. "Of course. I'll make you my deputy if you help me."

Addy looked at her father. "I'm gonna be a police girl, Daddy. So you're gonna have to listen to me."

"Good to know." Colton smiled.

"Addy, your dad tells us someone opened your window. Did you do that?"

She shook her head. "No, that man did that."

"Where did the man come from?" Tammy asked.

"I don't know. He was just standin' in my room when I woke up."

"What was he doing when you first noticed him?"

Addy yawned. "He was standing by my dresser, playing with the box Daddy made."

Tammy shot a look at an officer who had joined them. Colt did not miss that or the small head wag that sent one of the men toward his daughter's room. "Did the man open the box?"

Addy shook her head. "I didn't see him open it."

"What did the man say to you?"

A second yawn escaped from Addy. "He told me we were playing a game, and I had to be really quiet." She tucked her arms deep inside the quilt. "He said he was Santa's helper, and he was making sure I was being a good girl."

Colt tightened his grip on his daughter.

"Did he say anything else?" the woman asked.

"He asked me if I wanted to ride in his special car. He said it could fly all the way to the North Pole."

Officer Clarkson looked at Colt. "What did you tell him?"

"I told him I had to ask my daddy if I could go."

The woman smiled. "That was a good thing to tell him. It's important to always ask your parents for permission to go anywhere." Tammy leaned forward.

Addy looked at her dad. "I don't have parents," she said to the officer when she turned back.

The woman looked confused. "You don't have *parents*?"

She shook her head. "No. I just have Daddy."

Tammy nodded. "Well, he must be pretty special to take care of you all by himself."

Addy pressed her cheek against her dad's chest and patted his shoulder. "He is."

"Okay, police girl," the woman said, "when you told him you had to ask your dad if you could go, what happened then?"

"I jumped out of bed to go ask Daddy, but when I got the door open, the man grabbed me and told me he was just kidding."

Officer Clarkson looked at the other officers. "Where did he touch you?" she asked.

"On my shoulders." Addy crossed her arms and touched both shoulders. "I didn't like it. He squeezed them."

"Do you remember what he did then?"

Addy nodded her head. "He wanted me to go play in the backyard with him. But then he heard my daddy and said he had to go."

Tammy looked toward the chief before returning her attention to Addy. The little girl rubbed a fist against one eye. "How did he leave your room?" she asked.

Addy yawned and laid her cheek on her father's chest. "He went out the window. It was so cold in my room, I crawled under my blankets until Daddy found me." She tilted her face upward. "But he wouldn't shut the window. Bad daddy." She tapped her finger through the air toward him.

Colt smiled at his daughter as she closed her eyes. "Addy, you have to stay awake and help the nice officers. Remember, you're a police officer now too."

Her brown eyes popped open as she sat upright. "A police girl," she said. She turned toward Tammy and waited for another question.

"I just need to know a couple more things, Addy. You're doing so great!"

Addy smiled. "I know." Everyone in the room

chuckled.

"Can you tell me what the man was wearing?"

The little girl pursed her lips and tapped her forehead. "He had on a sweatshirt." She poked a finger into the air.

"Do you know what color?"

She shook her head no. "It was too dark in my room."

"Okay, Addy, this question is really important. Can you tell me what he looked like?" Tammy asked her.

Again, she shook her head. "He had his hood on. I couldn't see his face."

She looked up at Colt and his heart melted.

"I'm sorry, daddy."

"You did great, honey."

"Is there anything else you want to tell me, Addy?" Officer Clarkson asked.

Her face scrunched, and she again tapped her forehead. "Yes," she said quietly.

"Go ahead. What do you want me to know?"

"I don't want Santa's helpers checking on me no more," she said through a yawn.

Addy closed her eyes and rested the back of her head against Colt's shoulder.

Tammy smiled at Colt. "We're going to need her nightgown. I'll remove it from her to preserve any evidence." Colt nodded. Otherwise, we're done with her. We may have some other questions later."

Colt nodded before leading his daughter to his bedroom. Tammy pulled on a pair of gloves before carefully lifting Addy's nightgown over her head and placing it into a plastic bag and sealed it. When she left, Colt slipped one of his t-shirts over her head.

"You were so brave, honey," he whispered, laying her in bed. Addy's eyes were closed before he left the room.

By the time Colton returned to the living room, another officer had joined the mix. He wore rubber gloves and held a single sheet of paper.

"Mr. Stone, I'm Officer Carter."

Colt nodded. "There is a wooden box on your daughter's dresser, correct?"

"Yes. It was a gift I made for Addy's mom. We keep Addy's important papers and photos in it." Colton had too much energy to sit. Instead, he stood near the fireplace.

"The box has a steel lining. Yes?" Colt nodded. "Why the lining?"

Colt seemed confused. "In case of a fire. But how did you know that? The box was locked." He crossed his arms and rocked between his toes and his heels.

The officer looked at his chief. "Sir, the lock was broken. Could you or Addy have broken it?"

Colton shook his head no. "I just put her updated medical records in it two days ago. It was fine then."

"Colt," the chief said. "I think you might want to sit down."

"Why?" He glanced from officer to officer. His heart skipped a beat.

"Trust me on this one," the chief told him.

Colt moved to the chair he had been in before and lowered himself into it without taking his eyes off Officer Carter. He sat upright with his arms tightly wrapped in front of him.

"We looked through the box on your daughter's dresser. It was as you said—important papers and photos. But at the top, not filed like the others, was one item that…well, surprised us."

"What was it?" Colt's brow furrowed as he tried to imagine what could be so unusual.

The officer held up a single sheet of paper, an official-looking document. "We found this."

"What is it?" Colt asked.

The officer shook his head. "This is what has us so baffled. It's a death certificate." He paused and watched Colt's face before continuing. "For your daughter."

"What?" Colt said. "Addy? How's that even possible? You saw her for yourself. You talked to her."

Officer Carter turned the paper toward himself. "I know. But here's the thing. The certificate is dated with today's date."

Colt felt the chair cushion give way, as he fell backward into it. He had lost the ability to think, focus, ask questions, or even respond.

"Colt," the chief called. "Colt! Get him some water," he yelled.

Tammy twisted the top off her unused water bottle, wrapping her hands around his to steady the shaking as she helped guide it toward his mouth.

"Are you okay?" she whispered. An awkward movement resembling a nod was all he had in him. But he was not okay in any sense of the word.

"Colt," Officer Carter knelt on the floor in front of him. "We know it's a fake. It takes nearly two weeks after a death for a certificate to be available. Longer if there is an investigation." He rested a hand on Colton's shoulder. "Whoever was in your daughter's room was here for a purpose. Can you think of anyone who would want to get to you through Addy?"

Colt did not respond. Until Addy called out to him two hours later, Colt never left his chair. Officers walked through the house and all around him, but he never saw or heard a thing.

INTROSPECT

Chief Morales: "We found several size ten and a half Nike Air Zoom running shoe imprints outside the window and an exceptionally clean fingerprint and thumbprint on the left side of the window from when the man climbed in. The problem is, those shoes are common, and unless the guy's already in the database, what we have isn't going to be a lot of help."

Officer Clarkson: "That little girl was amazing! For four years old, she was exceptionally articulate."

Mary Perrine

Officer Carter: "I can't believe there was a fake death certificate in that box. I've never seen anything like that in my entire career, and I've seen a lot of weird stuff in my twenty-three years on the force."

Anonymous: "I almost pulled it off. I almost had her. Next time, I will."

THE VOICES WITHIN
(a choral poem)

NORAH	GRACE	COLTON
I am broken. I tell others I am fine.	I am broken. I am fine is just a group of words. I have lost my daughter.	I am broken. My daughter was nearly kidnapped from under my roof.
Under my roof is the only time I feel safe. It's where I can remember.		
	I can remember feeling her in my arms. But, losing her to death,	
It hurts too much.	it hurts too much.	It hurts too much to remember that I almost lost her, again.
I hide behind a façade of lies. I tell others I am fine, but I'm not. Smiling, laughing, loving.	I hide behind a façade. I tell others I am fine, but I'm not. Smiling, laughing, loving, I can't do it.	I tell others I am fine, but I'm not. I can't do it anymore.
I lie about my past.	I lie about my past. I am not okay. Can anyone hear me? Do any of you see me?	I lie about my past. Do any of you see me and all the pain I've suffered?
All the pain I've suffered, has to remain hidden.		
Bit by bit, I try to move forward.	I am falling apart, bit by bit.	Bit by bit, I try to move forward, but there are reminders everywhere I look.
Everywhere I look, I see my daughter, Lili	Everywhere I look, I see my daughter, Finley	Addy

PART THREE

TWO YEARS LATER

LIVING

Living without the child
you once held, loved, dreamed of
is like breathing
underwater,
drowning
in sea of
grief,
living a life
without air.

LIFE WITH NORAH—Norah Van Pelt

Life Without Air
Part three of a three-part series on the loss of a child

It has been two years. Two years since the grieving parent has felt their child's loving embrace; two years without sloppy kisses and childhood laughter. The unrelenting question of *why?* and the barrage of senseless jokes have gone silent. The intense pain that once knocked the wind out of the devastated parent has finally loosened its grip and a small slice of normalcy has fought its way back in.

For some, the days pass quickly; routine, friendship, and therapy help. For others, they drag on, eating away at their soul until they are nothing but a tightly wound barbed ball of grief. Their thoughts and emotions catch on everything and everyone, snagging those who are too polite to turn away. The anger they have tried so hard to control still periodically escapes if they do not stuff it deep inside. It is impossible to know which road a parent will travel until they are faced with this unimaginable loss.

For those who cannot move forward, sleepless nights stretch before them. Periodically, they wake with a start, drenched in sweat, unsure where their nightmare ends and reality begins. Their brain refuses to shut down and silent tears fall as they relive memories of their days as a family.

Life goes on for everyone around them. They watch from the sidelines, longing to be part of something they once knew. They finally take a deep breath and make a resolute commitment to belong to the world of the living. To smile, love, and laugh again is the promise they make to themselves. They have seen how short life is and have experienced the speed at which it passes. But often, smiling hurts, and laughter feels like a betrayal. Still, most of these parents will make it; they will push through the fortress walls the loss of a child has built around them. Yet, there will be some who are not so lucky. Their child's absence has destroyed their sense of identity, their belief in tomorrow, next week, next year. They have forgotten how to live without their child, without the pain and so, they cling to it like a poorly fashioned lifeline.

All these parents will tell you that life is too short. It moves too fast. There is never enough time to live in the moment and still consider the possibilities of the future. But regardless of our desires and plans, every child conceived lives a lifetime; it just may not be what we envisioned. Their experiences and their time here are exactly what was intended. Each child teaches us something priceless. Some teach us to laugh. Others teach us to dream. Still others teach us to feel—pain, love, and joy.

Once a parent finally hears that message, they are ready to face the future. That is when healing begins, and the Grand Canyon-sized hole begins to close. Parents tiptoe out of their darkness and begin to talk. They count their lost child among the members of their family. They tell their stories.

On that day, they begin to breathe again. They vow to never

let their child's absence steal one more day of living. It is not what their child would have wanted. For them, they live, laugh, and love. They give the best of themself.

Norah Van Pelt is a syndicated columnist

NORAH	COLTON
Hidden Past	Hidden Past
Single	Single
Newspaper owner	Custom Cabinetry Owner
Syndicated Columnist	Father
Afraid to Let Others In	Frightened of Losing His Daughter

CHAPTER TWENTY-THREE

Two years had passed since Addy's near-death accident on their first night in Podany and a year since she was nearly lost to the depraved intruder whose intent was still unclear. The first was an accident; the second was calculated and malevolent. The police had followed every lead; they interviewed everyone who came forward with even the slightest bit of information. The perfect set of fingerprints lifted from the window frame had not garnered a single match from the national database. For weeks, Chief Morales held daily press conferences and sent out messages via social media, but it was all for naught. During those first six months, Colt pored over the police reports searching for something that might have been overlooked.

At home, Colt created an unbreachable fortress. Deadbolts had been installed on both doors and security bars were mounted on every window. To ensure there was not an elusive key, Colt did the work himself. A top-of-the-line security system, complete with cameras on both the inside and outside of the house, was in place before he felt safe enough to let Addy return to her own bed. At times, he felt like a prisoner in his own home; other times, when he looked at his daughter, he was not sure he had done enough.

Except to attend daycare or to stay with Colt's next-door neighbor, who had been researched and vetted, Addy never strayed far from Colton's sight. Officer Carter had met with both groups and arranged for Addy to be released only to her father. It was impossible to know if a phone call with a verbal change of plans was from Colton or someone else pretending to be him. The daycare center was small and privately owned. In the unlikely event Colt could not reach the center before closing, Debbie agreed to stay with Addy until she could safely be handed off or dropped at a designated neighbor's house.

No matter where he went, Colt was aware of his surroundings. He took mental notes and images of people and their actions; he remembered details about cars and voices. Because he lived in constant fear, he carried his friend, Smith and Wesson, tucked inside an internal holster in the waistband of his pants. A private instructor had taught him to shoot to kill. No one would ever again attempt to take his daughter from him. If they tried, they wouldn't live to talk about it. It was that simple.

In those first several months, not a day passed that Colton did not experience a moment of panic. Walking into a movie theater, playing in the park, dropping Addy at daycare, grabbing fast food, or going for a walk all made the hair on the back of his neck stand at attention. Still, he was not about to keep his daughter from experiencing life. *His* job was to worry, to protect. Addy's job was to live; Colt did everything he could to make that happen—safely.

On Addy's fifth birthday, a milestone she asked about daily, she rose with the sun. She was beyond excited to start *big kid school* as she referred to it.

By 6:00 a.m., she was dressed and standing in Colton's doorway. "Hurry up, Daddy!" She watched her skirt billow as she twisted left then right.

"Hey, sweetie." Colt smiled at her as he crawled out of bed and pulled on a t-shirt. "Happy birthday, my big five-year-old. Why are you up so early?"

"Dad-dy," she whined, "don't be silly! I'm going to school today." Addy lifted her shoulders and grinned.

"You mean daycare?"

"No! That's for babies. I'm five now. I get to go to the big kid school," she said.

Colt scooped her up and planted a loud kiss on her cheek as she tried to squirm away.

"Don't mess up my dress, Daddy." Addy tugged the bottom of her dress from beneath his arm and smoothed it with her palms.

"Oh, Addy." He carried her to the kitchen and set her on a tall stool. "School doesn't start on the *exact* day you turn five. You have to wait for the new year to start."

Her smile slowly faded. "Why can't I go to school today? I'm five *now*, and you said when I turned five, I would start school." Addy leaned on the counter and pushed her lower lip out.

"Well, you got me there," he said. "I did say that, didn't I?"

Addy nodded; her long eyelashes fluttered at him. "Yes, you did."

He leaned across the island and pressed his forehead against hers. "Well, here's the thing, sweetie. I didn't mean *today*. I meant when the new school year starts."

"I don't understand." Addy pulled away from her father and swiped at her eyes with the back of her hand, brushing away the tears that rolled down her cheeks. "I want to go to school today, Daddy, just like you told me."

Colt slipped a pod into the Keurig and set his cup on the base beneath. He pressed two buttons and the coffee maker sprang to life. He pulled a carton of hard-boiled eggs from the fridge and peeled one for his daughter.

"Okay, sweetie, let me try this. So, remember last December when you wanted it to be Christmas, but you had to wait?" Colt smiled at her as he crawled

Addy nodded.

"Well, I told you it was still twenty-four more *sleeps* before Santa came. You didn't want to wait, but you did. It felt like it was never going to get here, right?"

Addy nodded.

"Well, you waited and waited, and every night, we crossed off one more day on the calendar. Then it was finally Christmas. Remember?"

Addy nodded again.

"Well, waiting to start school is kind of like that, honey. You just have to wait a little while longer, but when it comes, you will be so excited. It'll be better than Christmas."

His daughter sat quietly, never looking away. "Honey, do you understand?" Colt asked.

"I do," she said. The lines on her forehead deepened and her eyes narrowed as she crossed her arms in front of her. "You lied to me."

Colt chuckled. "I didn't lie to you, honey. I guess I just didn't explain it very well."

Addy huffed. "Well, Daddy, you better start practicing explaining stuff." Addy took a tiny bite of her egg. "Or else I'm gonna say you lie to me a lot."

"I agree." Colt laughed as he set two colorful, ineptly wrapped gifts on the counter. "Are you ready for your presents?"

A wide smile spread across Addy's face. She clapped her hands and sang, "Oooh! Presents! Presents! Presents!" Suddenly, her smile fell, and her eyebrows furrowed. "They better be good ones since I don't get to go to school today."

His daughter was well beyond her five years of age. She was an old soul who made a lot more sense than most adults Colton had ever known.

❦

Stone's Unique Builders had officially been in business for six months under their new name. After some negotiating,

Ned had agreed to sell his business under one condition: the crew stayed. Colt had no problem with that. He liked the team Ned had assembled; they were good at their jobs, and they felt like family. Other than Addy, they were the only family he had.

Colt had big plans for the business. By the end of the second month, it had expanded well beyond the projects that walked *in* the door. Colt's team quickly grew from a dozen employees to seventeen as he began taking on custom projects outside the workshop. The goal he had set for himself was steep, but he was well on his way to turning it into a reality. He often wondered if he was spreading himself too thin. Between his business and his determination to protect his daughter, there were days he barely had enough energy to make dinner.

The team was on break when Sonja called through the workshop door. "Hey, Colt."

She yelled his name a second time before he heard her. "Your ten o'clock is here."

Colt finished his discussion with one of his new hires and headed toward the showroom.

He was brushing the sawdust from his shirt when he reached the desk. "Hi," he said, extending his hand in greeting toward the woman. "C-Colton Stone." The lobes of his ears warmed before bleeding onto his cheeks. His knees felt weak. He could not take his eyes off the woman in front of him. There was something about her that fired every nerve ending inside of him.

The woman nodded, noticing his glowing cheeks. "Norah Burke."

A few seconds passed before Colt got his bearings back. "Let's, ah, let's meet in my office." Sonja poked him in the ribs as he led the way past her desk and through a set of handmade, ornate double doors. "Have a seat, Mrs. Burke." He pointed to a chair at the round table.

"Call me N-Norah." She looked into his blue eyes. Heat flamed her cheeks.

Sonja rolled her eyes at Colt as she set two bottles of water in the middle of the table and turned away. She muttered to herself, "Must be something going around. Nobody knows their name today."

Colton leaned back in his chair, creating more distance between him and Norah. His body tingled with the same warm sensation he had when he first met Brit, and it scared him. *No! Never again.*

"What can I do for you, Norah?" Her name slowly rolled from his tongue.

Norah studied his face for several seconds before the question registered. "Oh!" she muttered, taking a sip of her water. "I, ah, have a remodeling job I was hoping you would consider. You come highly recommended."

He cleared his throat, afraid of his voice cracking like a thirteen-year-old boy's. "How big are we talking?"

"I own the *Press*. I'm looking at doing some remodeling there," she said.

"Ah, the *Podany Press*. Because Truth Matters," he quoted the paper's tagline. "Never heard of it," he teased as a sideways grin lifted one cheek, exposing a deep dimple.

"Funny guy." She smiled, her breaths quick and shallow.

Colton sucked in a deep breath and released it. Just being in the same room as Norah was putting him on edge. He needed to get out of the office. "What are you thinking?" He clicked his pen.

"Well..." She smiled. "I'd like to restructure the office space with more collaborative spaces. I also want to have reservable private spaces for reporters to work as well. I'm looking for classy, yet comfortable. Casual, but sophisticated."

"Hmm, sounds like you've put some thought into this." Colt grinned. "You know, it would probably be cheaper to buy modular walls and furniture."

Norah shook her head. "Have you been in the building? It's beautiful. The original design is oak and black iron. I'd like to keep that look."

He slid his chair back and stood. "Tell you what. Let's walk down to the *Press* and you can show me what you're thinking."

"Makes sense." Norah picked up her purse and led the way outside. They walked the three blocks side-by-side, safely discussing the weather.

An hour later, Colton was back in his office working on preliminary sketches for the remodel.

INTROSPECT

Colton Stone: "Norah Burke is classy, casual, sophisticated, and sexy as hell. There's only been one other woman that made me feel this way. I can't let myself get roped into another relationship. Or can I?"

Norah Burke: "There was something about Colton Stone that stirred everything I thought I had safely stowed away. That frightens me. I don't trust myself. I failed at love before."

Sonja Blum: "Had I not just met Norah Burke, I would have told her and Colt to get a room. Those two put off enough electricity to run the workshop."

CHAPTER TWENTY-FOUR

A glass of wine and a quiet evening with the television remote had been Norah's plans for the night. But the more she replayed her time with Colton, the less the TV mattered. It was just background noise.

His intoxicating blue eyes had charmed her so much she found herself tongue-tied. She had stumbled on her own name. His deep voice was as smooth as the wooden samples in his showroom. And that sideways grin and one dimple that grew deeper the bigger he smiled made her heart almost stop. She'd had everything she could do not to touch it. She was grateful the receptionist was just outside the door; otherwise, she may have made a fool out of herself. Honestly, she could not remember ever experiencing anything like that before.

With Seth, love had grown slowly; they were friends who fell into marriage. The longer they were apart, though, the more she realized there had been no passion. She had mistaken comfort and familiarity for love. With Colton Stone, her legs grew weak, and her heart danced, fluttering inside her chest. She finally understood the story her dad told her about meeting her mom for the first time. Their story had been love at first sight. Was that what this was? Love? Was it something predestined or just a momentary infatuation? Had she been led to Podany for the reason of meeting Colt? Was he part of her new beginning?

Norah poured more wine into her glass and took a sip. Everything in her longed for a man she had known for…she looked at her watch, *nine hours and thirty-three minutes*. What was wrong with her? Hadn't she suffered enough? Or perhaps, what was *right*? Wasn't it time she found true happiness?

She set her glass on the coffee table and stretched out on the couch. It was rare she lounged around in her pajamas in the evening, but her column had just been submitted, and after a few nights of perfecting it, she deserved a night off. Through the open spaces in a pair of tall bookcases that leaned against two long windows, Norah watched the clouds shift in the evening sky. But suddenly, it was the unique bookcases that grabbed her attention. She marveled at their placement. Setting them against the window would never have crossed her mind—but that was why she had hired Tracy. She had done a marvelous job of decorating her condo.

As Norah rolled onto her side, she noticed a wooden box she had not remembered seeing before. It had somehow gotten shoved to the back of the lowest shelf. Clearly, her cleaning lady didn't get down on the floor to dust. She slid off the couch and crawled on her hands and knees toward the bookshelf. Lying on her stomach, she pulled the intricate box toward her.

It was stunning. Delicate finger joints created a checkerboard pattern along each edge. As Norah ran her hand over them, she was amazed by their smoothness. They were so tight, it felt like a single piece of wood instead of two. The lid was as thick as the bottom. The opening cut through the middle of the box. An intricate clasp lifted to the right to unlatch it. Norah's breath caught when she lifted the lid. The inside was lined with a deep blue velvet, the bottoms and the sides pillowed inward to protect any contents it may one day hold.

The more she looked at it, the more it felt oddly familiar. When she and Seth married, he had gifted her a box of nearly the same shape and size, but not nearly as beautifully crafted. For weeks, that box had caused heated arguments. Repeatedly, she moved it to their dresser in their bedroom, but Seth insisted it was displayed in their living room, near the front door. He wanted guests to be impressed with the gift he had chosen for his new bride. Finally, she gave up and let him place it where he wanted. After a while, she barely noticed it. When she was packing to leave their home, she threw it in the sale. It had been just another reminder of her past with a controlling man.

Norah flipped the box over. *Ned's Custom Cabinetry* was stamped onto the bottom of the box. The name sounded familiar, but she could not place it. The box would make lovely gifts for her staff. She would have to ask Tracy where she could order more. She moved a few things around and placed the box on an upper shelf. It was exquisite and deserved a place of honor.

She pressed the button on the remote and paused the show she had yet to watch before returning to the couch. Her phone lay next to her wine glass; she picked up both, one in each hand, drinking while she texted. One-handed texting was something she had perfected during her four weeks in a cast. It was the only time Seth had ever gotten physical with her. She honestly did not think he meant to hurt her; she wanted to believe it had been an accident.

Hey, she typed out. *Where did you find that lovely wooden box with the finger joints?*

Before her phone went black, she saw the dots encircled in a speech bubble and knew an answer was forthcoming.

Her phone whistled at her. *What box? Send pic.*

Norah zoomed in on the box and snapped a photo; she

forwarded it to Tracy. Another sip of wine warmed her throat as she watched the dots pass like marquee lights.

No clue. Don't remember it. A second text followed. *Will check with Mel. Give me a few.*

While she waited, Norah stood at the wall of windows watching the boats travel up and down the river. The sunlight was just beginning to lose its brilliancy as evening continued to march in. The windows were tinted from the outside so she could see out, but no one could see in. After spending fifteen years in a neighborhood fishbowl, where the neighbors knew everything within seconds after it happened, she felt great comfort in the condo.

Her phone whistled, announcing another text message. *Mel doesn't remember it. Might have been pulled from our warehouse. Don't recall putting it there. Doesn't mean we didn't.*

Norah set her glass down. Her thumbs flew as she tapped out her last text. *No worries. Love it. Glad it's here. Have a good night.*

A smiley face emoji appeared on her phone, ending their conversation.

⚭⚭⚭⚭⚭

"Hey, have either of you ever heard of Ned's Custom Cabinetry?" Norah asked Beth and Luke the following morning. Luke laughed as the two exchanged a knowing look. "What's so funny?"

"The guy you had in here to give you a quote to remodel this place, Colton Stone, he bought that place from Ned. He used to work for him."

"Really?" Norah seemed intrigued—a reason for another visit to Colton's shop.

"Why are you asking? Is there some juicy story about Ned Newton I should be researching?" Beth leaned in.

"Always the conspiracy theorist, aren't you?" Norah snorted. "No, I have a box in my condo that came from Ned's. I just thought they would make nice gifts for the staff."

Beth dropped back in her chair. "Well, that's boring." She sighed.

"I'm not interrupting anything, am I?" Colt asked as he tapped on her door frame.

Norah glanced at her team and smirked.

"Nope." Luke grabbed Beth by the hand and pulled her out of the office past Colt. "We were just leaving."

"But I…" Beth argued, looking back into the office.

"No, you weren't," Luke told her as he pulled her into his room and closed the door.

Colt tipped his head toward the door. "Interesting crew you work with."

"They're great." Norah laughed. "But they're always up to something. What can I do for you, Mr. Stone?" A shiver ran up her spine.

"Colt," he reminded her. "I just came to get a few more measurements before I draw up the final plans."

Norah wondered if Colt could hear her heartbeat. She was breathless as she stared into his eyes. "By all means," she said airily. Colt smiled and turned toward the outer office. "Wait!" Norah called after him. "I have a question. I have a wooden box at my place that was made at Ned's. I wondered if you still make them."

"We do custom work. So, I'm sure we could."

"I was thinking about ordering some for my staff as Christmas gifts. I know it's early, but I'd need more than a dozen of them." Norah grabbed her phone. "I have a picture of it. Just a minute." Norah showed Colton the photo she had sent to Tracy the night before.

Colt's face turned white.

"Are you all right?" Norah asked. "Can I get you something?"

"No," he wheezed. "Yeah, I can make up a bunch of those pretty quickly. Call the shop and tell Sonja what you want. Tell her it's the finger joint box. She'll know the one." Colt returned to the door. "I'll get out of your hair and get those measurements."

Something had changed. The air, which moments earlier had been electrified, suddenly felt murky and thick. Had she misjudged what she believed to be something between them? She got up and closed her door and paced around her office. Clearly, it was a wake-up call. *Stay the course, Norah. Let no one in.*

After Colt left the paper, he recalled the circumstances surrounding that box—the cop and the special order. He claimed he had ordered it for his wife—to keep tabs on their nanny. Norah, the one woman other than Brit who stirred emotions inside of him, the woman he had dreamt about last night, the one he had known for just over twenty-four hours—was married. His heart dropped into his stomach, and he felt like he'd been punched in the gut.

After her less than positive interaction with Colton Stone, Norah was committed to spending another night in front of the television. She pulled a black plastic takeout container from the fridge. She set the remaining half of a once toasted sandwich in a small cake pan and slipped it into the hot oven while she poured herself a glass of wine. This had become her life: takeout, TV, and wine. She shrugged. It was better than the alternative: letting someone in who would eventually leave. Or worse yet, someone who would control her entire life. Neither of those things could happen again.

Holding a napkin and the wine glass, she walked into the living room. She set them on the coffee table before glancing toward the shelf. Something was wrong. There was an empty space where the box had been. Maybe she had only thought she moved it, cleared the space, but never actually set it there. She bent down and searched the lower shelf, but it was not there either. How was that possible? Where had it gone? Had she moved it somewhere else and forgotten?

Norah wandered the living room, searching for the wooden container, but found it nowhere. Had it all been a dream? Had she only dreamt it into existence? No. It was real. She had a photo to prove it.

Smoke seeped out of the oven, and she grabbed a potholder and jerked the pan out, throwing it into the sink and running water on half of the sandwich she had not eaten the night before. "Dammit!" she yelled as she watched the burnt bread break apart and float in the discolored water. "Dammit," she said more softly as she waved a dish towel under the smoke detector to keep it from going off.

Her phone was splattered with droplets of water; she wiped the screen on her thigh before opening her photos. The last picture she had taken, the one of the ornate box, the same one she had shown to Colton that morning, was gone. Somehow, it had been deleted. She opened her text messages, but Tracy's contact and their entire conversation string were missing also. Norah dropped onto a stool. That old familiar feeling, the one of losing control, returned. She was confused. Nothing made sense.

Feeling woozy and out of sorts, Norah opted to go to bed before the sun dropped below the horizon. As she approached the bedroom, she began to shake. The door was closed. Norah never shut that door, not even at night. Why had she not noticed it before? The buzzing in her ears grew louder as her back straightened. Was someone in the condo? Silently, she pressed down on the levered handle and slowly pushed the door open. Silence rang out. Norah grabbed a heavy crystal vase from her dresser and dumped the fake flower arrangement onto the floor before she wandered through the rest of the en suite. Neither her closet nor bathroom looked amiss.

When she walked out of her bathroom, she was certain she heard the door to her condo latch. Had someone just entered or left? She ran to the door and jerked it open, but no one was in the commons. As before, there was nothing. She twisted the lock on the door handle and on the deadbolt before leaning against the solid wood. Either she had locked herself in with a crazy person or she had locked them out. Either way, the hairs rose on her arms as she walked back into her bedroom with a butcher knife, checking every spot large enough to hide.

Slowly, she spun around her bedroom. What she saw on her bed dropped her to her knees. The picture of Lili, the one she slept with every night, the one she tenderly packed away in tissue paper and tucked into her nightstand each morning, leaned against her pillow on the neatly made bed. Norah curled into a ball and sobbed—fearing she was losing her sanity.

INTROSPECT

Luke Simon: "It is so obvious Norah has a thing for the builder guy. And I'm fairly sure the feeling's mutual."

Anonymous: "Sometimes people need to experience something horrific to understand what could have been, what still should be. I have no qualms about helping Norah see that."

CHAPTER TWENTY-FIVE

After four drinks, two books, and a story in which Humphrey saved the day, Addy was finally asleep. Colt dropped onto the couch with his computer and a bottle of beer, the first of a handful. With his feet propped on the coffee table, he started his search. It was a proverbial rabbit hole; he knew that. Everything inside of him screamed to *leave it alone*, but he could not let it go.

Colt pulled up the archived orders on his computer, combing through them for a good twenty minutes before he found what he was searching for. He checked the date. The box with the finger joints had been ordered around the same time the stranger had broken into Addy's room. Had the two incidents been connected? Could the man who wanted the box, be the same one who breached his daughter's bedroom? Was it possible he left the fake death certificate? What connection would there have been between the two? What would he want with Addy? It had to have been some sort of freak coincidence.

The order had been placed by a man named Seth, a man

with no last name. Sonja had left handwritten notes on the top of the order: *cop, beyond creepy, buying it for his wife to spy on the nanny.* Like always, once the project was completed, she snapped photos, scanned everything, and electronically filed it.

Colt scrolled through the pictures of the plans and the notes the man had written. Norah had shown him the same box described in the order. If this guy could be trusted, and everything he claimed was true, then Norah was the woman he ordered the box for. So that meant she was not only married, but she had a kid. And if she did not, whose nanny were they spying on?

Colton got up and grabbed a second beer and popped the top into the sink. Sonja had told him it was for the guy's wife, to spy on their nanny. Somehow, he was falling in love with a married woman who had a child.

He dropped back onto the couch. Was it possible Norah had gotten the box another way? A garage sale? A gift? Colt could not leave it alone. He had to know more.

He typed *Norah Burke, Podany Press* into the search bar. An article from the *Press*, introducing her as the new owner, mentioned nothing about a child or a husband. It did, however, say she had previously lived in Mason Hills, California. Colt narrowed his search: *Norah Burke, journalist, Mason Hills, CA.* A *Norah Van Pelt* popped onto his screen but, after digging through images, there was no photo, just a generic drawing of a woman that looked nothing like Norah. How could that be? Norah Van Pelt was a syndicated columnist, a public figure. How had she kept her picture a secret?

He left that tab open and tried a new search, linking the two names he had with the location: Norah and Seth Burke, Mason Hills, California. Several articles populated the page. He scribbled notes on a yellow legal pad, linking information in a convoluted web of curved lines and circles. Periodically, he turned to a clean page and recorded random details that did not quite fit his disorganized mess. Once he had exhausted every lead on the web, he flipped through the pages of the notepad, focusing on significant facts, committing them to memory.

Seth was a police officer in Mason Hills, or he had been at one time. There was no way to tell if he was still there without calling the station. LinkedIn showed Mason Hills as his last location of employment, but that meant nothing. People often overlooked updating their profiles and resumes.

In Mason Hills, Norah had worked for the *Clearwater Chronicle* writing under the name of Norah Van Pelt. The syndicated columnist and owner of the *Podany Press* were one and the same. It was clear Norah didn't want this to be public information, or she would not be using her married name at the *Press*. Another link had revealed a birth announcement for a little girl named Liliana; Seth and Norah were listed as her parents.

Hoping beyond hope, Colt typed in California divorce records. Seth Allan Burke and Norah Elizabeth Burke had been divorced eighteen months earlier. The information put a smile on Colton's face, and an audible sigh indicated his relief. He celebrated the find with another beer.

It was nearly 2:00 a.m. when he uncovered an obituary for Liliana Daisy Burke. Norah had lost what appeared to be her *only* child. He could not even imagine the grief she must have suffered. When Colt thought he lost Addy, his world came crashing down. How much worse it would have been had she died. Suddenly, his heart ached for Norah.

Colt took a long drink from the bottle and relived the night he found out Addy was not his biological daughter. He had lost her too, just not in the same way. He still had the child he fell in love with the minute Brit told him she was pregnant. Maybe Addy was not his flesh and blood, but she was his daughter. He could see her and hold and kiss her every single day. Norah could not.

As the minutes pushed toward daylight, Colt tore the pages from the notepad and spread them across the coffee table. He looked through them again. Something bothered him. Seth had ordered the box under the premise of spying on a nanny. But he and Norah had been divorced by then and their daughter had already passed away. Maybe Seth had had an affair and the box was purchased for *another* child with another woman. But, if that was the case, how had Norah ended up with the box?

There was no doubt about it; Seth ordered the box for one reason: to spy on his ex-wife. Colt couldn't remain silent.

<hr>

Beth stood in Norah's office doorway. "Boss, Colton Stone just walked through the door," she whispered, pointing a thumb over her shoulder. The two of them had had a lunch date the day before. Norah had tried to hide her feelings for Colt, but Beth was Beth and Norah had come to know that the researcher in her could pull information out of anyone. The woman should have been a detective.

Norah froze. "How do I look?" She ran her fingers through her hair.

"Like you just walked off the cover of a magazine. Stop worrying. He'll keep coming back. Just stop playing hard to get," Beth whispered.

"Hard to get what?" Colton asked, suddenly appearing behind Beth.

Beth smirked. "Wouldn't you like to know?" She pushed past him. Once she was out the door, she gave Norah a covert double thumbs-up and a goofy grin.

"Paper business," Norah lied. Her heart was already racing. No, that was not true; it had not stopped since the previous night when she realized the box had disappeared and she found Lili's photo propped against her pillow. She had not called the police because she wasn't even sure the box had ever existed. Just as it was entirely possible, she had left Lili's photo on her bed unintentionally and did not remember. Or maybe the whole thing was simply a nightmare that came off a little too real.

"Hey, do you have a few minutes?"

Norah glanced at her watch. "I do. Did you bring the final plans with you?"

Colt pushed the door shut and laid a manilla folder on Norah's desk before settling into the chair across from her. "I'm still working on them, but I'll have them soon." He shifted in his chair. "There's something else I need to talk to you about."

"Oh." Norah squirmed uncomfortably.

"That box, the one you asked about yesterday, there's something weird about it."

Norah's throat tightened. It had not been a dream. She knew she was not crazy. She reached for her water bottle and took several swallows. "W-what about it?" She faked a cough she hoped would justify the higher pitch of her voice as it squeezed between her nerves.

"Well, there was something odd about that box. I'm sure you noticed the lid and the base were nearly the same size." Colt slid to the front of his chair. His forehead wrinkled and his mouth twisted. "Well, the reason the lid is so thick is because it has a hidden compartment." Colt pulled an enlarged photo from the folder. "See?" He watched Norah as she studied the picture. "And here," he pointed to the latch, "there's a small hole in this circle. It was designed to disguise a camera."

A chill ran down Norah's spine and she shivered. Had someone been spying on her, watching her every move, listening to her calls? Her eyes did not leave the photo. Sweat beads formed on the back of her neck, but yet, she felt cold, blisteringly numb. Her stomach trembled as much as her hands. She tucked both hands beneath her legs so Colton would not notice.

"The cop..."

"Wait! Did you say *cop*?" Norah was bordering on a full-blown panic attack.

"Yes. The cop who ordered it said it was for his wife to

house a nanny cam in."

Norah let out a small sigh. Her shoulders fell forward. A sense of relief flooded through her, leaving her weak and shaky as the adrenaline dissipated. It wasn't Seth; they wouldn't have needed a nanny cam. Maybe there had been no recorder in the box while it was in her apartment or, if there was, perhaps there had been no one on the other end of the video stream watching her every move. But where had the box gone? Had she simply misplaced it or hidden it during a bout of sleepwalking she was prone to during times of stress?

Colt leaned toward her. With one foot, Norah pushed her chair backward again, making a slight turn to the side. She crossed her arms across her chest.

"Norah, the man who came into the shop and ordered the box wore a police uniform from another city. Sonja couldn't tell which city. He also had no name on his uniform, and he only gave her his first name. *Seth.*"

Her arms dropped into her lap and her body went limp. Every part of her felt like rubber. She tried to make sense of what Colton had just told her.

"We-we don't need a nanny cam," she said, clearly confused.

"I know. I did some digging last night. I connected Seth Burke to you—Norah Van Pelt, the syndicated columnist." Her face paled. "And… I'm not proud of this, but I, ah, know you were married and divorced." He stared down at the floor before looking back into her eyes. "I also know about your daughter Liliana."

Norah sprang up. Her chair thudded against the wall as it rocketed backward. "Get out," she hissed. "Get out, now!" Colt did not move. "How dare you dig into my past. How dare you!" She angrily pointed toward the door. "You're no better than my ex."

Colt stood. "Norah, I can check the box and remove the recording device. Or, if you'd prefer, I can destroy it."

Slowly, Norah walked toward the other end of her

office. She paced back and forth across the room. "The box is gone."

A heavy sigh came from Colt. "Good. I don't care what you did with it, but I'm glad it's not in your place anymore." He turned to leave but stopped when he heard her admission.

"Someone took it." Norah turned toward Colton. "Someone took the box, deleted the photo, and removed at least one of my phone contacts."

Colton awkwardly pushed the chairs out of the way to get to her. He wrapped his arms around her and held her tightly as she trembled.

"Listen to me. I've had some experience creating a stronghold no one can subvert. I can make sure your place is safe."

Norah planted her face against Colton's chest and sobbed. Colt held her until she was ready to talk about an escape route through the warehouse where no one would see what a mess she had become before the day even officially began.

INTROSPECT

Beth Ramos: "It's so obvious Boss and Colt have a thing for each other. I may research facts, but that doesn't mean I can't see what's right in front of my face."

Seth Burke: "Norah thinks she's so smart. She found the box, but don't think for one second I don't have other devices planted. Norah will never belong to anyone else. I will destroy anyone who gets in my way. Hell, I followed her from Iowa to California. This is just a little detour in getting what I want."

GRACE

Estranged Daughter
Ex-mistress
Mother of a daughter who drowned
Ex-Patient of the Greensboro Psychiatric Hospital

CHAPTER TWENTY-SIX

Grace clutched the handles of a small plastic bag filled with the few belongings she had with her when she was admitted to the Greensboro Psychiatric Hospital. She wore the same sweatshirt and blue jeans she had on when she arrived, but after a year of purging her pain and eating regular meals, she no longer swam inside of them; the fabric did not fold over on itself. The marred leather belt she had worn the day she frantically tried to steal another poor woman's daughter, mistaking her for her own, was not among her things. It had been removed, considered unsafe for someone so out of touch with reality. It did not matter; she no longer needed a belt. It was one less reminder of her destructive past.

For the first time in just over two years, Grace felt almost normal. She could marvel at the sun and the blue sky without carrying the guilt of still being alive when her daughter was not. Her days were not measured by the level of the emotional pain she felt or the number of times she wanted to join Finley in the next world. It no longer hurt to draw a breath. She could finally appreciate the smells she had once enjoyed with her daughter—buttery popcorn, cotton candy, puppies—and not feel a crushing sense of loss. Because of her time at Greensboro, she could watch other women with their daughters and not feel cheated or bitter. She had finally come to accept she was not defined as an abandoned child, or the daughter of a man who had chosen a new family over her. Neither was she just the mistress of a psychiatrist who loved her only until she became pregnant, breaching some pact he made with the universe to remain fatherless. She also was not defined as the mother of a child who drowned or, for that matter, a *mother* at all. She was Grace, simply Grace Wilson—a person worthy of giving and receiving love.

Jen, a colleague of Grace's, waited at the far end of the pale green hallway. A smile drifted across Jen's face when she saw Grace turn the corner. She cast a warmhearted wave in her direction, and Grace returned the greeting as she hurried toward her. Twenty-one days before, when she had been notified of her release date, she hadn't known who to call. It was a day for celebrating, but with whom? Her father had once again abandoned her, and Daniel clearly was not an option; he was the last person she wanted to see. Her ex was an enormous part of what was wrong with her life. Her hand trembled when she had dialed Jen's number and asked for the favor of sacrificing four hours of her time to come and get her.

But before Grace even finished with the request, Jen cut in. "Yes, of course. Thank you for asking me."

Grace knew there would be numerous relationships to mend and bridges to rebuild when she returned home. In her life journal, she made relationships her priority and circled it in red.

All those years she had spent with Daniel had done nothing but destroy her self-esteem. Instead of making her more independent, he had simply shifted her need to feel loved and accepted from her mother and father to himself. And the pain of her parents' rejection paralleled what she received from Daniel. He had not helped her as a therapist should have; he had controlled her—continued the cycle, dragged it out and ground it into the dirt until Grace's life was tatters of what it should have been. Through intensive counseling, Grace had learned to break the negative cycle, eliminate the people who manipulated her, and focus on the ones who were there for her, those who loved her simply as Grace. So far, the woman waiting at the end of the hallway was the only person on her friend list. In the coming weeks, months, and years, she hoped the list would become immeasurable.

When Grace got closer, Jen rushed toward her, past the line separating patient from visitor. The two women tightly embraced. "It's so good to see you, Grace," Jen said softly. "Thank you for calling me. I feel honored."

Grace chuckled. "That's probably the first time these people have ever heard those words." She pointed to the few staff who had gathered around to wish her goodbye.

Maybe it was because she was an English teacher at heart, but, as she stood near the door leading to the next chapter of her life, she felt like Dorothy from the *Wizard of Oz*. She shook hands and hugged staff members who had been part of her progress. The moment felt dreamlike, and Grace did everything she could not to utter the words that raced through her head. *And you were there, and you were there...* Instead, she just smiled and waved, locking the memory inside.

Jen grabbed the plastic bag from Grace's hand and hooked an arm through hers as they turned and walked out of the hospital. Under a double umbrella, on the way to the car, they chatted about nothing of significance. For that, Grace was grateful.

On the day Grace was admitted to Greensboro, Daniel's business card had been in her wallet. Because of that, her doctor had contacted him, assuming he was her psychiatrist. Daniel informed the doctor she was no longer a patient of his; she had moved on. Grace was positive he had left out the truth—that she had been his mistress, his friend, and the mother of his child; just as she was certain he had conveyed an abundance of false accusations about her.

Shortly after her arrival, a thin typed white envelope with no return address was delivered. The postmark was from *Hollister*, leading her to believe it was either from her father or Daniel. Whatever bull either of them was pushing, she didn't care. But, out of curiosity, she opened it anyway. They were Daniel's words. The envelope contained a small sheet of paper torn from the notebook he used to record his patients' innermost thoughts. His message was terse. His one request: that no one know he was Finley's father—*ever*. That word was underlined several times in dark blue ink, emphasizing the importance of his message. But it was too late. The people at Greensboro knew the truth. She could not get better by hiding her past. What they did with the information about Daniel was in their hands. That chapter of her life had been detonated before it fizzled out.

From the minute Grace shared the exciting news of their impending parenthood, she and Daniel had quarreled about Finley's paternity. There was no doubt Daniel was the father; Grace had never been with another man. But, even so, he did everything he could to try to destroy Grace's conviction in the news—drunken nights when he claimed to have seen her with other men, drugged states she couldn't remember, blackouts, etc. In her heart, she knew none of those had happened, but Daniel was so good at making her doubt everything that, in her head, she wasn't sure. All she had wanted was a father for Finley, but the space for the biological father's name had been left blank. Protecting his practice was far more important than claiming his daughter.

"I am so tired of rehashing this with you. If push comes to shove, no one will believe you anyway," he had told Grace. "I am a well-respected psychiatrist. You, on the other hand, have been in therapy since you were seventeen and at the ranch before that. Others would see you as nothing more than my patient." He warned her that if she ever told anyone their relationship had gone beyond professional, he would claim *transference*. She was just another of his patients who had transferred her feelings for her father to him.

Grace had been too weak to see how he had manipulated her. So, in the end, she just accepted it. Daniel did not care how it made her look not to list a father: cheap, a hussy, a slut.

When she told him as much, he had laughed. "You *are*, Grace. You're a weak little girl who was after only one thing, a father figure. You came on to me, remember?"

But she did not remember it that way at all. Daniel had forced her to do things she would never have done—things, in the beginning, she did not want to do, but he had insisted. At first, he claimed he only did them in the name of helping her push past her fear of stepping out of the comfortable box she had put herself in. Later, he told her it was in the name of love. She now knew Daniel was a liar.

At Greensboro, Grace never acknowledged his demand to remain quiet. After intensive therapy, she was relieved she had not listed him on her daughter's birth certificate. Now that she could see things more clearly, she realized Daniel was nothing more than a sperm donor—number one on a list so short, he was the only member. He had walked away with her virginity and her self-worth.

"I'm kind of afraid to go home," Grace admitted to Jen as she stared out the wet window, seeing nothing at all. Soft music played on Jen's car radio as she talked. "What if all the demons I worked so hard to leave behind are still there? What if they find me again?"

Jen laid her hand on top of Grace's as they traveled along the four-lane highway. "You know, Grace, you're not the same person you were a year ago. You're stronger now and you'll continue to get stronger every day. I'm here when you need someone to talk to."

Silence no longer scared Grace. It didn't drag her to the depths of darkness like it once had; it didn't pull her into her own head where she only saw things as negative. Instead of feeling the need to keep the conversation going, she counted her breaths and the few blessings she had. Jen was number one.

"Thanks." Grace's smile was thin. "I guess the first thing I'm going to have to do is find a job. And then, a house." She looked at Jen. "I don't mean to impose any more than I already have, but would it be possible to stay with you for a few weeks until I get back on my feet?"

"Grace, your house is waiting for you. Some kind soul stepped in to help you out while you were...well, away. And as for your job, school starts in a month or so," Jen reminded her. "If you need money, I can lend you what you need until then."

Grace sighed. "I highly doubt I have a job to return to."

Jen shook her head. "You still have a job. I talked to Bart last week. He said because you were tenured, you can return if, and when, you feel up to it."

"Really?" Grace sighed. "That's incredible. I know I'll have to prove myself to everyone again—especially Bart, but I'm more than ready. I want to be the teacher I know I can be, the one I should have been all along. And lord knows, with Finley gone," Grace exhaled loudly, "I'll have more than enough time to commit."

"Then that's what you'll do." Jen maneuvered the car around a rusty white boat-of-a-vehicle driven by a gray-haired man who could barely see over the steering wheel. "I always saw the potential in you. I think a lot of people did. If you can stay focused and committed, you'll be an amazing teacher."

Grace smiled at Jen. "Okay. That will give me something to work on."

The rain had cleared, and the sun was just beginning to peek through the clouds by the time Jen drove into Grace's driveway. Thin ribbons of fog floated in the damp afternoon, creating a heavenly view. "The house!" Grace cried. "It's, it's..." She looked at Jen and back at the house. "What happened?"

"Your neighbor. Not long after you left, your landlord was hauling your stuff to the corner of your yard to give it away, but Sam convinced him to sell him the house on the spot. While you were gone, he remodeled it." Jen grinned. "I think he kind of likes you, Grace." Jen winked at her.

Grace looked toward Sam's house. "I met him one time. All I know about him is that his name is Sam."

"Well, Sam's a pretty stand-up guy."

"How do you know all of this?" Grace asked, turning her attention to the new stone walkway and steps.

"A couple of months after you...left."

Grace laughed softly. "Call it what it is, Jen. Went crazy. Lost it. Came unhinged or unglued. I'm okay with it. I am so much better. I feel so much better."

"Okay," Jen said, laying her hand on top of Grace's. "So, while you were...gone." She turned toward Grace and smiled. "I can't do it." Both women laughed. "Anyway, I stopped in to check on your place about once a month. One of the first times I stopped, I ran into Sam. He told me what happened and what he was doing. He asked if I wanted to help."

"Did you?"

Jen nodded. "I did. I figured if he could do all of this for someone he barely knew, I could help someone I considered to be a friend."

Grace grabbed Jen's hand. "Thank you. I can't believe you guys did all of this for me."

"Don't lump me in with Sam. He paid for everything. I was just free labor."

"Wow!" Grace said. "I honestly can't believe it."

"Do you want me to come in with you?" Jen asked.

"No," Grace said softly. "I need to do this on my own. I need to face my demons head-on."

Jen nodded toward the house. "Okay,' she smiled, "but they may have moved out with all the pounding, sawing, and sanding." She shifted in her seat to face Grace. "If you need anything, anything at all, please call me. I'm going to start spending some time at school next week. That might be a good time for you to connect with Bart and the few other teachers who stop in. Besides, I'd really like to spend some time picking your brain about some of our themes."

"I'd like that too," she said, still staring at the house. Grace held her hand on the car door handle, but she didn't open it.

Jen's face clouded. "You're sure you don't want me to come in?"

Grace's chest rose as she drew a deep breath and slowly released it. "You've done enough. I'm okay. Really." Grace awkwardly hugged Jen over the center console. "Thank you, Jen. You'll never know how much I appreciated today."

"You're a good person. I just think you drew the short straw. Things *are* going to get better. You just have to believe they will."

"I will," Grace said. "I do," she said more confidently.

"Oh, wait," Jen said. "Sam changed the locks after he bought the place. Your new keys." Jen dropped them into Grace's hand.

Grace stared at them. An engraved metal keyring had been attached to the set. It read *Home is where your story begins. –Annie Danielson.* The keys were a metaphor for her life; from this day forward, she would be writing her own story. "Thanks, Jen."

"Welcome home, Grace. Call me, because if you don't, I'll be checking in with you more often than you want me to."

Grace nodded and climbed out of the car. "I will. I promise."

❧❧❧❧❧

Grace unlocked the door with one shiny gold key and slowly pushed it open. The last time she had walked out of the house, she had been on her way to reclaim her life. However, rather than coming together that day, it had fallen apart in the parking lot of the grocery store. That day still haunted her.

Stepping through the door, she fully expected to see the remnants of her old self; the one she had left behind a full year before. Instead, for the second time in just a few short hours, she felt like she had stumbled into a dream. The inside of the house gleamed in the afternoon sunshine; not an item was out of place. The previously scratched oak floors had been sanded and refinished. Sam had replaced the old birch kitchen cabinets with the broken doors and hinges with new gray, sleek ones. Granite countertops lined three walls of the kitchen, instead of the chipped and scarred Formica ones. New stainless-steel appliances stood where the mismatched ones had always been. Grace ran her hand down the front of the fridge handle; she pulled it open and gasped at the array of fresh food. "Who?" she said out loud, but she already knew. Her new landlord lived next door. It made sense to remodel, but why would he fill her fridge?

The rest of the house had been remodeled as well. New paint, blinds, and flooring brightened every room. The door to Finley's room was closed. A note had been taped on the yet to be refinished door. *Grace, I didn't know what you wanted to do with your daughter's room, so I left it as it is for now. When you are ready, I will redo this room also. Sam*

Grace put her hand on the lever but did not open it. Instead, she walked into her oversized bathroom, which, most likely, had once been a bedroom. Her mouth dropped open. The new bathroom was better than anything she had seen on HGTV. In place of the cracked fiberglass shower was a beautiful ceramic stone-tiled one, surrounded by glass on two sides. The chipped antique tub had been replaced with a soaker tub and wavy glass blocks replaced the old moldy window and frame. Two walls of open shelving were filed with wicker baskets and towels. Grace couldn't believe she lived here.

She pushed open the door to her bedroom. It had been redone similar to the rest of the house. Grace pulled off her boots and socks and wiggled her toes in the nap of the thick brown rug. New beige vertical blinds were closed, hiding the view to the backyard. A smile lit her face as she twisted the wand and the blinds separated. The cracked window had been replaced with a sliding door that led to a beautiful private patio, complete with a resin wicker couch and two chairs surrounding a low concrete gas fire table. A round glass-topped dining table and four chairs sat to one side near a built-in gas grill. Heavy white flowerpots displayed a brilliant array of summer flowers. She slid the blinds to the side, opened the door, and stepped onto the patio.

We're not in Kansas anymore, Grace thought as she dropped onto the couch. She had walked away from a broken life and returned to a magical one—complete with its very own wizard. But why? Why had Sam done this?

Grace glanced toward his house, but it was quiet. When she returned to the bedroom, she stopped. Her eyes grew wide. She clapped a hand over her mouth and gasped. On top of her dresser, tucked into a small alcove, sat the biggest bouquet she had ever seen. Grace knew flowers. In high school, she had worked for a florist. She was certain the arrangement had cost as much as one of her new appliances. The vase was filled with roses of every color, white lilies, red and lavender alstroemeria, and delicate sprigs of Queen Anne's Lace. Greenery of all shades filled out the bouquet: ruscus, Ligustrum, and variegated English ivy. She wrapped her arms around the huge bouquet and pressed her face into the sweet smells. Had she died and gone to heaven?

Grace returned to the kitchen and dug her phone out of her purse; she flipped it over and stared at it. For the first time, she wondered how her phone had worked for an entire year. Who had paid the bill? She pressed Sam's number, the one he entered the night Daniel had appeared from the shadows.

"Hello?" The voice was deep and soft at the same time.

"Sam?" Grace had never called him before. She wasn't even sure the number was the same.

"Yes. Who's this?"

"Grace Wilson, the, ah, your, ah, renter next door." She was uncertain what to call herself.

"Grace! How are you? Jen said you were coming home today. I wanted to make sure everything was perfect."

"Oh, Sam, it's more than perfect. It's beautiful. I can't believe all the work you did."

"Well, I can't believe the previous owner left you in that dump."

"It's amazing!" she said.

"Well, it's what I do. I buy and remodel houses. Sometimes I sell them; sometimes I rent them out."

Grace's stomach sank. "I assumed as much. But... Well, I'm sure you'll need to get more for this place than I was paying, so I'll start looking for a new rental tomorrow."

Sam laughed. "No, Grace. I didn't remodel your place for more rent. The house was falling apart. You deserve better."

"But, Sam..."

"No buts," he said. "Just enjoy the house."

Grace cleared her throat. "I, ah, have another question. Did you happen to pay my cell phone bill while I was in the...well, you know?"

"I did," Sam said. "I had a cousin in a similar situation once. I wanted to make sure you had access to the outside world."

"Thank you." Tears rolled down her cheeks. "I want to pay you back once I get back on my feet."

"I'll take payment in home-cooked meals," he said.

"Well, you're taking your chances there." She hiccupped as she cried and laughed at the same time.

"Anything's better than *my* cooking."

"I wouldn't say *anything*." She moved toward the bedroom. "The house is amazing, but the flowers are absolutely gorgeous!" She tucked the head of an iridescent white rose between her fingers and breathed in. "I've never seen a bouquet this big. It must have cost you a fortune."

Sam was quiet for a few seconds. "What flowers?"

INTROSPECT

Jen Heppel: "When I started teaching in Ponderosa Falls, Grace was the first person I met. She was so kind and helpful. Then things started to fall apart for her. I've always believed that's when people need friends the most, not when their lives are going according to plan."

Sam Hall: "The only time I met Grace, that guy was with her. I knew he was no good for her, but she insisted things were fine. From the time I was young, my mom told me that *good people lift others up in their time of need; selfish people do everything they can to hold them down.* Every night after school, she would ask me what I put out into the world—good or bad. The older I get, the more I think about her message. Grace needed a hand."

Anonymous: "Life is supposed to be interesting. If it can't be interesting, then it should be over."

CHAPTER TWENTY-SEVEN

During the year Grace spent in Greensboro, her dad married another woman who had teenagers. Tinder had provided him a platform to share his best traits: a big house, a good income, and the ability to put his new wife on a pedestal, even if she did not deserve it. Grace did not know if she was a gold digger or a perfectly wonderful woman with well-adjusted children. It didn't matter. Grace promised herself she would not go through another *mommy-dearest* situation.

The one time her father visited her at the hospital, nearly six months after she arrived, she begged him to just let her go, not make her suffer through what might very well turn into another ill-fated stepmother-stepdaughter relationship. It had been a dreary Tuesday morning in December when she watched him trudge through the slush and out of her life. Even though he had done so at her insistence, her father was just another person to leave. It was a long line that began with her mother. Her stepmother and siblings left her before they ever moved in. Daniel and Finley had left too. What was one more? She had to learn to be enough on her own.

If Sam had not sent the flowers, then it had to have been her father—a final goodbye. He had known when she was leaving the hospital; as her next of kin, they had notified him. Getting the huge bouquet into the house without being seen would have taken nothing short of a miracle for anyone else, but her father was a locksmith. He would have had the motive and the means to make one final attempt at trying to reconnect on the other side of their great divide. She was sure he was waiting for her call and with an apology, waiting for her to change her mind. He could wait until the end of time; it was not going to happen. For her own sanity, she had to cut people from her life who did not put her first. Unfortunately, the man she had once called *Daddy* was one of those people.

The psychiatrist at the hospital had connected her to a therapist in Ponderosa Falls: Dr. Laura Connelly. Grace looked forward to their Friday afternoon sessions. Dr. Connelly listened and asked questions; she did not tell Grace how to do things or that she was doing them wrong like Daniel had. Their time together was exhausting, but it also set the course for the weekend—the two days Grace spent the most time inside her head.

Workshop Week for the beginning of the school year had just ended, and for the first time in many years, Grace felt good about facing a new batch of learners. Her room was ready, her plans were on point, she had reconnected with her colleagues, and she had just had a great session with Dr. Connelly. But when she walked into the silence of her still spotless home, doubts began to peck at her. A dark cloud hung over her, and she could not shake the anxiety she felt.

Grace wanted nothing more than a glass of wine, but when she had arrived home from the hospital, she had opened every bottle and dumped them down the drain. She was not an alcoholic, but she couldn't be sure. There was a lot of uncertainty in her mind, enough to make her decide to stop drinking for good. Unsure whether to reach out to the sponsor she had connected with at Greensboro, she wandered the house, making the same loop several times before stopping in front of Finley's door. Her palm gingerly rested against the door, and she was deep in thought when her doorbell rang. She silenced the end of a scream with her fist pressed to her mouth.

"Grace? Oh my God! Are you okay?" Sam ran down the hall.

She was bent over, sporadically drawing in deep breaths. Sam stood behind her; one of his huge hands covered much of her back.

Her entire body suddenly began to shake.

"Grace?" Sam said again as he knelt next to her.

When she stood up, he saw it was laughter that had caused the shaking, laughter so deep, the sounds were trapped inside. Her eyes watered as she wrapped one arm across her stomach and held on to the wall with her other. The moment spread, and soon Sam's booming laugh filled the air as well. By the time their fits of laughter ended, they had both collapsed onto the floor in the hallway, struggling to catch their breath.

"Ahhhh," Sam let a deep sigh escape as he watched Grace. "You want to tell me what was so funny?"

Grace wiped her face on the sleeve of her shirt. "Oh my God! I needed that. "I haven't laughed like that in—I don't know how long. It felt so good."

"Good to know, but why were you laughing? And what was the scream about?"

"You!" Grace said. "You scared the bejeebers out of me when you rang the doorbell."

"Okaaay?" Sam asked, dragging the word out. "Most people don't laugh when they're scared."

Grace shook her head. "Before you rang the doorbell, I was in kind of a...well, a bad place. I was struggling with myself and the school year and two days of quiet."

"Got it."

She nodded her head toward Finley's door. "I was

actually thinking about going in there."

Sam slid across the hall and sat next to her. "Do you want me to go in with you?"

"No. I'm not ready. If I had been, I wouldn't have been contemplating it for so long when you rang the dang bell." She laughed again.

"Have you been in there since you got home?" Sam asked.

She slowly shook her head. "No. But I will. I just need to prepare myself." Suddenly, she turned toward Sam. "So, do you have dinner plans?"

"Are you kidding?" Sam told her. "I can build a magnificent kitchen, but remember, I can't use it. I am the king of TV dinners eaten on my lap in front of *Jeopardy*."

Grace smirked. "Oh, so you know a lot of random crap, then?"

"No." He laughed. "But I've mastered the phrase *I was just going to say that*." He grinned as he stood up and extended a hand toward Grace.

"Ah, you're one of those." She looked into his eyes.

A shiver ran down Grace's back as Sam bent down, took her chin in his hand, and lightly brushed his lips against hers. Suddenly, he pulled back.

"I'm so sorry, Grace. I didn't mean to…"

"You don't see me complaining." Grace shrugged. "But just so you know, if this is going to lead to a date or something, you're going to have to feed me first."

Without a moment's hesitation, Sam took her hand and led her to his truck.

~~~

Thunder rumbled in the distance as the rain beat against the windows. This was not the day the weatherman had predicted. His twenty percent chance of thunderstorms had somehow blossomed into the real deal.

"Hey, looks like our picnic is off for today," she said into her cell.

"Yeah, I was going to call you about that anyway. I got a call from a buddy about a used fixture sale. I try to buy everything used or cheap when I refurbish houses."

"Really?" Grace said slowly. "So, you're telling me you remodeled my house with used goods?" She snickered.

"You'd think that, right? But ah, no. You got new. I mean, come on, the remodeler lives next door? How would it look if I put in cheap crap? You got the good stuff."

"Good to know it won't fall apart anytime soon."

"Alright, now that we've cleared that up, I thought you might want to go with me."

Grace chuckled. "Well, as fun as that sounds, how about instead I have dinner ready when you get back?"

"Yeah, about that, the sale's not until tomorrow, but it's down in Durango, so I was going to head down there today."

"An overnight date, then? Mr. Hall, you're taking our relationship rather fast, aren't you?" She grinned.

"Date? Yes. Overnight? Yes, but you can have your own room."

Grace laughed. "I am not a prude, Sam. But I still think I'm going to pass. School starts on Monday, and I still have some things to prep for the week."

"Well, have it your way, then." From his voice, she could tell he was smiling. "Are you sure you're going to be okay this weekend?"

"Sam, I'm going to be fine. We've gotten to be friends in the past several weeks, but you don't have to worry about me. I'm in a much better place than I've been in a long, long time."

"Okay, I should get going. It's a good six-hour trip, and it's going to take me longer with this storm."

"Be safe, Sam. Call me later, will you?"

"Yes, Mother." He laughed.

INTROSPECT

Sam Hall: "I waited almost five whole weeks before I

kissed Grace. I have to confess; for much of that time, while we sat in her backyard talking, I didn't hear a lot of what she said. I couldn't take my eyes off her. She's beautiful. And, according to my mom, I'm to be a gentleman at all times—which basically equates to: treat a woman with respect and make sure your intentions are pure. Mom has been gone for nearly seven years, but I can still hear her voice in my head."

CHAPTER TWENTY-EIGHT

The storm brewed on and off all day long and well into the evening. Thunder and lightning blew through and, just when Grace believed it had finished, it returned with a vengeance. For much of the day, she worked on schoolwork, getting a jump start on the second week when her classes would begin a unit on *control*. If anyone knew about control, she did.

Around 7:00 p.m., she threw together a turkey sandwich and called Sam. His phone rang several times, but he didn't pick up. She flipped on the television to pass the time but quickly turned it off when the ring of her cellphone cut into the show she had settled on.

"Hey, Grace. I saw you called," Sam told her. "I'm still on the road. I've been in and out of shops all day long."

"No worries. I just thought I'd check in. Is it raining wherever you are?" she asked.

"It just started again. It's coming down pretty hard."

"Well, then, I'm going to go so you can drive safely. I'll talk to you Monday night."

"You don't have to go," Sam said. "You could keep me

company."

"Nope, not if you're driving in heavy rain. Night, Sam."

"Night, Gracie," he said.

Grace smiled as she stuck her plate in the dishwasher. *Could Sam be the one?*

The gray day shifted into a dark, starless night. Grace decided to turn in early and read. She shut off the lights in the living room and ran her hand along the wall as she made her way through the dark hallway toward her bedroom. A shiver ran down her spine when she touched Finley's door. She froze, staring toward it, catching glimpses of the wood grain each time lightning flashed and sent slivers of light down the hallway.

Slowly, she pressed the lever and pushed the door open. Her heart pounded against her ribcage like a xylophone mallet as she stepped inside. The curtains were open, as they had been since the day her daughter had drowned. Lightning lit the room, illuminating the yellow striped wallpaper. Grace felt a time warp press in, pulling her back to that last day. Suddenly, the dark felt heavy. She had always had an aversion to the night, a fear of the unseen. She wanted to turn on the lights, but the longer she stood in the center of the room, the more the need faded away. Seeing the room muted made it all feel less real.

A sharp flash of lightning instantly followed by a thunderous boom made her scream. She flipped on the light. Her eyes darted around the room, quickly at first and then more slowly as she let the memories wash over her—her daughter's laughter, her beautiful smile, the way she chattered on about nothing at all. Another brilliant bolt of lightning flashed, illuminating the backyard nearly to daylight. Someone stood in the center of the backyard. Quickly, she flipped off the light and moved to the window. Another sharp flash captured whoever it was jumping over the fence. By the third, the person in the hooded sweatshirt was gone. Was he real or had she only imagined him?

Grace pulled the curtains closed and stood very still. She lifted the edge of one of the yellow panels just enough to peer into the backyard, but she saw no one. According to the digital clock on Finley's nightstand, several minutes had passed before she moved. Grace took a deep breath. She knew she was being ridiculous. There was no one in her yard; there had been no one in her yard. Her brain was waterlogged from the storms. *Face your fears, Grace.*

She turned on the lamp that hung next to Finley's bed. A soft light washed across the middle of the room, leaving the edges deep in the shadows. The bed was still unmade from one of her early meltdowns. But the rest of the room was exactly as it had been the day her daughter died.

Grace flipped off the light and headed toward the door. Another bolt of lightning snuck in around the edges of the curtains and cast shadows across the room. One of the bifold closet doors was slightly ajar. From the time Grace was small, she had a fear of open closet doors. She knew for a fact she would never have left it open, no matter how much of a hurry she may have been in. She flipped the ceiling light on and stood before the door, fighting the irrational fear from her childhood, the one that still haunted her. No one was in there, not the person from the yard, not anyone else. *Grace, get a grip. Push the door shut or open it. You're an adult. Grow up.*

She reached forward and pushed the door closed, but she didn't move. Something inside her told her to get out, but she could not. Two forces fought; the second told her to open the door. Cautiously, she pulled the door open. "See," she said. "Nothing." The breath she had been holding rushed out. Grace drew another breath and held it, just to remind herself she was fine. But as she started to push the door closed, a flash of red caught her eye. The red sundress she had worn the day Finley drowned hung at one end of the closet. *Why would I have put my dress in Finley's closet? Did I do it? Did I hide it from myself?* She didn't remember doing it. *Did Sam do it when he was cleaning? How could he have known that was the dress she was wearing when her daughter drowned?*

Grace lifted the hanger from the clothes rod. Goosebumps ran through every inch of her body as she stared into the closet where the dress had been. Her vision grew foggy as she reached for a second hanger. On it hung the red dress Finley had been wearing the day she died. *How?* Grace collapsed to the floor, hugging the dress and sobbing nearly as hard as the day she lost her daughter.

INTROSPECT

Sam Hall: "I know, Mom. Your voice is coming through loud and clear. I know gentlemen take things slowly. That's why I didn't push Grace to come with me. Knowing what I know now, I wish I had."

Anonymous: "Eminem once said, *'The truth is you don't know what's going to happen tomorrow. Life is a crazy ride; nothing is guaranteed.'* He's right. This woman knows what happened to her in the past, but she has no idea what still lies ahead."

Mary Perrine

THE VOICES WITHIN
(a choral poem)

NORAH	GRACE	COLTON

NORAH

I am broken.
I tell others
I am fine.

Under my roof
is the only time
I feel safe. It's where
I can remember.

It hurts too much.

I hide
behind a façade
of lies.
I tell others I am fine,
but I'm not.
Smiling, laughing, loving.

I lie
about my past.

All the pain I've suffered,
has to remain hidden.

Bit by bit,
I try to move forward.

Everywhere I look,
I see my daughter,
Lili

GRACE

I am broken.
I am fine
is just a group of words.
I have lost
my daughter.

I can remember
feeling her in my arms.
But, losing her to death,
it hurts too much.

I hide
behind a façade.

I tell others I am fine,
but I'm not.
Smiling, laughing, loving,
I can't do it.

I lie
about my past.
I am not okay.
Can anyone hear me?
Do any of you see me?

I am falling apart,
bit by bit.

Everywhere I look,
I see my daughter,
Finley

COLTON

I am broken.

My daughter
was nearly kidnapped fro
under my roof.

It hurts too much
to remember that
I almost lost her, again.

I tell others I am fine,
but I'm not.

I can't do it
anymore.
I lie
about my past.

Do any of you see me
and
all the pain I've suffered

Bit by bit,
I try to move forward,
but there are reminders
everywhere I look.

Addy

NORAH	COLTON	GRACE
Moving Forward	Moving Forward	Moving Forward
Falling for Colton	Falling for Norah	Falling for Sam
Newspaper owner	Custom Cabinetry Owner	Teacher
Syndicated Columnist	Father	

CHAPTER TWENTY-NINE

Colton unloaded the brown canvas bag, setting items on Norah's coffee table. After much discussion, they had agreed Norah would stay away while Colt searched for listening devices. Like always, he had done his research. He disconnected Norah's router and all WIFI devices before turning on the bug detector. Slowly, he went from room to room, carefully listening for a beeping sound. He found one in the smoke detector in her bedroom and a second near the television in her living room.

Next, he set about checking every cord in her apartment, ensuring it was connected to the correct appliance and did not lead to a recording device. He found nothing.

Norah had gone to a hotel and his neighbor had agreed to keep Addy for the night. As darkness rolled in, Colt turned off all the lights and waited for the wall of blinds to close. He stood in the darkness with only a narrow beam flashlight. Slowly, he began aiming it toward the vents, the ceiling, and into light fixtures. He traveled in narrow zig-zag sections as he scanned for reflective lenses. Methodically, he moved from one room to the next in search of concealed video devices. He found nothing—until the last room. There, stuck in the bathroom fan, wired into the electricity, was a camera so tiny, he almost missed it.

Colt's cheeks grew red as he realized this device had been purposely placed to watch Norah shower. Listening to her conversations was one thing, but this was another. Seth was a disgusting pig.

"You see me, you sonofabitch? Do you see me?" he yelled into the lens of the camera before he yanked it down. "You'd better hope you never find yourself within a hundred feet of me. Cuz I'll kill you myself."

As dawn eased in, Colton continued his work in Norah's condo. He replaced the locks on the door, installed a couple of extras, and mounted hidden security cameras near the inside of her front door. If her ex-husband set one foot into her apartment, both he and Norah would receive a notification on their phones. Should he tell Norah he would also receive the alerts? If he didn't, did that make him as bad as her ex? Not even close, he decided.

Around 6:00 a.m., he stretched out on the leather couch and called Norah.

"Hi," Norah said. The pitch of her voice was slightly higher than usual. Colt could hear her distress. "I was awake all night. How did things go? Did you find anything at all?"

All night long, Colton had contemplated what to tell her—the truth or a lie. For her sanity, he wanted her to believe nothing had been found, but he had to be honest. He just didn't need to tell her everything; the video feed in her bathroom would destroy her. "I found two listening devices." He heard Norah's soft sigh followed by a deep breath.

"I can't believe it. He heard everything I said, every noise I made," she cried. "Please tell me you didn't find cameras. Please," she begged softly.

Guilt churned the several cups of coffee Colt drank to stay awake. He could not tell her the truth, or she would never feel safe in her condo again. "No video," he lied. "I replaced the locks and set up some cameras that I'll connect to your phone." A chill suddenly raced down his spine as he jumped off the couch. "Norah, I'm leaving here right now." Colt tried to conceal his panic, but his voice shook.

"Colt? What's going on? You're scaring me."

"I'll be there soon. Just wait for me."

He grabbed his loaded tool bag and locked the three new locks. The fourth could only be secured from the inside.

The sun had barely appeared above the horizon when Colton got to the hotel; an arc of orange spread above the tree line, painting the sky with golden streaks that seeped into the deep purple above. Colt hurried through the double doors of the hotel and toward the elevator. He didn't need the room number; he had been with Norah when she checked in. *407.*

As the steel doors separated on the fourth floor, Colt caught sight of someone in a gray hooded sweatshirt, jeans, and tennis shoes halfway down the hall. The person turned slightly toward him before shoving something into his pocket. Colt could not see the face hidden inside the hood of the sweatshirt, but based on size and shape, he was sure it was a man.

"Hey," Colt called. "Who are you?" The man raced down the hall in the opposite direction and hit the push bar on the heavy metal door at full speed. He saw the man stumble down the first couple of steps before the door closed. Colton followed, but, by the time he got the door open, there was no one to see. Footsteps echoed in the staircase as the man descended. Colt could tell he was skipping stairs; he heard the slapping of the person's tennis shoes hit the landing with a thud as he jumped the last few steps each time. He bent over the railing, trying to peer down the narrow shaft, hoping to catch another glimpse of the runner, but he saw nothing.

Maybe it was just a coincidence; perhaps the person had nothing to do with Norah. But Colt's gut told him he was wrong.

Colton let the door slam shut as he returned to Norah's room. "It's me," he said as he softly knocked on her door with his knuckle. He heard her push the swing bar to the side before unlocking the deadbolt and pulling the door open.

"You have me petrified." Norah bit her lip as she pulled Colton inside and turned the deadbolt behind him.

Colt pointed to the phone in her hand; he held his hand out, palm up. Norah handed it to him but said nothing. He pressed a finger to his lips before shoving the phone between the mattress and the box spring. Laying a hand on Norah's back, he guided her into the bathroom. He flipped on the fan and turned on the shower.

"What's going on?" Norah's eyebrows knit tightly together as she waited for an answer.

"Your phone's bugged." Norah's face went white. "Remember when you said someone removed Tracy as a contact?"

She nodded.

"I am pretty sure your phone was hacked or somehow Seth got himself added to your account."

"Crap," Norah whispered. "So, besides hearing what I said when I was at home, he's heard every phone call I've ever made?"

"That'd be my guess."

"What do I do?" A single tear trickled down her cheek and fell into the line of her lips before seeping into her mouth. Colt pulled her into a hug and held her. "Why did you shove my phone under the mattress? Why didn't you just shut it off?"

Colt stepped back. "Did anyone knock on the door before I got here?"

Norah shook her head. "No, but I swear I heard the door handle jiggle."

"There was someone in the hallway when I got off the elevator. I'm not sure who it was but, if it was your ex, he knows you're here and knows I got rid of the listening devices in your apartment. Shutting off the phone as soon as

I arrived may have pushed him over the edge."

Norah's face turned white. "What-what do we do now?"

Colt felt an intense need to protect Norah surge through him. He leaned his head close to her face and whispered, "New cells—one for work and a second for personal use. I'm the only person who will have the second number. You can only use it to call me or the police. Got it?" Steam billowed from the top of the glass-enclosed shower. He jerked the door open and turned the temperature to cold. "We'll also make sure your carrier lets no one else join your plan, ever."

Norah nodded.

"I'm sure Seth got on it because you were married. Is it the same phone you had back in California?"

"Yes, but I had him removed long ago."

"Well, Seth's a cop. Somehow, he finagled his way back on. I would guess he's had access to all of your text messages too. He's likely using a parental control app to monitor everything."

"Oh my God. I can't believe he'd sink this low."

Colt shrugged. "I think you underestimated him, Norah." He took a deep breath. "When we leave here, I want you to turn your phone off."

Norah looked confused. "But?"

"He would have been more suspicious had you done it as soon as I arrived. We've given him a little time. We'll go get new phones." Colt put his hand on the door handle but didn't push the lever. "But before that, we're going to the police station."

"No!" Norah yelped.

Colt pulled his hand away from the door. "What? Why?"

"I can't trust the police." She twisted her hands before folding her arms across her chest. "I just don't know who I can trust. The cops back home had a good old boys' network; they protected each other no matter what. I can't chance it."

She rocked between her heels and her toes. "For all I know, he has the police here on his side as well."

"I can't believe..." Colt stopped when he saw fear cloud her eyes. He wrapped his arms around her. "Okay," he nodded. "For now, we'll wait. But at some point, we may not have a choice."

Norah tilted her head back and tenderly kissed his cheek before laying her head against his chest. "Thank you," she said.

INTROSPECT

Hotel Manager Rick Hawley: "On the morning of August 24 around 6:35 a.m., I had just entered the back stairway from the lobby when some guy in a hooded sweatshirt and jeans came barreling down the stairs and almost knocked me over. I yelled, but he blew through the doors without a word. I was curious about the man, so I checked the security camera. About ten minutes before, he had entered the hotel through the parking ramp with another guest. From the lobby camera, I could see they got into the elevator together. The next camera showed him exiting the elevator on the fourth floor; the other man got off on another floor. He stopped outside the elevator, read the room signs, turned right, and headed down the hallway toward Rooms 400-410. The video showed he stopped in front of room 407. He removed a small item from his pocket and inserted it into the keyhole and proceeded to move it around. I'm guessing it was a pick of some kind. We've never gone to card readers because we've tried to stay true to the design of the original hotel. So, yes, we still use metal keys. Anyway, when that didn't work, he tried another. The only registered guest for that room was a female. The video showed he ran when he saw someone step off the elevator. That man chased him down the hallway and through the door at the far end. However, within seconds, the new person returned to 407, knocked on the door, and it opened."

CHAPTER THIRTY

After Colt discovered the devices, Norah felt vulnerable and insecure. Whether at work or home, she looked over her shoulder constantly, trying to read the minds of anyone who came within fifty feet of her. She catastrophized every situation she was in. Life no longer felt safe.

Clearly, Seth was a bigger threat than she had imagined. Before she left Mason Hills, he had warned her he would never give up. It had not been a warning; it was a promise. So far, he had kept his word. Going to the police was not an option; Seth was one of them. Shortly after their divorce, she had tried to file a report, but it backfired. After that, instead of being afraid of just Seth, she lived in fear of every officer: the ones who tailed her, those who laughed when they pulled her over for no obvious reason, and the officers who taunted her with visits to her office at the *Chronicle*. The MHPD was tight—a *one-for-all, all-for-one* mentality. On the day Norah watched the Mason Hills sign fade away in her rearview mirror, she thought she was free, but that had been another part of Seth's surreptitious plan. He wanted her to believe she was free, but he was everywhere, including in her condo. She knew it. But proving it was something entirely different.

In the nearly three months since Colt had removed the bugs, he and his daughter Addy had become a constant in Norah's life. It had started out slowly, but, as time passed, it blossomed into more than friendship. If the father and daughter duo were not at her condo, the three of them were at Colton's. Every day, Norah felt more and more enamored with the prospect of her new little family. Falling in love again had never been part of her life's plan. Relationships took too much emotional bandwidth; they were too risky. After losing her own daughter, she was unsure it was safe to grow so comfortable with Addy. Losing another child would break her. But Colt had assured her the two of them were going nowhere.

Norah had hidden her past from Colt for far too long. He knew only a thread of her previous life, only what Google and social media wanted him to see. Being a journalist, she had controlled a great deal of what was out there. If they were moving into a relationship, she had to be honest. She had to tell him everything, but opening up wasn't easy. One evening, after downing a large glass of wine while Colton put Addy to bed, she closed the Jenga spaces of Norah Van Pelt Burke.

"Lili was my everything, and when she got sick, Seth left us. I watched her die alone. I saw it every day: her life leaving her, her fighting spirit breaking into a million tiny pieces. The joy she was filled with just disappeared. She never smiled. She never laughed. She no longer cried out in pain." Norah drew a deep breath. "It was there, though. I saw it—the pain she covered up. Lili gave up long before I ever did." Colt slid next to her and held her tightly. Norah leaned her head on his shoulder and wept.

"A few days before she died, Lili told me the birdies had visited her. 'Just like all the birds who visited Snow White,' I told her. 'What a sweet dream.' Her tiny smile, the first one I had seen in months, drifted away, and she told me it wasn't a dream. She insisted the beautiful birds told her they would come for her soon, and she could fly away with them. She said they told her she could leave her tired body behind because she would get a new one." Norah sniffed as she swiped at the tears with the fingertips of both hands and slid away from Colton. "Lili took her last breath three days later."

"On the morning she died, Seth asked to come back home. He wanted to move on as if Lili had never existed. He thought I should forgive him since everything was over, and we didn't have a mountain of trouble in front of us." Norah's jaw tightened as she looked into Colt's eyes. "He actually referred to Lili's life as a *mountain of trouble*." A ragged breath ripped through her. "After everything that happened, why would I ever let him back into my life?" Norah looked at her hands, rubbing her thumb along the back of her finger where her wedding ring had narrowed it. "Now I wonder what I ever saw in him, how I ever loved him."

"I am so sorry, Norah. The guy sounds like a scumbag. It's guys like him who give men a bad name." He lightly kissed her forehead. "He's clearly not playing with a full deck."

Norah laughed loudly. "He isn't playing with *half* a deck." She pulled a small blanket up and over her shoulders and turned sideways. "Okay," she said as she stared at him. "I shared. Now tell me your story."

"Really?" He seemed surprised.

"Yeah, I want to know how you and Addy became a duo; what happened to her mother? Unless you aren't ready to share." She gently touched his arm.

Colt bit his bottom lip. Norah could tell he was carefully considering her request.

"Well," he paused, "the truth is I was madly in love with a woman who didn't love me back. She cheated on me and then committed suicide because she couldn't live with it." He gently shook his head as he recalled the exact moment he had learned Addy wasn't his daughter. "On the night of Addy's accident, our first night in Podany, I found out I wasn't her biological father."

Norah's mouth dropped. "Oh my gosh, Colt. That's terrible. But I'm sure your wife loved you at one time."

"Well, I'd like to think so." He stared off into the distance, through the wall, into his past. "It sounds like neither of us made a good life partner choice." His words were whisper-quiet.

"Well," Norah wagged a finger between the two of them, "what does that say about our relationship, then?"

Colt gave her that sideways grin. "Fifty-fifty chance," he said. "I mean, you flip a coin enough times, and eventually, you're going to get it right."

Norah shook her head and laughed.

Long into the evening, Norah and Colt talked about Brit and Addy. It was nearly 1:00 a.m. when Colt finally surrendered the story of his mother abandoning him at the amusement park.

"Her name was Sunny?" Norah asked. "Was that her real name?"

Colt shrugged. "I doubt it. How many people named Sunny do you know? There was nothing really...*normal* about her at all. She was always dancing and playing this small tambourine she had." Colt's eyes darkened. "I don't even know if her hair was actually blond or if Stone is even my real last name."

"Where was the last place you remember living with her?" The reporter in Norah was digging.

"Somewhere in Colorado. A town with the word Crystal in it. I only remember that because my mom loved crystals. Sometimes I would wake up and she would have them lying all around her, in a huge circle." Colton grew quiet. "The only time I asked about them, she took my face in her hands and, in that airy voice of hers, she told me, 'Colt, baby, don't you worry about that. Mama's gonna take care of everything.' Then she jumped off the bed, scooped up the crystals, and danced around the room in her skirt of ribbons and lace that flared out like a rainbow when she moved."

Norah reached over and took Colt's hand. "It sounds like she was a free spirit."

Colt snorted. "Yeah, a free spirit who smoked a lot of weed and popped a lot of pills. I didn't know that as a kid, but I do now."

"Did you ever look her up?" Norah asked.

He clenched his jaw. "No. I don't know if I could have taken the rejection again."

Norah held his hand and rubbed it. "When you look back, was there any indication she was going to leave you on the day she did?" Norah could hear the clock ticking as she watched Colt's face relive his last day with his mom. His eyes gave away the exact moment he could not find her.

Slowly, he shook his head. "Nothing. She just told me to be brave. Then, when the merry-go-round circled again, she was gone."

"I'm so sorry, Colt." Norah wrapped her arms around him. "Some people just don't understand how precious children are."

Colt pushed her away and quickly stood up. "I don't believe that for one second. She loved me. She treated me like I was her everything. I just don't understand why she left."

Norah shook her head. "I'm sure you were important to her. I didn't mean she didn't love you." She stood up and faced him. "But maybe your mom *had* to leave. Maybe she didn't have a choice."

Colt walked toward the hallway. He picked up a Barbie doll from the floor and whipped it across the room. It ricocheted off the floor and into an overstuffed chair. "She *had* a choice," he seethed. "We all have choices," he said. "Hers was between me and her drugs." Addy's Barbie car flew into the wall on the other side of the room after meeting Colt's foot.

Norah flinched.

"I lost," he announced loudly. He stared at the indent in the sheetrock. "I was five," he whispered as he left the room. "Five."

Norah jumped when she heard his bedroom door slam. He needed time. Maybe she had pushed him too hard.

She tossed a throw pillow onto one end of the couch and clicked off the lamp. She threw the thin throw blanket over herself, tucking it under her feet before lying down. The gas fireplace and her cellphone were the only lights in the house. Her thumbs moved with lightning speed as she texted Beth. If anyone could find Colton's mom, it was her.

❦

Beth and Luke were sitting side by side in Beth's office when Norah arrived. They each had a laptop open in front of them. Norah handed a white paper bag with an expanding grease spot to Luke before setting a cardboard tray of steaming paper coffee cups on the corner of Beth's desk.

"What are you two up to?" Norah asked.

"What were you doing texting me at two o'clock this morning?" Beth asked without looking up from her screen.

Luke took a sip of his coffee. "It's amazing the things you can accomplish when you come to work before daybreak."

"What?" Norah asked. "What are you talking about?"

"Well, after you texted Beth, she got it in her head that I needed to help her find information on Colt's mom—immediately. So, I've been sitting here since 3:07." He lifted his coffee cup toward Norah and winked. "Thanks for this. I needed it."

"Beth, I didn't mean you had to look into Colt's mom immediately. I figured you'd work on it when you had spare time." Beth continued to study her screen and stab at keys, seemingly unaware Norah was speaking to her.

Luke grunted. "Well, obviously, you don't know Beth very well. She never sleeps. When we were married, she would try to engage me in these deep conversations in the middle of the night. All I wanted to do was sleep." He looked at Norah before tilting his head toward Beth. "She always won."

Without looking up, Beth punched him in the shoulder. "You two either need to help or go away."

"What have you found?" Norah stepped behind Luke.

Beth finally stopped typing; she grabbed a roll from the bag and spun her chair toward Norah. "Colton's mom's real name was Sunlyn Stone. She passed away just months after she abandoned him." Norah watched a dollop of red goo fall from Beth's jelly donut and splat onto the hardwood floor, narrowly missing her jeans. Beth scooped it up with a napkin. "Other than her obituary, there isn't a lot of information about her."

"Does it mention how she died?" Norah asked.

Beth shrugged half-heartedly. "Not really. It just said she died at home."

"Overdose?" Luke asked.

Norah tipped her head sideways and nodded. "That wouldn't surprise me based on how Colt described her." She turned back to Beth. "Does the obituary say anything about family?"

"Mmm-hm." She nodded as she wrangled with an extraordinarily large bite of roll. She pointed toward her mouth and then to Luke.

Luke clicked on the second of a dozen tabs he had open. "It says her parents lived in a town called Ponderosa Falls, Colorado."

"Wait! Ponderosa Falls? I have an aunt who lives there. That's so weird. She used to live in Boulder, but she and my Uncle Denny wanted something a little less... How'd they put it?" Norah closed one eye and looked toward the ceiling in thought. "Oh, yeah, like a madhouse."

"Have you been there?" Luke asked.

Norah took another sip of her coffee. "Boulder, yes. Ponderosa Falls, no. I always planned to go, but with everything... Well, you know. How big's the town?"

Luke flipped the page of a yellow legal pad he had been writing on.

"It's about 8,000," Beth said. "Give or take." She swiped at her mouth with the same paper napkin she used on the floor.

Luke raised his eyebrows and looked at Norah. "She forgets nothing."

Beth ignored his comment and again focused on her computer screen. From time to time, she tapped out a few words. "According to the obituary, her parents' names were Ziggy and Harmony Stone." She shrugged.

"You're kidding, right?" Norah asked. "Those were their real names?"

Beth nodded. "As far as I can tell. I'm still working on that. But, somehow, it appears responsible Colton Stone came from a long line of hippies."

Luke laughed. "You're sure their last name wasn't *Stoned*?"

Norah smirked at him. "Are they still alive?" she asked Beth. "You keep talking in past tense."

"Harmony is. Turns out, she's the owner of a store called the Happenin' Hippie in Ponderosa Falls." She laughed. "The woman looks like an eighty-two-year-old *stoner*." She chuckled as she high-fived Luke. "That's how you pull off a joke, Luke."

"I concede to the master." He bowed toward her.

"Boss, come check out her website."

Norah moved behind Beth as she clicked on an open tab. A woman popped onto the screen. A headband decorated with brightly colored peace signs was tied tightly around her kinky long gray hair. She wore round, orange-lensed glasses and a matching neon t-shirt with the word *Peace* embroidered across the front. Her fingers flashed a peace sign. Norah reached over Beth's shoulder and enlarged the picture. The woman's eyes were at half-mast. She turned her head from side to side and studied the photo. No matter what angle she looked from, she could not see

Colt.

"She doesn't look at all like Colt, does she?" Beth asked. "Of course, she would have been his grandmother, so they may not look a lot alike."

Norah nodded. It was nearly impossible to pull her eyes from the woman on the screen. "What about Zig...?" She shook her head. "It just seems so odd to call a grown man Ziggy."

"He died just over two years ago after a short battle with cancer. That's according to the obituary. There's no mention of any other kids. As a matter of fact, there was nothing about any relatives, period."

"Other than the store, did you find a home address?"

Beth shoved a sheet of paper over her shoulder toward Norah. "I knew you'd ask. That's the store address. From what I can tell, that's where she lives."

Norah stared at the paper. "Anything else?"

"Not really. I checked the newspaper archives, but it's a small town. There really wasn't much in it."

"Wait," Luke said. "Why wasn't Colt listed as a survivor?"

Beth frowned. "She left him, Luke. Maybe her parents didn't even know she had a kid." She bit her lip. "If I'd deserted my kid, I'm not sure I would have wanted anyone to know."

Luke nodded. "Fair point."

"Thank you, both." Norah draped her arms across their shoulders and pulled them into a hug. Not sure what I'd do without you two."

"Well, I'd like to bank this *helping you out at 3:00 a.m.* for the next time I screw up," Luke told her.

Norah laughed. "I'll remember that."

"You won't have to," Beth said. "He'll remind you."

Norah stared at Harmony's address as she walked into her office. What she planned to do with the information was still up in the air. It was more than she had just a few hours ago, more than she had expected at all. She folded the piece of paper and tucked it into her wallet.

A stack of mail sat in the middle of Norah's desk where Maxine had placed it the night before. Norah sorted through the pile, tossing junk into the recycle bin beneath her desk. A hand-written envelope grabbed her attention—most likely a news tip. Often, when someone wanted to report a story anonymously, they sent it by mail or shoved it under the door in the middle of the night. The letter opener cut through the top of the long envelope. Norah fished out a small sheet of paper. In exquisite, flowing handwriting were five words: *She is not your daughter.* She studied the missive. *Seth?* Of course, it was from him; he had obviously gotten someone else to write it for him. She had grown close to Colt and Addy. He would never stand for that; he would take great pride in reminding her their daughter had died. Crumpling the paper and the envelope into a ball, she tossed it into the trash as her stomach lurched.

INTROSPECT

Luke Simon: "I complain about Beth all the time, but she has no idea that I have never fallen *out* of love with her."

Beth Ramos: "Norah has become a good friend. So has Colt. Luke and I hang out with them from time to time. We have so much fun together. I could picture them getting married."

Maxine Lonsdale: "I saw the handwritten note in the stack of mail. It was awfully thin to be a letter. I'm the world's biggest snoop. Everyone knows that. So, when I saw the word *personal* written across the bottom of the envelope, I took it into the bathroom and held it up to the light. I saw what it said. *Why would someone write that?* you might be asking yourself. But I know."

CHAPTER THIRTY-ONE

Colt adjusted his headphones and started the orbital sander. He ran his hand over the pale maple. The wood was smooth, but it still needed to be fine-sanded.

It was well before dawn when he snuck out of Norah's condo, leaving a note propped against his pillow. *Meet me for lunch at Cullen's after church.* Nearly every weekend, they had gone rounds over attending church. She might have forgiven God, but Colt was bound and determined not to let Him off the hook. Leaving before Norah woke meant he could avoid the conversation for another week.

He had checked on his daughter before he left; she was asleep in Norah's guest room—*his daughter*—the one he had loved since long before she was born. DNA did not matter; it didn't determine a real family. Addy was the love of his life. She and Norah were the only good things God had done for him lately and, after everything he'd been through, that wasn't nearly enough. He had once thought Brit was the best thing to happen to him, but that relationship had ended in a suicide and a lie. Colt could depend on nothing in his life being permanent. Everyone left eventually. Joy always ended, and that scared him. If he honestly believed that, why did he want Norah in his life?

A dust cloud swirled upward toward the filtration system. Addy's Christmas gift, a maple desk designed to grow with her, was beginning to take shape. Colt grinned as he recalled Addy's fifth birthday and her insistence she was starting school *that day*. It must have felt like an eternity between then and her first day of kindergarten. Now that she was finally there, she loved it. It didn't matter if he or Norah dropped her off, she always jumped out of the car and ran through the front doors—often forgetting her backpack, lunch, or some other item one of them would have to haul into her classroom.

The night of the intruder had slowly faded into a distant memory; he believed it was simply a happenstance that would never occur again. With all the security measures Colt had put into place, he felt safe, and, best of all, he believed his daughter was safe. Addy's safety was the one thing he no longer worried about.

Even though Colton spent much of his life waiting for the other shoe to drop, there were moments, sometimes weeks, when he honestly believed everything was going to be okay; he and Addy and Norah were going to be a real family—one that would go the distance. In one of those stretches, when he plainly saw a future, he had purchased a ring for Norah. He had planned to ask her to marry him, but something always happened whenever he came close, sending him spiraling into a well of doubt.

They had only been dating for four months, yet he knew he loved her. He had not felt that way about anyone since Brit. But then again, Brit had broken him, destroyed his ability to trust. No, that was not fair; his mother abandoning him when he was five had done that. His deceased wife had just compounded the problem.

At 11:00 a.m., Colt cleaned up the workshop and headed to his desk. The mail was carefully stacked to one side. Most of it was junk. He tossed it into the trash. Only two envelopes remained. The first was from a customer who sang the praises of his company. He immediately took the letter to the breakroom and pinned it on the bulletin board for his crew to see. When he returned, he opened the second envelope. It was clearly from a female. The letters were large and curvy, and it smelled of perfume. The word *personal* was scrolled across the bottom. Colton tore off the end and blew into the envelope before upending it and dropping the small sheet of paper onto his desk. *She is not your daughter!* was all it said.

Colt flipped the paper over but found nothing on the back. He stared at the words, whispered each one out loud. Someone knew. Someone else knew Addy was not his biological daughter. Who? Besides the surgeon who gave him the news on the night of the accident and, of course, Norah, he had told no one. Had she told someone? Or was she the one who had sent the letter? Had he been wrong about her the entire time? Was this the other shoe he had been waiting to fall?

He picked up his cell phone and texted her. *Can't make lunch. Too busy at shop. Go without me. Be back around 7:00.* He knew she was in church and would not respond until later. That would give him time to develop a plan.

Thirty minutes later, his phone chirped. *Glad you have time to work on Addy's gift. We'll miss you at lunch. Girl shopping this afternoon. Love you.* He returned only a thumbs-up.

Colton did not return to the shop. Instead, he listed everyone who might know about Addy: Norah, Dr. Theelin, his lawyer, the police, maybe someone in the lab. Data privacy allowed neither the police, the hospital, nor his lawyer to share the news. Would Norah's right-hand people know? Maxine? Luke? Beth? It was not Norah's news to share; it was his. He hadn't even confided in Sonja, his receptionist. So how had his secret gotten out? Or more importantly, *who* had shared it?

Suddenly, his shoulders dropped. There was one person he had not even considered—Addy's biological father. Had Brit confided in the unknown man from the beginning? Had she told him she was expecting *his* baby? Maybe, but they had moved to an entirely different state, and Addy was five. If the letter were from him, wouldn't he have come forward years before? Norah had to be the leak. How could he ever trust her again?

⸙

At 7:03 p.m., Colt knocked on Norah's door. He never knocked, but somehow, he didn't feel at home in her condo any longer.

"Hey, Colt," Norah said as she rose to her toes and kissed him. "Did you forget your key?"

Colt shrugged. "Sorry, I was reading a phone message." He looked around the living room. "Is Addy ready to go?"

Norah looked confused. "She's in her bedroom reading. Aren't you planning to stay here tonight?"

Colt yawned. "It was a long day and I've got a full week ahead of me. I think we'll go home so Addy can sleep in her own bed tonight."

Norah looked toward the extra bedroom. "O-okay," she said awkwardly. "Do you want me to stay at *your* place tonight?"

"Nah." Colt shook his head. "I'm exhausted. Let's just see how this week goes."

His words hurt her; he saw the sadness in her eyes and the way the corners of her mouth dropped. He felt a tightness across his chest. But, after discovering she had betrayed him, this was just the way it had to be.

Colt scooped Addy from her bed; she was already in her pajamas. "How about we sleep at our house tonight?" Addy squirmed and giggled as Humphrey licked the bottom of one foot.

"Norah too?" his daughter asked as she reached down to grab her nearly hairless teddy bear from the bed.

247

"No, Norah's tired. I think we should just have a daddy-daughter sleepover tonight."

Addy squirmed until Colt set her down. She stamped her foot on the ground. "Daddy, I thought we were a real family. You said we were." She leaned her back against Norah, who had begun picking up Addy's clothes and stuffing them into a small pink duffle bag. "A daughter, a daddy, and a mommy." She spun around and wrapped her arms around Norah's waist. "I want you to be my mommy. I want to call you Mommy, and I want you to love me."

Norah knelt next to the little girl. "I do love you, honey. But sometimes things don't always work out the way we want them to." Colt met her confused stare over the top of Addy's head. "Don't you worry, though. I have the best Christmas present for you."

Addy giggled; she tucked her fists against her mouth and scrunched her shoulders up until they nearly touched her earlobes. "And we have the best Christmas gift for Daddy too. Don't we, Norah?" Addy tried to wink, but she still had not mastered keeping one eye open.

Norah was broken; she could not even smile at the little girl. Her heart ached. "We do, honey—the best gift." She turned Addy around and pointed her at Colt. "I think it's best if you go home with your dad tonight, sweetie. Get a good night's sleep, and we can talk about our secrets later this week."

Addy threw her arms around her dad's hips. "I love you, Daddy," Addy gushed before she ping-ponged back to Norah and locked her arms around her. "And I love you, Mommy," she whispered.

Colt cringed.

INTROSPECT

Addy Stone: "I want Norah to be my mommy. All my friends have moms. Since I don't have one, why can't I pick someone to be my mom? If Daddy lets me, I'll pick Norah."

CHAPTER THIRTY-TWO

For three weeks, Norah's phone was silent; there was neither a text nor a call from Colt. The silence was monumental. Each night, she fell into bed with an emptiness that nearly pulled her under. Mornings were worse as she faced sixteen hours of loneliness. She could have called him, but she refused to chase him.

Norah felt battered and broken. Her heart clashed with her head—flip-flopping between logic and love. Useless at work, she often left early to drive by their house, hoping to catch a glimpse of the two people she had fallen head-over-heels in love with. From the shadows of a park restroom, she spent an hour watching Colt and Addy build a snowman, make snow angels, and play on the playground. Another day, she followed them to the mall and slipped in and out of the shops not far behind them. From the second floor, hiding behind the fake branches of a Christmas tree, she snapped a photo of Addy sitting on Santa's lap. It was not a close-up, and it wasn't at a good angle, but she knew it was the most she was going to see of the little girl that Christmas.

As Christmas morning dawned, Norah was overcome with the possibility of a miracle. She was confident she would hear from Colt, but as the day dragged on, the silence only grew more overwhelming. The day before, Norah had wrapped the gift she had helped Addy make for her dad, a personalized photo book called *Addy and Daddy*, and left it on his doorstep along with three gifts she had bought for the little girl. The box wrapped in silver paper, a special edition newspaper she had created with fun articles about the three of them, still lay on her coffee table. It was too personal. After everything that had happened, she couldn't give it to him. Shortly after dropping everything except the silver box on his doorstep, she texted him to let him know what she had done, but there had been no response.

The massive wall clock ticked away the seconds, drumming like a death march. By noon, she had already downed two glasses of wine. She slapped together a crudely made peanut butter sandwich and poured herself a third glass before retreating to the living room to watch TV—anything not Christmas-related would do. She wanted nothing that reminded her of Colt and Addy or of her Iowa childhood: the hundreds of brilliant lights on the fourteen-foot tree, presents stacked nearly to the ceiling, and a ham dinner with all the fixings. If she closed her eyes, she could smell it. If she kept them closed long enough, she could see her mom and dad sitting side-by-side on the long couch, laughing about the kissing cows her Aunt Linda and Uncle Denny had sent as a gag gift. Norah stopped closing her eyes.

Her condo was devoid of Christmas, except for a small silver bell her mother had given her when she turned eighteen. It hung from the upper corner of a picture frame near the windows. The day before, when she had finally accepted that Colt and Addy were not going to be part of the special day, she angrily tore down the tree and the lights, shoving it all into a storage closet. Remnants of a dozen or more broken ornaments were trapped among the garbage in her trash can.

Around 9:00 p.m., Norah shut off her lights. With her forehead and one shoulder pressed against the long window, she stood in the dark and watched the boats filled with families celebrating Christmas on the water. An ache grew in her throat, and she could barely swallow. She had loved so many people, but each one had disappeared. She was alone, truly alone.

There was a sudden noise at the door. Everything in her prayed it was Colt, but she knew better. More likely, it was Seth. She tiptoed toward the door but stopped when she noticed an envelope lying on the floor. She jerked the door open but saw no one in the shared areas. The elevator bell dinged as the doors slid shut. Whoever it was had escaped.

She closed the door, locking all the locks before turning on the lights and picking up the envelope. Had Colt left the note? The envelope was sealed; not a single word was written on the front of it.

Norah tore it open and pulled a small piece of paper from within. *She is not your daughter. I will not warn you again.* The paper fluttered to the floor as she clasped her hands together to stop the shaking. The handwriting was identical to the other notes. All of those had arrived at her office during the past few months. Whoever this was had invaded her home; it was personal now. She had told no one about the messages, not Colt, not Luke, not Beth. This one was different. It frightened her. Clearly, it was meant to be a threat.

Seth had crossed the line this time. She was not going to put up with his games any longer. From her work phone, she entered the last number she had for her ex-husband. "This is Seth. You know what to do." The message had been the same since before they started dating. But the beep never came. His voicemail was full. She tried a second time, but again she received the same message. It was typical of Seth to ignore something so simple.

Like she had done with the others, Norah crumpled the message and tossed it into the recycling bin.

For the second time that night, she turned off the lights and headed through the dark toward her bedroom. Suddenly, there was a loud knock on her door. Her heart jumped. Had Seth returned? Again, she tiptoed toward the door.

"Norah, it's us," the familiar voice called.

"Addy and Daddy," a second muffled voice giggled.

Her heart raced as she flipped on the light near the door and ran her fingertips under her eyes. She pinched her cheeks and pulled the door open. Addy toppled into her, nearly knocking her down. Colt grabbed the back of his daughter's sweater to keep them from plummeting to the ground.

"What's going on?" she asked quietly. Colt wheeled a load of gifts into the condo on a dolly.

"We're having a sleepover," Addy announced as she clapped her hands.

Norah locked eyes with Colt. "Hey, Addy," he said. "How about you go get ready for bed so I can talk to Norah?"

Addy looked from one adult to the other before she started toward the guest bedroom. As she passed Norah, she leaned her head sideways and pressed the back of her hand to her lips as if she had a secret to tell. "He just wants me to leave so he can get all lovey-dovey with you." She rolled her eyes and giggled as she pressed her fists against her lips. "Somebody better come and get me before Norah opens her presents." Then she skipped off to the guestroom. She slowly closed the door, her face getting smaller and smaller as the opening narrowed. "Lovey-dovey! Lovey dovey!" she sang as she finally shut the door.

"What's going on?" Norah demanded. "Why are you here?"

Colt pulled her toward the couch. "I made a huge mistake, Norah."

Norah's eyes narrowed. "Yeah, you did. And I've spent the last couple weeks wondering if I made a huge mistake by letting you in my life." Norah moved to the opposite end of the couch.

"I deserve that." Colt folded his hands in his lap. "That and a whole lot more." He slid toward her. "Norah, I haven't stopped thinking about you the entire time we were apart." Colt swallowed hard. "I love you. I think that scared me. I've been deceived and abandoned so many times in my life that I was afraid it was happening again."

Norah's forehead creased. "What was happening again? Me leaving?"

He drew a deep breath. "Not leaving but putting distance between us—making me not trust you." Colt looked down. "I thought you told others about Addy."

"You mean about her paternity?"

Colt nodded.

"Why would I do that?" she asked.

He reached into his jacket, pulled a letter from his pocket, and handed it to her. "I've been getting these notes. Very few people know I'm not Addy's biological father, so someone must have shared that information. And the police and the hospital have to follow data privacy protocols, so I doubt it was them."

Goosebumps grew on Norah's arms. She felt her head prickle as the hair stood at attention. The handwriting was the same on Colt's note as it was on the messages she had been getting.

Colt stared out the wall of windows. "I thought maybe the notes were from you or someone you had told."

Norah balled her hands into tight fists, stood up, and moved toward the window. "Why would you automatically assume that?" She turned to face him. "Why didn't you just ask me?" She paced back and forth in front of the couch. "What if the person who's sending the notes *is* someone on the police force?" Her voice softened. "What if it's Seth?"

Colton's shoulders fell. He looked as if his bones had turned to rubber. He leaned against the back of the leather sofa and his arms dropped to his sides. "Oh my God. Seth?" He nodded. "Of course, Seth." Then he looked at Nora. "But how? How would he know?"

"Do you even have to ask? He's already proven he can't be trusted. He spied on me and had access to my phone. He's a cop. He can find anything and get away with ten times as much. Do you see why I can't go to the police?"

Norah dropped onto the couch next to Colt. "I love you, Colt, but I can't be with someone who doesn't trust me, someone who leaves when the going gets tough. I had that with Seth. I won't have it again. I deserve better than that."

Colt wrapped her in his arms. "I know, sweetheart. I know," he whispered in her ear. "I am so, so sorry. It will never happen again."

The guest room door opened a crack. Addy's cheeks pressed against the door and the frame. "Can we open presents yet?" she whined.

Norah laughed as she went to meet her. "You bet, honey."

"Good." Addy giggled as she skipped out of the room. "I was getting tired of pressing my ear to the door, listening for kissing." The three of them laughed.

"Colt," Norah whispered, "we'll finish this later." Colt nodded his agreement as Addy passed out gifts.

INTROSPECT

Addy Stone: "I knew it. I'm going to have a daddy *and* a mommy soon."

Anonymous: "When life gives you lemons, make lemonade. When life gives you liars, destroy them."

254

CHAPTER THIRTY-THREE

Spring in Iowa always brought muck and the stench of manure as the farmers prepared their fields for planting. While the farmers worked the soil, the birds began their chorus of songs. The temperatures finally hit the sixties with random days in the seventies and eighties thrown in to keep things interesting. Spring in Podany did not arrive with such a drastic change. The days warmed, but, because it was nice year-round, the change in seasons did not have the same remarkableness as the Midwest. The birds did not suddenly reappear; they were always there, sharing their melodies. There was not the aura of a new beginning you felt in the Midwest when the buds of the trees suddenly burst open. There, the snow had covered the earth for so long that the minute the tulips, irises, daffodils, and phlox bloomed, people felt like they could breathe again—even if the air did smell of cow pies and anhydrous ammonia. In Podany, people did not notice the slide into spring, nor did they get excited by the shift. But Norah did.

The letters continued to arrive every couple of weeks. Both she and Colt received them. They agreed to keep them rather than toss them, just in case. Norah still did not want to go to the police. Fear of police officers was embedded in her so deeply that she trusted none of them.

Just before the spring solstice, Colt sold his house, and he and Addy moved in with Norah. As before, he checked the house for listening devices, but, this time, he found nothing. It was clear Seth was not spying on them from the inside; he was keeping tabs on them from somewhere else.

⁙

As soon as Norah walked out of the conference room, Maxine was at her side with another letter. Norah had kept the contents of the letters a secret. Even Beth and Luke had no clue of their existence. But as each arrived, Norah grew more and more unsettled. She was certain her assistant noticed how her smile fell away and her forehead wrinkled, how her eyes grew dark when she saw the envelope.

"Another one," Maxine whispered as she slipped away.

"Thanks," Norah muttered.

"I know you don't mean that," Maxine called from her desk.

Norah entered her office and closed the door. She already knew what the letter said. She had an intense desire to run the sealed envelope through the paper shredder and throw the pieces into the river, but she had promised Colton she would keep them. Why she had agreed to it was beyond her. After dealing with Seth and the good ole boys who protected him, she wasn't going to the police, no matter what.

With a long letter opener, she tore the top open. This time, instead of a note, there were eight scraps of torn paper inside. It appeared to be some sort of puzzle. Norah quickly arranged the pieces, matching the tears until the picture took shape. Her mouth fell open. Drawn in a thick black marker was the crudely drawn outline of a female with a hole where the heart would be. What appeared to be blood was scattered everywhere. She covered her mouth and fought the tears. Her hands shook as she tucked them into her lap. This time, Seth had gone too far. If he was fighting to get her back, this made no sense. This message was threatening. How had her ex gotten so out of control?

A sudden knock on her door made her jump. She pulled her top drawer open and swept the pieces inside as Maxine opened the door and poked her head into her office. "Norah, there are two police officers here to see you," she said. Maxine's eyes were wide, and her jaw tightened as Norah nodded for her to let them in.

"Hello, Mrs. Burke," the female officer said as she entered the room.

Norah cleared her throat. "It's Ms. Burke." She tried to feel braver than she felt. "What can I do for you?"

The male officer nodded. "I'm Officer Sonner. This is Officer Whitehurst." He pointed to his partner. "You were once married to a man named Seth Burke, is that correct?"

Norah crossed her arms in front of her chest and pulled them tightly against her to disguise her shaking. "Yes, but we've been divorced for a few years."

Officer Sonner fished out a small notebook from his front shirt pocket and flipped a couple of pages before he stopped. "He was a police officer in Mason Hills, California?"

Norah nodded. Her mouth felt like cotton. She opened her water bottle and gulped down nearly a third of it.

"When was the last time you spoke to your ex-husband?" Officer Whitehurst asked.

Do terrifying messages from him count? "I've tried to call him a couple of times since Christmas, but his voicemail's been full." The officers looked at each other. Norah's heart skipped a beat. "What? What was that look?" She held on to the edge of her desk with both hands.

Officer Whitehurst pulled a photo from her front pocket and handed it to Norah. "Is this your ex-husband? Seth

Burke?"

Norah nodded. "Why? Has he done something?"

"I'm sorry to tell you this, but your ex-husband is dead," Sonner said.

"What?" Pressure built inside of her, and she felt like she was going to explode. Tears welled in her eyes. "Seth's dead?" It was one thing to wish him dead, but to hear it had happened was surreal. "How?"

"I'm afraid he was shot—six times."

"Oh my God." Tears streamed down her face. "Where was he? Did it happen at work?"

"A woman walking her dog along a path not far from here came across his body."

The room began to spin. Norah squeezed her eyes shut to keep the movement at bay. She was aware the officers were watching her, but she didn't care. She laid her forehead on her desk.

"Mrs.—I mean, Ms. Burke, are you okay?"

"I can't believe this," she whispered as she sat upright. "When did he die?"

"The coroner has the body, but it looks like he's been dead for several months," Sonner told her.

Norah froze. "How's that possible? What do you mean, *several* months?"

"Based on the condition of his body, it appears he died sometime around the end of last year."

"That can't be," Norah said. "That's impossible."

Officer Whitehurst sat down in the chair across from Norah. "Why do you say that?"

Suddenly, Norah released a deep breath, and a tiny smile bent the corners of her mouth upward. "He hired you to tell me he was dead, didn't he? This is all a big joke to him, another of his power plays to get me back. He wants to know if I still love him enough to take him back—if I'm distraught enough to fall into his arms again." Norah pushed her chair back and stood. She squeezed her hands into tight, white-knuckled balls. "Well, you just go back and tell him enough is enough. I wouldn't take him back if he were the last man on earth."

Again, the officers exchanged a look. "Ms. Burke, I don't think you understand. This isn't some game. Your ex-husband really is dead. Someone shot him nearly four months ago."

"That's impossible," Norah said.

"Why do you say that?" Office Sonner asked again.

Norah opened her top drawer and pulled out the envelope and pieces from the latest message and slapped them on her desk before she furiously folded her arms across her chest. "Because of this." She nodded toward the pile.

"What is it?"

Norah quickly rearranged the pieces and turned them so the officers could see. "He's been sending me and my...well, my new boyfriend, messages for months now. This one arrived just before you got here."

The officers stared at the paper puzzle on Norah's desk. "I'm afraid these haven't been coming from your ex, Ms. Burke, unless he's got some pretty amazing powers."

Norah could no longer control her trembling. "He has powers you don't even understand."

Officer Sonner sat next to Officer Whitehurst. "I think you better tell us everything."

INTROSPECT

Officer Sonner: "Being a cop, I've seen some pretty unbelievable things. I didn't think anything could surprise me anymore, but this did. When I finished with Ms. Burke, I called the Mason Hills PD. It turns out her ex-husband hasn't lived or worked in Mason Hills in almost three years. He left around the same time as his ex-wife."

Office Whitehurst: "Based on everything Ms. Burke told us, her ex stalked her from the day they met back in college. He even followed her to California. Listening devices are a woman's worst nightmare. But, if he wasn't sending those letters, who was?"

Anonymous: "If too many people know a secret, you have to get rid of some of them to protect it."

CHAPTER THIRTY-FOUR

Colt sat on the bed and watched Norah arrange her clothes into a Michael Kors suitcase. "Are you sure you want to go? I'm sure your aunt would understand if you didn't make it to the funeral. It's such a long way up there."

Norah dropped onto the bed next to him and laid her head on his shoulder. "You're only saying that because you're going to miss me. I know it."

"And you're going to miss me," Addy said. Her pink suitcase bounced behind her as she walked into the bedroom.

Colton scooped her up. "I am, little one. It's nice of Norah to let you tag along—even if it is to a funeral."

"Colton!" Norah said. "We're going to have fun while we're there too."

"I'd feel a whole lot better if the two of you were flying rather than driving."

"It's not that far. We'll have lots of fun. Won't we, sweetie?"

Addy jumped onto the bed and bounced up and down. "Yes. We. Will." She giggled. "Did you pack my teddy bear,

Mommy?" Addy hesitantly asked. She tipped her head down and watched her dad out of the corner of her eye. Norah grinned at Colton.

Colt grabbed his daughter in mid-jump and pulled her onto his lap. "If I know your *mommy*," he said, winking at Norah, "she's packed everything, even the kitchen sink."

"Daddy, that's silly. Why would we need the kitchen sink?" Addy giggled.

"Just in case you have to do dishes, little one." He tickled her until she screamed.

Norah zipped her suitcase and set it on the floor next to Addy's. "Why don't you fly up next weekend? Then, we can drive back together. You'd only miss a couple of days of work, and it would give you a chance to meet my aunt."

Colt plucked his phone from his pocket and pulled up his calendar. He stared at it for a few moments, playing out scenarios in his mind. "Yeah," he said. "Okay, I'll fly up on Saturday morning, but I have to be home by Tuesday night."

"Yay! Daddy's coming too," Addy said. "Daddy's coming too."

"You ready, sweet pea?" Norah asked.

"Yep." She threw her arms around her dad. "Fly safe," she said.

Colt laughed. "I'll do my best."

❧❧❧

Norah eased down the ramp and onto I-8 East toward Phoenix. It would be nearly five hours before they would make their first *planned* stop, but traveling with a six-year-old guaranteed only one thing: the unknown. They would be lucky to make it half that far.

After a rousing rendition of "The Wheels on the Bus" and several other silly songs, a ten-minute spurt of Addy-told stories that made absolutely no sense, and a string of equally awful knock-knock jokes, silence was all Norah wanted to hear. But when Addy sang out, "iPad, Mommy. I want to play a game," Norah wasn't so quick to give in. The little girl kicked her feet in excitement, jarring Norah's seat.

"Honey, we've only been on the road for an hour. We have a long way to go."

Norah glanced into the rearview mirror. "Please, Mommy?" Addy begged as she folded her hands together and cast an exaggerated, lopsided grin toward the mirror.

Addy's *mommy* line was going to get her whatever she wanted. Norah reluctantly handed the little girl the iPad. "Put on your headphones, please."

Within seconds, Addy was engrossed in the iPad, and Norah's hope for a long mother-daughter bonding trip had come to an end.

The early morning sun drifted through the open driver's side window, warming Norah's soul as she traveled the nearly empty freeway. Saturday morning was the perfect time for a road trip. Traffic was so light that she set her cruise control and allowed her mind to wander. It happily skipped through her childhood, danced across the waters of her relationship with Colt, and slogged through the fen of muck and weeds that had begun in Mason Hills—or even as far back as Parkerville, Iowa.

Seth had been the common denominator in nearly every hurt she had experienced. Looking back, she now saw that the man who had once been her everything had in fact, been her undoing. He had destroyed their marriage. He had left when she needed him the most. And, once she moved to Podany, his destruction had continued. Seth had always been controlling. She had seen glimpses of that before they married, as far back as college. But the listening devices, and the camera Colt had finally admitted to finding, were too much. Seth's controlling ways had escalated to an entirely new and unforgivable level.

Since her ex's body had been discovered, the notes had stopped. The police could not explain how or why they had continued to arrive months after his death. Someone knew more than they were letting on; perhaps they were working with him, or for him, continuing to deliver notes in his absence. She was sure it was his friends at the MHPD. But it no longer mattered. Every day without one of Seth's horrifying notes felt like a gift. It was finally over. Norah no longer looked over her shoulder; she didn't conjure up horrifying scenarios.

Still, the sense of peace she felt did not stop her from remaining somewhat vigilant.

As she sped down the highway, a blurred rainbow of vegetation drifted past her window. The sun dusted the tops of the colorful wildflowers with a thin layer of gold; tall clusters of weeds in green and amber poked through the ground. The brilliance of the flatland was a stark contrast to the brown and white snow-capped mountains off in the distance. Norah drew in a deep breath. Not since before Lili got sick had she felt this happy.

By late afternoon, they reached Durango. On the outskirts of town, she pulled into the Belle-Mère Hotel. She helped Addy out of her booster seat before passing her keys to the valet. He removed their bags, placed them on a cart, and wheeled it all into the lobby before returning to park her car. A tuxedoed bellhop waited next to the cart while Norah checked in. Addy winked at him with her awkward double-eyed blink and smiled. He winked back before leading them to the elevator and to their room, where he unloaded their bags and threw back the curtains. Norah thanked him and held out a ten-dollar bill before he left.

"Why did you give him money?" Addy asked after Norah ushered the bellhop from the room and closed the door. "Doesn't his boss give him money?"

"Well, he does, but it's not enough. When you stay in a hotel, you give money to everyone who helps you. It's called good manners."

"Hmmm," Addy huffed, "if I ever own a hotel, I'm going to pay them all a whole lot of money. Then they won't have to beg."

Norah laughed. "Honey, they aren't begging. It's just a nice thing to do." Addy shrugged and turned on the TV. "No

TV for now." Norah took the remote and shut it off. "Let's order room service and eat on the balcony. Okay?"

"What's room service?"

"Well, it's where you order what you want to eat, and someone brings it to us."

Addy shrugged. "Daddy and me ordered room service a lot before you became my mom, but we got ours from McDonald's, and we had to bring it to ourselves."

Norah laughed. "That's not quite the same thing, honey. With room service, we don't have to go anywhere. If we want, we can eat in our pajamas."

Addy jumped up and down. "Yippee! I wanna do that. But do we have to pay room service money too?"

"Yes. It's called a *tip* for helping us," Norah said.

"A tip? My teacher told me a tip is something you give someone to help them know how to do something better." Addy had her hands pressed to the sides of her waist. One hip jutted outward defiantly.

"Well...yes, that's one kind of a tip," Norah said.

"Well then, I have a tip for them." Addy waved one finger through the air. "They should get a job that pays more money."

Norah laughed. "Someday, you will understand, sweetheart."

Addy huffed. "Can I watch TV while I wait for my food?"

"Go ahead. I'm going to call your dad. He may want to talk to you." Addy nodded as she hit the power button on the remote control.

It was nearly seven before their food arrived. "Room service," the voice called.

Addy shut off the TV and ran to the door. She jumped several times, trying to look through the peephole. Finally, she gave up and pulled the door open. A man in a tuxedo wheeled the cart inside. "You're gonna have to wait for my mom to get out of the bathroom if you want your tip," she said. She whispered behind her hand, "She had to pee."

The man laughed. "No worries, little lady." He smiled at her. "This time, I won't take a tip. How's that?"

Addy raised her eyebrows and nodded. "I think you should tell your friends they shouldn't take tips either."

The man laughed out loud, "I'll do that."

"O-kay." Addy held her hand out and pulled the man's hand down once—as an agreement. "Thanks for being a good guy." She walked him to the door. "Don't forget to tell your friends."

The man nodded. "Absolutely," he said.

Addy closed the door and jumped back onto the bed and waited for Norah.

"The TV was kind of loud, Addy." Norah opened the bathroom door.

"The TV wasn't on," the little girl said. "I was talking to the hotel man. He brought our food. And you know what?"

"What?" Norah opened the door, hoping to catch him.

"He said was gonna tell all his friends they shouldn't ask you for tips no more."

"Oh, Addy." Norah glanced up and down the hallway. "They aren't *asking* for tips. It's just something people do to be kind."

Norah jumped when the door across the hall opened.

"Good evening," the man said.

Norah nodded toward him. She had the oddest feeling she had seen him somewhere before.

Addy poked her head under Norah's arm. "Are you one of those people we have to give a tip to too?"

"Shhh! Addy." Norah pressed her finger to her lips. Something about the man made her uncomfortable.

He stepped into the hallway. His eyes never left the little girl's face. "Your daughter—Addy, is it?—is such a cutie pie."

Addy wiggled out from under Norah's arm. "I'm not

really a pie," she said. "But if I was..." she tapped the side of her face. "I'd be pumpkin."

The man chuckled as Norah pulled Addy inside and closed the door. She twisted the deadbolt and flipped the security lock. Everything inside her screamed to run, but she didn't know why.

✦

Norah's alarm went off at 3:30. Her plan had been to leave early, but not this early. Her chance meeting with the man across the hall had kept her tossing and turning much of the night. She didn't want a second encounter with him. Just before 4:15, she escorted a very tired little girl down the hallway and into the elevator. It wasn't until they were in the car and back on the road, with Addy asleep in the backseat, Norah began to relax.

✦

Twelve hours after they left Durango, they pulled into her aunt's driveway. The white front door opened and a grandmotherly-looking woman with short, gray hair and frameless glasses rushed toward the car. "My Goodness! It's so good to see you, honey." She pulled her niece into a long hug.

Addy jumped out of the backseat. "Is it good to see me too?"

"Oh, my gosh, yes." The woman wrapped her arms around the little girl. "You must be Addy."

"Yes, I am. What's your name?"

"You can call me Aunt Linda," she said.

"Okay, Aunt Linda, do you have a potty I can use? I gotta pee." Addy clenched her teeth, grabbed her crotch, and impatiently squirmed.

"Right this way, honey." Aunt Linda steered Addy into the house as Norah removed the suitcases from the back of her car.

"I made hot dogs and macaroni and cheese for dinner.

Is that okay with you?" Aunt Linda asked Addy when she came out of the bathroom.

"It sure is." Addy smiled and pointed toward Norah's aunt. "Now there's a lady you should give a tip to."

Norah rolled her eyes and shook her head. "Did you wash your hands, Addy?" Norah asked.

"Well, of course, I did. It's the right thing to do when you're not at home," she said.

Norah scowled in her aunt's direction before looking back at the little girl. "Honey, it's the right thing to do no matter where you are—even at home."

Addy shrugged. "Well, no one ever told me that before." Her cheeks turned a dark shade of pink, and her eyes grew glassy. "How was I s'posed to know if no one ever told me that?"

Norah hugged her. "Oh, honey, don't cry. You're at an age where you learn something new every single day."

Addy looked at Aunt Linda over Norah's shoulder. "Wow! So, when I get as old as Aunt Linda, I should be really, really smart then."

"Addy!"

Linda laughed. "Yes, Addy. That's true. But when you get as old as me, you'll forget a lot of stuff too."

Norah gently laid her hand over Addy's mouth. "Aunt Linda, you didn't have to cook for us. We came to take care of you." Norah handed Addy the iPad. "Go sit on the couch and play some games so Aunt Linda and I can talk." The little girl tucked the iPad under her arm and skipped to the couch.

The top of her aunt's kitchen was painted yellow; the bottom half had been wallpapered in a light blue plaid. It reminded Norah of her childhood; the farmhouse had been decorated in similar colors. "Have a seat, honey," Aunt Linda said as she poured them each a glass of iced tea. The two women talked about her uncle's funeral before Norah shared the news about Seth.

"I never did think he was good enough for you, Norah.

There was always something a little bit off about him." Her aunt frowned. "I don't know what it was, but he just didn't seem quite…right. You know?"

Norah frowned as she swirled the ice in her glass. "I know that now. Back then, I seriously thought I loved him. I think I mistook love for…I don't know." She shrugged. "Something else, I guess."

Her aunt nodded. "Something *like* love, but not real love. Honey, you had just lost your mom. You and your dad had moved across the country in search of something new, so when Seth showed up, he felt comfortable—like home." Linda folded her arms and rested them along the edge of the old table. "He felt like home, honey. Nothing else."

Norah smiled sadly. "You're right." She tilted her head. "You're absolutely right. Seth was there when I needed comforting. He reminded me of Iowa and Mom and the life we'd left behind." Tears began to well. When she blinked, a single tear trickled down her cheek and into the glass she was holding.

Her aunt took a long draw of her tea. "Well, we all have our moments of weakness, honey," she said. She aligned the bottom of her glass with a damp ring on the tablecloth. "You can't kick yourself for falling for someone who tricked you into loving them. It wasn't your fault." She raised her eyebrows and chuckled. "Your Uncle Denny made me laugh. That's why I fell in love with him." Her eyes grew distant.

Norah knew she was remembering him. Finally, her aunt laughed.

"Of course, there were a lot of times the things he said and did were completely inappropriate, and I'd send him this annoyed look. He called it *the flicker* because my eyes would rapidly blink when I looked at him." Again, she grew quiet. "But I kept loving him because he made me feel safe."

Norah wiped her tears away and smiled before taking a sip of her tea. "That's the way Colton makes me feel," she said. "He makes me laugh and he holds me when laughing is too painful."

Linda patted her niece's hand. "Then you found yourself a keeper."

"But how do I know? Clearly, I was wrong before."

Her aunt smiled. "You're older and wiser now. You know so much more about life. This time, listen with your heart *and* your head."

Norah nodded. "Like always, you're right."

"Well, I'll tell you this, that little girl in there, she can never replace Lili, but she sure is a cutie."

"Yeah, she's a six-year-old cutie headed straight into adolescence." The women laughed until they cried.

INTROSPECT

Gary with Room Service: "Oh, my goodness, that little girl in Room 515 is adorable."

Linda O'Neil: "Norah is going to have her hands full with that little Addy. She's a doll, but... Denny and I never had kids. Norah's the closest I have to a daughter."

Anonymous: "A woman and a child really shouldn't be traveling alone. You never know what could happen."

CHAPTER THIRTY-FIVE

Monday and Tuesday were long days. Norah stood by her aunt's side, holding on to her arm, as she visited with those offering condolences both during the visitation and the funeral. On Tuesday evening, Linda collapsed into her recliner shortly after they returned home. After settling Addy in front of the TV, Norah retreated to the kitchen to make her aunt a cup of tea. "Are you doing all right?" she asked. She slipped her shoes off and rested her feet on the oak coffee table in front of the couch.

"I am, honey." Linda took a sip of her tea, set the cup back in the saucer, and rested her head against the colorful handmade crocheted blanket on the back of her chair. "This is when I wish Denny and I had had kids. I've got my church friends and the volunteer work I do at the library, but I'm afraid this house is going to get really lonely from time to time."

"Why don't you move down to Arizona? I've got lots of room and…" Norah's eyes widened. "There's no snow."

Linda nodded. "No snow, huh? I might have to give that

some serious thought. I just have to see how the next few months go."

"Well, think about it. I would love to have you live with me."

A sad smile crossed Linda's lips as she closed her eyes. Within seconds, Norah could hear tiny puffs of air passing through her aunt's lips. Tea sloshed onto Aunt Linda's saucer and her slacks. "Goodness," she said as she brushed her hand against her pants. "I must have dozed off." She shifted in her chair as she held her cup and saucer above her lap.

"It's okay, Aunt Linda. "You sleep. I'll take care of dinner tonight."

"If I sleep now, I'll be awake all night." She yawned. "I promised Addy I'd take her out for breakfast and to see the flowers in the park tomorrow. Do you want to come?"

"I'd like to," Norah said, "but tomorrow I have to check in with someone in town."

"Newspaper business?" her aunt asked.

Norah bobbed her head in a random pattern. "Yeah, something like that," she agreed. "But I can take Addy with me."

"Nonsense," Linda told her. "After we get back, Addy and I are going to make a pan of apple bars for tomorrow night's dinner."

"I always loved those apple bars. They remind me of Aunt Lucille. But you don't have to entertain Addy. I can take her with me."

"I want to make apple bars," Addy said. "Are they *metal* like the climbing bars on the playground at school?" She smiled.

"See?" Norah said as she shook her head. "Either she's wise beyond her years and has perfect comedic timing or she's a little bit off." She laughed.

"Let's hope it's the first." Linda grinned at Addy.

At 8:48 a.m. the following day, Norah pulled out of her aunt's driveway. Linda and Addy stood on the porch hand-in-hand when she drove away, waving until she turned the corner. The address Beth had given her months earlier had already been loaded into her phone and was providing turn-by-turn directions to The Happenin' Hippie, the shop belonging to the grandmother Colt didn't know existed.

No other cars were parked on either side of the street near the store when Norah arrived. The neon *open* light turned on just after 9:00, drawing her out of her car. Joni Mitchell's "Big Yellow Taxi" played in the background as Norah stepped into the store.

"Peace." The old woman waved two fingers above her head. There was no mistaking who she was; she looked exactly like her picture on the website. Only the headband and the neon shirt were different colors.

Norah pretended to look at the 60s and 70s merchandise while she watched the woman from behind a Bohemian floor lamp that splashed a rainbow of colors across the shop as it spun in a slow circle. She randomly picked up items, jumping when the yellow smiley face ball started to laugh.

"Scares a guy, doesn't it?" the old woman asked.

Norah wagged her head. "Say, are you *Harmony*?"

"It depends." The woman's eyes narrowed as she stared at her. "Who's asking?"

"I'm Norah." She wiped her sweaty hand on her jeans and extended it toward the woman.

The old woman smiled. "I'm a hugger." She grabbed Norah in a bear hug. "So, why's a girl like you coming into a shop like this?" Harmony's brand of uniqueness was something she had never experienced.

Norah drew a deep breath. "Did you have a daughter named *Sunny*? Sunlyn Stone?"

The old woman stood perfectly still; the lava lamp she had picked up leaned precariously to the side. Norah was certain the glass would fall out of its base.

"How did you know my daughter?"

Norah could hear the caution in her voice.

"I didn't actually *know* her," Norah said, "but I'm dating her son, Colton." She watched Harmony's face, trying to read her reaction.

"Colton? Wow!" she shook her head. "Now, there's a blast from the past! I never expected to hear that name again." She side-stepped behind the old oak and glass counter, set the lava lamp a little hard on the surface, and plopped down on a stool. "So, you're dating Colton, you say. He's what?" Norah watched the woman put the numbers together. "Forty-one?"

Norah nodded.

Harmony reached to the far side of the long counter and picked up a half-eaten brown banana. She broke off a piece and shoved it into her mouth. "Is there something you want?" she asked. Banana pieces shifted between her teeth and her tongue as she spoke.

"Yes. Answers." Norah couldn't believe she had even asked that. "Your daughter abandoned her son at an amusement park when he was five. Colton has never gotten over that. There's still a lot of pain inside of him because of what she did that day."

Harmony shrugged as she leaned on the counter. "We all do what we have to do. Does the boy know you're here?"

Norah bit the inside of her cheeks before answering. "Well, he's not a boy anymore; he's a man. And no, he doesn't know I'm here. He doesn't know I know anything about you or his mother at all. I own a newspaper in Arizona, and my researchers and I were able to put some of the pieces together. I didn't want to tell him I was coming to see you until I had some information." Norah moved her purse to her other shoulder. "What can you tell me?"

The song "All by Myself" by Eric Carmen began to play as Harmony stood up and limped toward the front door. She turned the deadbolt and flipped off the open sign. "Come with me."

Norah hesitated but eventually followed her up a set of

rickety stairs that led to what she assumed was Harmony's apartment. The higher she climbed, the more the air grew stale. A wisp of marijuana drove out the incense from below.

At the top of the stairs, Harmony laid a hand against her chest. Her shoulders rose and fell in time to her rapid breathing. She was still struggling when she pulled a photo album from an overstuffed, unorganized shelf. Opening it to a dog-eared page, she laid it across her forearm and pointed to a young woman who sported a baby-bump.

"Sunny?" Norah asked.

"Yes," Harmony said through a ragged breath. "Sunlyn Harmony Stone, Colton's mom—my only child."

"How old was she here?"

"Sixteen." Harmony turned the page and pointed to another picture. "That's Sunny and Colton."

Norah wanted to cry. "Would it be okay if I snapped a picture of these photos?"

Harmony shook her head. "You don't need the photos. You can take the book."

"Really?" Norah was surprised. "Don't you want to keep it?"

The woman shook her head. "Ain't nothin' in that book that I don't already have committed to memory. And when I start to forget, it ain't gonna matter no more."

Norah smiled at her. "Thank you." She took the book from Harmony. "If you don't mind me asking, what happened? To Sunny? And to Colt?"

The lines on Harmony's forehead blended into a deep, single V. "Well, you came for answers, didn't you?" She pulled a photo of a young boy from the shelf and handed it to Norah. "Sunny was a driven child. She wanted a lot more than what her dad and I had. To her, we were just a couple of hippies who smoked pot and owned a junk store."

"Is this Colt?" Norah held the framed photo toward Harmony.

"Yup. Sunny took that photo the morning she left him." She stuck a cigarette in the corner of her mouth but didn't light it. "The family of the boy who knocked her up had more money than the whole damn town. They were highfalutin folks who wanted nothing to do with the likes of Sunny, and they sure as hell didn't want anyone to know their son had cheated on his girlfriend with trash like my daughter."

Harmony opened another photo album; she paged through it until she came to a newspaper article. "This was the boy's father: Richard Wellington the third."

Norah leaned closer to the paper; she saw Colt's eyes.

"The third!" Harmony scrunched her nose as she repeated it. "His family paid handsomely to keep us quiet. But Ziggy, that was my husband, God rest his soul, said it was Sunny's money since she was the one who was gonna have to take care of the kid." She pulled the unlit cigarette from her mouth and dropped it into a cup. "Dumbest decision he ever made." She handed Norah the second album. "The day after he gave her the bankbook, she was gone."

"Where'd she go?" Norah asked.

Harmony's shoulders rose slightly. "We had no idea. She left a note sayin' she wanted more for her kid."

"I'm so sorry. That must have hurt."

The woman tilted her head and raised her eyebrows. "It did. But, hey, life goes on. I had the business to run, and Ziggy had his job with the city."

Norah grinned. "I just don't picture a guy named Ziggy working for the city."

A familiar sideways grin appeared on Harmony's face. For the first time, Norah saw Colt in her. "His real name wasn't Ziggy, hon." She took a sip from a cup that had been sitting near her chair since before they arrived upstairs. "His real name was Bob. Robert Bradford Stone. Everyone knew him as Ziggy, though. Even the guys in his office. You can't own a hippie store with a name like Bob."

"And your name? Is it really Harmony?"

She nodded. "It is. *Harmony Freedom Clarkson Stone.*

I had a couple of weirdos for parents. I mean, I was born back in the 40s, long before all the peace and love scene. My folks traveled. They worked a little here and there to buy food and then we'd move on. We slept in our car or under the stars most nights. They were free spirits. Me? Not so much back then."

She stuffed the cigarette back into her mouth and bit down on the filter. "Then, when they arrived here, they joined the beatnik crowd and settled here in Ponderosa Falls and opened this store." She laughed. "Wouldn't figure there'd be too many beatniks in a town like this, would ya? Not sure how they thought they were gonna make a living, but there was enough. Can't say as I remember ever goin' hungry." Harmony spit the cigarette across the room. "I like the feel of those things between my teeth, but since Zig died, I can't smoke 'em no more." She took a sip from a different cup and closed her eyes as she swallowed. "If you're thirsty, grab any cup you see. But check it before you drink from it. There's a surprise in each one."

"Sounds interesting." Norah silently counted the cups in view.

"The store wasn't called the Happenin' Hippie back when my folks owned it. They made that change in the 70s."

"I figured as much." Norah looked around the dark, crowded room. "Do you have any idea why Sunny abandoned Colt?"

Harmony leaned her head against her chair. "She loved that little boy more than anything. Evidently, they lived in grand style on the money Richard's family gave her. But, like I always say, if you're too dependent on the world, it has a way of kickin' you in the ass."

"What do you mean?" Norah eased forward on the antique couch.

"Sunny got cancer. Money only goes so far when you're paying for doctor visits and medication. When traditional medicine didn't work no more, she tried all that hokey crap from crystals to incense."

Norah looked confused. "But you sell that stuff in your store. I saw it downstairs."

Harmony rolled her eyes before she got up and grabbed a different cup. She scrunched her face as she swallowed. "Woo! Whiskey." She held the cup out to Norah. "Wanna swig?"

Norah put her hand up. "No thanks. I'm good."

"Where were we?" Harmony asked as she settled back into her chair. "Oh, yeah. Nothing worked. She started smoking pot to ease the pain. Of course, we knew nothing of this until the day she hauled her ass through our door." She picked up a green cup from the floor. "Tea," she shrugged. "Cold as hell, but ah, it don't matter."

Norah smiled.

"She came home to die. She didn't want her son's last memory of her to be a shriveled-up dishrag. More than anything, she wanted him to remember her the way she was. So she left him in the greatest place on earth, an amusement park."

Tears built in Norah's eyes. They burned as they threatened to fall. "Colt always believed she abandoned him because of something he did. He loved her so much. His last image of her is on the carousel. One minute she was there and the next she was gone."

Harmony snorted. "Do you have kids?"

Norah shifted in her seat. She cleared her throat. "My daughter died of cancer also—when she was four."

"I'm sorry to hear that, kiddo." Harmony sucked down another swig of tea. "We want our kids to remember us as the best version of ourselves. Sunny wasn't that anymore. Oh, she felt guilty as hell about leaving that little boy, but she knew he would find a good home, and he'd remember her the way she wanted him to."

Anger gripped Norah. "He *never* found that family," she said, "the one Sunny thought he would. Colt spent his entire childhood in the foster care system, in and out of seventeen different homes. Seventeen times he prayed that the one he was in would finally be his forever home, but seventeen times he was disappointed, abandoned—just like the day his mother left him."

Harmony shook her head. "Well, you can't spend your whole damn life looking backward. You gotta move forward at some point. Sorry about the kid, but I don't think Sunny would have done anything different had she known what life would be like for him." She pointed at a glass orb in the middle of a dark wooden table. "Crystal balls don't work, you know."

Norah's stomach burned as she glanced at her watch; she'd had enough of Harmony and her cavalier attitude. Maybe Colt had been better off after all. "What happened to Colt's father?"

Harmony smirked. "Well, money don't buy everything, but it bought that boy a fancy car on the day he graduated from college. But then he crashed it not more than twenty minutes after driving it off the lot. His folks buried him with the hood ornament from the Jaguar in his hand."

Norah swallowed hard. "I'm sorry to hear that." She smoothed the front of her blouse. She and Colt had one more thing in common: neither of them had parents anymore. "Well, thank you. I should let you get back down to the store."

"Honey, there ain't been no real customers in the store for probably thirty years. Snoops walk in from time to time. But I'm lucky if I make twenty dollars a week. It just gives me something to do. I'll be down there 'til the day I die."

Norah stood and moved toward the stairs.

"Wait. I want you to have this album too." Harmony plucked a random book from the shelf. "There's a picture of Sunny in there on the morning she died. If the boy truly wants to see what he missed out on, show him that picture." She handed the old dusty album to Norah. "It wasn't pretty."

"Thank you." Norah's lips trembled. "I'll make sure he gets these." She tucked the albums in the crook of her arm and set the photograph back on the shelf before she walked down the steep stairs. Harmony followed her, descending the steps backward, one at a time, holding on to the railing on each side.

Before Harmony reached the last step, Norah had tucked a hundred-dollar bill under the lava lamp near the old black and gold cash register and left the store. The bell rang when she exited, and all she could think was *another angel got its wings*. Was that angel *Sunny*? Had Sunny saved Colt or had she destroyed him?

INTROSPECT

Harmony Freedom Clarkson Stone: "I ain't talked about Sunny in a long time. I haven't thought of her boy in years. When that woman left, I lit a candle and prayed for my grandson. You would think I'd have thrown some salt over my shoulder or stroked a lucky rabbit's foot as I thought about him. But Harmony is only the façade I show others. God knows the real me."

CHAPTER THIRTY-SIX

A flyer had been tucked under the wiper blades, against the windshield of Norah's car. She grabbed a corner and pulled it out. Without looking at it, she dropped it onto the passenger's seat as she climbed in. "Siri, route me to the nearest coffee shop," she said into her phone. Norah looked at the options and selected one just a couple of blocks down the street. Walking would do her good, but, after her meeting with Harmony, her nerves were frayed, and her stomach churned. She needed coffee and something to eat immediately.

She pulled into a spot that had just been vacated near the front door. The shop was bustling with moms and young children. The solitude she had expected could not be found even in the corner booth, the only seat available. For nearly five minutes, she sat in silence, watching the children skipping, laughing, and fighting. Finally, she slipped the slice of lemon poppyseed bread back into the bag, grabbed her cold brew, and headed for the door. More than once, she had to swerve to avoid a collision with a rogue child. Her heart ached for what might have been.

Norah drove around the block and pulled in next to a small park; she saw only a few children and a couple of parents. With her windows rolled down, she picked at the slice of bread while she watched the kids play. Lili would have been older than the children she watched, but the child she remembered, four-year-old Lili, would have fit right in. She missed those days—the days of taking her daughter to the park, pushing her on a swing, or waiting for her at the bottom of the slide. Until Lili grew too weak, they never missed a day filled with adventure.

After shoving the last bite of the bread into her mouth, she repeatedly pressed her fingertips into the paper wrapper, collecting the crumbs. Once satisfied, she crumpled her garbage and shoved it into the white paper bag. Norah grabbed the flyer from beneath her purse and flipped it open. Her blood ran cold. A scream threatened to escape, but she tightly clenched her jaw. A rush of adrenaline pumped through her, burned her stomach, and set her brain ablaze. Her need for air was overwhelming, but she could not draw it in fast enough. Frantically, she grabbed the small bag and shook the garbage onto the floor before cupping it and pressing it to her mouth. *Breathe in, breathe out.* She repeated those words over and over in her head until the dizzy feeling passed.

Again, she stared at the flyer. It was a missing child poster. The little girl had disappeared three years before at a place called Halston Park, just outside of Ponderosa Falls. Side-by-side photos showed the girl as a three-year-old and an age-progression photo of how she might look today. But the second photo did not look computer-generated. It looked like Addy. Norah held the paper closer. As a matter of fact, the older girl wore the same top Addy had on when Norah left her with her aunt that morning. And, on the right side of the photo, the girl's fingers were laced with some else's hand. She was positive it was her Aunt Linda's.

Norah grabbed the bag, clutching it in her fist; once

again, she used it to ward off her battle with hyperventilation. How could this be? Who was messing with her? Who was taking pictures of Addy and passing them off as photos of a missing child? Seth was dead. So, if not him, who?

Not wanting anyone to overhear her conversation, she rolled up the window and called Beth's cell phone.

"Hey, Boss. If you're calling to check in, everyone's behaving except Luke," she said.

"She's a liar," Luke yelled. "It was an accident. Who knew a bag of popcorn would set off the fire alarm?"

Norah ignored their banter. "Put your phone on speaker and close your door," she said quietly. "I want you both to hear this."

"Luke, shut the door," Beth told him. "You're scaring me, Boss." Beth pushed the speaker button. "What's going on?"

"I need you two to research something for me. This has to be off the record. As a matter of fact, leave the office. Go to one of your homes. I don't want anything traced back to the paper, and I don't want anyone to know what you are looking for."

"What's going on? Are you okay?" Luke asked. "You don't sound like yourself."

"Take notes," she said. "I need you to find information about a girl from Ponderosa Falls, Colorado named Finley Wilson. She presumably drowned in April, three years ago. I want everything: names, addresses, police reports."

"Finley Wilson. Got it," Luke said. "But why is this so important?"

"I don't want to say anything else until I hear back from you two."

"Okay, but…" Beth said.

"No questions," Norah told her. "How soon do you think you can get me the information?" She could feel her heart racing again; her panic was firing potshots in her stomach.

"If we focus solely on this, we should be able to have everything you asked for tonight."

A rush of air escaped from Norah and her shoulders sagged forward. "Okay, listen, I'm going to have you send the information to my aunt's computer. I'll call you later from a different number. So, answer your phone, even if you don't recognize the number."

"A different phone, your aunt's computer? Boss, be careful. Somehow I have a feeling you're in way over your head." Norah could hear the concern in Beth's voice.

"Well, we'll find out. By the way, I don't want Maxine or anyone else to know what you're researching. I don't care what story you concoct about why you're leaving, just don't say anything that leads anyone back to what I asked. Understand?"

"Got it," Luke said. "Norah, please be careful."

Norah returned to her aunt's house shortly before noon. She closed the door and turned the deadbolt.

"Oh, my goodness, girl. I can tell you've lived in a big city far too long." Her aunt laughed.

Norah chuckled, but it sounded hollow and fake; her aunt didn't react. "Sorry. Habit," she said.

"Where's Addy?" she asked as she looked around the living room, drawing her aunt's attention away from the still locked door.

"She's in the back bedroom watching TV."

Norah hurried down the hallway, her stride longer than normal. A thought passed through her. Who was Addy? She wasn't her daughter. And according to the surgeon, she wasn't Colt's daughter either. Had Colt kidnapped this girl? Had he taken Finley Wilson three years before, letting her mother believe she had drowned? Hopefully, Beth and Luke could put her fears to rest. She trusted them. She had to. She didn't have any other choice.

To keep from diving into the abyss of fear, while her

aunt made lunch, Norah brought in flattened boxes from the garage and taped the bottoms. Then she stacked them on the floor in her aunt's bedroom before returning to the kitchen.

"Would you mind if I use your house phone? My cell phone reception is rather spotty," she said.

"By all means. Go ahead and use the one in the den. It's a little more private."

"I know this is a huge ask, but would it be okay if I use your computer later today too? I'm working on a story."

"Of course. Computers and I don't mix. Your Uncle Denny was the computer guy. As far as I'm concerned, that thing could be dropped in the bottom of Bass Lake. It would make a fine anchor."

Good. Bullet dodged.

Before grabbing Addy for lunch, Norah called Beth and relayed her aunt's phone number and email address.

"Shall we eat on the patio?" Aunt Linda asked.

"I don't want to," Addy whined before Norah could concoct an excuse. "I like sitting in Uncle Denny's big chair."

"Well, okay, then," Aunt Linda relented as she turned back to the stove.

Norah spun around, closed her eyes, and sighed. If Addy's picture had been taken that morning, someone was watching them closely. She couldn't take any chances.

After lunch, Addy returned to the back bedroom, where she curled up on the bed and read. Norah went with her. She pulled the blinds and turned on the bedside lamp. "You can always take a nap, sweetheart."

Addy crossed one leg over her knees. "Naps are for babies," she said as Norah left the room, leaving the door slightly ajar.

Norah and her aunt spent the better part of the afternoon sorting through and packing her Uncle Denny's clothes. Each item carried a memory or story her aunt needed to share. Norah was grateful for the distraction. She frequently cheeked on Addy, who had fallen asleep with her legs still crossed and the book lying across her chest.

Once the hanging clothes and dresser were boxed, Norah moved to her uncle's nightstand. Books, cards, a small cross, and various mementos removed from the top drawer brought more stories. The bottom drawer held only one item. Norah lifted a black plastic box and set it on the bed. She knew it was a pistol before she even opened the case. Her aunt dropped onto the bed next to her.

"That was Denny's gun." She gently touched the top of the box. "He bought it about ten years ago when there was a string of burglaries in town. I don't think he ever took it out of the case, though."

"Where are the bullets?" Norah opened the plastic container and peered inside.

Aunt Linda laughed as she pointed to the top of the closet. "He kept the gun in the drawer and the bullets in the top of the closet. I used to ask him what he would do if someone broke in—ask them to wait while he got his bullets and loaded his gun? I think it was all for show. He couldn't have shot anyone."

Norah picked up the gun. "What are you going to do with it?" Her dad had taught her to shoot back in Iowa. They shot at tin cans and the occasional animal that made its way into the chicken coop. By the time she was fifteen, he had begun referring to her as *Hotshot Norah*.

"I don't want that thing in the house." She patted Norah's knee. "I'll have one of the neighbors get rid of it for me."

"I can do it," Norah said. "I'll get rid of the bullets too." She dug through the top of the closet until she found the box of ammunition tucked inside one of her aunt's old purses.

"Well, if that don't beat all." Her aunt laughed. "Can you picture it? A robber in the house and Uncle Denny digging through my purse looking for his bullets?" For the first time in hours, Norah's laugh was genuine.

She took both the gun and the bullets back to her bedroom, removed the gun from the case, and wrapped them inside an old t-shirt of her uncle's before putting them in the bottom of her suitcase. They were there if she needed them. She hoped she wouldn't.

Norah taped and labeled each box before hauling them into the attached garage, where she stacked them against the far wall. A community group was scheduled to pick them up the following week.

Sweat rolled down her back, and she stopped on the top step in the garage and pressed her back against the cool metal door. The narrow windows at the top of the double-wide rolling door gave her a view outside. Two cars passed by while she watched, but it was the small gray Toyota parked on the corner that piqued her interest. From time to time, she thought she saw movement. It was too hot to leave a dog inside a car.

Norah scanned the garage. A pair of binoculars hung on a pegboard wall filled with tools. She turned the dial so she could see the car clearly. Suddenly, a camera popped up above the steering wheel. It pointed directly at her aunt's house. She dropped onto the step. Her heart banged inside her chest and a shiver ran down her spine.

The door between the house and garage unexpectedly opened. "Oh, there you are. I went outside looking for you. I thought you'd gotten lost somewhere," her aunt said.

"Whoa, you scared me!" Norah pressed a hand to her chest. "I was just straightening some things out here."

"Oh, don't worry about the garage, honey. Keith's son is coming next week to give me a price for all of it."

"That sounds good." Norah looked around the garage, visually searching for tools she could use to defend herself if needed. "How's dinner coming?"

"It should be ready in an hour or so." Aunt Linda wiped her hands on her apron. "Just need to make the salad. Did you want to use the computer before or after dinner? Or both? I can always entertain Addy while you work."

The house phone rang. Norah grabbed the garage phone before her aunt could. "Hello," she said. "Yes, this is

Norah." She pressed her hand over the mouthpiece and whispered to her aunt, "It's work."

"Well, by all means, you go ahead and take it."

Norah waited for the door to close. "What'd you find?" Her nerves buzzed as she pulled the long cord toward the workbench. "Hold on a second." She dug through drawers in the workbench searching for paper and something to write with. "Okay, go ahead," she told Beth.

"Finley Danielle Wilson was three years old when she drowned," Beth told her.

"Well, they assumed she drowned. Her body was never found. They did, however, find a sock and a sweater," Luke said. With a crudely sharpened carpenter's pencil, Norah scribbled down the information as fast as it was relayed to her.

"Her mother, Grace Marie Wilson, was never married. She's an English teacher at the high school in Ponderosa Falls."

"Her address is 1152 Cordie Avenue," Beth said. Norah stopped writing. She had driven on Cordie Avenue. The park was on Cordie.

"It looks like the mom did some time in a psych hospital." She could hear Luke flipping through pages. "Greensboro. She was there for over a year. She was admitted after trying to grab someone else's daughter and claim her as her own."

"She seemed to have had several other legal issues after the kid drowned," Beth added. "The police were called to her home a total of six times before she went to rehab."

"For what?"

"Miscellaneous complaints. Noise. Drunkenness. Domestic."

"So, there's a father, then?" Norah whispered.

"No. We were able to call in a favor to get that information."

"Please tell me you were careful."

"Come on, Boss. You know how the newspaper

business works. *You scratch my back...*" Beth told her.

"I do, but still... Is there anything else you can tell me about the mother?" Norah asked.

"She grew up in Hollister, about two hours northwest of Denver."

"Her dad was divorced and remarried by the time she turned eight. He's remarried again. Other than that, everything else seems rather benign," Luke said.

"Do you have photos to send me?" Norah asked.

"We already did. We sent a zip file to your aunt's email address."

Luke cleared his throat. "Now, are you going to tell us what's going on?"

"Not yet, but I will. Soon, I promise. For now, can you keep looking for information on who Ad-Finley's father might be?" She slammed a fist through the air, angry at herself for nearly spilling what she needed to protect.

"You bet," Beth told her. "Luke just ordered a pizza." She laughed. "He should be good for several more hours."

"Thanks." Norah hung up the phone before the word even left her mouth. She tore the pages from the notebook, folded them, and stuffed them into her front pocket. Something didn't add up. If Colt had kidnapped Addy, why were her sweater and one sock found in the water? Or had that been part of his plan? She didn't know what to believe. All she knew was she would protect that little girl no matter the cost.

INTROSPECT

Linda O'Neil: "Norah has been a lifesaver. And that little Addy is the gift Norah needed."

Beth Ramos: "I'm really worried. Something's not right. I think Boss might be in over her head."

Luke Simon: "It's not what Norah's telling us; it's what she isn't saying that worries me."

CHAPTER THIRTY-SEVEN

After dinner, Norah withdrew to the den, leaving her aunt and Addy to an evening of card games. She softly pushed the door shut and flinched as the sound of the lock echoed in the sparsely furnished room. The silence afterward was earth-shattering. Norah stood against the door, calming her nerves before she made her way to her aunt's computer.

She unzipped the file and waited for it to open. Inside were scans of photographs and newspaper clippings, each carefully labeled in Luke's neat block printing. Tears filled her eyes as she studied the *after* photos of Grace. She was waif-thin, almost skeletal. Her face was drawn into what could only be described as permanent sorrow. She looked brokenhearted. But even with all the pain etched on her, there was no mistaking her as Addy's mother. The two looked so much alike, it was shocking. Why hadn't her aunt noticed that some woman in the town looked just like Addy? Why hadn't the townspeople—at the funeral or when Linda took her to breakfast or to the park? It wasn't like she had been hiding her.

Norah tucked Addy into bed before returning to the den. She read through every clipping several times and analyzed each photo. She took notes, then sequenced and highlighted them. Somehow, Finley hadn't drowned that day. Somehow, she had come to be Colt's daughter. *The two had become a family in a faraway town, in another state where it wouldn't be so easy to discover the switch.*

Had Colt lied to her? Had he ever had a daughter? Or was he staking claim to a child that was not his? Was this the way he was dealing with being abandoned? Or was it part of something far deeper?

Norah grabbed the desk phone and dialed Beth's cell.

"Free researchers at your service," Beth sang into the phone.

Norah swallowed hard. "I suppose I deserve that."

"It was a joke, Norah. You know Beth," Luke said.

"I know," Norah said softly. "I just… Never mind."

"Sorry," Beth said. "I didn't mean it. Besides, you're paying us, so we're not actually *free*." She awkwardly chuckled at her own joke. "Are you okay, Boss?"

"I hate to ask, but I need another favor. Can you look up Colton Michael Stone from Hollister, Colorado?"

"Didn't we do that once?" Beth asked. "I swear…"

"This is different," Norah interrupted. "This time, I'm looking for a birth announcement for his daughter, Addison Lynn Stone. I'm also looking for information on a Brittany Stone."

"On it. Of course, Luke's on his third beer in the past hour, so he might not be as productive as you'd like."

Norah ignored Beth's comment. If she was right, there was more to Colt's background than *he* even knew.

〜〜〜

It was well past midnight when the computer pinged, indicating a new message. Norah crawled off the loveseat in the den and wiggled the mouse to bring the screen to life. A new email appeared. This one contained another zip file.

Norah extracted the file and opened it as she dialed Beth's number.

"Hey, Boss. Have you even read it yet?" she asked. "I just sent it."

"Can you give me the overview before I start digging in?"

"Yeah, but you're not going to like it."

"I don't like any of this." Norah took a sip of wine.

"It turns out Colt was married to a Brittany Ellen Stone, maiden name of Lopez. They had a daughter named Addison. When their daughter was three, his wife lost control of the car and plowed into a tree. The little girl was killed." Beth waited while the news sank in.

Norah coughed. "So, Addison Stone died in the car accident?"

"Yes. And not long after that, Brittany died. The obituary just said *suddenly*. In newspaper speak, and given the circumstances, I would say it was most likely a suicide."

"Yes," Norah confirmed. "I knew she committed suicide. Colt told me that. But he thought it was because she'd had an affair and she couldn't live with the knowledge that Addy wasn't his daughter."

"Norah, this is freaking weird. You're telling us the kid Colt's been raising isn't even his kid? How could he not know that?" Luke's skepticism seeped across the phone line. "And if he honestly didn't know it, how did he find out Addy wasn't his biological daughter?"

Norah sucked in a deep breath. "He found out the night he moved to Podany. Addy was hit by a car that night. Colt tried to donate blood, but he couldn't; he wasn't a match."

"Holy crap!" Beth exclaimed. "I kind of remember that accident. It was so long ago I didn't connect Colt to it. The whole thing is crazy."

More than you know. "Thanks for all your work." She bit her lip. "I have to figure out how to handle this. Until I do, I'm swearing you both to secrecy. I'll be in touch soon. I owe you guys, big time."

"Send more beer and pizza," Luke said.

"Sorry, Luke. You're on your own." Norah set the old-fashioned corded phone back into the cradle.

Norah spent the rest of the night reading through the files. Something still did not make sense.

❦❦❦❦

The following morning, after convincing Aunt Linda that Addy wasn't feeling one hundred percent and should lie low for the day, Norah climbed into her car and crept past 1152 Cordie Avenue. It was too cool to run the air conditioner but too warm for the windows to be closed. She finally settled on the air, keeping her windows rolled up so she could hide behind the special-order tinted glass. She needed to see Grace Wilson for herself, not just in photos.

While she watched the house at 1152, the door of the adjacent one opened. A man and a woman stepped onto the front porch. The woman's back was to Norah as she kissed the man's cheek before walking down the steps and across the lawn, where she entered 1152. From the back and the side, Norah got her answer. The woman's curly brown hair belonged to Addy too.

Norah took a right at the end of the block and parked near the coffee shop. Again, amidst the chaos, she ordered a repeat of the day before. With the white bag in one hand and a cup in the other, Norah passed her SUV and walked toward the park, choosing a bench near the playground, one that faced Grace's house.

She slowly broke off tiny crumbs of the sweet bread and drank her iced coffee as she covertly watched the house with the green shutters. Norah blended in; she looked like any other mother watching her child play in the park. Sitting to the far left of the bench, she milked her breakfast for the better part of an hour before a woman plopped down next to her.

"Hi. I'm Nor-een," Norah lied, almost spewing her real name. Her mission was to learn anything she could about

293

Grace. If she played her cards right, she might get answers to the questions that ran through her head during the middle of the night.

"Hi. Heather," the frazzled woman said as she stared at the playground. "Do you have boys?" she asked without looking at Norah.

"No, I have a daughter."

"Which one is yours?" Heather asked.

Norah tucked her hair behind her ear and rubbed her nose, quickly piecing together a believable story. "Oh, she's not here. I dropped her off for a tennis class. I thought I'd stop here and have my breakfast while I wait for her."

Heather turned toward Norah. Her eyes narrowed and her brows pressed together. "And you picked a park with screaming kids over a quiet coffee shop? What's wrong with you?" She laughed.

"Well, to be honest, the coffee shop had its share of screaming kids this morning too."

"Ah, the *mommy crew*." Heather nodded. "They tend to take over everywhere they go. They won't come to the park because they would have to actually watch their kids. If the kids are confined within the four walls of...say a *coffee shop*, they can spend their time gossiping instead."

"Well, that explains it." Norah nodded. She slowly sipped the last of her coffee. "Nice neighborhood," she said, tipping her cup in the direction of Grace's house. "Small and quaint. It seems pretty peaceful here."

Heather looked across the street. "Most of those homes are rentals. There's a few that are owned, but not a lot."

"Rentals? Hmm. I've been considering a move," Norah said. "It would be nice to have the park so close."

"I suppose." Frantically, Heather jumped up. "Ephraim, leave that little girl alone." Norah watched the boy race off before his mother reached him. "Be glad you don't have boys." She fell back onto the bench. "What I wouldn't do to have a sweet little girl."

Norah cringed but quickly pulled herself together. "Do

you know anyone in the neighborhood?" Norah questioned, lifting her empty coffee cup to her lips, feigning a drink.

"Well, the guy in the tan house owns the ones on either side of his. One of the teachers at the elementary school lives in the house with the blue shutters. And, ah, oh…" Heather cast a sad look in Norah's direction. "Well, the lady in the white house with the green shutters, the one on the end of the block, next to the tan house, well, that's a tragic story."

BINGO. "Oh my gosh, what happened? If you don't mind me asking."

Heather leaned against the back of the bench. She lifted a hand above her eyes and searched for her son. When she spotted him in the sandbox, playing cars with another little boy, she launched into the story of Grace Wilson. From the beginning to the end, she shared it all—including the woman's year at Greensboro Psychiatric Hospital. Norah learned nothing new. But hearing it from a local's perspective made it feel more real—less like an impersonal newspaper article.

"Hey!" someone yelled, loudly clapping their hands. Norah and Heather looked toward the woman heading in their direction. "Does that little boy belong to either of you? He's bleeding." Heather ran to her son as Norah watched. Her heart ached for the daughter she had not been able to comfort in more than three years.

When Heather walked away with the boy, Norah turned her attention back to Grace's house. A gray Toyota drove down the street and parked in the middle of the block. She couldn't be positive, but it looked like the same one that had been outside her aunt's house the day before. Pulling her handbag close to her on the bench, she laid a hand on top of it and pressed down against the buttery leather until she felt the outline of the gun. It was loaded and ready. As much as she loathed the idea, she would use it if she had to.

Norah picked up her garbage and tossed it into a tall green barrel. She lifted her purse strap over her shoulder and power walked the two blocks to her car, acutely aware of every sound around her. With the doors locked, she pulled out of her parking spot and drove back to her aunt's house, remaining hypervigilant.

INTROSPECT

Linda O'Neil: "If you ask my opinion, Norah works much too hard. I know she came for Denny's funeral, but it should have been a vacation too. It seems that paper of hers can't do without her for five minutes. She has spent an awful lot of time on the computer or the phone since she's been here. And if she's not doing that, she's out chasing some story or another. Don't get me wrong, I love spending time with Addy, but it's just not right she has so little time for the girl.

Heather Harstad: "I feel terrible I got so involved in the story of Grace Wilson that I forgot to watch my own son. What kind of a parent lets their guard down for even a second? Children need to be watched like hawks or they can get hurt or disappear. That's what happened to the Wilson girl. I mean, Ephraim just knocked a tooth loose. That's not even close to what happened to that little Finley. At least I still have my child."

Anonymous: "People say the end of something is just the beginning of something else. I don't know if I believe that. I can see the end from here and it looks pretty final to me."

CHAPTER THIRTY-EIGHT

The following day, Norah refused to leave her Aunt Linda's house. Repeatedly, she checked the locks on the windows and doors and tilted the blinds as much as possible without stirring her aunt's suspicions. The beginning threads of a migraine and fear of Addy going outside without telling her first served as excuses for her odd behavior.

Multiple times, she noticed the gray Toyota parked in various places across the street. As the afternoon dragged on, anger bubbled up inside Norah until she thought she would lose her mind. Finally, she had enough. She tucked the pistol into the waistband of her jeans and headed out the front door and across the yard. With her hand resting awkwardly on the handle of the gun, she walked directly toward the mystery car. Her eyes were glued where the license plate should have been, but it was missing. As she got close, the vehicle sped away, nearly bumping into her in its hasty retreat. A man and a woman had been inside, but she could tell nothing about them. "Who are you?" Norah muttered as she stood in the middle of the street and watched them turn left. "What do you want?"

"Are you talking to someone, honey?" Her aunt's sudden appearance startled her. "I'm sorry. I didn't mean to startle you. You seem so jumpy today."

For the second time in two days, Norah threw her hand to her chest and drew a deep breath. "It's okay. I was so engaged in watching the, ah, birds pull up those fat angleworms. I remember watching them with my dad back on the farm." Norah's cheeks burned.

Her aunt laughed. "Uncle Denny used to do the same thing." She hooked her arm through Norah's and turned back toward the house. "Dinner's almost ready. Do you want to grab some veggies from the garden and make a salad?"

"I do," Norah said, thankful for even the slightest distraction. Her arm bumped the gun as it swung backward. "But first, I have to take care of a little business in the house."

"You go ahead. Dinner can wait a few minutes."

<hr/>

Norah heard the phone ring. She kept one ear toward the hallway as she read to Addy.

"Norah, honey, someone's on the phone for you," Aunt Linda said as she shooed Addy over and crawled in next to the little girl. "I answered it in the den." She turned her attention to Addy. "Now, where are you?"

Norah walked into the den and closed and locked the door. Her hands were shaking as she picked up the receiver. "Hello?" It was more of a question than a greeting.

"Well, well, well." The voice was high-pitched and youthful, making Norah believe it was a female. Goosebumps rose on her arms.

"Who is this?" Norah asked.

The woman laughed. "I'm your worst nightmare, Norah Van Pelt Burke. I imagine you're hoping to make it Stone soon." The woman snorted. "We'll see about that."

"Who is this?" Norah asked again, this time much louder. She was shaking inside and out. Whoever was on the line had done a great deal of research into her life. "Why are you calling me?"

"Are you rattled? Feeling a little nervous? Maybe even scared?" the woman on the other end of the line cooed. The questions ran together before she paused. "Well, you should be." Then the line went dead.

"Hello?" Norah called loudly. "Hello?" But there was nothing. The caller had already hung up. Norah pressed *star sixty-nine* but knew it was all for naught. The number had been blocked.

Addy was asleep and her aunt was sitting in the living room working on a crossword puzzle when Norah left the den.

"What's a nine-letter word ending in a D for scared?" Aunt Linda asked without looking up.

Norah stared down at the floor. "Petrified," she said, not talking to her aunt at all. "Petrified," she whispered.

Linda set the folded section of the newspaper on her lap. "Are you okay, honey? Was that phone call bad news?"

"I'm fine." Norah cast a weak smile in her aunt's direction. "I'm just struggling with a story I'm working on. I'm sure things will work themselves out tomorrow."

"I hope so. You've seemed rather distracted lately."

Norah kissed her aunt on the cheek. "I have to pick Colt up around 10:00 tomorrow morning. Can you keep Addy?"

"Oh, sweetie, I'd love to, but I have a meeting at the church in the morning and a luncheon afterward."

Norah felt her stomach lurch, but she put on a brave face. "That's fine. Don't give it another thought." She waved a hand in her aunt's direction. "Addy can come with me to pick up her dad. She'll want to see him anyway. I don't know what I was even thinking."

"Are you sure?"

"Absolutely. We'll see you sometime after you get home." *Depending on how things go.*

Sleep eluded her as she thought about her plans. She had spoken to Colt only a few times since arriving in

Ponderosa Falls, but it was never for longer than a few minutes. Addy or her aunt had always been her excuse for hanging up. The real reason had been to keep him from hearing her anxiety. There was too much at stake. Addy had not been the child of her mother's affair as Colt thought, but rather the daughter of two entirely different people. *His* daughter, the real Addy Stone, had died in a car accident when she was three years old. Her death had been the reason his wife committed suicide; it wasn't because she had cheated on Colt. Everything he had told her was a lie. *Every. Single. Word.*

Norah finally gave up trying to sleep; she threw back the blanket and wandered into the room where Addy slept in a twin bed, covered in her aunt's handmade mint, pink, and white quilt. She sat on the edge of the bed and listened to the little girl's rhythmic breathing. This would be the last night Norah would ever watch her sleep. It would be the last time she would smell the scent of night sweat and Dove soap, strawberry shampoo, and cotton candy bubble bath. And the last time she would think of her as Addy.

She lay down next to her... There it was again. What was Addy to her? Norah's heart was breaking; she felt like a weight had been dropped on her chest. Lying next to the little girl brought back a flood of memories from Lili's last days. She pulled Addy close and snuggled tightly against her. *I don't want to let go. I can't. This was supposed to last a lifetime. I want to be your mommy, and I want you to be my daughter.* A sob shuddered through her, and she clenched her teeth to silence it. *But it can't be. You belong to someone else and it's killing me.* Tears rolled down her cheeks as she held Addy. "I love you, little girl," she whispered. "I wish you could be mine forever."

In that moment, Norah began to pray. She had returned to church after Lili died, but she had not truly started to pray again. She had hoped, through some sort of osmosis from just being among the believers, she would find God again— or He would find her.

INTROSPECT

Linda O'Neil: "*Petrified* was the nine-letter word Norah gave me for *scared*, but I have this unsettled feeling she was talking about something else entirely."

CHAPTER THIRTY-NINE

Dark shadows and puffiness mushroomed below Norah's eyes. Their edges were rimmed red, and the bloodshot color gave away her lack of sleep. She had spent much of the night crying or worrying; most of the time, it was both. Neither the miracle of make-up nor the promise of drops that cleared the red lines masked her misery. Finally, she tossed her cover-up into her black and white striped bag and shoved it to the end of the counter.

Addy brushed her teeth in the other sink in the vanity. "Duh yuh tink…"

"Honey, wait until you're done brushing."

Addy spit the white sudsy toothpaste into the sink and scooped water into her mouth with a cupped hand. She sloshed it around before spraying a milky stream through the small hole in her pursed lips. She giggled when it hit the spigot.

Norah rolled her eyes and handed her a towel. "Okay, now, what were you going to say?" Norah asked.

The young girl wiped her face before swiping at the

faucet. "Do you think Daddy missed me?"

Norah felt tears swell. After the previous night, she could not believe she had any left to fall. "I think Daddy will always miss you, honey, no matter where he is or where you are." She swallowed a sob and cleared her throat as a cover. "I will too."

Addy grinned. "I know." She hoisted herself onto the countertop and scooted toward Norah's sink. "I like it here with Aunt Linda, but can Daddy come with us next time?"

A tear rolled down Norah's cheek as she hugged Addy for what might be the last time. She swiped at the tear and sucked in a long, slow breath and gently released it. "We have to get going or we're going to be late picking up your dad."

"Okay!" Addy jumped down from the counter and skipped from the room.

In her bedroom, Norah picked up her purse and felt for the gun. She closed her eyes. *Petrified,* she thought, the exact nine-letter word that explained how she felt.

⛬

The baggage claim at the Denver airport was busy as they waited for Colton. Addy held a fancy sign she made that read *Daddy*. When they had talked about picking Colt up, her aunt mentioned all the things she might see while they waited. When she told her about people holding signs with names on them, Addy insisted on making one. Her aunt found paper and markers, and the little girl spent the better part of an hour creating her sign.

"Usually, people have those signs so the person arriving knows who is giving them a ride where they need to go. But typically, the people don't know one another," Norah said.

"Well, I think I grew some this week. Maybe Daddy won't know who I am anymore."

Norah wanted to laugh, but she couldn't. The irony of that statement was like a blade to her heart. Colt knew who she was, and he knew she wasn't Addy—at least not *his* Addy.

"There he is! There he is!" She jumped up and down and waved her arms. "Daddy! Daddy! It's me, *Addy*. Do you see me?" Colt smiled and waved as he ran down the escalator steps taking them two at a time.

"It's my girls," he said as he picked up Addy and wrapped an arm around Norah. "This was the longest week of my life. I missed you both so much."

"We missed you too, Daddy. Did you see I made you a sign? That's so you'd recognize me and know we are giving you a ride home." Addy shrugged. "Well, not home, but back to Aunt Linda's."

Colt dug his finger into his daughter's side. "I sure did see you. It's always good to know who you're getting into a car with," he said as the little girl giggled and squirmed.

It sure is. It's important to know who's driving you away from the people you love.

Colt set Addy down and looked at Norah. "Are you okay? You seem kind of quiet."

"I'm just drained. I haven't gotten a lot of sleep this week."

"Missed me?" he asked as he held her.

"Yes, something like that," Norah said. She untangled herself and walked toward carousel eleven.

<hr>

Norah pulled out of the airport parking and pointed her SUV toward Ponderosa Falls as Colt chatted with his daughter. From time to time, he threw a question in her direction.

"Wait! Doesn't your aunt live *in* the town of Ponderosa Falls?" Colt asked when Norah turned off the freeway and headed in the opposite direction.

"She does, but she won't be home until later this afternoon. I thought we'd stop at a park before going there."

Colt nodded. "That sounds good. What do you think, Addy? Want to go to the park?"

"Yessiree, Bob!" Addy yelled from the backseat.

Colt's eyes narrowed and his lips pressed tightly together as he turned and looked at his daughter. "My name's not Bob!" He teased in a grizzly voice. "It's Daddy!"

Addy squealed in delight.

"Where in the world did she learn that phrase?" he asked Norah.

"Aunt Linda," Addy sang. "She says it allllll the time. Right, Mommy?"

Norah nodded, "Yes, she does." She slowed for the recently unmarked road that led to the park and flipped on her blinker, letting the string of cars behind her know her intent. The small, tan sedan directly on her tail whizzed past on the right.

"Unbelievable!" Colt exclaimed as the car picked up speed and continued down the highway. "Did you see that?" he asked Norah.

She shook her head and made a left-hand turn, focusing on the loose gravel and sections of washboard road that pulled the car sideways. She had researched the park, knew the exact distance from the turnoff, but she hadn't realized the dirt road would be in such bad shape.

Norah slowed for the entrance to Halston Park. She watched Colt's face as she pulled into the empty lot. He bit his lip and his eyebrows furrowed. Something registered. A glint of recognition or a spark of fear?

She opened Addy's door and the little girl jumped out and ran toward the playground. Suddenly, she stopped and turned in a circle. "Hey! I've been here before," she said. "I remember the river."

Norah gauged Colt's response. "Honey, we've never been here. I would remember. Maybe you dreamt about it. Rivers all look the same. Maybe you remember a different one we visited."

Addy shook her head. "No, Daddy. I've been here." She firmly pointed to the ground. "I remember it."

Colton laid his arm over Addy's shoulder, bent

forward, and whispered in her ear. She looked at Norah and nodded. *He's lying. This is where he kidnapped Finley Wilson.*

"How about you, Colt?" she asked. "Do you recognize this place?"

"He should." The booming voice came from near the riverbank. There were three heads visible, but only one of the people was close enough to see clearly; only one moved toward them. It was the man from the hotel.

Norah grabbed Addy's hand, bent down, and whispered to her, "Addy, listen to me. Get in the car and lock the doors. Crawl into the backseat and get down on the floor. Do not come out or look up until we tell you to. Okay?"

"Why?" she whispered.

While Colt walked toward the man, Norah turned Addy around and aimed her toward the car. "Please just do as I ask. I'll explain later." Addy ran to the car and did as she was told.

Standing sideways, Norah watched both the little girl and the new arrivals, before turning back toward the car for a few seconds. She pressed her elbow against the soft leather of her purse. The sharp metal outline of the gun dug into the skin on the inside of her arm.

"Do I know you?" Colt asked the man as the two of them drew closer to one another. Suddenly, Colt smiled. "Dr. Fischer?"

"So, you remember," the man said. "I'm rather surprised."

"Really? I spent almost a year with you, working through Brit's suicide. I wouldn't have made it without your help."

Daniel released a maniacal laugh. "Is that what you think? Then I'm better than even I knew."

Norah stepped closer to Colt. Other than knowing he was the man from the hotel, she knew nothing about him, but she had to trust someone, and based on the man's last comment, she chose Colton.

Colt looked confused. "You don't remember? My wife, Brittany Stone, committed suicide in Hollister several years ago. I saw you once a week for many months. Then, the last week before I moved, you saw me every day," Colt said.

Daniel's grin broadened as he spoke. "I saw you, yes, but my goal wasn't to *help* you, Colt. I needed something *from* you, and you were so weak, I could convince you of anything."

The hairs lifted on Norah's arms, and they prickled in the breeze. She stepped between Colt and Daniel. "Hi, I'm Norah Burke," she said, trying to intervene. As he removed his baseball cap, she stepped back, bumping into Colton. He wasn't just the man from the hotel, he was also the driver of the gray Toyota.

"I know who you are. I've been following you for months."

Norah swallowed hard.

Dr. Fischer continued. "You just couldn't leave well enough alone, could you? You had to go and fall in love with this loser, but that wasn't enough. You got your damn team to dig up dirt on him. I'm sure Colton here doesn't appreciate that. Do you, Colt?"

Colton stepped closer to Norah. "What's he talking about?" he whispered.

"I'll explain later," she told him. "Doctor Fischer, is it? Who are you and what do you want? Why have you been following me?"

"It's Daniel to you. You know what I want. I want my *daughter*. Addy, is it?" He turned toward Colt. "Isn't that the name of your *dead* daughter? The one your wife killed in the car accident?"

Colt's face flushed and his hands tightened until his knuckles whitened. "My daughter's not dead. She's right here." He spun around. "Where's Addy?" he frantically asked Norah.

Norah and Daniel spoke at the same time. "She's safe," Norah said softly.

Daniel yelled, "That girl is not Addy! Her name is Finley, and she's *my* daughter."

"What's wrong with you?" Colt asked him. "Addy is *my* daughter!"

Daniel laughed. "You always did have a screw or two loose. What do they say? Lost your marbles? Run amuck? Not the sharpest tool in the shed? All statements people use to describe crackbrains like you."

Colt ran toward Daniel. "Shut up!" He closed in on him.

Daniel swung his arm forward and pointed a pistol directly at Colt. "I wouldn't come any closer if I were you."

Colton stepped backward and raised both hands in the air. "Put the gun away," he said. But Daniel only laughed. "What makes you think Addy is *your* daughter?" Colt asked.

"Because she is. Because DNA proves it." He glanced back at the two people still standing on the riverbank before turning back toward Colt. "And because, during our sessions, I convinced you she was *your* daughter." He laughed loudly. "It didn't take much. You were so pathetic." Daniel lowered his voice to mimic a whiny version of Colton's. "Oh, Doctor Fischer. I don't know what to do. I miss my wife. I miss my daughter. I can't go on. Blah, blah, blah."

Norah watched Colt grab the sides of his head and press inward. "Colt? Are you okay? Colt? What's happening?" She moved toward him.

"He's remembering," Daniel told her. "Your boyfriend here was an easy target. He'd just lost his daughter and his wife. He'd hit rock bottom. In the right hands, mind control is a wonderful tool." Daniel laughed. "I perfected it in the service." He snorted.

"*You* did this? You made Colt kidnap your daughter and believe she was his?" Norah asked.

"Oh, it wasn't like that at all. I *helped* him kidnap her."

"How?" she asked as she watched Colt writhe in emotional pain.

"It was easy. Grace, my muse at the time, got pregnant

with Finley. I didn't want to be a father, but I played nice—for a while. But child support isn't cheap, you know." He wagged his gun toward Norah. "Oh, that's right. You wouldn't know. Your kid died—suffered a terrible, prolonged, soul-sucking death. Didn't she?"

"How dare you?" Norah yelled.

"Shut up." Daniel grinned.

Norah pressed her arm against her purse again. The gun was still there; it hadn't only been in her imagination. She inched her hand up toward the opening.

"Stop!" Daniel yelled. He stepped near her and jerked the purse from her shoulder. He hung the strap over his extended arm and reached into the bag and pulled out Norah's gun. "Well, well. You were prepared for a gunfight, huh, Norah?" A smirk curled one side of his mouth as he shrugged and threw her purse to the ground. He tucked her pistol into his waistband. "But there can only be one winner. Stupid woman. The thing is, it sure as hell isn't going to be either of you."

Daniel was intent on making them hear his entire story; he picked up right where he left off. "No kid, no child support." He shrugged. "It was the perfect plan. And Grace, well, she just fell apart. That was a bonus I hadn't counted on. I so enjoyed finding new ways to make her suffer." He wildly flung the pistol between Norah and Colt. "I enjoyed making you *all* suffer. That last week, I fed Colt a time and a place—this park. It was embedded so deep inside his brain, he wouldn't have missed it. And right on time, he pulled into the parking lot. Right after Grace stormed off." He smiled.

Norah knew he was recalling the exact moment he forced Finley into Colt's life.

"That's the thing; I have the power to make whatever I want happen. You were all so predictable."

"Why? Why would you do that when you're supposed to help people?" Norah asked.

"Pay attention. Child support. I already told you. Colt needed a daughter, and I needed to get rid of one. It was the perfect match-up. While Grace was off licking her wounds, I threw Finley's sweater and her socks into the river. I changed her clothes and hid around the side of Colt's truck and pushed my daughter toward the dog. Dogs were the one thing she could never resist—especially one she'd become familiar with." He laughed. "It wasn't just Colt I messed with." His voice rose and he mimicked Addy. "Oh, Hum-fee! I love you, Hum-fee!" Daniel shook his head. "Colt fed me everything I needed. The pieces all fit. In Colt's mind, my daughter became his and he drove off with her to another state, far enough away for no one to know or care."

Colt had not lied. He'd been tricked, manipulated into believing Finley Wilson was his own daughter. "So why do you want her back now?" Norah asked.

"Well, damn if I didn't actually fall in love this time. Turns out my new wife can't have kids. So…well, you get the picture. I almost had Finley long ago when I slipped into Colt's house that morning, but…" He swung the gun toward Colt. "But you had to ruin it for me."

"It was you? Why?" Colt asked. His face was almost gray; his eyes were clouded and dark.

Daniel snorted. "No wonder you were so easy to manipulate. You're dumber than a box of rocks. You and Grace are quite a pair." Colt stepped toward him. "I wouldn't if I were you," he told Colt. "Let me explain this to you in simple terms. I gave her away. Now I want her back. It's that simple."

"But what about Finley's mother?" Norah asked, trying to buy time.

"What about her? The woman's daffy. We have nothing to do with one another. She'll never know I have Finley. A change of name, maybe…Addy Fischer, and she'll never suspect a thing. And, of course, that little girl will be easy to manipulate into forgetting her past—just like before." Again, he swung the gun between the two of them. "And dead people don't talk."

Colt looked at Norah. "Run!" he mouthed.

She refused. "Dead people?" she asked, hiding her shaking hands behind her back. "You're planning to kill us?"

Daniel looked at Colt. "Well, look at that; she catches on a whole lot faster than you do. Here's the thing, if I shoot you, that's on me. If you fall into that river and die, that's on you." He circled behind them and pointed them toward the river as the two people on the hillside moved deeper into the shadows of the giant trees.

The incline of the riverbank was rutted where the water had overflowed its boundaries over the years. Colt watched the car over his shoulder as he eased his way down the bank. Clearly, his mind was on Addy.

Norah stopped at the top of the hill. The water roared as it raged over the sharp boulders and bounced against the edges of the bank. "What's the matter? Can't you swim?" Daniel laughed as he shoved the pistol into her back. "Won't matter! Move it."

Colt was already standing at the edge of the river. *Had he given up? Did he think any of this was his fault?* He looked at Norah and toward the ground in front of him. A large rock lay at his feet. She knew what he was thinking. She carefully made her way down the bank, moving slightly away from Colt. Daniel was on her heels, shoving her as she descended the bank. When they neared the edge, Daniel gave her a push. One of Norah's feet dropped into the water, but she threw herself backward, landing on the overgrown grassy edge.

"Just a taste of what's coming." Daniel snorted loudly. "I did my research. No one who has fallen into this river has ever survived. I bet the trip is pretty damn exciting, though."

Norah saw Colt's face. His chin moved slightly toward the car, and he mouthed *Finley*. She nodded her understanding.

She stood up and turned toward the parking lot. "Finley!" she screamed.

Daniel spun around, looking for his daughter, but saw

311

nothing. Nor did he see Colt sneak up and hit him in the back of the head with the rock. Blood gushed down his back. Norah watched Daniel's eyes roll back into his head, showing only white before they closed. He dropped to one knee and fell forward onto the grass. Those last twenty seconds felt like slow motion.

Colt grabbed Norah and turned her away from the ghastly sight Daniel had become.

"You okay?"

Norah only nodded.

Loud voices rang out from farther down the trail before a pair of officers made their way down the bank from the parking lot side; both were holding a gun pointed at Daniel, who lay motionless on the ground. "Everyone okay?" the younger of the two asked.

"I don't think he is," Colt said, jerking his head toward Daniel. He turned toward the trail. "There were two other people back there."

"We know," the other cop said. "We'll sort it out at the station."

A siren's wail came to a stop at the top of the bank as an ambulance jerked to a stop. The younger officer sat on his heels next to Daniel.

"How did you know we were out here?" Colt asked the officer. His arms were still tightly wrapped around Norah.

"We got a call from a woman in Arizona." He looked toward Norah. "That was a pretty impressive maneuver."

Colt laid his hands on Norah's shoulders and pushed her out at arm's length. "What did you do?"

She stepped forward and dropped her forehead against his chest and collapsed back into his arms as she fished her cell phone from her front pocket. "Hey, Beth," she said, "maybe you should explain. I don't have the energy."

"Boss called me when you got to the river. I've been on speaker the entire time. Luke recorded the call while I got a hold of the police up there."

Colt took a deep breath. "You're brilliant." He gently

pressed his lips against Norah's forehead.

Norah laughed. "No, but I've been a reporter long enough to know when something's worth recording."

"Glad to know you guys are okay. We're going to hang up now. The police know we have the recording," Luke said.

"Thank you," Norah cried. "You literally saved my life."

"Our lives," Colt added. He looked around. "Where is Ad... Finley?" He coughed.

"She's safe. She's with an officer up by the car," one of the paramedics said as they strapped Daniel to a spinal board and carried him up the bank.

"I don't even know what to call her," he told Norah. "How do we even know Dr. Fischer was telling the truth? Could he really have manipulated me and...his own daughter?"

Norah wrapped her arms around Colt's waist and looked at him with as much warmth as she could muster. "I'm sorry, Colt. She truly is Finley. And she looks just like her mom." She pressed her head against his chest again. "I'm afraid it's going to take a long time for you to get over losing Addy—again."

Tears rolled down his cheeks; Norah could tell he was having a hard time breathing.

She held him tightly. "But that little girl was so lucky to have had you in her life...even if it was just for a short time."

"I'm going to need you two down at the station," one of the officers told them. "You can ride in the squad car. Officer Grant will drive your car."

Norah nodded as she continued to hold Colt.

INTROSPECT

Beth Ramos: "I'm typically on the research end, not part of the story. But for Boss and Colt's sake, I'm glad I was there—or rather *here*—to help."

Luke Simon: "Well, I'll tell you this, for a woman who worked so hard to keep her identity a secret, she sure made headlines today."

Anonymous: "In my nearly sixty years of life, I've learned that the things we want the most aren't necessarily the things we need or the ones we get in the end."

CHAPTER FORTY

It was dark when Grace ran through the front doors of the police station. A custodian flattened himself against a wall to avoid being hit as she raced past the front desk, around the corner, and down the hall toward Sergeant Pollack's office.

"Ma'am!" the woman at the desk yelled. "Ma'am!"

"Let her go," the man behind her said. "We're not stopping her."

"Where is she?" Grace yelled before she reached Pollack's door. "Where's Finley? Where is she?" She grabbed the door frame and slid into the sergeant's office.

Pollack walked in after her and closed the door behind him. "Ms. Wilson. I know you're excited, but we have a lot of preliminary work to do before you can see your daughter."

"See her? I'm taking her home. You can't keep her from me. She's *my* daughter," Grace shouted as she poked at her chest. "My daughter."

"It's going to take a little while to sort this all out," the officer told her. "We aren't even sure she is Finley."

The woman from the front desk opened the door and ushered Sam into the office. "They won't let me see her," Grace told him angrily. "They won't let me see my daughter."

Sam wrapped his arms around her. "I'm sure they're doing everything they can to make it happen, Grace. You've just got to hang in there a little while longer." He walked her backward and lowered her into a chair.

Grace looked at Pollack. "Who did this? Who's the scum of the earth who kidnapped my daughter and made me think she was dead? Who is it? I hope they die in prison."

The sergeant scowled. "Well, it's not quite that cut and dried. It's complicated."

"Complicated?" Sam asked. "What does that mean?"

Sergeant Pollack folded his arms across the top of his desk. "Grace, do you know a Dr. Daniel Fischer?"

Her cheeks instantly burned. "He, ah, well, he was my therapist when I lived in Hollister."

"Nothing more?"

Grace looked at Sam before answering. "What does this have to do with Finley?"

Sam grabbed Grace's hand and nodded toward Pollack. "Don't protect Daniel, Grace. He's not worth it. Finley deserves so much more."

Since she had gotten the phone call, her heart had not stopped banging in her chest. Admitting Daniel was Finley's father would mean bringing him back into their lives. He was a doctor, a highly respected psychiatrist. Who would believe her over him? Because of her stint in the psychiatric hospital, they would most likely give him sole custody of their daughter.

Grace defiantly folded her arms across her chest. "Why are you asking? What difference does it make?" She inched forward on the sticky black chair.

Pollack stared at her for several seconds. "Is *he* Finley's father?"

Life without Air

Grace said nothing, even though the sergeant continued to stare at her.

Finally, he closed the manilla folder in front of him. "Fine. We can run a DNA sample. It'll take a couple of days to get the results back. In the meantime, your daughter goes to foster care."

"Yes!" Grace shouted. "Yes, Daniel is Finley's father!" She closed her eyes and twisted her mouth. "What does this have to do with..." Suddenly, she stopped talking. She planted her hands on the sergeant's desk as she leaned closer to him. "Has Daniel had Finley this entire time?"

Pollack leaned back and crossed his legs. "Not exactly. However, according to what he admitted today, he's known where she was the entire time."

Grace leaped up. Her hands sliced through the air before she squeezed them into fists. "What? You're telling me Daniel knew Finley wasn't dead?" Sam pulled her back into her chair and wrapped his arm over her shoulder to hold her down.

"I think we need to have some pieces filled in for us," he told Sergeant Pollack.

For the longer side of thirty minutes, Pollack relayed what he knew—from the day Finley disappeared until hours before when they believed they had enough information to substantiate Addy Stone was indeed Finley Wilson.

Sam shifted in his chair. "So, this guy who had Finley, honestly had no idea she wasn't his daughter? How's that possible?"

"No, he didn't." Pollack shook his head. "It's crazy, but based on Daniel's confession to him, he set this poor guy up. His daughter looked an awful lot like Finley. And being a psychiatrist, Daniel had the ability to make him believe Finley was actually his daughter—Addy." Pollack shook his head. "Mind control is scary."

"And Daniel did this? You're sure?" Grace asked.

The sergeant nodded.

"Not once did this guy ever believe my daughter wasn't

317

his?"

"Ms. Wilson, we're still unraveling all the pieces. We've called in a team of experts to work with this man. We want to get to the truth."

Sam looked at Grace. "Just playing devil's advocate here, but how do you know this girl is Daniel and Grace's kid? Maybe she's not, and he was trying to kidnap her from this man?"

Pollack looked at Grace. "I lied. We've already collected a DNA sample. We should have a definitive answer tomorrow. But we're fairly certain she belongs to Grace." He held Grace's stare. "She looks an awful lot like her mom."

Grace's mouth suddenly felt dry; she cleared her throat, trying to push down the huge lump that had begun to grow. "Can I see my daughter?" she whispered.

"She's asleep right now, Grace. Social Services has been working with her all afternoon. She's pretty wiped out. We want to get the DNA test back before we release her to you." Pollack looked at Sam. "We need to wait until tomorrow. It's late. If you go in there all frantic, you're going to scare her."

Tears streamed down Grace's face. "I just want to see my baby girl," she cried.

"I understand, but the likelihood she's going to remember you is pretty slim. I'm afraid she sees the man who has had her as her family."

She pointed to her chest. "But I'm her mother," Grace said. "Me. A child never forgets their own mother."

"I wouldn't say *never*. Your daughter was only three when she disappeared, Grace." Pollack stood. "You go home, get a good night's rest. Spend the morning getting things ready for your daughter's return. I'll see you around 1:00 tomorrow afternoon."

Sam put his hand on top of Grace's. "It's not even twenty-four hours, Grace. You've waited three years. You have to do what's best for Finley. Okay?"

Grace opened her mouth, ready to object, but she couldn't. She wanted what was best for her daughter. "Okay. But I'll be back tomorrow, and I want my daughter."

Officer Pollack nodded. "Get a good night's sleep, Grace."

Sam pulled the door open and led Grace down the hallway and out of the station.

INTROSPECT

Sergeant Pollack: "What a mess. I'm not sure who I feel sorrier for: the woman who thought her child was dead and learned she isn't or the guy who was tricked into believing his dead daughter was still alive. Either way, someone wins, and someone loses."

Sam Hall: "Grace was finally in a good place. We were supposed to get married next weekend. I love her. I have since the day I laid eyes on her. I really worry about her mental state now. Either way, I'll be here to support her and her daughter."

CHAPTER FORTY-ONE

It was nearly midnight when Norah left the police station. After talking with the team of doctors they brought in to work with Colt, they decided to hospitalize him for further evaluation. It was around 8:00 p.m. by the time the transport arrived to take him to Greensboro.

Norah met with the officers and the social worker, trying to help with the transition of Finley back to her *real* family. That thought made her want to cry. She, Colt, and Addy *had* been a real family. But, like before, she and Colt were walking through the heartbreak of having another daughter ripped away. Her heart ached—for Addy, for Colt, and for herself. How could it not? But it also ached for the little girl's mother, Grace.

Aunt Linda was still up when Norah walked through the door. She didn't utter a sound; she just wrapped her arms around Norah and held her while she sobbed. When she had no more tears left inside, her aunt led her to the bedroom and helped her get ready for bed.

Norah slid over as her aunt sat next to her and turned

off the bedside lamp. They sat in silence for a long while.

"Norah, honey, do you remember when Lili died? Do you remember thinking you could never love again? That you would never let anyone else into your life?" Aunt Linda asked.

"Mm-hmm," Norah said softly.

"But then you let Colt in, and you let Addy in. Even though you thought you would never love again, you did. You opened your heart, honey. Good always comes from that." She gently rubbed her thumb across her niece's arm as she spoke. "Hearts are meant to love, honey. *We* are created to love and to be loved. We need others, just like they need us. We can't shut people out."

Norah sobbed softly. "Sweetheart, love is meant to be experienced and shared. And just when you think you have no love to give, that's when love finds you."

The moonlight streamed into the room; a yellow glow spread across Norah's face. "Love found me," she said softly.

"I know, honey. Love found you many, many times. Love gave you the most amazing parents, then Lili, and Colt, and Addy."

"And you," Norah said as she took her aunt's hand.

"Yes, and me and Uncle Denny. And you loved each of us with all your heart—and we returned that love just as fiercely. I'm so sorry you've had so many disappointments in your life, but all you have to do is open your heart and wait for love to find you again."

Norah laid a hand on her stomach. "It did," Norah whispered. "I'm pregnant."

"Well, praise the Lord!" Aunt Linda said. "That's the best news I've heard in a long time."

Norah sat up and leaned against the quilted headboard, another of her aunt's handiwork. "Colt doesn't even know. I found out the day before Addy and I left to come up here. I figured if he knew, he wouldn't have let me come." She took her aunt's hand. "I'm just so scared. What if this baby gets cancer too?" She sobbed. "What if I can't save them? What if I end up all alone again?"

Her aunt ran the fingers of one hand through Norah's hair. Her eyes looked soft in the moonlight. "If you worry about everything before it even happens, you'll miss out on all the good things life has to offer."

Norah smiled and slid over in the bed. "Will you sleep with me tonight?" she asked.

"Of course, honey."

❦

Norah arrived at the police station at four minutes to one. As she passed through the hallway, Grace entered the ladies' room just ahead of her. Small beads of sweat popped up along Norah's hairline. She pushed the bathroom door open and waited for Grace to leave the stall.

"I'm Norah," she said as Grace dried her hands on the rough, tan paper towel.

"Should I know you?" Grace asked.

Norah was not sure what she had been told the day before, but it was clear names had not been exchanged. "I'm Colt's girlfriend."

Grace tipped her head slightly to the left and shrugged. "Colt…"

Norah ran a hand across her forehead. "He's the one Dr. Fischer, well…brainwashed into believing Finley was his daughter Addy."

Grace took a step backward. "Oh." It was more of a sound than a word until she repeated it louder. "Oh. So, you've been with Finley all this time?"

"No. Colt and I didn't start dating until a year or so ago. I met Addy… I'm sorry, I mean Finley, not long afterward." The room suddenly felt too small. Norah uncomfortably wrung her hands as she debated what to say. "Your daughter is the sweetest little girl. It's clear you did a wonderful job with her when she was young."

Silence hung in the air like a dense fog.

"I, I don't know what you want me to say," Grace said. "Because if you think I'm going to forget your boyfriend stole my daughter, I'm not. I've lost three years with her."

"But it wasn't Colt's doing. Dr. Fischer manipulated him into believing your daughter was his," Norah said.

Grace softly snorted. "Manipulation is a matter of..." She looked down at the floor.

"What?" Norah asked. "What were you going to say?"

Grace sighed. "I was going to say we let ourselves be manipulated by not being strong enough." Her shoulders fell and she shifted her eyes to the wall above Norah's shoulder. "But when I started to say it, I realized Daniel manipulated me for years—including this entire time when he knew where Finley was." She tossed the paper towel into the trash can. "I don't suppose you want to help me learn who my daughter is again, do you?"

"I'd like that, Grace. I know Colton would too."

INTROSPECT

Linda O'Neil: "When I lost Denny, I was afraid I would lose myself. But when Norah and Addy showed up, they helped me see that love never really dies. Our loved ones live on in our memories. Just because they aren't physically with us, doesn't mean we stop loving them, and it doesn't mean we stop living. We just need to make new memories."

Mary Perrine

THE VOICES WITHIN
(a choral poem)

NORAH	GRACE	COLTON
	I ached for my missing daughter for three years.	
		For three years I loved a child I believed was mine. Now
Emptiness churns in me. Another child entered my life, but she was torn away.		emptiness churns in me.
		She was torn away. The same way I ripped her from her mother.
	Mother! I am a mother again.	
Again, I feel the devastation, the loss.		
		The loss is more than I can bear.
	All this time, we were blind to the truth.	We were blind to the truth.
We saw what we wanted to see.	We saw what we wanted to see— the best in people.	We saw what we wanted to see— the best in people.
People can destroy those who are weak and vulnerable.	Those who are weak and vulnerable can be led to believe everything.	
Everything seemed lost. Lili is gone. Now, Addy is gone.	everything.	Everything seemed lost.
		Addy is gone.
	But Finley lives on, and our new life begins	
And our new life begins mom and dad and baby.		And our new life begins mom and dad and baby.
	Finley and me.	
A family.	A family.	A family.

PART FOUR

TWO MORE YEARS HAVE PASSED

LOVING

Love is not silent.
It is loud and glorious.
It is found in a kind word,
a helping hand, a listening ear, a smile, or a hug.
So, open your arms;
spread them as wide as you are able.
Let others fall inside and experience
the warmth, the joy, the hope.
Love passionately. Love unceasingly.
Love without expectation of something in return.
Lead with love.

LIFE WITH NORAH—Norah Van Pelt

Life's Greatest Moments

Rose Kennedy once said, "Life isn't a matter of milestones, but of moments." A *moment* in medieval time was considered approximately ninety seconds long. Using that measure, each person experiences nine hundred sixty moments a day. Those moments could be small: a smile from a friend or stranger, the arrival of a well-timed text message, a hug from a child, or a quick prayer cast in need. Or they may be bigger: a much-needed conversation, a walk through the woods enjoying nature, or time spent snuggling a child before they fall asleep.

Each of those moments impacts who we become. Negative ones feed negative people. And, of course, the opposite is true as well. A person who is ignored carries a much heavier burden through life than someone who is loved unconditionally. A child who is bullied quite often becomes a bully themselves or sees life through the eyes of anger and pain—always doubting, always questioning whether they are good enough. Often, they lash out at others, even without cause.

Therefore, what if, for one entire day, we made all our moments count? We can't control how someone treats us, or if the gas pump drips gas while we're filling our tank, or if the bottle of ketchup we just dropped explodes all over our kitchen; those things just happen. But we can create positive moments for others: buying someone coffee, sending an anonymous note to a person who needs a pick-me-up, calling a friend, handing a flower to a child, or leaving a positive note on a public mirror, car window, fitting room, or bathroom stall. And what if *ding-dong ditch* became a joyous moment where the homeowner was rewarded with a special gift on their porch when they opened their door? Think of the impact it would have—the lives it could change.

Our sole purpose in life should be to make a positive difference for others. Because once we start treating them like their life matters, it does.

Most of us will never win the lottery or earn a massive amount of money for a talent we were born with or one that was nurtured. Instead, we have been bequeathed with nine hundred sixty moments each day, nine hundred sixty opportunities to have a positive impact on someone else. Besides, big wins are fleeting, small wins touch the soul.

Put good into the world and see what comes back to you. Make every moment count. Make every moment one of life's greatest.

Norah Van Pelt is a syndicated columnist

NORAH	GRACE	COLTON
Mother of an angel	Mother of a miracle	Father of an angel
Missing Lili & Addy	Loving Finley	Missing Addy
Engaged to Colt	In a relationship with Sam	Engaged to Norah
Mother	Grateful for life	Father

CHAPTER FORTY-TWO

The sun was out, but a stiff, cool breeze pushed out the warmth of the April day. Norah was grateful to step out of the cold.

"Norah Stone," she told the woman at the desk. It was still a bit awkward to connect the two names. During one part of her life, she had been Norah Van Pelt, and then, Norah Burke. One name she cherished the other she loathed. But that no longer mattered. She was now Norah Stone. This was the name she knew she would keep forever.

"Sign in and have a seat," the woman told her. "Someone will be out to get you in a few minutes."

She sat on one of the blue plastic waiting room chairs and flipped through a magazine, not really reading, just staring absently at the photos.

"Mrs. Stone," a gray-haired man in a uniform called to her. She dropped the magazine and walked toward the door. "Right this way," he said, stepping back and allowing her to enter the narrow room. "Put your purse and everything else in the bin. We'll put it in a locker until you're done." Norah did as she was told, then stepped into the scanner and held her hands in the air as the poster on the machine instructed. "Okay," the man told her, beckoning her with his fingers.

Norah walked through the next door and into a room with glass walls that separated the incarcerated from the visitors. She sat down on a black swivel stool and waited. Finally, a woman in an orange jumpsuit walked in and sat opposite her. They picked up the phone at the same time.

"How are you?" Norah asked.

The woman looked down and drew a deep breath. "Embarrassed," she said. "Embarrassed I let my life get so out of control. Embarrassed I was manipulated into doing things I knew were wrong."

Norah slowly nodded. "I understand. Colt feels the exact same way."

The woman shook her head. "Yes, but Colt never killed anyone." The woman's lashes grew damp. "Why are you here, Norah? Why would you ever come to see me?"

"Because you worked for me. Because you are a friend. And, like Colt, Dr. Fischer manipulated you too, Maxine. You were an excellent receptionist, but you got pulled into his web of deceit."

Maxine nodded in agreement. "He brainwashed me too, just not the same way he did to Colt. He played mind games—subtle messages and comments to get me to do what he wanted. And I let myself get caught up in his charm."

"I know. It's easy to do. As mothers, we'll do anything for our children. Your daughter couldn't have a child and you wanted to help. And when she married Dr. Fischer, he had the perfect solution—to reclaim his daughter."

"And I fell for it." Maxine released a sharp breath. "To this day, whenever I close my eyes, I see your ex-husband lying on that path. I'm a good person, Norah," she said, pointing to herself. "Before I met Daniel, I wouldn't have hurt a flea, but when your ex found out about Daniel's plans, Daniel convinced me he had to be stopped. One too many people knew the secret. I can't believe I killed him. Before that night, I'd never fired a gun in my entire life."

Norah leaned one arm on the counter. "Seth was not a good person, Maxine." She sighed. "But he didn't deserve to die. But then again, I didn't deserve the things he did to me all those years either." Norah folded her hands and tucked them into her lap. A weak smile crossed her face but was gone as quickly as it appeared. "Dr. Fischer controlled all of us—including Finley's mother."

"Norah, I hope you know this was never about you. Once you started dating Colt, I wanted out, but Daniel wouldn't let me. Remember, I even talked about moving away, making a fresh start on the east coast. I never meant to hurt you." Tears filled Maxine's eyes.

"I know," Norah told her. "The only consolation is you don't have to worry about Dr. Fischer anymore. He got what he had coming. By the time he leaves prison, he'll be too old to manipulate anyone ever again."

"That's the only thing that keeps me going at night in my cell. I wish my daughter had been assigned here instead of in Minnesota." A long sigh passed across the line. "That day at the park, when Daniel held you and Colt at gunpoint, I couldn't even watch. I wanted to stop him, but instead, I pulled my daughter farther into the woods." Tears streamed down her cheeks. "I'm not as strong as you are. If I had been, I wouldn't have allowed Daniel to manipulate me the way he did."

"He manipulated all of us." Norah frowned. "Do you need anything before I go?" she asked.

The phone cord wiggled as the older woman shook her head. "No. Nothing. I just wish I could turn back time."

"I think we all wish for that." Norah placed the phone back in the holder and pressed her hand against the glass. Maxine did the same. "Take care of yourself," she said out loud, knowing Maxine could not hear her. Then, she turned and walked away.

Life had a funny way of connecting the dots for you. It didn't always follow a simple pattern; most of the time it was much more complicated.

INTROSPECT

Maxine Miller: "Norah was a wonderful boss, and Colton Stone was a kind man. I respected them both so much—until I crossed paths with Dr. Daniel Fischer. One person, *the wrong person,* can destroy you. And sometimes, that person can destroy everyone and everything you love."

EPILOGUE

"Hey, Mom. Do you think I should invite Becca to my sleepover?"

"Why?" Grace asked. "I thought you'd already decided who to invite."

The little girl pressed her lips together and scrunched her face. "I did, but she hasn't exactly been nice to me lately."

"Honey, it's your party. Invite who you want, but be nice about it," Grace warned as she watched her daughter. She would be eight soon; she was in second grade and growing like a weed.

"Morning, girls." Sam walked into the kitchen scratching his stomach. He had morning hair and breath.

Grace pulled away as he tried to kiss her. "Go brush your teeth, hon."

"Hurry back, Dad. We're having pancakes."

Sam grabbed the little girl and rubbed his day-old whiskers against her cheek.

She giggled as she tried to escape. "Whew!" she

complained as she flapped her hand in front of her face. "Mom's right. You need to brush your teeth."

"Critics," he said as he walked toward the back of the house. "Everyone's a critic."

The front door opened. "Hey, guys. Everyone decent?"

"Dad's not," the little girl yelled.

"Addley sandwich," Colt called as she walked into the kitchen. Norah handed her year-old son to Grace before they plastered the girl with kisses.

For the second time that morning, she screeched in laughter. "Ooohhh, someone's ticklish," Colt said.

"Daddy," Addley whined. "I am not. You and Mommy just surprised me."

Norah moved toward the counter. "I'll finish the pancakes if you put him in the highchair," she said. "Make sure you tie him down. He's taken up highchair diving in the last week."

Grace held Porter in the air. "Are you a diver?" she asked as she brought his face close to hers. The little boy drooled into her mouth. "Seriously?" Grace asked as she tucked him under one arm and wiped her mouth with her sleeve. "Gross!"

"Oh, yeah," Colt said. "That's his newest trick."

Sam reappeared; he'd put on a shirt and run a comb through his hair. "How's the house working out for you guys?"

"It's great. It's nice to be right next door. It's so much better than being across town. And Aunt Linda loves the backyard."

Sam wrapped his arm around his wife's ever-growing belly. "It's great for us too." He winked. "By the way, where is Aunt Linda?"

"She'll be here soon. She and Harmony were in a deep conversation about the fine art of ironing when we left," Norah told him. "We'll be lucky if Addley's dress doesn't have a giant scorch mark on it when they get here."

"Did you bring the paperwork?" Grace asked.

"Right here." Colt held it in the air.

Grace smiled. "Perfect! We're scheduled for 10:30."

Norah looked at the clock as she flipped the last pancakes. She turned toward the table and smiled at the little girl. "In just a couple hours, sweetie, you will officially be Addley Samorah Stone-Wilson. What do you think about that?"

"I think," Addley said, holding one finger in the air, "you'd better hurry up with my pancakes, Mommy. Otherwise, we're going to be late."

INTROSPECT

Harmony Stone: "I never knew how much I missed my family until Colton appeared in my shop. Now, I have so much family to love."

Linda O'Neil: "There are moments that take you by surprise. Moments you never expect to happen. Two years ago, when I lost Denny, my only family was Norah, and she lived over a dozen hours away. Since then, I have more family than I know what to do with, and my heart just keeps growing."

Luke Simon: "It's so good to see Norah happy again. She can't hide that smile in our daily Zoom meetings. But then, neither can I."

Beth Ramos: "Alright, you may as well know. Luke and I are giving it another go. Life is strange sometimes. But I'm really happy."

Addley Samorah Stone-Wilson: "I have four parents who love me, a new name, two bedrooms, a baby brother, a sister who will be born soon, and the best aunt and grandma anyone could ever have. Do you know how many presents I'm going to get on my birthday? A lot!"

THE VOICES WITHIN
(a choral poem)

NORAH	GRACE	COLTON
Life has a way of knocking us down before picking us up.	Life has a way of knocking us down before picking us up.	Life!
		It's not as it was, but now life is so much better!
Life is so much better! Different, but definitely better! I'm finally at peace.	Life is so much better! I'm finally at peace.	Different, but definitely better! Peace is an amazing feeling.
It's not easy to get there.	There is such joy in sharing my life with others.	There is such joy in sharing my life with others.
I once felt alone. Now, I see only joy, love, and family.	Now, I see only joy, love, and family.	
		Family isn't who lives in your house.
Family is who you choose to let in.	Our daughter is	Family is who you choose to let in.
Adley, will never take the place of Lili. I will never forget what once was. But for the rest of my days, I will choose joy! And I will always remember to love, to breathe, and to enjoy life's greatest moments.	Adley. I will never forget what once was. But for the rest of my days, I will choose joy! And I will always remember to love, to breathe, and to enjoy life's greatest moments.	Adley, will never take the place of Addy. I will never forget what once was. But for the rest of my days, I will choose joy! And I will always remember to love, to breathe, and to enjoy life's greatest moments.

From the first time I picked up a chubby Crayola crayon, I have been writing stories. I always wanted to be an author, but my mom told me I should get a job that made actual money. So, after four years of college and $2,500 in student loans—it was a long time ago—I spent thirty-six years honing my writing skills. Clearly, I am a slow learner. During most of that time, I taught middle school, because I fall in about the same place on the quirkiness scale as they do, and trained teachers to help students personalize their learning.

I was an award-winning Minnesota teacher. Some of my awards include the 2006 Fox 9 Top Teacher, 2010 Eastern Carver County Teacher of the Year, and 2011 Minnesota Teacher of the Year—Top 10 finalist. I also present at educational conferences across the United States as well as freelance for educational companies.

I hold a master's degree in education, but, while I loved teaching, I jumped ship three years ago and retired to a small Minneapolis suburb. I now have time to spend with my husband, Mitch, a retired principal, my son, Brandon, and my daughter, Taylor, who both still come home to see what's cooking in my pots and pans, my Parti Yorkie, Harper, and my two grand pets: Baxter, a Wheaten Terrier, and Guinevere, a tabby cat.

We spend a great deal of time at our cabin in Northern

Minnesota, where I lose at waterskiing, but win at Cornhole. We enjoy boating, ATVing, and entertaining our massive group of families and friends. Of course, there is never a lack of food due to the fact I was raised by the Food Devil herself.

My husband has a gold personality, planner, and I have an orange personality, spontaneous. That makes us the perfect pair. We love to travel. He likes to plan, and I don't ask where we are going until we get on the plane.

Between all the family shenanigans and laughter, I spend time spinning tales—stories that entertain, inform, and teach. So, stay tuned. There will be many more to come.